AWARD-WINNING AUTHOR
J.L. DELAVEGA

ASH LIKE
VENGEANCE

THE REVERE TRILOGY

AWARD-WINNING AUTHOR
J.L. DELAVEGA

ASH LIKE VENGEANCE

THE REVERE TRILOGY

ASH LIKE VENGEANCE
The Revere Trilogy, Book Two

CITY OWL PRESS
www.cityowlpress.com

Cover Design by MiblArt. All stock photos licensed appropriately. Map illustration by Cartographybird Maps.

Edited by Tee Tate.

For information on subsidiary rights, please contact the publisher at info@cityowlpress.com.

Print Edition ISBN: 978-1-64898-357-3

Digital Edition ISBN: 978-1-64898-358-0

Printed in the United States of America

 CITY OWL PRESS
Escape Your World ● Get Lost in Ours

PRAISE FOR J.L. DELAVEGA

"*Ash Like Vengeance*, the follow-up to a brilliant first book of the series, this doesn't disappoint. Here, the author delves deeply into the inner workings of the characters. The actions are there but it is the thoughts that drive them that carry the meaning. The rich detail done in intricate fashion makes this a book you can sink your teeth into. There are times when you feel you are trying to survive on the rim yourself." — N.N. Heaven, author of *Princess of the Light*

"An action filled adventure with a core of strong-gunned and stronger-willed female characters, I couldn't put it down. In essence a story about staking a claim in a world that aims at crushing you, *Smoke and Other Storms* shows that no matter what sparkles in the desert, it's family that you need to survive." — Florence A. Bliss, *Taken by His Sword*

"Each character in the cast is strong, clever, and flawed in their own way, but the ways in which they work together and supported each other was truly the heart of the story. We need more creative, thoughtful, empowering books like these." — Lilla Glass, author of *The Unseen*

"A thrilling and substantial page-turner of a fantasy adventure, set in a rough and gritty frontier where mining is king and a weapon might be a girl's best friend. A solid debut and beginning of a series!" — Karen Eisenbrey, author of *Daughter of Magic*

"Delavega has an incredible knack for worldbuilding and character development that doesn't feel forced. You're dropped into the world right off the bat, and J.L. just keeps adding more coal (or in this case, crystals) to the train boiler and doesn't let up. I have a whole new appreciation for the Western genre because of *Smoke and Other Storms*, and I can't wait to see where J.L. Delavega takes us next in the series!" — Derek Borne, author of *The Ultimate Agent*

For my grandma.

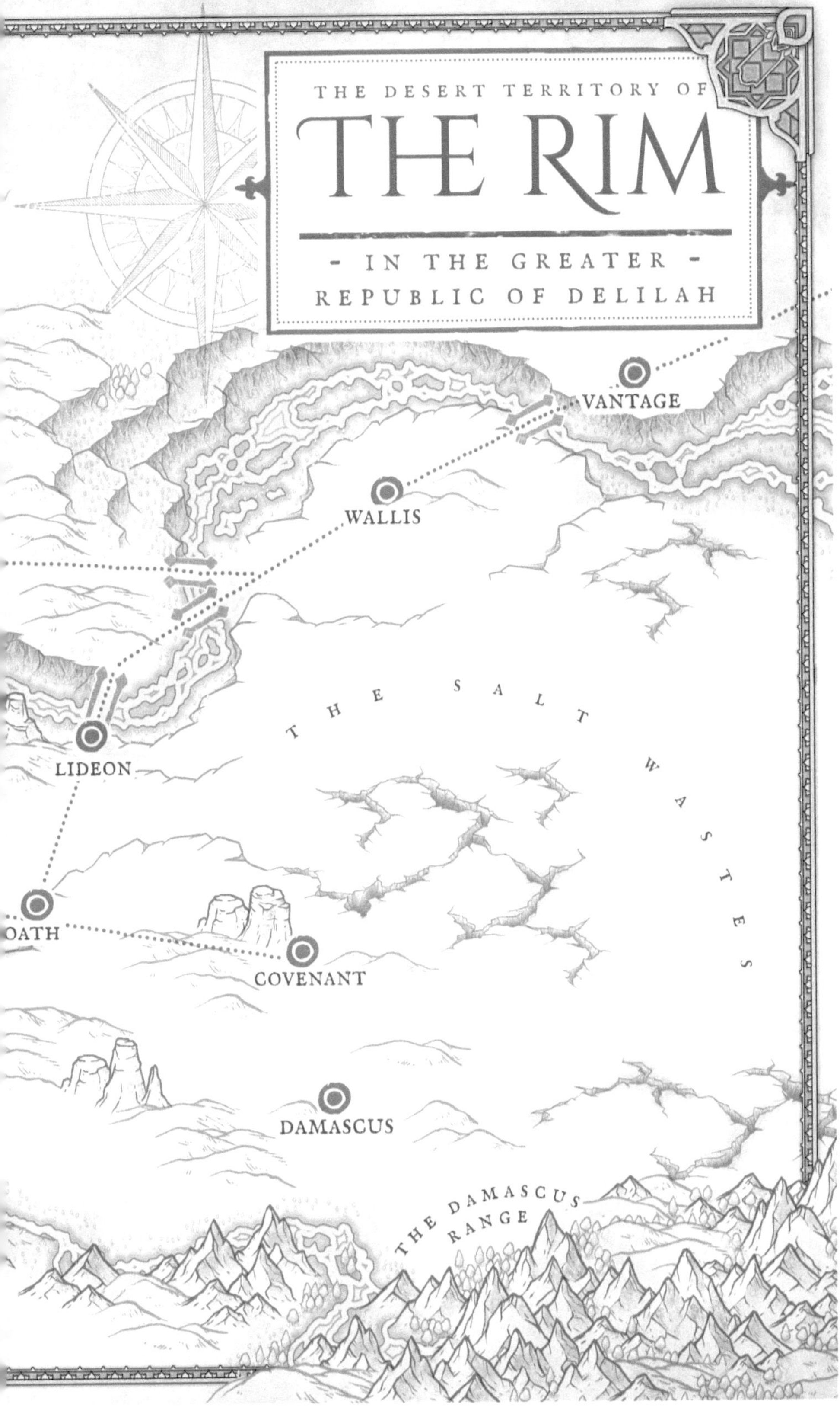

THE DESERT TERRITORY OF

THE RIM

- IN THE GREATER -
REPUBLIC OF DELILAH

VANTAGE

WALLIS

THE SALT WASTES

LIDEON

OATH

COVENANT

DAMASCUS

THE DAMASCUS RANGE

ARRIVAL

My name is Adelaide Revere.

I am twenty-two, hair like moonlit bone.

It's been one hundred and twenty-six days since I buried my sister Vesta outside Winchester, and my eyes are still gray. I don't have the pestilence. But all this time I've been seeing blood, breathing smoke.

There are only two colors now. The ground in Hannah, black. Everything else, steeped in red.

But red is the color of revenge.

Welcome back.

PART ONE

STORMS AT DUSK

ONE

ADELAIDE

THE STRANGER SPLAYS UP THE FOUR CORNERS OF THE ALLEY, IRON SMOKE. NOT a dead end, it just looks like one. Four corners make people buying dangerous things feel safe. She spills out of me more often these days, blacking out edges, tired of this bullshit. So am I.

My spoon chime lists outside the curtain clouding the alley entrance from the air market and soup camp, empty promises. Never sell from the same spot two days in a row. People who want what I have just have to know what to look for.

Sunlight comes through breaks in the wall and over the peaked roofs, red, slanted. It's always dusk in Hannah. The refinery towers on the fool-made hill breathe out black smoke with a stability even the wind doesn't have the strength to clear.

Every crack bleeds black ash, lips and fingernails crusted with it. A second skin that never washes off.

The man in front of me breathes heavily, and I draw my thumb around the pommel of the knife hidden against my back. *Four passes. Five...*

He doesn't really see me. His gaze drips across the muzzle locked around my jaw to the gray skin of my neck.

"Fool's gold, fox, stop holding out on me."

On my table lie the things I've stolen. Two clip-point knives and one folding. A string of keys for those who can't pick locks, sleeping tablets, sugar, a tin of butter, my last two Ven crystals. They look black, not blue, in this wasted light.

This picker doesn't get to know about the revolver I stole yesterday. I know what he's after.

You can spot a powder licker by the gray stain on their lower lip and tongue, clearly under the skin, unlike the flat black of refinery ash discoloring me.

There are many.

I show a corner of the waxed paper packet stuffed up my left sleeve, hold up five fingers, then open my palm. Fifty, gold standard. This is a solid week's wage for a second-shifter like him, gone like water.

He reaches back. The Stranger locks my hand around the knife until his reemerges from his pocket with money, not a weapon. I count it by touch, eyes not leaving him. Gold standards weigh more than silver.

He follows the powder with his tongue, the buzz under his skin a hive of stone beetles. He grabs the second it lands on the upturned crate between us, fingers rubbing the package the way men touch women.

Courage powder.

My mother was a user.

"You're a devil—" The cough turns on him, retching phlegm onto the ground. The refinery dust gets into everything. I taste it in my throat, in my lungs, in my sleep. There's no escaping its touch. The curse of industry.

"When will you get more?" His weight shifts to the other foot like a mood. "You're cheaper than the other dealers."

Then you shouldn't have told me what it's actually worth.

Unfortunately, getting this powder isn't like picking rocks off the ground. I know where to find it, but bodies used to being dulled by chemicals become sharp like the Stranger when they're not. I'm careful. Wait, take these little envelopes from pockets when it's safe and sell it back to them.

Miners buy this more than alcohol, more than knives or stolen meat and sugar. They give me every last string in their pockets for this gray dust that weighs less than the wax holding the paper shut.

I drop my wares into the pockets lining my skirt.

He doesn't even bother to leave my sight before ripping through the wax. His tongue flicks across cracked lips, gray and filmy.

It's my mother, his body, melting and becoming hers. Her face is a blur except for the gray-blue stain on her mouth as she turns her back on me. She couldn't hide it from me then, when I wasn't even old enough to reach the countertop of the sideboard. She can't now.

The Stranger crashes over me, my thoughts a glass shattering. She's black and rolling, water that's sat in sun, become warm.

I blink her out of my eyes.

The miner hunches on the ground, the blood pulsing from his neck a little weaker with each heartbeat. Red spray coats my right side, itches down my shoulder, an arrow pointing to my hand and the knife in it.

The lines between the Stranger and I have grown so thin. Why waste my energy stopping her? He was here buying from me to numb his worthless existence, slow death.

He got what he wanted. Faster.

I empty his pockets, then reach past the curtain and remove the spoon chimes from the crusty nail protruding from the overhang, clenching them before they jangle.

The air market swallows me with smoke and carpet tents. No one follows, the Stranger is sure. But they will, the boss's men.

The alley level drops off at the Slash, the packed road of old slag that splits Hannah like a scar. My cold ash gaze runs up it to the source. The refinery hill, built on the bones of old Hannah. The Slash Gate, small below it, but it's not. Nine massive logs pinned together by steel bands, sealed with black taffy pitch, and crowned with glass and twisted metal shards. Behind that, the tracks and chutes of the rail loading yard and snipers who keep watch from the raptor towers.

I keep my shoulder between me and that side of the street, always. My mother's ghost drags nails against splintered walls as she wanders, blind, faceless. Old Hannah is where she sleeps. I don't go looking for her, the Stranger a hard, direct wind that erases me when I come this close.

Six hundred and fifty steps.

The spike-toothed outer wall doesn't just keep pickers out of Hannah. It's a belt circling another world. This one is singed like air after a lightning strike. Leather and skin salt, the hard muzzle encasing my jaw.

I've been here four and a half cycles. That's four and a half months if you're from the east. I made them bring me in after the ambush in Winchester, the boss's men, sent to collect the crystal everyone thinks we stole. I lied. It was the only way to keep them from killing me.

The sun is a scarlet blot in a dishwater sky, staining stacked dwellings red and people to shadows. I've been outside all day, but it can't burn me past the ash cloud.

I pass under bottle chimes limp on the eaves. The sound of glass breaking is supposed to scare off ghosts, but there are too many people. We're all haze ghosts in a bloody nightmare.

The low twang of strings escapes through a saloon's lattice door. Always music and drunken voices in the air. Moaning and laughter. No escape from the pressure of noise in my head except for the Stranger's black.

The triangle bell strikes behind the uneven rooftops, followed by the salesman's yell. "Fresh hanging! See a ration thief hang, only two silver standards!"

Arson used to be the Rim's only real crime. In Descendants, you pay right people to have someone hanged. The rest of the Rim, you do it yourself. Here, you pay to watch.

The offer fades into another. Cabbage, flesh, moon readings. Behind it all, the throb of the refinery heartbeat, ceaseless and crushing me from the outside in.

Nine hundred.

The plank stamped with a thousand black dust handprints wobbles when I open the bathhouse door, just like yesterday. *Miners ONLY. No Refinery fuckers.*

Sweat and moisture are flaying the paper off the black walls.

The long room creaks, even under my soft feet, privacy stalls made of calico sheets and the crack of dice hitting the throw boxes between tubs. I go through the coats foolishly abandoned on hooks inside. Ammunition and silver standards, one protection skin and a comb. No courage powder today, but nine of the eleven people here wear the stain on their mouths. Wool scrapes my hand as I withdraw from the pocket.

Twenty-two.

Deeper, down where the shadows breed with each other, the last stall that belongs to the girls is made of real walls. I pull the chain attached to the overhead pipe and flush stale water into the shallow sink basin. It turns from yellow to brown as blood and ash melt down my neck and arm.

The Stranger catches on the gaze of the wheat-haired girl who always rocks in the hammock. Smoke on her lips, crochet hook in her hand, red ink star points and constellation lines running up her arms to her chest. She smiles at me.

A line of loose water runs inside my cotton camisole, biting like an itch the deeper it travels.

The door at the top of the unbalanced stairs peels open. Thadie lets her client out first, hiking the shawl of crocheted lace up her bare shoulder. She doesn't skip a breath as she notices me and closes her fist, slowly bringing it to her smile. He paid.

I let him pass, steps bowing above and below me as Thadie hops over the unlucky twelfth stair.

"I wasn't sure when you'd get here, so I had to start without you," she says.

That's why the first thing I sold her was a knife, even though I doubt she'd be able to use it on something alive.

"Got anything good today?"

Eight.

Her room is sticky with wax, lit by candles not crystal, bundles of herbs bound in cloth dangling from the eaves, jars of dirt sold to miners for protection underground. The scents leak out and snag on the loneliness stuck in me, twisted as roots. Dried sage and powdered minerals, Navy's lab.

I hope she and Raleigh made it out of the *Delta Sol* canyons. I hope they don't feel guilty for leaving me behind. It was the only way. I wouldn't want Navy here, even to have her with me.

"I'll take this." Thadie exchanges my sugar for a glass vial, orange with flash fire.

I twitch as she reaches toward my head.

"Sorry, I wasn't—that was instinct."

So was mine.

"You have something in your hair... Oh, wait, I think it's—blood?"

Probably.

Feet startle the stairs.

"I'm taking a ten-minute break, so keep your pants on," Thadie calls. "I'll come get you when I'm ready. It's been so nice..." She closes her eyes with a little sigh. "Not having to fight with anyone. Especially nice not getting punched in the face and robbed."

The bruise that made her hire me is almost gone. Only a thin yellow moon haunts her eyelid below a break in her eyebrow where it split on impact.

She rubs the dark brass globe of her moon diviner, cradled in the drape of her skirt like an egg. "Will you *please* let me tell your future today?"

I shake my head. You don't see anything with diviners, you lie with them. Grandma is special enough to see through this world to whatever's on the other side of it. She's the only one I would maybe let look into my future, and she's never offered. If she's seen anything, she's never bothered me with it. She's always let me be what I am, never tried to make me into anything for her own satisfaction.

"They never stop, do they? That was not ten minutes." The shawl drops off Thadie's shoulder again as she stands. "Hello there, handsome."

The buckle clank of his steel-toed mine boots halt. He smells like fear to the Stranger. Piss to me. "Why is that fox up here?"

Because I want you to see me.

"Don't worry, she protects me." Thadie offers her hand. "Come on, I'll take care of you."

My shadow on the stairs makes them think twice about slitting her throat when the door closes.

"She won't hurt you."

Unless he tries to rob her.

Thadie sets the bell clock hanging by the door. "This five-minute sleep will be the best you've ever had." The swing of her solar quartz pendulum snags shards of blue out of candlelight before the door shuts me out.

This is the difference between people like her and people like us. We would have sold him this hypnosis lie and robbed him of everything else he carries while he slept. The missed opportunity still rubs me against the grain.

I set my leg against the opposing rail.

Thadie's door opens again. She rubs her customer's back as he leaves, every step a quake, another one already lurking near the bottom of the stairs.

Thadie shows me her closed fist.

I draw my leg back, let him pass.

Someday, one of them might kill her anyway, me here or not.

TWO
TESLA

WE RODE A TRAIN.

Not so very long ago, only a lifetime of empty space between that life and this new one.

The long, cool whistle eats a hole in my bones. They remember the sway of wheels on rail. The rumble casting through the ground isn't the same as riding the engine, being the one in control of a beast so mighty, so fast. This train is an unending freight creature, spooling off the salt-white horizon toward the town called Covenant.

The wind rolling off the cars unsettles my hair, pulls at me, stirring the orange seed grass.

It would be easy to assume the cargo is Ven quartz. Most of the cars are made of wood and iron, and the cold burn of Ven crystals corrupts hardened steel, even unlit. But Covenant is goat country, remote enough that resources aren't wasted on personal comfort like cooled rooms.

Vesta and I played this guessing game together since she was a child. Where did the train come from, what did it carry, and where was it headed?

My guess is cattle and grain from the South Rim's Windust ranches by way of the station in Oath.

"I hope you don't come here just to torment yourself." The grass swishes as Evangeline crosses off the path to stand where I'm waist deep in it, beetles and all.

The damaged nerves that web off my scar pinch as I flick away the loose tear. Even my oldest friend shouldn't have to feel the weight of my sorrow all the time. "You know me."

"That I do." Evangeline places a hand against my back. "What makes you punish yourself so mercilessly today?"

Looking into the sun doesn't help my eyes to stop burning, either. I stop squinting at the bright sky like a fool and sigh. "Raleigh's late." Never a good sign. Not here on the Rim, at least.

"Everything has its time."

"That's why I like machines. They have to be logical to work." Everything has a place on a train, a purpose, a function. When a piece breaks sometimes the rest can go on, and other times damage to a single five-pound rod is deadly enough to stall an entire engine. "I'm not patient, not with things out of my control, at least."

Sometimes I wonder if we're lost without Mother. Every day I still miss my Vesta so much it hurts to exist inside my body. The sun sits hot on my back, but under my skin I'm so unseasonably cold and running with a current that never lands anywhere. When I get like this, I have to ride up into the hills behind the Damascus Sanctuary and scream at the full blue sky until the pain of my raw throat shuts me up and I've frightened away every bird for ten square miles.

Leagan and I may have survived the bounty hunters who came for our heads and burned us out of Fort Emmaline, Navy, the expedition to the West Rim with Kane's crew, but some days I don't recognize myself.

Heartbreak leaves you fighting for survival of a different kind.

I witnessed Mother's grief after my sister Liza was killed. Now I understand it. I wish I didn't, but I am eternally glad to find I'm strong like she was. As deep as the loss of both Vesta and my mother roots into me, I still have too much to lose to give up. I have three other girls I love, and like hell if I'm going to roll over and give our old friend Green what he wants—our defeat.

This isn't the end. Someday I'll ride another train, someday I'll see my Vesta again.

Someday, I vow to myself, then turn my back on the flowing train to smile at Evangeline.

Hers is always straightforward. She doesn't hide things behind it like I do, and I appreciate that about her. Honesty is rare, even in people who claim it as a virtue. *Especially* in those people. They're usually the deepest liars because they lie to themselves about what honesty even is.

Evangeline plucks a seed pod stuck to my sleeve and examines its identity before throwing it away. "From time to time I like to remind myself this life is the most I'll ever suffer. Providence has made a place for me where all things are good and pure, and none of this will matter. Your mother and daughter are already there with your sister." She brushes the scar dividing the left side of my face in two parts, still violent and pink, a souvenir from the day the *Absolution* derailed three cycles ago. Her touch shimmers down my spine like a ghost's hand. "Momentary suffering, my friend. And it's okay to feel it."

"That is comforting, actually."

Yes, I was a mother, but I have more to offer than that. This is my story, and I will not make it one about grief. I prefer love, nice clothes, and a respectable amount of blood.

Up the next ridge pools the spring well the church was built around. Water offered freely from the ground is a miracle, you know, and the white and blue backdrop of the mountains is Godlike. A church makes sense here, unlike most places on the Rim, where they always look out of line.

If I look very deep into the pale desert, I believe I can see the purple smudge of Evangeline's lifework, the Damascus Sanctuary of Sisters, all the way from here, but that could just be a heat lie.

A single-horse wagon stands beneath the bell arch's fluted shadow, the preacher's door dangling to the wind.

Evangeline walks a little faster. The chickens that didn't see us coming past the dying vegetable garden pick up their feathered skirts and flee with cackles.

"Reverend Phillips?" she calls.

A windowpane still in its frame leans against one wagon wheel, and the suitcase dumped in last will get tossed out when they hit the first big rut.

The preacher comes through the back graveyard hauling a second windowpane, the unbuttoned dust collar of his long brown coat flapping against his square nose. His chin is done no favors by the shave he's given it.

"Is something wrong, friend?" Evangeline says.

He sets the window with the other, replacing sweat with dirt when he wipes. "I'm tired."

"I'm sorry to hear that."

"If it's all the same to you, Sister, I'd rather not discuss it," he says.

"At the very least let me help you with that." She points with her eyes to the windows as Reverend Phillips fails to cover all four corners as he wraps them in a woolen blanket.

"No, thank you, I have it." He unfurls the wagon canvas, as if that can hide the evidence of his pillaging.

Evangeline helps him buckle down the corners despite him getting in her way on purpose.

"Going somewhere then?" I say. It's obvious he's not coming back.

"Home. Where I should have listened to my mother and sisters and stayed."

"And so you find this a fair reason to pick apart Providence's house," Evangeline says. "Would your mother say a kind word to that?"

"I've taken nothing more than my due. I deserve something for the time I've wasted here unpaid, speaking to an empty room every Sunday eve. Someone will buy these. I need the money for my ticket east."

"Only if they make it to someone in one piece," I say.

"Then I'll take them to the glass refinery in Wallis. You haven't seen the prices on the grains that just came in."

"Being out of the way makes things expensive."

Things are generally cheaper in places like Wallis, Descendants, or Junction. And by cheaper, I do mean by the Rim's standards. Food is always a valuable commodity, often stolen, expect to pay.

"The vendor was going to charge me three times what he offered the man standing right in front of me," Phillips says.

"Yes, they've been known to do that." I can't avoid the jab of spite, it's too sweet. "You should hear the prices they've tried to charge my Tov niece." Then you'd have something real to complain about.

"Is there anything I can do to ease your burden?" Evangeline asks him.

"Not likely. I'm tired of being hungry and hated, and so wretchedly hot. I wasn't called here for this. If these are the current fair-weather prices, if I stay, I'll be forced to eat my own arm next Moon Season when the storm prices hit."

"Well, that would be unfortunate," I say. "But you do realize what's really to blame, don't you? It's not just because merchants hate a man of Providence pointing out their sins, it's the security fees, coming out of Vantage. We have a merchant named Mr. Green and their new sheriff to thank for that. You should do it if you happen to see him."

"Let's not bring politics into this," Evangeline says. "The law saves lives."

"So they say."

Someone has to pay for him and Green's railroad bullies. Who did they think it was going to be? The Commerce Guild? The Von Kane company? Absolutely not, they have their cut to take too. We tried to warn our protection contracts last Season. Protection from law costs more than anything. I fucking told you so.

Phillips drops onto the plank seat with a grimace. "I used to think everyone deserved redemption and the opportunity to welcome it. But I was mistaken."

Evangeline strikes her tongue past her top lip and whatever she's holding in with it. "That bad."

"If you like talking to yourself in an empty room, or better yet, getting rocks thrown at you, the church is yours. They come to me when they want favors and selfish prayers answered, but the rest of the time I'm a worm in the bread. No, these pickers can enjoy hell. They won't find it much different than this when they get there." He slaps the reins. "Providence and His mercy protect you, Sister."

Evangeline holds her silence, and I stand away to avoid getting my feet run over by the irritated horse as it circles the blue pool.

"You're not thinking of going with him, are you?" I joke. She wouldn't, she'll never leave her sanctuary.

"No, little darling." Evangeline wakes from her disillusion to secure the door the former Reverend Phillips didn't bother to close. "I prayed for him. A tired soul needs mercy."

"Well, he's not the first preacher to get run off the Rim by us wretched heathens. Not you, of course."

"And he won't be the last." She says, very grim.

White dust billows to the sky as a rider gallops out of the cut between hills from the opposite direction. I circle the church for a better view as he comes in, hand on my revolver, heart up in my ears.

Raleigh wouldn't be caught dead in a ditch wearing clothes that ragged.

He dismounts at the split stone fence before the red horse stops moving, running to open the church door. When he finds it locked, he rips off his moth-nibbled hat and pounds.

"Reverend Phillips! Open up, it's an emergency!"

"The Reverend just retired, I'm afraid," Evangeline calls. "Retired" being her polite word for giving all of us sinners the middle finger and running back east.

"Retired? Well, when will he be up?"

"Never. But what can I help you with, friend?" She holds up the silver prayer pendant from under the collar of her double-breasted men's shirt.

The man rushes down the steps. "We got a collapse at Cutter's mine. At least eight men broken up real bad. Two of them are just boys, orphan pickers, but still."

"Fool's gold," Evangeline mutters to her boots. "This is why children don't belong in a mine."

"If you know anything about stitching, we could use the help."

"You go," I say. "I'll take the supplies back."

"Blessings." Evangeline winds up her scarf and draws the goggles from the crown of her hat to her eyes. "Be careful out there, Tess. Fresh cattle always drive out the roadmen and other hungry creatures."

"I know."

I was one of them.

◐

Navy and Leagan meet me at the sanctuary gate, the black and white goat born last week lounging in Leagan's arms, a yellow sweater hugging his stubby little body.

"Look who's so fancy."

"Della made it for him."

The stars are out early, lovely bands of pink aura light drifting over the mountain peaks.

"Any news?" Navy asks, fear under the halt in her throat.

"No pickers were stupid enough to attack me. And Raleigh wasn't there yet."

"He's always late, that bastard. Probably wasting time matching his ascot with his socks." Leagan stalks over to me. "Give Dilly a kiss."

"Contrasting his ascot with his socks is more likely." I rub the twist of white hair on Dilly's forehead and put the kiss on Leagan's cheek.

"I said Dilly!"

"I know."

Leagan turns, pressing her lips to Navy's cheek.

"Nasty!" Navy twists away, a black print left on her skin. "You're wearing your lipstick, aren't you?"

"Aunt Tess started it." Leagan gets away before Navy can get hold of her.

"You did this, go get me a rag to wipe this off!"

"No."

Sister Beth who never smiles bars the gate up again behind the wagon, pivoting with her rifle like a well-trained soldier. I salute to see if she'll crack this time. Still no.

"Let's get this into your room, ma'am," I say.

Navy finds the corner of the wagon with a hand, following it around the sacks of beans and rice to the crate of medical supplies and what glass vessels I was able to find at the Covenant trading post.

"Not University-approved equipment, but I assume they'll hold liquid."

"I'll make them work." She runs her fingers around a jar, then a coil of brass pipe attached to a still drum. "Did you get the notebooks too?"

"Yes, and the cotton and ghost quartz, but they didn't have any Ven, but Raleigh said he'd bring some. So hopefully, what you have now lasts."

"If he ever gets here," Leagan mutters to Dilly's ear.

Bottles click as I lift the crate. "*Farce*, that's heavy."

"Don't hurt yourself."

"I'll try not to." I bow my head before crossing the main threshold to the inner courtyard, but recite the grace and keep walking because, fool's gold, my hands are burning from the weight of this crate. "Providence, God of Mercy, in these walls we find rest."

In these walls I find the green smell of tomatoes.

The candles flutter in the prayer alcove below everlasting smoke stains, halls growing shadows like weeds, but in the day, so much light comes through the star lattice windows.

"Tess!" Megdaline calls across the gold light of the kitchen door. "I made the cabbage hand pies."

"Save me one, I'll be right there."

The salty dust isn't ready to let go of my boots even after being scraped on the boot brush. Megdaline can scold me for leaving a trail, but I did try.

The bed has been cleared out of Navy's room into mine, a long worktable created from planks and crates. She keeps the storm shutters locked and a sheet of tenting canvas nailed over the reformed glass. It keeps out the sun out of her failing eyes, the wind and dust out of her work, and everything else in permanent twilight.

My scar prickles as I pass the wardrobe.

The cracks are fuzzy with goat wool insulation, doors bound with a padlock only Navy holds the key to. The room has a different kind of chill because of it. Inside lie the samples of Vesta's blood, skin, hair, and clothing, sealed in glass tubes since the night she died.

Leagan built the cooling apparatus from Ven quartz, an iron stove belly and copper coil shipped from back east for a scandalous price.

There's a certain strangeness I can't get away from whenever I'm in here, that fragments of Vesta remain when the rest of her doesn't. And this base piece of machinery is the only thing saving them from rotting away forevermore.

I haven't looked at them, and I won't. I'd rather remember her the way she was—absolutely perfect.

THREE
ADELAIDE

THE BOARDING HOUSE RUN BY MADAM CHARLENE LEANS LIKE A DRUNK. IT survives only on the support of two other inebriated buildings, one storm away from failure.

Across the street a Company man rocks in the chair. Gray like the smoke sky, pipe blush on his face as he breathes it in, waiting for me to return.

I let him see me before I dissolve again, swallowed by the night beyond the door.

Eleven.

The hall funnels past the warped stairs to the kitchen. The backside of that, Madam Charlene's private rooms. Black dust thickens the skin on the walls and eats the fragile light that dares to leave the dusty lanterns. It sticks to my throat the same way.

The two girls cutting potatoes at the long kitchen table turn their shoulders in so there's no chance of me brushing them as I pass. Blue bodices, guaranteed to work indoors, services sold for at least seventy empty gold.

Top drawer. Spoons and knives. Second. Salt and tea leaves. The kettle screeches like a once-mountain cat, faded by the pestilence.

First cupboard. Cups, five of them. Plates, seven.

The Stranger lets my thoughts go quiet once I've opened everything. Nothing has changed since this morning.

Twenty-seven.

Weak light splays from the gap in my door. I closed it when I left.

The flounce of Copper's bustle rasps against my brass bedframe as she lets the mattress go. My room is too tight for that much silk. It splays like an emerald bloodstain as she squats in front of the bedside cupboard, picking fingers through my single change of clothes.

"Sweet Jezebel!" She knocks against the cupboard then the wall when she turns and sees me. "You scared the thunder right out of me."

I circle past her to the cupboard, use my heel to press it closed.

This is why I don't leave things with value lying around here. It's all inside my skirt, or buried in the bone well.

"I'm sorry," she says. "I didn't mean for you to catch me snooping."

Liar.

Someone who doesn't want to be caught shuts the door and listens for footsteps. But she'll have to do better than this if she wants to find something hidden by a smuggler.

"Don't look at me with those eyes, fox. This is the only way I can catch you before you sneak upstairs and lock yourself in here," Copper says. "I had Jordina wake me from my nap so I could come visit you."

The Stranger flicks out of me, acidic. The sear a close lightning strike leaves behind on the air.

Get out.

But Copper's too blunt to hear her hiss.

I worm a finger under the muzzle to the undying itch it leaves on my cheek.

"Maybe I'm beginning to like you, did you ever think about that?" Her smile flashes like the gold thread in her green bodice. "The other girls wouldn't be so afraid of you if you said a word now and then and stopped creeping around like a ghost and turning up with blood on your clothes. You know when you first came here, I thought you were a mute. Then I realized you're just a bitch with a stick up her ass."

Better that than something else.

She works the Company hotels and dance hall. The foremen, shopkeepers, and investors. But those men have hunger in them, same as the second and third shifts I'm supposed to service out on the street.

She pulls her lips back again, teeth black as river pearls. Apparently, that's the style if you're a popular whore in Jezebel. What a freight car of *farce*. "I saw you in Hangman's Yard today."

The Stranger rises past my head, touches the ceiling.

There are secrets in Copper's eyes. The venomous kind. They shine like the black gold resin painted on her teeth, whisper with the tongue of the Stranger. She already knows the answer to whatever she's trying to trick me into admitting. But I knew I shouldn't trust her the day we met. I haven't.

"And lasterday." The corner of her smile twitches. "They do say to keep death away from you, you have to stand in death's shadow and it won't see you."

Eyes distracted by death make pockets easier to pick. They don't notice my brush with so many others happening at the same time. I don't go because I like to watch.

My mother died by a rope in Hannah. One she tied herself.

The itch spreads off my jaw to my spine like a shiver.

The muzzle has a slit just wide enough to slip a spoon through to eat and drink. But I wasn't raised a thief for nothing. I take the pin from my braid.

Copper's brows lift as she watches me pick the lock, peel the muzzle off like a dead jaw.

"I thought so."

A woman needs practical skills.

"At least you wash the blood off your lips," she says.

I'd shoot someone for their bar of soap if I ever got someone else's blood near my mouth.

"Why do you let them keep that thing on you if you know how to take it off? It looks hideous."

I finally look at her straight and let the muzzle drop off my fingers. "It serves a purpose."

It says one thing: I bite. On these streets, this mark counts more than a visible weapon, halts hands faster than my white hair. Those who might mishandle me think twice. And the others can't expect my mouth to do anything for them.

Copper nods, but it's the flat kind. She doesn't understand.

My washrag changes from gray to storm black as I pour the last water in my jar onto it and scrub my face, neck. *Farce*, it feels good to be clean underneath the muzzle. The dirt entombed under my nails doesn't come free, all of them dark crescent moons. But you won't know where I've been digging just by seeing it.

"I could teach you some better tricks." Copper steps in, rusty perfume on warm skin, hand scraping cotton as she passes it across my waist. "First of all, don't flinch. It shows you're scared, and an amateur."

The Stranger resents that.

I step around her so she has to move toward the door again. She's wrong about me. Why I have to wear this muzzle, what scares me. It's not hands. Not anymore.

"Second, if you're going to bite people, at least have the brains to be sensual about it. Some men do like rough play. But fool's gold, stop looking at them like you're going to rip their throat out, because they'll just want to do the same thing to you. And stop looking at *me* like that."

You don't survive the Rim by following other people's rules.

You don't survive the Rim by following any rules.

"What do you want?"

Copper drops onto my unmade bed, springs popping, dust catching in her throat. "You know there's alkaline money here, fool. Plenty to go around. But you won't get it from the kind of men who want to fuck an animal. You'll get a black eye." Her eyes point out the bruise on my forearm. "So be nice, smile for the gentlemen, unless you're happy fucking on the ground behind Miner's Row. Which I doubt."

I've never fucked anyone on the ground. And I never will.

"Your services will be worth more once you get out of the white bodice," Copper says. "You're actually prettier than I thought a fox would be. I heard you all had red eyes and pointed teeth. You look... disappointingly average, but I think you could do all right. Word of advice, all you have to do is pretend. I tell all my customers they're the best I've ever had." She waves off a biting fly, lurching off my bed as it returns for vengeance. "Men will believe almost anything that makes them feel good about themselves."

Any fool will believe something if it makes them feel good. Men and women. Flattery is an easy tool.

"Trust me. A little moan or two is usually all it takes. Lie. Why make your life harder than it has to be?"

Because I don't want to be you.

I do not accept this life as the only way because it's all I'm believed to be good enough for. I am more. It's been six cycles, three since they let me out of the cell under the Company compound. Long enough. I'll get out of here, even if it's the last thing I manage to do.

There's blood under my nails with the dirt. The Stranger put it there.

"By the way, I have the money to promote to scarlet bodice. I paid Charlene today, so you will call me Madam now." Copper slides the blotted mirror aside to check behind as if I'm not here, tilts her head and adjusts how her emerald bustier displays her breasts. "Plus, I've earned a favor or two. I've also considered moving to Jezebel when I get tired of the meat here. I can get one of these crystal barons to take me back east for good. He'll set me up in a sweet little manor by the sea and visit when he's tired of his wretched wife."

You fool.

"You've never seen that much water, have you?" she asks. "I'll have to learn to swim. Doesn't that sound fun? Drinking the sea and bathing at the same time, none of this dirt sticking to me."

You can't drink salt water. And this is the desert. Unless you're a pearl diver, swimming isn't a skill you need to learn. It won't save you in a *Solace* flash flood.

Copper arches her dense eyebrows, still hoping for a word from me. "A little fly told me the Company brought you in to service an east blood baron a few cycles ago."

Who told you that?

I recede a little deeper into the Stranger. Black in the corners of my eyes, her shadow large enough to cast one on me even in the dark. I thought Madam Charlene was the only one in here who knew my connection to the boss.

I won't make this mistake again.

It's too late. Copper saw my face before the Stranger blurred it out. "Did he want something special from you? Maybe you've got something you can teach me." She offers a smile of conspiracy, to turn gossip into currency like Aunt Tess and Vesta. But they were actually good at it.

I don't enjoy giving people what they want. I enjoy keeping it from them.

The meal bell rings.

"Oh yes." Copper sighs. "About time. I hope there's butter, otherwise you can't call it toast, it's just crusty bread. Providence knows we're paying Charlene enough for better than that. Cheap bitch." She plants her arms across the doorframe. "By the way, I'll be collecting the rent tonight, so I hope the poor pickers have been paying you. Agnes will be so disappointed if we have to wait another cycle to evict you. Let's ruin her day."

I don't move.

"You coming, fox?" The sting of the Stranger finally connects. Copper's arms drop, gaze slipping off my narrow shoulder. "Don't forget to put your little muzzle back on."

The sudden smell of potatoes and eggs fills my room in her place. Hunger pushes up my throat, sour as bile. But my heart pounds.

Copper's steps go cold as they fade. As much as I despise her, at least she was a distraction.

The mattress sags under my weight. I pull my knees up to my chest, hug them, and count how many overstretched wires I feel through the mattress. I don't want to be here.

One tear escapes before I feel its wetness. Painless and down my cheek so fast, melting into my skirt. Gone.

Not now.

I know.

The first fled painless. The rest would rather burn than let me stomp them down. But I do.

I WAIT ANOTHER FIFTEEN MINUTES FOR AT LEAST HALF OF THE GIRLS TO FINISH eating.

Silence drops like beads off a necklace as I enter the kitchen. The Stranger mixes with the smoke escaping their lungs on its own strength.

Twenty-eight.

Music seeps from the yellow gap underlining Madam Charlene's door. It's the only reason I don't think she's dead in there. We're a skin disease she's trying to peel away, and looking at us might reinfect her.

"Relax, you fools." Copper extinguishes her cigar on her dirty plate. "The fox is in a muzzle. She can't bite you, but if you don't pay your bills on time, I might let her." She licks open Charlene's pocket ledger as her laugh chitters, a spiteful bird. "Let's see who still owes rent... Fox, Suzanna, and...Agnes. Let's see gold, ladies."

Suzanna hangs back, like I do. A memory forgotten in the corner with its back turned.

If she isn't going to move first, I guess I have to.

Six.

I let the standards go on Copper's dirty plate. Some stolen, some earned from the protection I sold to Thadie and others. They spread, unstacked and slipping in the grease left by her dinner.

Leagan could make me some kind of fool's trap to keep her out of my room—but I kill that thought where it stands before it gets into me.

"*Gold.*" She lifts her eyebrows to me. "Maybe I underestimated you."

A common mistake.

"Suzanna." Copper snaps her fingers.

Her voice is a whisper made to the floor. "I need more time."

"I didn't hear you, mumbler."

"I said I need more time." Suzanna throws her head back, hood of her shawl dropping off her rust-brown hair. The left lens of her glasses is shattered, cheek swollen under it like an overripe fruit. "Just one more night. I had the money...it's not my fault."

Copper's tongue crosses her lips, a snake sampling the scent of its prey. "You got robbed."

"Please."

"Sorry. I don't make the rules."

"Please. Please don't make me sleep outside."

"You don't have to sleep. You probably shouldn't." Copper snaps the book closed. "Be smarter with your customers next time."

"Copper, don't do this to me. You know I'm a hard worker. This will never happen again, I swear—"

"And how about you?" Copper turns on Agnes. "I heard you lost your promotion money playing dice lasterday. I hope you have your rent. It would look bad to lose two girls in one cycle."

The heat off Agnes's glare is almost breathable. "You'd better get out of my face, you ugly bitch."

"Or what? I won't have one?"

The chain lock falls behind Charlene's door. The click of her peg heels runs one step ahead of her, like stone beetles clapping their wings on the skewed floor.

She's a spider, pronounced at the elbows with powdery florals in her wake. But the hiss of silk on floorboards knocks the lie away. The truth is a sour body wrapped in a shell of watered jasmine perfume.

"How long has she been in there this time?" someone whispers.

"Two weeks," Agnes says.

"Keep talking," Copper says. "That's a good way to get promoted."

"Shut up."

"No one is getting put out on the street." Gold shadow paints the caved lid of Charlene's empty right eye socket. The one that remains is bloodshot and yellow. "Get your business in order and pay me by the end of the week."

"I will, Madam." Suzanna drops her head. "Thank you."

"Thank me by not letting it happen again. Albino."

The Stranger passes right through her, until the tether attaching me to her pinches my stomach.

Charlene stands aside, points a lock-joint finger to her room.

Whispers follow me, they don't matter. I don't want to die—it makes me consider the things the Stranger loathes in others. Shriveling to something less dangerous in hopes of mercy, running like a rabbit.

You are not that weak.

She's right. I'm not. I made Vesta a promise when we buried her in Winchester. Everyone responsible will die. If they decide to kill me, I go bloody.

Eleven.

Ammonia hits my eyes, chemical heat. Charlene uses a spit bucket as a toilet, and it is definitely in here, full.

Her desk lamp radiates the dirty, yellow light of bastard fire quartz that always bleeds from under the door. But inside the room, closer to its source, the light gets swallowed by the drapes that cling to half the wall like the refinery dust in the rest of the house.

What lurks behind them? I hate that I may never know.

The Stranger compresses my spine, and I try to stop seeing these things she wants. It only makes her demand to know what's inside more violent.

Desk drawers that scream to be opened, the echo of forgotten things, and what's changed since last cycle.

The top of her desk has been buried deeper under paper and wads of orange-stained cotton holding their balled shapes. The pen, out of its brass holder. Empty bottles of perfume. Three loose, yellow pills. Cigarettes.

A wax packet pokes from between her account ledger's pages.

Hidden beneath her blood orange lipstick, courage powder's telling gray ghost haunts the inside of her mouth. The same shadow that lurked inside my mother.

I try not to blame myself for not noticing it before. I've only seen her three times, here in the dark, but once usually is enough for me.

The fear boiling in my throat melts for the second it takes to flick the powder packet to my palm and then my pocket.

"You know why you're here."

Yes.

The Stranger catches on the key as Charlene pulls it from the lock and drops the tarnished chain it rides between her breasts.

"The boss has asked to see you tonight—" Her collarbones jut up through her skin suddenly, and she chokes black lung phlegm into her palm.

The refinery poison settles in my lungs every time I go outside. But the stench of her piss bucket is worse.

She wipes her palm with one of the already-used cloth scraps, her lips, smudging the lipstick caked into the crevices. Two more crusted balls dislodge from the desk when she drops this one, Charlene not minding as they catch on the frayed tail of her skirt.

She shifts aside the curtain that covers the back-alley door. Someone's already out there, the Stranger feels it.

"I've never asked who you are or where you came from because I don't care," she says. "Whatever bad blood you have with the boss, you haven't caused me any real trouble, as the Company pays me to keep you here."

And that makes me tolerable. At least it's an honest motive, nothing hidden inside it to sabotage me like whatever Copper is looking for. Gerard Rafael, boss of Hannah, didn't give me somewhere to live because he didn't want me living on the street. He wanted to be sure he knows where to find me.

Charlene turns the key. The lock crunches, tries to stick. It's probably full of ash.

My lungs strain against the top of my ribcage, and I can't hold my breath anymore. I press my arm up to my muzzle but still taste the burn of Charlene's piss bucket.

The Stranger quick judges the men waiting for me outside.

Two revolvers each.

Black-dust clothes and steel-toed boots. One is a sliver, carrying a long, skull cracker cane. The other is Nelson. He watches me on the street for the boss. He was there when they cornered me on the way out of Winchester six cycles ago. The Stranger put her shadow on him.

"Ladies first, she's all yours." Nelson motions the other man inside.

"Bastard cheater." He reaches for my arm, but I walk on my own.

Nine.

"It was dice." Nelson keeps his eyes on me, his hands off. Sad welds blister the knuckle duster knife on his thigh that Leagan wouldn't take off his corpse for free.

"How in sweet Jezebel could I cheat you?"

Aunt Tess can cheat at dice three different ways.

"Have her back by sunup," Charlene calls through the wedge of light left in the door.

"The boss will send her back when he sends her back."

"I'm tracking the overtime."

The black refinery fog smothers the top windows of buildings. Heavier than the storm clouds above it, bellies growling full of red lightning. I turn my face away from the wind, but the blowing dust still hits my eyes, draws water.

"Keep moving, milk-bastard. We don't have all night."

"Careful." Nelson cuts an arm across the alley before he gets too close to me. "You don't know who this is, do you?"

"I don't care who the boss wants to fuck tonight, so long as it's not me."

"Does the name Revere mean anything to you?"

"Should it?"

"They did most of the back market transport on the Core Rim. Some South. If you weren't buying something moved by them, you were paying for their protection."

Past tense.

"A fucking smuggler?"

"All I'm saying is take care."

"What is she going to do? There's two of us, and she's wearing a muzzle." He goads my spine with the cane's steel cap. "I bet she hits like a girl too."

Try me.

"Even with that muzzle, she's feral. She killed a man with her hands tied."

"Now that's an old fool's tale if I ever heard one."

"I was there, I saw it." Nelson breathes a little faster into his scarf, eyes pointed everywhere but directly at me. "They rode a train, six of them. All women. If that's not unlucky enough, people say their boss had the sight."

I hope Grandma hasn't had to see what's happened to me. Even if her dreams haven't told her, as a woman she knows. I just want her and everyone to know I'm not dead.

"I didn't realize you were such a superstitious female."

"I'm not. Maybe they're lying, but why would you want to fuck around with that? A female diviner, a gang of six...that's halfway to twelve."

"You're pathetic."

"And her...they call her the Stranger."

"Why?"

"I don't know."

The Stranger swells inside me like a deep breath.

Old Hannah lies around the next corner, east where I always keep my shoulder pointed and my gaze away from, but never my fully turned back.

"Why do they call you the Stranger?"

Turn your back on an enemy and die.

"Hey. Milk-bastard I'm talking to—"

It doesn't matter.

I walk faster. With enough speed I can slip through this place a shadow. She won't catch me.

Seventeen.

"Get back here." He has to yell.

In sunlight I see her. Before the refinery was born and covered Hannah in smoke. Before any of the buildings that exist here now. But the ground remembers, the Stranger does too.

She walks the street in a long dress, white hair, pale and burning in old sunlight.

My mother's ghost.

. . .

I've never known why she's been the only thing the Stranger allowed me to forget. It's because I was wrong. She's still here in my head alongside everything else. The Stranger just let me bury her face down so I wouldn't have to look at her.

I still don't. Not now.

Then look away.

The cane whistles against air.

Move.

He misses my spine, but the burst of pain across my hip takes my next breath.

"Come here, you." He grabs my shoulder. "Stay ahead of me where I can still see your ass. Try to slip me again and I'll beat some fear into you. Turn right."

Fool.

I know where I'm going.

They don't know I was born here. They don't know I'm going to turn this place to ash.

FOUR
TESLA

Leagan wanders into the kitchen, pipe smoke trailing her wake like coattails. She slides into the seat at the far end of the bench, an armload of space between her and the Damascus Sisters.

"There you are." I look to Evangeline. "I told you the bread would bring her in."

"I can smell a good bread from a mile away." Leagan stretches arms across the wasteland she made for herself down there and still barely manages to scrape the dish of goat cheese beans with her fingertips. "And shoot it from that far."

So, she's in that mood.

"Why are you sitting all the way down there?" Della pushes the dish closer, the tablecloth fighting back. "We already blessed your food for you and said an extra prayer for Adelaide."

Oh, sweet Della, you still don't know better.

Leagan sneers, rearranging the fried rice on her plate. "Like that's going to help."

"You shouldn't ask Raptor too many questions when she's hungry," I say.

"You don't mean that," Della says, like I didn't warn her.

"And don't take anything she says too personally either."

"I said it." Leagan glares, candy-black lips and hazel eyes. "And I meant it."

"No, you don't."

"I'm not going to pray until I see Adelaide again. And maybe I won't ever do it again."

"Evangeline!" Della looks to her for help.

Evan laces her fingers with a simple shrug. "Little darling, where's your sister?"

Leagan's gaze finds me. "Upstairs."

Oh fuck.

"Was she still working? Or does she not know it's time to eat?"

"I rang the bell," Della says.

"Maybe you didn't ring loud enough and it got covered up by all the praying." Leagan slices her spoon around the inside rind of a rock melon. "I was taking a nap and it didn't wake me up. That's why I'm late. I wonder what excuse Raleigh will use. It better be something good, like being dead."

"A nap?" I give the clock a glance, but I did not misread it the first time. Leagan's always been a dawn girl, and if she's telling the truth not simply goading Della, it did her foul mood dirty. "This close to your bedtime?"

She avoids looking at me now. "Who made you the boss of sleep?"

"Suspicious."

"Should we make a plate for Navy?" Della asks. "I'm sure she'll be hungry when she finishes working."

I should be a good aunt… Don't sigh.

"I'll go check on her." I squeeze Leagan's shoulder on my way out. "Be nice."

"No."

"Then keep your mouth full and your dirty hands off my pickles, ma'am. I'm coming back for them."

Della's a kind girl who makes the goats' clothes, remember?

Dusk fades the sky, not quite dark, not quite anything. Sugar bats whistle overhead, but that was a definitively human sniff slipping across the courtyard. I backtrack my last few steps into the garden.

"Navy?"

The air tastes green, lamplight and thickening shadows tangling between the reach of leaves. Another breath shakes the dark on the other side of the tomatoes.

She sits on the lip of the stone herb bed, a strand of lemon thyme being twisted apart between her fingers.

The retaining rocks push warmth through my skirt as I sink onto them. "Is there something you want to talk about?"

"Not really." She turns her face away to wipe it.

"Do you want me to leave you alone?"

"Not really."

I pull her against me. Her forehead is smooth to my cheek, and her hair carries the essence of dust. Or science. "You're my favorite chemist."

"I'm the only chemist you know."

"That wouldn't guarantee you're my favorite." I wait for her to take a better, less shaky breath. "I'm here to listen."

"My eyes...they've gotten—I couldn't read tonight." The defeat in her voice stings. "Usually it's better when it's darker, but I can't see you right now either. I can't see this." She holds her hand close to her nose, then scrubs the palm heel against her eye as if she can wipe out the damage that's been done to them by the lab accident.

"Stop." I pull her hand away. "Leagan and I will read to you. We'll be your eyes and hands, and you'll be the brain that guides us."

"You can't solve this problem for me, Aunt Tess. I wanted to be the one who cures the pestilence, but maybe it can't be done."

"You have Amnesty Wells's notes, and she's the bitch who made the pestilence. No one has ever had a better chance than you."

"I don't have any real training. What if I can't do it?"

"Well, what would you rather do instead?"

"I don't know."

"Say you try, and your theory is wrong, the West Rim isn't any more poisonous than it already is. Trying never hurts."

"Unless someone else dies." Navy tightens the hold she has on me. "I left her."

Adelaide.

I know the touch of that guilt. It's got hooks that worm their way deeper the harder you struggle to get away. It's not a burden she deserves, but even knowing that can't stop the way it cuts you.

"To play fair Adelaide is...known for doing things on her own, in her own way."

"You weren't there, Aunt Tess. We wouldn't have been there at all if I'd been more careful with my experiments and hadn't had my accident. Vesta wouldn't be..." She breaks. "I miss Grandma so much."

My bruised heart breaks too, it's so close to the surface it doesn't take much these days. I hold her tighter as raw tears spill down my cheeks.

"Adelaide would never admit it, but she was scared," she whispers. "I could tell. We had time to pull her off that ledge after the stovepipe separated us, I know it... She told me to leave without her. I said no, but she didn't listen to me. Raleigh didn't listen. He listened to her, and I just stood there like a fool."

"So, she made her own choice."

Damnation. Adelaide did what all of us like to say we'd do for the ones we love, secretly praying we never have to choose, because so few of us really are that selfless. Adelaide, the girl who loots warm corpses and walks by most who insult her without acknowledging a foul word, because survival is logical not emotional. The thing that makes women like her so terrifying isn't her Tov hair or glass skin. It's the ruthless wall built so high around her heart, most fools don't even know it's there. They have no idea what they're missing. If those bounty hunters killed her, then she went out as the fucking loyal sister I still wish I could have been.

"She chose wrong," Navy says. "I just rode away with Raleigh and... left her." The sob leaves her gasping, whisper so small yet so wide with guilt. "Maybe to die...and worse."

My fingers tremble as I run them down her back. While I don't like to doubt Adelaide's ability to survive alone, there's a price to live in a place without rules. We all know women pay double. In my opinion the risk is worth it, but even if we manage to slip past the horrors the Rim keeps for sport, in the end none of us will be leaving this life alive.

"This is not your fault," I say. "You didn't make us go to West Rim for you. We all agreed, remember?" Mother was the only one who didn't, and I still want that black gold out there in Eden. I still believe we have a chance to get it.

"I told Adelaide Vesta's death wouldn't be in total vain because I could learn more about the pestilence from studying her body. It made sense back then. What if she chose to save me because I had those samples? If I don't figure out a way to cure the pestilence, then I let both of them down again."

"She would have chosen you either way. You can't put so much on yourself." What she sees as a survival debt is still a thousand times less selfish than my choices the last time I saw her mother, my sister Liza.

"I still wonder if I could have saved your mother's life." I go numb inside the memory, so distant yet still so close it will always be a part of me. "She thought the Crow job was wrong, but I told her we weren't quitters." I think that made her want to prove herself to me. "I could have easily talked her out of going and just done the job myself." The same way my pressure talked her into going. "She was my little sister. I wanted to protect her the way Adelaide protected you. I always said I would but..." Then I ignored what Liza wanted to get what I thought we deserved. "Our last conversation wasn't very kind."

"You didn't know they were going to shoot her," Navy says. "Even Grandma didn't know what her dream meant until after it happened."

"Exactly. But Grandma used to blame herself for that day too." And I regularly ordered her to stop accepting the guilt, a hypocrite to my own advice. "Some things you can't stop because they're supposed to happen, even if you see them coming. Even if you hate them."

"Even if they're awful... Am I bad for also being relieved I didn't get captured? Or killed?"

"Absolutely not. Don't be sorry," I say, but it's Mother's voice, her words tried by time. "It's not worth the effort."

There's only one person who deserves the blame for how horribly east our life went. In a very unprovoked manner, I might add. His name is Mr. Carrson Green.

"Adelaide loves you," I say. "She also loves exploring new places, robbing fools and messing with things that don't belong to her. She could be having the best time of her life."

Navy comes close enough to a smile that I can feel like I've done my job.

"We made you a plate. Wait here, I'll go get it and we'll go back to my room and eat."

"Thank you, Aunt Tess."

"Anytime, Rook." I pat her knee as I rise. "Don't worry. Raleigh will come back soon, and we'll find out if Adelaide's in Hannah or not."

We'll know if she even survived the rest of that day, but obviously I don't say that to Navy. Truthfully, I'm just as scared for Raleigh to get here as I am anxious for the news he's supposed to deliver. Waiting is always worst.

FIVE
ADELAIDE

GERARD RAFAEL FACES THE BANK OF WINDOWS IN HIS OFFICE, THE ONES THAT look like teeth from the ground. Hannah pulses red, a bed of hot crystal below. The walls of the Company compound create a dense and oiled den of halls and rooms. It has plenty of glass, but his apartment feels more like a cupboard than mine.

The garlic traces I smelled on the way up the stairs come alive in here. Fool's gold, I'm hungry. Behind him waits the tea table, two covered plates.

"Come in, wayward fox." Rafe sucks the ivory pipe in his hand, smoke a sick caramel haze around his silver-flecked beard.

I reach for the memory of Grandma's rose tobacco. She and I sit on warm steel of the parked *Absolution*, the two moons and stars all over, her hands softer than petals. The Stranger lets me live in it a few seconds. I flood with the longing that makes me wish I'd never gone on Kane's expedition. The truth that I had to, and I will again.

"The supply train came this morning." Rafe doesn't turn immediately. He waits until he's produced a few more smoke plumes. "There's fresh oranges and plums from Eos."

Plums are one of Leagan's favorite treats, especially the sour red ones.

Rafe's eyebrows pull the skin of his thick forehead as he approaches, the mix of sage and mint in his pocket meant to ward off fell spirits. But they don't work on me.

"You don't look too happy to be here. Are you well?" He eyes his men. "She's right on time, but were you polite to my guest?"

"Absolutely, sir."

"I asked Revere." The hinge of Rafe's lower replacement jaw clicks when he talks. "They didn't manhandle you?"

I start a count of the number of times I catch the glint of copper teeth.

"Never touched her, sir." Nelson again.

The welt from the cane hit still rages hot under my skirt.

Not yet, the Stranger cautions me. *Soon. His guard will come down at some point. That's when.*

I'll be waiting.

I lean away as Rafe reaches for me.

"Alkaline." He drops his hand on my shoulder anyway, thumb rubbing absently across my exposed collarbone. The touch fires through the hair on my arms, neck, to the black beds of my fingernails, the blood under them. "Are you hungry?"

My jaw waters. Right now, I would even eat corn pudding, or the soup from the soup camp. I hate corn pudding. The camp soup kills people.

The Company gun jabs me with his cane. "Speak up, you disrespectful whore."

My grip tightens against his as I remove the pointed skull cracker from my neck. East blood weapons. Any bone picker can swing a stick.

"That's not necessary." Rafe pulls the square muzzle key, and his man drops his stance. "Revere, you'll join me for dinner."

The mask peels off my face, freedom and cool emptiness. The Stranger flares, fills the room to the corners like a set of hard wings.

Fool.

"There." Rafe's palm scratches against my bare cheek. "That's better. Smile for me? No? Maybe later." He winks at his men. "She's just shy."

The Stranger drifts behind him, a shadow he can't see. Her attention strokes drawers and shelves along the grain, picking and twisting like a screw while Rafe shifts pages on his desk.

"Revere, Revere...Adelaide, the Stranger, Revere."

I hate his voice. It vibrates, the low rumble of wheels. The way he softly mispronounces my name like an east blood on purpose. If the Stranger could kill alone, her darkness would choke him, fill until his eyes and stomach squeezed out. But she has no tether to this world except me.

"Go have a seat. We have a load to discuss." Rafe looks up, waits for me to obey him.

My stare is hard as his.

The ridge of his top lip twinges, the muscle unsure if it should snarl or smile. "You know that feeling when you're being watched, all the hairs on your body twitching? You look, but there's nothing there…"

But there is. He just doesn't see her.

"Such a curious thing."

"I feel it too, boss," the hired gun says.

"Damnation." Rafe shakes his head. "Now you are being an impolite guest, giving us a spook. Have I been disrespectful to you at any point? Sit. You're making me nervous."

Outside, it starts to rain. The roar of thunder can't compete with the weight of water crashing onto the steel roof. The glow of Hannah beyond the windows disappears in a river of ash.

"I sent my man Kasey to Descendants last cycle. I believe you know him." Rafe comes back around the desk, tapping a folded letter on his palm. "He just got back. I'd heard a rumor, but I wanted to be sure it was true before I spread it to you." His hand is hot as he wraps it around the back of my neck, big enough to reach the front, and pulls.

Thirteen.

Rafe draws the chair and seats me in it, impact startling the porcelain. The Stranger runs her gaze up the front of him like cold water.

I am in deep with this fucker.

"There. See, your legs aren't broken. Sit, relax."

I don't want to give him the satisfaction of eating his food, but I need to eat something. It might as well be this over something rancid or flecked with ash from the air market.

Steam floods my face, creamy cheese and spices spill over rice as I uncover the bowl. The first bite scalds the whole way down, but I don't stop.

It's a flash memory of being younger, eating without stopping to breathe because I don't know what my next meal is going to be. And to finish before someone tries to take it.

"Should we go, sir?" Nelson asks.

"Stay there." Rafe takes the seat opposite me, clears his throat while he picks open the letter. "Gut her if she stabs me."

I'm already a third through my plate, but my hunger-shaken limbs haven't noticed yet.

"This is from Tesla. In it she calls me an impotent bastard and hopes—" Rafe perches reading spectacles on his shovel nose. "—that I bite my big toe off and swallow it. I'm not sure how that would possibly occur, but she certainly has an imagination and a charming way of expressing herself, doesn't she?"

He only wants one thing from me. Same as the day I got here. The thing he sent his men after us to find. The thing we don't have anymore.

"Signed 'Absolutely yours, Tesla the Widow Revere.'" He folds the letter and stuffs his napkin deep into his linen collar to protect the black floral ascot.

This worries me. Aunt Tess being the voice of this. Most of our business has been her ideas, but Grandma has always been the one to speak our decisions, even if we all had a vote in making them.

Rafe looks past his spoon at me. "She did not tell me where my stolen crystal went."

Of course, the time I'm not lying is the one time someone's convinced I am. *Farce.*

"We left it with St. Paul, Mr. Green's pocket man in Descendants. Warehouse thirteen. He paid us to bring it back to you and get caught."

"You've told me this story before."

"I'm not lying."

"In my experience, a person who must announce they're not lying is."

Well, not this experience.

"And in response to that, I've told you, several times, Green's an investor in the railroad expansion. Governor of Vantage, licensed with the Commerce Guild now. Thievery doesn't advance a man like that."

Yes, it does.

The Stranger twitches. "How do you think he got that way?"

"Irrelevant. Your family has accepted the terms of my ransom, but so far you're about fifty thousand standards short of meeting the debt. You'll likely be here for a while, so you might as well do yourself a favor. Tell me the truth and I can improve your living arrangements. Wouldn't you like that?"

Vesta and I moved that chest Green asked us to deliver for him. It was heavy, but not big enough for fifty thousand standards' worth. Black gold goes for two hundred per pound back east, copper standard.

"It was maybe worth fifteen."

"The amount is circumstantial. Black gold is not your business, Miss Revere, I can't expect you to know the market value. It goes up. Moreover, they haven't said a word yet that sounds sorry."

We don't apologize for things that aren't our fault. Grandma taught us that.

Rafe plucks the lemon garnish off his plate, twisted into a rose. "The deed is done. What matters to me is the contract your family and I had. We were on the same side of the coin. Bone pickers, come from nothing. You were whores, and I was the son of one. Now I was born in a Jezebel slum, but it's all the same on an auction block when you have no power to offer. People disrespected me for a long time too."

Not like this. You're still a man, and different rules apply, even on an auction block.

"We all worked hard, and we all became something. Then you betrayed me. Now it's time to pay the gravedigger."

I've eaten as much as I can stomach. Now I feel sick. I wipe the oil from my mouth on the back of my hand.

"You made a smart decision, coming here to see me yourself. Now I can't kill you from a distance with impunity. I have to order it, knowing what your face looks like."

I'll let him know what the Stranger looks like someday too.

"I want to read that letter." See if he lied.

Rafe smiles down at me, copper bottom teeth on full display.

Some say it was a mining accident that ruined his jaw. A saloon brawl. Others that he modified it on purpose. The Stranger remembers all his real teeth were present the day we left Hannah nineteen Seasons ago.

"I thought you might."

I stand as he does. My spoon flips off the edge of the bowl, splattering cream across the linen table.

Six—

Rafe plucks the brass cap off the desk lantern behind him. I grab, but he shoves my hand inside. A burst flares behind the green glass as the letter ignites on quartz. Flames kiss my knuckles with needles.

Bastard. The Stranger lashes out, darkness.

I twist my arm, latch onto his thick wrist. Rafe turns on me, back knuckles connecting with my cheek. While I'm still stung by the impact, he forces me to a seat on the desk, shoving my legs apart, dragging back on my hair. His false jaw clicks against my ear. "It wasn't addressed to you."

Or it wasn't from Aunt Tess at all.

Rafe finishes hiking my skirt out of the way, undoes his belt. "Gentlemen, I think it's time for you to call it a night. Miss Revere and I will settle this alone."

"Right, boss."

The door scrapes to rest in its frame, and Rafe steps back. Belt threaded back into place, he picks an etched decanter from the bookshelf.

I clench my legs together, arms against me, watch the last flakes of Aunt Tess's letter crumble away. Red and black. All that's left, the not knowing if he lied.

"To keeping appearances." Rafe lifts the glass my way. "Your silence has its uses. At times."

The hotspot left on my cheek has a pulse.

He knocks an account book off the desk, a dull slap for them to hear outside. "There's one other matter, and I thought you might appreciate this being said in private. It regards what Kasey found in Descendants."

I go unseasonably cold.

"A portion of the bounty on your family name was claimed. Around the time you arrived here."

Rafe drops the same book on the floor a second time, but it lands without sound. The black swells up past my ears, the Stranger's beating heart, shadowy to the tips. I could take its hand and fall into her before this horror latches onto me.

I know which of us it's not.

Not me. Not Vesta. Not Aunt Tess, if the letter really was hers. But refusing to hear something won't make it untrue.

"On Moira, the Raven."

"Prove it."

He can't.

But Rafe takes a small object from his vest pocket with a sigh that's almost real. Grandma's river pearl ring. The black mirror shine, fixed in a scalloped and oblong copper setting.

Focus, the Stranger says.

I try. Nothing good comes past my cloudy judgment.

"They claimed her dead."

I wait to crack, the Stranger's feral blackness pouring out of me like it did when Vesta died, ready to murder everyone in my path. But it doesn't happen. Nothing happens. This ache is raw. A sour seed planted inside me in a dream. Dull, a blade that's been hammered against a wall too many times. Even the Stranger's voice fades to the back of my head.

Rafe drains the last of his whiskey and comes back to me. "I'm sure you want this over with so you can be left in peace."

So many things burn through my heart that I don't have time to pick them apart, and I'm made of wax.

Rafe wraps my hand around the block of refined black gold, his hand enclosing both. With a hammer's repeat he brings the crystal down on the papered desk.

There was a time when Grandma was the only person in this world who wanted me. I've always been afraid of this day, at the same time recklessly believed she would live forever. She gave me everything. A family. Value. Love. Without her, I wouldn't have survived.

The desk lurches as I rip my arm free, glass clattering over, trailing whiskey vapor. There's nowhere to run in here, or out there.

Vesta was infected with the pestilence, but she wasn't dead yet. He set his men on us in Winchester because of a lie spread by Green. Grandma kept her word to Rafe for almost twenty Seasons, but he was too lazy to ask why she'd break it now.

He killed them both.

There's no impunity in distance. Only proof you're a coward. He as good as pulled the trigger himself, just wasn't willing to see the blood.

I saw it. I held Vesta as she died, her beautiful face split open like a melon, still wake up at night with the weight of her in my arms and the bone chill of that death rattle in her chest. That's all I have left of her and Grandma now. Memory. It's a good thing the Stranger has a perfect one.

"I have been merciful to you." Rafe squeezes my arm, red spots left behind on top of pain. "You still have value to me, but don't force me to change my mind, understand?"

No, I don't. His idea of mercy can't scrub out what I want. What I'm going to do. It only makes me want it more.

He should have killed you when he had the chance.

I am a wretched enemy. One with fire and no remorse. And I will burn this place down to the dust.

I bring my hand around to the knife sheathed at the base of his spine. The oiled blade slips noiselessly.

"Don't." His hand clamps my wrist. Iron.

Three. Four.

My legs hit the desk as his body moves mine, impact firing through my bruised hip.

Rafe peels my fingers back one at a time, and I pick Grandma's ring from his vest unnoticed.

"I can see you're upset by this news, and I don't blame you for that. But don't make me hurt you tonight." He leans into me harder, the desk crushing the blood from my legs.

My arm shakes as I push back.

"Say yes, so I know you understand me."

Make him trust you. The Stranger echoes Aunt Tess's familiar words back to me. The gamble I've somehow survived by.

All I have is a whisper. "Yes."

Rafe pats my cheek three times, the last landing as a slap. "You're free to go. I trust you can find your own way home."

Yes, I plan on it.

SIX
TESLA

THE WIND SOOTHES LIKE MINT BALM TODAY, LIKE YESTERDAY AND THE DAY before. No *Solace* rains, no livestock raids, and no Raleigh. Just the bleat of the goats and their bells as I gather them off the hillside with Della and Leagan.

From the rooftop terrace, the Salt Waste glows like the constant moon's mirror surface. The silver skin stabs my eyes, even at this distance.

Deeper south, the Damascus Mountains rise eternal. It defies logic that something cold as snow manages to cling to rocks the color of fire when the heat takes on a life of its own. But it does. The low slopes near us are clear, but as the rocks rise higher, white cloaks the red. The highest ones, a blue and unbreakable promise. Someday I will feel that proud summit snow with my own hands. I've heard it stings. I wonder if it has a smell.

"Did you know," Leagan says, "Damascus means sanctuary in Old Root, the base language Tov, Cairosh, and Eosin emerged from back when—"

"You're distracting me," Navy says.

"That's why you keep me around."

"You're supposed to be copying Amnesty's journal."

"I am. I'm just taking a break. Calm your pits." Leagan wanders out to the rooftop balcony, pointing at me. "Did you know—"

"I heard. So, calling this Damascus Sanctuary is like calling me Tesla Tess."

"Yes." She snaps her book shut. "But most people don't know that. Now you do, so don't make the same mistake twice."

"I wouldn't dare. Thank you, ma'am."

Leagan slides a shoulder against the mission's stone wall, drawing Mother's pipe from her coveralls. To the rose tobacco she adds drops of the bergamot and redweed oil Raleigh brought her the last time he was here. After the initial flash of empty pain as she lights up, the familiar scent spills the good memories over me. I don't cry this time, but that itself makes me sad. Am I already forgetting to miss her?

The bergamot catches up to the rose, the sour note redweed puts under it changing the smoke scent into a new memory creature, Leagan's flavor.

I clear a hungry fly off my page. "I see you've accepted Raleigh's peace bribe. That's nice."

"I have not." She exhales, the first deep cloud pouring from her open mouth as she flicks the blue vial of oil between fingers. "And I'm not nice. I don't have to forgive him to use the gift. He should know better."

"Fair enough." I stretch my arm overhead with a groan, using a finger to keep the wind from collapsing the rest of Kane's stolen journal on my page.

When I turn back, his alkaline handwriting blurs to meaningless shapes again, the cramp in my neck something livid. I could keep sitting here, but if I'm not comprehending this, then I'm just wasting my time.

Navy sits with her back to the light outside, rubbing her knuckles on her brow as she smooths her magnifying lens across her calculations. She's rubbed the front end of that eyebrow right off. She keeps writing as my presence looms over her, even as I pull the hand away.

It wouldn't be nice to laugh, so I lean over her shoulder. "Go look at yourself."

"What, do I have a bug in my hair? Please take it off."

"Missing something?"

Navy squints close to the washbowl mirror, running fingertips across her forehead until they sense a bald patch at the start of her brow. "Fool's gold, Leagan! Why didn't you say something?"

Pale tendrils taint Leagan's breath and slip past her flared nostrils. "You didn't ask." She holds her fingers to Navy's face. "What would you look like with no eyebrows? Hmm, not very good."

"How dare you. Will you please go find something else to do and let me work. Go look for some scavenger lizards."

"No, I like it here with you."

"You like bothering me."

"I think we've all been up here breathing our own breath too long," I say. "Time for a break."

"I'd better not, I have too much to do."

"You'll work better if you relax."

Leagan grabs her hat. "I'm going to visit the goats. They miss me."

"Navy Revere." She flinches as I plant my hand on her book, peeling it away from her nose. "The pestilence isn't going anywhere. I know you're not much of an outdoor girl, but at least go downstairs and stand in the sun for five minutes. It'll be good for your brain."

"You're right." She sighs, searching out her veil among the other scarves and coats on the rack by touch.

I swing my arms as I walk, my footsteps resonating down the stone corridors and clearing the dust from my head.

Gentle prayer twists off a Sister's lips and escapes through the star lattice wall of the lower hall, the top of a dusty white hat moving behind the pattern of green leaves in the courtyard garden.

Damascus is safe because it's removed from most of the Rim's excitement, most of the Rim still unaware of its existence. We could stay here under the mountains, raising goats and spinning yarn. I could pretend I'm satisfied, but it would always be a lie.

It wasn't a lie when I told Mother I'd like to retire someday. I long for peace like this, but this is Evangeline's sanctuary. I am a guest in her home, and the lure of black gold still calls to me too loudly to ignore. When I retire, it will be for the right reasons.

I can't build us a safe place while we still have enemies who will try to take it.

The steady clap of leather grows clearer and sweat thickens as I descend into shadows of the cellar, emerging from them into rose-gold quartz light.

Evangeline paces around the stuffed leather dummy hanging from the support beam, throwing bare-knuckle punches and swerving imaginary blows. Sweat runs through the crevices in her arms and back, undershirt soaked from the neckline to belt.

The thick cadence of strikes doesn't stall as I rest a shoulder to the shelves of pickled vegetables. "He just insulted your form and called me a bitch."

"Did he now?" Evangeline pulls a breath past the moisture dripping off her nose. "Well, that's low dignity, even in a ring fight. We should show him some manners. Would you like to go a round with me?"

"Not today. I washed my hair last night. It would be a sin to get all sweaty and waste that water."

"An admirable assumption." Her last two punches leave the bag swaying on its rope like a loose tooth.

"Do you ever miss boxing for money?"

"Not particularly." Evangeline wipes her slick hairline with the back of her forearm and smiles with her teeth instead of just her lips this time. The brass canine and molar replacement teeth her everyday reminder of small mercies, because it could have been all of them, she's said. "But the exercise still relieves my soul and body."

She rubs a cloth over her arms and face before setting to the buttons of her work shirt. The sleeves were made for practical things, plain cuffs and no tucks or gathers. "Speak your mind then, darling." She hauls up her suspenders. "I can see you have something on it."

"I always have *something* on my mind... I want this someday."

She nods, awaiting my next thought.

"But it won't be right unless I've earned it."

"Not necessarily. You don't earn mercy. The Rim could use more sanctuary, more compassion, and someone willing to defend those things. And you, my friend, have the gift of making a vision reality."

"You understand my side of things." I swallow the glass in my throat. There are knots six inches deep in my head. "Obviously we're not going to abandon Adelaide."

"Of course not. I never meant to suggest that."

"Green took everything from us." I stop to collect my runaway breath. "I don't walk away from unfinished business."

"I know..."

"And you have some kind of advice for me, don't you?"

"Did you come looking for advice, or a friend to listen?" she asks.

"Both." I value her insight second only to my own, and my mother's. She is the second wisest woman I've known—Mother the first, obviously, but I know she can't tell me how this will end. I have to make the choices that will steer me to the outcome I want. Good thing I've always been crafty. "Just know I will make my own decision."

"Have you allowed yourself to grieve your daughter and mother? Or are you running from that toward this revenge?"

"They might appear similar." But running and striving are still two very different things. I rebuke the idea of sitting in my bedroom with the storm shutters closed, crying my pain to the dark. That does nothing and honors no one in the end. "Keeping busy is so much more productive, and it hurts less."

She clears the exercise from her throat. "Hate and greed are easy. Forgiveness is one of the hardest things there is, and Providence never promised that it would be painless. Be better than your enemies."

"Why? What backwards justice makes forgiveness my responsibility? I shouldn't have to be better than my enemies. By the time I'm done with him, it's Green who will be begging for mine."

"Judgment is mine," she quotes. "As is mercy."

"Blessed are those who pass through the fire."

"Indeed. You've lost more in your lifetime than I can imagine, and I would never hold the desire for justice against you." Evangeline looks at me with nothing but kindness. It doesn't make the lump of iron in my chest any less painful. *Farce*, even at her absolute worst, I'll never be wholly good like her.

"You say Green took everything from you, but I have to disagree," she says. "He took much, yes, but not all. I'm not asking you to forget what happened to your family, or even to lie down and accept it. Adelaide needs your help, and I know you'll use every gift you have to bring her home. I'm just reminding you to be kind to yourself, and to remember everything you still have."

Vesta's memory, my mother's love that made me strong. Navy and Leagan, my sister's clever-at-science daughters. And Adelaide, the one my mother loved first, despite what anyone else said. Our family is incomplete without her unique blend of insight and apathy.

I owe them the chance to fight back. I owe Mother, Vesta, and Liza whose lives were cut from under them. I owe the women who will be born to the Rim after us, and because of what I've done, see they are more than what they're told to be.

Most of all, I owe myself.

"I know you, Tess, and you are a schemer. Whatever you're planning to do, I do not ask, just remember Providence is God of Mercy, and His mercy will always remember you."

"And that's a very good thing, because I like doing things that are considered wrong, by preacher's standards, at least. But this isn't one of those times."

"I've said my piece, you know where I stand, and I thank you for hearing it even if you don't agree." Her hand touches mine. "But when you come to end of this road, and Adelaide is safe and back with us, if you still choose vengeance, consider the cost."

"I have."

I'm not going to be better than my enemies. I'm going to be much, much worse.

"You have so much to offer, my friend," she says. "Both fire and compassion. Your heart is gold, and no matter what you do or say, I will always love you."

"So will I." And that will always mean so much to me, her compliments given with no ulterior motive, and her strength not a mask.

"I would hate to see you lose yourself to this. These men are not worth that—"

The bell outside the wall rings.

"I'm sorry." I pull away so fast, I accidentally scratch her. "I'm sorry, this can't wait."

My steps hammer on the aging stairs, air kissing my knees as I gather my full skirt over one arm in the courtyard to run.

The iron teeth of the wheel lock pull out of each other, allowing me to lift the bar and sweep the gate open.

Raleigh stands at the well, the iron bell like a dead melon over it, salt dust boiling off his clothes as he slaps them.

"Where have you been?" The uneven ground jars my bones, and my voice with them.

Farce, he's not smiling. This is not the kind of news I want to be surprised by. God of Mercy, brace me.

"I know." Raleigh halts at the line of yellow tile crossing broken dirt that divides women-only Damascus from the rest of the Rim. "The Express Rider got butchered. We're lucky we even got this. One of my pearl divers happened to be in the area and decided to strip the thief." His words tumble on the loose wind as he struggles to remove his goggles and dig the other hand into his pocket simultaneously.

"And?"

He holds up a letter, all ice and stillness like that snow up on the mountains. With it is Adelaide's skystone ring.

"Fucking Jezebel." I can swear in five different languages, but this one feels most appropriate right now.

Leagan overtakes me, a shadow I didn't know I had, the sound that floods her throat more animal than girl.

"She's alive—" Raleigh trips over exposed roots as she slams into him. "*Farce*, Raptor!"

"Give it!"

"Get off of me." He shoves her back, waving Adelaide's ring to draw her off his soft bits as meat does to a feral dog. But he can't crawl fast enough to get away from her, and she grabs his hair.

"Don't break him." Fool's gold, I can taste my stomach. "There wasn't a finger to go along with this, was there?"

"No, it's not—"

"Shut up, you *traitor*!" Leagan lunges again, two of her strikes connect with Raleigh's head before I grasp the back of her collar.

"Raptor!"

"For the last time, I had *no choice*!" His voice breaks.

"Snake!" Her chest heaves, tears rolling from her eyes.

I drag her back over the Damascus side of the tile line, shivering like she's the one who got hit. "Both of you stop it or I'll slap you so hard you go out of existence."

Raleigh turns away, wiping his face.

Leagan jams Adelaide's ring onto her hand, sinking to her knees, head buried between them. "Don't read it, Aunt Tess. I don't want to know."

"We have to." I lift the envelope's gray wax seal because it's already broken. "Your pearl diver read our mail?"

"I read your mail." Raleigh finds another streak of dust-laced spit left on his cheek. "Nice. I had to know, I'm sorry."

I stretch out the double-sided sheet. "I would have too."

To The Reveres:

Moira, Tesla, Vesta, Navy, Leagan:

Let this letter formally notify you that I have Adelaide "The Stranger" Revere in my possession, if you were not already aware. She is alive and in what can be regarded as reasonably fine health, considering her disposition.

I am deeply pained to write this ransom, and this position brings me no pleasure. I had the highest hopes our agreement would stand as a testament to mutual respect, no matter how many Seasons eclipsed between us. I don't know what changed, or what fell moon compelled you to cannibalize our peace, but I thought you among the few spirits who could be trusted. It seems I was gravely mistaken in the honor among thieves.

Not so, sir.

If you really believed this load of bullshit you're trying to feed me, you'd give us the chance to explain ourselves.

However, I am willing to consider a trade, provided proper restitution is made for your collective betrayal. I wouldn't offer this chance to anyone else. However, as once-partners I still feel I owe you the courtesy, as well as the opportunity, to apologize. I hope you feel the same, and that this can be resolved without an end written in blood.

Doubtful.

Until we come to such an arrangement, I will keep the Stranger at my discretion to ensure you take no further action against me or my business. I'm confident you see the reason in this, not malice. In the meantime, she will be treated reasonably and will not be fatally harmed by my hand.

Not by *your* hand, and not fatally. I understand how these word games are played, Rafael.

Mr. Kasey, my right-hand man, will be in Descendants two cycles from now to give you my full terms. That should allow enough time for this letter to reach you, and for you to meet him, wherever you may lurk.

Bring my crystal, or whatever you sold it for. You will only be given this one chance to negotiate. Do not be foolish with it.

Sol,

  Gerard Rafael

Son of a bitch.

"Motherfucker!" The yell doubles me over, blood scalding through my ears. I've got nothing else. We lost everything, but the Rim and all its pickers still demand more. If this letter had gotten lost like it almost did...

Evangeline places a hand on my back, the weight a relief like one being lifted. I hadn't realized she was standing beside me. "Forgive her, she needs mercy now more than ever."

"*What?*" Leagan claws the letter from me, despair bleeding from her eyes.

"What are we going to do?" Raleigh asks.

He's asking me. I'm in charge of this shit fight, but do I look like I have answers?

I barely finished reading and had time to take a breath, and he wants a clever plan.

"Let me think, damnation!"

Raleigh puts his hands up.

I know, I usually have the plan, but aren't I allowed a moment of weakness like the rest of them? Maybe I don't want to be the one responsible this time. All I want to do is scream.

"There is nothing lost that can't be found, Tesla." Evangeline steps between us, her rock-steady hand a support for my arm while she holds her other against Raleigh. "Your toe is awfully close to that line, my friend. Women-only past this point. You seem pleasant enough, but I can't bend these rules, even for you, so please step back so I don't have to take action against a good soul."

"I appreciate being given a warning." Raleigh retreats to the well, the beaten curve of his shoulders exactly what I feel between mine.

Evangeline squeezes my hand. "May I see this news?"

Navy emerges from the sanctuary, wind flowing through the black veil that protects her eyes from the sun. She walks careful on the stone path, uneven and pitted by *Solace* rain.

"Have it," I nod, wiping my cheeks clean. "I'll be back."

"Is that Raleigh?" The tremble in Navy's voice is smaller than the other night, readier. "I got down here as fast as I could, I didn't want to trip on the stairs. Not that I blame Leagan for being in a hurry... What did he say?"

"We got a letter from Hannah."

Maybe it's Navy's hand on my arm or simply the act of repeating the words out loud to her, but the bigger plot clarifies in my head. The information I've just absorbed isn't the end of our line, despite what it made me flash feel. It's an opportunity to show why Green sought to eliminate us. We are the name you should fear, and Adelaide isn't dead.

The plan must be mine not because everyone else doesn't have a brain without me, but because plotting is what I do best.

Really, though, they would be sad without me.

Leagan rocks herself while Evangeline strokes fingers over her back to the pace of Raleigh circling the well.

They turn to include us as Navy and I reach the line in the dust again.

"Holding Adelaide alive gives Rafe leverage over us," I say. "He's smart enough to realize this, and in my experience, he's not a liar. He won't kill her until he gets what he wants."

You fool, Rafe. You met me when I was only a girl. A clever girl, but now meet me as the woman with experience I have become.

Fear glistens, liquid in the corners of Leagan's raptor eyes, the shadows under them deep as bruises. "You'll make sure that doesn't happen?"

"Absolutely. Raleigh?"

"Yes, ma'am?"

"We'll be making a savings withdrawal from the vault." *Farce* if I don't find some insane pleasure buried in the middle of this. The worst part is over for me, the waiting, the shock. "Get your best guns ready, ladies. We're going to Descendants."

SEVEN
ADELAIDE

WHEN I LEFT FOR THE WEST RIM, LEAGAN ASKED ME TO BRING HER BACK SOME bones or a live armadillo.

I lift the rough planking covering the bone well behind the soup camp. She'd appreciate this. Animal bones float with bare white shadows in a bottomless void as the Stranger probes the darkness below. They clatter, teeth and heads, eye sockets snagging on the end of the firebox rake, and ribs slipping off it. It's possible some are also human.

Somewhere behind the clotted sky and refinery stacks, the sun has gone down. It's been so long since I've seen the moons.

The wind turns, infesting the air with fresh ash particles like flies. Don't breathe. My chest doesn't rattle like Charlene or wake me up in the night choking on phlegm like Agnes.

The rake catches on the drawstring of my bag among the bones.

I won't be here long enough for that.

A vial of flash fire, three fire quartz crystals and wax-dipped string. Nothing taken, nothing added, but now it all goes into my skirt.

The women who run the soup camp feed their kettles unknown carcasses and rotting vegetables. Whatever doesn't melt is picked out and fed to the bone wells. Dirt-covered fools gather around the pits of bastard fire quartz to drink from oily bowls for single silver standard. The air has texture. Sour, like a wound.

Forty-seven.

Margorhett hangs her long-reach ladle on the end of her cauldron spit, arms spotted with grease burns, hair and face wrapped up with cotton to keep the ash out. "Hello, fox girl. Did you bring it?"

I'm not here to eat.

I follow her around the two bins of bastard fire quartz used to keep the pits burning, bucket topped with potato skins bumping weight against my leg with every step.

The chop tent is more rancid than the soup, the troughs dripping carcasses and deflated gourds. Another woman smiles at me from across the bench of knotted intestines.

"It's time to stoke the pits." Margorhett grabs an empty bucket off the hook.

My shoulder clicks under the release of weight as I let the bucket go to the ground, soft with fluids under my feet.

Margorhett delves in hands first once we're alone. The layer of cabbage and potato skins lifts away, lands in the empty bucket with a slap. A sack is the real core beneath.

Sugar. Coffee. Stolen from the Company-owned general store.

She undoes the top, dips a finger, and giggles. "You are a clever one. I didn't think you could do it."

The Stranger doesn't believe she can do what she promised either.

With a blood-rust hand, she picks one of the stomachs dangling from a chain. It hits the table with a glass thud. Piss-yellow corners of bastard crystals poke from the membrane as she spreads a slit at the top with her fingers and adds three more vials of flash fire.

"I put in an extra," she says. "I want this to be worth your while if they catch you. And if they don't, I want to deal with you again."

It's worth it. I smile at her from behind the muzzle, place the stomach in the other bucket and leave the one I brought in with her.

SIX MEN TRAPPED ME, NAVY, AND RALEIGH ON THE WAY OUT OF WINCHESTER last Season. One of them died on the bank of the *Delta Sol* that same day.

Five remain, the ones who brought me here.

The mask I wear tonight is made of bone. A lower jaw like a crescent moon wired to the upper of something with needle canines, drawn from the depths of the soup camp bone well to live again. My black scarf dissolves my hair and skin. The true face of the Stranger, born in Hannah, like me.

Nelson returns to the Company boardinghouse, his room on the bottom floor, the bed next to the window.

He's a gray shadow, removing his scarf and suspenders, the glass sticky with ash between us. Thunder groans across the walls, the air like mud.

He drops onto the bed to remove his boots, the curve where the mattress sags from his ass every day. His weight crushes the twin glass vials I put under it.

One with four drops of flash fire. One of clear pine.

Blue-hot rage sprays across the pine floor under him, the tree made of fire that sprouts from those roots midday gold. Nelson, his scream, both collapse inside it.

He told the others they should kill me, not bring me here where I'd cause trouble.

The Stranger smiles.

Four.

He was right.

EIGHT
TESLA

Everyone can agree Lideon smells like dead fish, but Descendants reeks like the unwashed armpits who dwell here. An armpit some fool attempted to cloak with the perfume of sweet black taffy pitch that coats the warehouses. Let me tell you, it does not help.

But there's something irresistible about a place so unsavory even a lawless bastard like the Rim is afraid of it, and I respect Descendants for that.

Our bounty poster clings to the Lucky Sol trading post. With my fingers I spread the curled edges, and from them comes the heat that boils up my forehead.

Return dead or alive to Japheth Ames.

While I'm here maybe I should root him out of whatever snake hole he's curled in and slit his throat. Good luck collecting any bounty gold then.

Raleigh grabs the poster out from under me and crumples it into his pocket. "*Farce.*"

"That one was old."

"Not old enough, I could still read it." Raleigh shifts the basket of food to the opposite shoulder so it shields his face from the street. However, it also blocks his view of the street. "I saw another one down the row outside a room full of murderers."

"Was it fresh? Don't worry, I'm also a murderer, and I am much older than that paper."

"Your age has no bearing on this situation."

"Well, I'm older than you. You too can brag when you breach the Rim's life expectancy of thirty-five, my dear."

"Alkaline, now you hexed us and we're both dead."

Oh, I do love teasing him.

Flies land on the walls to lick the black taffy pitch and then get stuck. The incessant buzz of their flightless wings mixes with the cadence of stone beetles and voices arguing over bets. In the wind, the vague rise and fall of gunfire and an auctioneer's pitch selling flesh.

We're just two more bodies in the mud ruts they call streets here, but Raleigh won't stop looking over his shoulder, so obviously veering out of the way when anyone passes us.

"Stop it, you look like an east blood. You do know hexes are just to frighten little rabbits."

"I know the feeling where everyone is staring at you just a moment too long. It's called intuition and you might want to try it on sometime—"

I shoulder check the next man who passes us.

"Watch yourself, lady!"

"Gravest apologies, sir. I'll go flog myself." I bend falsely at the waist, his barometer watch in my hand. "See? We're fine. He would have said 'whore' if I wasn't wearing this widow's lace. My disguise is working. In the meantime, let my aged wisdom protect you."

"The irony of your disguise isn't lost on me either, *Widow*. Wait until we run into someone with a shard of sobriety and sense."

"Do you need to eat something, sir? You are awfully grumpy, I almost thought you were Leagan there."

"She'll resent you for that."

"Let her." I tuck the hem of my skirt into my holster belt as the boardwalk ends in naked street and horse shit. Possibly human shit too.

"Since you said it, you're a little too cavalier for this situation."

"I can't help it, I enjoy Descendants. And the only reason people are staring is because you're so good-looking. Descendants is a dangerous place, you know, for a pretty face like yours."

"Don't be foul, but thank you. Do you like this coat? I just had it made. Feel this leather…"

My steps halt at a woman and her moon diviner set out on a barrel branded *Eel skins*. The shade of my widow's lace hides me but also distorts her.

"Fortunes, lovely?" Her voice is too young and too high, spun thin like thread. "Good? Bad? That depends on the moon."

"No." Raleigh hooks my arm, pulling fast. "Put away your occult obscenity."

"An alkaline discount for the gentleman."

"I said no, so thank you."

"*Farce.*" There are hundreds of fortune tellers spinning webs across the Rim. I know she's gone, but my first glance under that woman's quail plume hat, I honestly expected to see my mother, and I wasn't expecting that.

"I know..." Raleigh says, as if he can sense exactly what I'm thinking without saying. "It's happen to me before too."

"That was an evil trick my mind just played." I swallow and let myself laugh at him. "Occult obscenity?"

"It's all that came to mind—" Raleigh veers away as two men wearing the long-skull neck ink of the Handsomer Gang come out of a dining hall. "This is a nice tragedy waiting to happen. I should have come alone and negotiated for you."

"Excuse me? What kind of bullshit is this? Shame. You're the one making these fools suspicious. I'm the boss of this operation now, darling, and I'm already here."

"Rafe isn't even bothering to show himself, why should you?"

"Because I'm better than he is." Better at pickpocketing, cards. Much better at manipulation. "Better at just about everything now that I mention it."

"And you want him to know it."

"Yes, I do. Fool's gold, look at me." I open my arms, the sun snatching at the brass buttons on my vest, the rust-red fire against the contrast of my black sleeves. "I've been shut away in a women-only sanctuary for a while now. It's been a long time, Raleigh."

"I can't help you with that...but you look successful, and that's the problem. We're both too attractive and look like we have too much money to be seen together, especially around here. Next time we travel, let's go somewhere we can sit by water and get some good cheese, like Eos."

"I've heard Rafe hasn't left Hannah in fifteen Seasons." And I believe it. "At least we do our own dirty work."

"I would have happily done this one for you," Raleigh says. "Nobody else would have to know. *And* you promised me. You said you'd stay away from bounty hunters."

"I said I wouldn't show my face here, and I'm not. I never said I wouldn't come. Beware of the syntax."

Raleigh groans, much like the hotel stairs as he follows me up. "Fucked by details."

"Always, darling. You should know better. In this line of work, details are the very fine rail between success and failure." I give our door three fast taps, then three careful ones.

"What's the password?" Leagan says, muddied by the wood between us.

"Free food."

"Wrong." She draws the dead bolt. "It's 'neutered.'"

"I don't like that one," Raleigh says.

"That's why I picked it. That's what it is." Leagan flounces to the bed where her ammunition and boar rifle lie, the name *Verdict* etched into the barrel, a skull breathing poppies like smoke on the stock. Gun oil soaks the air, rigid to breathe, but hopefully not into the quilt.

Her red sniper's lens covers one eye, two of the four magnification arms already adjusted over it, naked tripod at the window awaiting her gun.

My watch says five past three. I nudge the lace curtain. Red-headed crows land on the flat rooftop beyond the slanted one and the red muck street below.

Leagan cracks open the box of fresh rifle rounds and breathes them. "They're late."

"Well, you can't make an entrance if you're the first one to the party." I unpin the widow's lace from my hat. The sharpened bodkin glides from the lining of my button sleeves without trouble, but I test it several more times because it's fun. Around my knee rides the iron spike, my full skirt hiding the surprise. Fight dirty to win, my friends. Rafe may not have anything planned, but he can bet his ass I do. "Maybe they're watching us too."

My ribcage holsters already hold two revolvers and a seven-shot pistol around my hip. Descendants respects firepower, and the more guns you carry, the less you have to reload before you're empty. I bring the strap of our repeating rifle overhead. Liza, Mother, and now it's my turn to carry it. The argument could be made this gun is bad luck, but I think it's got a vengeful spirit, one I can put to good use. I call her *Misfortune*.

"I hope you can climb with all that iron," Raleigh says.

Leagan bolts *Verdict* to the tripod. "I hope you can climb with those two lumps of coward between your legs."

"I'm ignoring that."

"If you were ignoring it, you wouldn't make an announcement."

"You know what, it doesn't matter." Raleigh replaces his new coat with an old duster and a full-seal miner's respirator, the filters looking like two wrinkled elbows. "I'll see you over there."

Leagan plops on the footstool behind her setup, a stack of cheese in her hand, black lipstick prints on the crackers. "I'll see you, looking like a fool, but you won't see me."

"I have one request, Raptor." I squat down, an arm around her. "If I die over there, make sure there's a decent crowd for my funeral and everyone has a morbid time."

"I want a big cake at mine," she says, cheek to the rifle stock, dials of her scope clicking with each adjustment. "Half of it will be made with salt instead of sugar, but you won't know which. And everyone has to wear makeup so you know if they cried."

"Yes, ma'am. But tell your sisters, because you're going to outlive me by a long time."

"Wait." She turns to kiss my cheek. "There."

"Thank you, I needed that." I know she left a black lip print on my face, but I think I'll leave it. "Stay nasty, my dear."

Just past the shared bathroom, the back door and steps take me down sharp to the street, wagon ruts hard and deep enough to break an ankle in.

The backside of our meeting place peels voluminous curls of green paint, the horizontal sign reading *Land Survey Office* just for *farce*. It's a clear pine still below and nobody from around here is pretending like it isn't.

Raleigh waits for me at the end of the ladder, drifting to look over one side of the flat roof, then the other.

"Look at me, I made it with all the extra lead weight."

"You don't think this guy will stand us up, do you?" Raleigh asks.

"Absolutely not, he probably just doesn't know how to read a watch." Everything seen from above is still the Descendants we count on. Filthy, soulless, worse from up here actually—the stink rises.

I'm careful of my knee spike as I sit on the raised ledge. Don't want to cross the wrong leg and impale myself, that would be unfortunate.

You can see the pink and yellow flowers blossoming from the hillside cactuses thanks to the *Solace* rains.

Raleigh lifts a hand. "Wait, someone's coming."

His fingers split. Two of them.

"In the alley. One o' clock…"

The weight of all my guns settles on the base of my spine as I stand again.

They have horses. One man dismounts at the ladder, but his backup stays in his saddle to catch the reins tossed at him. All right, they know that, at least. No fool leaves their horse unattended in Descendants anymore. Though they haven't been seen in Seasons, the Five Sons were known for helping themselves to free animals.

"Deep breath." I brace my hands on my belt, feet planted wide. Men stand like this to intimidate each other. As long as we stay behind the tin stovepipe protruding from the planks, Leagan has the rooftop.

"To use some of your favorite words on you, don't tell me how to live."

A hat appears first, the black leather worn shiny where he grips the crown to tip it to the ladies. Or the gentlemen. There are more of them around, and that spot looks awfully well polished.

"Oh, he might like you better than me." I barely get the words out before he's close enough to hear, Raleigh not given enough time to respond.

"Afternoon." He grasps the hat exactly where it shines. Graying stubble protects his face, paper crackling somewhere within his clothes as he moves.

"Mr. Kasey, I assume. I am Tesla Revere, otherwise known as the Widow."

"Yeah, yeah, I know who you are." He smirks at me first, then Raleigh. "And you are…not a Revere woman."

"Not relevant," Raleigh says.

Kasey scratches his cheek where my scar is still hard pink and in the process of healing. "You have a little accident there?"

Just watching his action is enough to make that side of my face comes alive with sparks.

I let my head roll as I laugh. "No, actually, I paid to have this done. Don't lie, you love it."

"You're a confident daughter of a whore, I'll give—"

"I'd like to see some proof before we talk about anything else." Raleigh crosses his arms. "It would be easy to say the Stranger is alive, even if she isn't."

Kasey's woody eyes narrow. "The boss is a man of his word. Unlike some of you."

"It's nothing personal. We just don't know you."

"True."

"My friend does make a valid point," I say. "And Rafe sending us the Stranger's ring is rather ominous."

"Well, I didn't bring her along, if that's what you're hoping for. I'll let you imagine how that would have gone." Kasey peels open the paper bag I heard crackling within his corduroy vest and pops a candy into his mouth. "She was your associate—"

"*Was?*" Raleigh's voice shoots dangerously close to a crack.

"Is. You know how she is."

"Ah, but that's not what you said." Maybe he's not as conscious of his phrasing as I am, but I'm not in the mood to fuck with an amateur. I check the rapid escalation of my heart with a long breath. Nothing foolish now.

"It's what I meant." The candy shatters between Kasey's back teeth.

Is there a worse sound than someone chewing? I think not.

"She's not exactly pleasant company," he says. "However, in spite of that no one's killed her yet. You do want her back? I assume that's why you're here?"

"No, I heard *you* were pleasant company and came here just so we could meet. Tell Rafe I had the respect to come myself, and I'm offended he couldn't bother to do the same. We are old friends, after all."

"I'll mention you're hurt."

"Offended, not hurt, darling. There's a difference."

"As you like it. As you know, Gerard *Rafael* is boss in Hannah, and a business owner has better things to do than ride to the armpit of the Rim to visit former acquaintances who like to backstab. No matter how pretty they were." Kasey's eyes flick over me like a widow snake tongue. "He described you as unnaturally beautiful. I don't see the same, so don't get familiar, woman."

"Oh, I didn't realize how hard he must have to work. What a busy schedule of ransoms he must have." Fuck, I'd forgotten how much Rafe enjoys collecting ass lickers who tell him he's wonderful and deserves the world. I suspect it's only gotten worse being the black gold boss of Hannah all these years. "Next time I ransom one of his family members, I'll try to remember he won't have time. But oh, that's right, his mother is dead."

"Is that a threat?"

"If he chooses. She's still dead. I didn't make her that way… You didn't know that, did you?"

"What can we give Mr. Rafael in exchange for the Stranger?" Raleigh says. "We came ready to make a deal."

"Pardon me." Kasey puts up a hand. "I'm familiar with these bitches, they have a reputation for all being female. The Widow, the Raven, the Slip…"

My jaw tightens, the blood flushing from my heart. You really shouldn't say her name, you bastard.

"But you… I wasn't told anything about a friend with balls, unless you don't have them."

"Well, I could take my pants off and show you, would that help?"

Kasey steps closer. "It would be mannerly for you to take off that mask and introduce yourself."

"He's our brother," I say. "What's left of his poor face is too unfortunate to show. We don't bring him out much, and we don't talk about the accident. It would be mannerly of you to not embarrass him."

Kasey doesn't look convinced, but this rooftop overflows with the fucks I give about that.

"You want proof?" He shifts the leather pack off his shoulder, spreading the top. "Have at it."

My stomach falls into my groin as Raleigh recoils.

"What? You asked."

Oh, *krossus*. One of us has to.

I drop a hand behind my back, palm open to grasp the other wrist, Leagan's signal not to fire, and I make myself look.

Adelaide's crossgun.

"You snake fucker." Yes, I thought it was her head.

"Satisfied?" Kasey cinches the top of the backpack with a smirk. "Or did you expect something else?"

"Fuck you." And fuck how damp my armpits suddenly are. "God of Mercy."

"That's not proof," Raleigh says. "She'd never hand over that gun."

"Not willingly," Kasey says. "She's got a strong spine, I'll give her that. She didn't break."

"Don't," Raleigh says. "I don't want to know."

"We had to try, but I'll spare you the details."

"You're too kind." And I can taste metal, my smile rigid as a snapped blade.

"Now that we've got that sorted, the boss expects you to return either his stolen crystal or its equivalent value in another form. In addition to that, he deserves reparation for the damage done to his reputation."

"Naturally."

"His price is seventy-five thousand, copper standard. Along with your apology, he'll also accept your train. A gift of good will. Accept these terms, we'll give you your Stranger back, and we can all move on with our lives." Kasey clicks the fresh candy floating around his mouth against a tooth. "I don't think there's been this kind of money on a fox head since the war."

"Watch it," Raleigh says. "That's my sister you're talking about."

"Is she now?"

My laugh hurts like cold water as it comes up. "I have sad news. We don't have that crystal, as far as I saw we never did. As for my train..." My chest burns. "You can go pick her out of the Boneyard yourself. Mention my name there, and they might cut you a deal on her parts."

"Then why are you wasting everyone's time?"

"Dear Mr. Kasey." I smile, sweet poison. "I never said I had *nothing* to offer you." At my glance, Raleigh unshoulders the bag, its weight hitting the roof with a dry smack. "Bring me the Stranger, alive, with all body parts attached and your fucking hands kept off her, and you can have thirty thousand all to yourself, player's choice of standard."

Kasey's gaze stays pointed up at me as he tugs open the satchel's top. "That's not what's in here."

"You didn't bring the Stranger because you don't trust her. I didn't bring thirty thousand standards because I don't trust Descendants. Neither of us is a fool. That's five as a deposit. You're welcome."

"The boss warned me you might try to bribe me." Kasey rises off his spurred heels. "Actually, he said you'd do it with sex. Do I put you off that much?"

"If that's what you'd rather get…and no, I've done worse."

"Not interested."

"That's because you don't know what you're missing. I'm one of the best."

Kasey kicks our money back at us. "My loyalty isn't up for sale."

"Neither is mine." Unfortunate for Rafe, he's now on the wrong side of it. "My mother taught me everything about loyalty, and she'd gut you for this, so be grateful you're dealing with me and not her. I negotiate. Fifty thousand."

"Damnation. You do love that fox. The world is full of mysteries, isn't it?"

"Everyone's got a price, Mr. Kasey. What's yours? I'll beat it."

The hesitation starts in his hand, a trembling thread that flickers initially, then wraps around him like a melon vine. This kind of money, easy money, so hard to say no to.

You want it, I silently will him. *You want it so bad. Say yes.*

"Sixty-five," Raleigh says.

"And I'll fuck you." My smile slides, slick and fast as a card trick. "Deal?"

Raleigh removes his hat and lets Kasey see his full head of copper curls that gleam like money in the sun. "I will too, if that's what you'd prefer."

"Enough," Kasey snaps. "Offer me one more standard, and I'll shoot that milk-bastard the second I get back to Hannah. You're not as charming as you think you are. Neither of you."

"Fine then." Fool's gold, he was bitterly close to saying yes. Flirting with betrayal always leaves the aftertaste of anger.

I won't lie, the defeat stings. I wanted this to be over easy, especially for Adelaide's sake.

"You're the kind of loyal bastard a boss can only dream of." I kick the satchel at him. "Give that to your beloved Rafael. Tell him it's a deposit. And this." I yank the envelope from my inner breast pocket. "My apology."

You can go fuck yourself with it.

"See, now that wasn't so hard." Kasey stoops to catch the satchel's shoulder strap. "Now, what will you give me so I won't tell the boss you tried to buy me?"

"Oh, I think your loyalty is its own reward. Go ahead, tell him I tried everything to bribe you, but you were true to the core. He's lucky to have a man like you."

"I'll tell him you have at least sixty thousand stashed somewhere, thirty in copper."

Farce, I fucked myself with that one, didn't I? Like I told Raleigh — details, darling, they kill.

Kasey shoulders our gold. For the life of his balls, he'd better deliver it. "Before you claim it's not safe to move that much gold at once, the boss will kindly allow you to make the ransom payments in installments at fifteen percent interest. The reoccurrments will keep your fox alive, as long as they're timely and not offensively small."

Like you. The retort stings my tongue to hold back. Cheap, but I've never claimed I was above things like that.

"I'll also pass on the word about your train's fate. Now, I believe this concludes our business."

"I can tell you really wanted to say something there," Raleigh says. "Whatever it was, holding it in was most likely the right decision."

"Maybe, but I'll regret it later."

"I'm proud of you."

Kasey snaps his fingers just as he turns his back on us. "Oh…one more thing. Speaking of your mother…we happened to hear a share of your bounty was turned in on the Raven a few cycles ago. The boss also asked me to find out if it was true."

"You lie." The words lunge out of my mouth before I ever had a prayer of stopping them. I spent all my self-control too soon.

"I wouldn't. Not about someone's mother."

Raleigh puts a damp hand to my arm.

I knew it was wrong to abandon Mother's body like that in Fort Emmaline. I fucking knew. What was I thinking? Damnation, I—

Don't be sorry, she always said. *It's not usually worth the effort. Do better.*

Oh, I intend to.

"Where is she now?"

Kasey smiles, tipping that fool's gold hat. "You both have yourself a pleasant afternoon."

I'd love to shoot him in the back of the head, but then there'd be no one to deliver the ransom to Rafe, and no reason for him not to kill Adelaide. I can't do that to her.

So let it be three times as bloody when I destroy him later, since I can't have it now.

"*Jezebel.*" My arms shake as I grip myself, rage on fire between my lungs.

When I was younger and heard people describe heartbreak, the way it saws through your chest, physically painful, I always thought they were being dramatic. They weren't. It cuts me open again, jagged and bloody as the night Mother died. And it hurts just as bad as the first goddamn time.

"I should go piss off the roof on—" Raleigh comes back to me. "I'm sorry, I'm so sorry."

"So am I. I need to talk to Adelaide myself."

"You can't go to Hannah."

"Like *farce,* I can't."

"I'm serious—"

"Oh, I'll find a way."

Fuck manners, you want to twist the knife, Rafe? I'll twist so deep the point comes out the other side.

NINE

ADELAIDE

Steam like sweat drips off the beams of the bathhouse, landing on me, on the dice boards, on pooled water. Moisture rot reveals pipes beneath the floorboards of the bathhouse. They're what bubble the water into the tubs and recirculate back to the heart, the boiler and turbine vibrating through the wall at my back.

The tattoo-smith has a line piled up for his stool coiling around the tubs like a worm. His lips aren't gray, but the mouths of nine of the eleven people in line are. His foot rocks down on the pedal that drives the needle, wire tethering him to the little boiler that powers it. Double lines of ink cuff both his wrists and each knuckle joint, letters running up into his sleeves like coordinates.

How far does the pattern travel? The Stranger needs to know.

The door at the top of the stairs breaks open, lavender and sage smoke escaping.

"The diviner down the row only costs silver."

"She's probably who you should visit next time then." Under her painted-on flush, there's a red mark on Thadie's skin. "I can't guarantee her results."

He shoves my leg out of his way. "Move."

She winks at me and shuts her door.

I stand.

"You have something to say to me, milk-bastard?"

I do not.

With both hands I brace the wall, snap my knee up and bury my heel in his stomach. The back of his head cracks on the beam crossing the stairwell before he hits the floor, jelly.

You asked why I was here?

Silence, breathing, nothing but the pipes gurgling.

Learn from this.

Nine.

The girl with the crochet hook and star lines inked on her skin rises from her hammock.

Open buttons run the length of her sleeves, trousers, and an etched ivory revolver is on her ribcage for everyone to see. For me to see. She can pay the pistol tax.

"Whoever drags him out of here can have what he's carrying," she calls.

Nothing, because I empty him first.

"Can I talk to you outside?" Up close her voice is a razor grass blade. Sharp-edged.

Walk away, the Stranger warns her.

"Blood doesn't wash off so easy, does it?" She points out the stain on my bodice. "Don't look so nervous, I'm not the one wearing a muzzle for biting."

Nervous isn't the word I'd use.

"Come on, I have a job for you."

No.

But the Stranger's tick speeds up, same as it does for the cupboards and drawers I don't look in.

I can still say no after I hear what this is. If Kane taught me anything, it's that jobs that make me feel like this aren't worth it.

Forty-two.

"I like your style. It's effective, to the point." She stays out of arm's reach, safe as long as she keeps that gun in her holster. "I'm Saraline. I already asked Thadie about you, she calls you the Stair Ghost. You're not a real ghost though—I've seen one. She said you can't talk, but you'll understand me."

I don't know why "can't" and "don't want to" confuse so many people.

Thadie doesn't mind if I choose not to answer her. We can just exist in the same space. There's a difference.

"How much would you charge me to take care of someone?" she asks.

Not worth it.

"By take care of, I mean…make it permanent, wink wink."

Yes, I got that. But the Stranger is right.

Four.

"*Sol, so, doxx vos,*" she says in Tov. Louder. "I'm sorry, that's all I really know. I read Tov better than I speak it."

"I understood you the first time."

"Aha! So you *can* speak. Good, then we can talk." She smiles, and unlike most people here, she looks happy. There has to be a lie. "Like I said, my family and I need a few people…well, I say taken care of, but Soli doesn't like that. Anyway, our competition needs to be taught a lesson."

Now we're up from someone to several.

"I'm not a bounty hunter."

"And I'm not a chemical dealer." She laughs. "I thought you might like to make a little extra money."

Don't get distracted.

She's right. I have my own things to take care of.

Seven.

"You'll change your mind," Saraline says. "You know where to find me."

That's what you think, but I won't.

If I'd gone with the Stranger's instinct and stolen Kane's journal while he was on the *Absolution* last Season instead of taking the long way to it, I wouldn't be here. I don't blame Aunt Tess, but sometimes she overcomplicates things. It's easier to go for the throat.

TEN

TESLA

I peel back the sheet covering the dead woman, drawing the Sign of Blessed Deliverance across my chest in an X. "Providence, take this soul. Ash to ash, dust to dust."

Blessed are those who pass through the fire, for they shall be refined.

"Close enough?" Leagan says.

Her hair is black like mine, skin roughly the same tone. Maybe her jaw is a little too round, and her nose slightly tilted to one side from breaking, but I don't think that will matter too much. Faces…change once they're dead. They don't quite stay the person they were when they were alive—the soul adds something.

The hole ripped through the woman's cheek and eye socket will be the most distracting evidence—and cover-up.

"Close enough."

Raleigh braces the door with his back, even though we paid for an hour in the room. Someone could still decide to walk in, and locks aren't safe for the usual patrons of such places. With his other hand he pins the fabric of his scarf to his nose. "This is a new low, even for us."

"We don't know her." Leagan shrugs. "And she was already dead."

"Would you like it if this was done to you?"

"How would I care? I'm dead."

At least I can have the two of them in the same room without Leagan actively trying to rip Raleigh's face off anymore. I call that an improvement.

"She's not wrong..." I remove the plain, silver band from the corpse's middle finger and replace it with my amber and silver setting. A shame to let it go, but a worthy cause. Green is a man for details, like myself. "We all serve a higher purpose. If we weren't supposed to use her for this, she wouldn't have been put right in our path."

"That feels overly simple, considering the facts."

Better than being left behind the outhouses to bloat in shit like we found her.

Her plain cotton overskirt rips as it comes off, but I leave her bone underbust corset and open-seat bloomers alone. Whore's clothes. That's what they all think of me anyway.

"Help me turn her over."

Leagan rolls the woman to either side so I can maneuver both arms through a soiled shirt, then face down to drag the bell skirt over her hips. Anyone even moderately observant and acquainted with me should know I only like nice things. The mud caked between the diagonal silk ruffles completes the lie that I died in these clothes.

"Good enough for me." I wipe the tracks of what I hope is mud off my hands. "Find your rest, Tesla Revere."

"This is fool's gold," Raleigh says. "I don't think Moira would approve."

"Mother did a lot of things that you don't know about. And probably a lot of things that I don't know about."

"If you say so. But when I die, you give me a nice burial and don't you *dare* touch me for any other purpose, all right? I'll get the horse."

"There will be no fighting today, children." I pass the pair of them a warning glare. "When I'm not around, both of you stay away from each other."

"I wouldn't." Leagan turns up her nose. "This matters."

THE LONG DRAPE OF WIDOW'S LACE HANGS OFF MY HAT LIKE BUG NET. IT CUTS off my peripherals and makes my neck stiff. But I promised...

Leagan and Raleigh walk a safe distance behind me and the horse, and a safe distance away from each other, dropping to their cross position as Green's warehouse comes into view.

The sweet black taffy pitch that protects the warehouses against fire melts under the sun. Fresh, and so is the fence that now connects Green's original warehouse, number thirteen, to warehouse eleven. He's expanding his business on our dead family and murdered reputation. And they say kindness doesn't exist out here.

I raise my fist to the slide door before giving it a tug.

"Locked, but I won't look like a fool for not trying." The horse is less than impressed by my effort. I pound a little harder. "Open up, in the name of Japheth Ames!"

Someone unlatches the iron gun hole in the warehouse's second floor. "I heard you the first time. State your business, woman."

"I have a delivery." The angle of the building is too sharp, like the sheer morning sun, so I can't see him. This widow's lace, it pulls my hair and almost drags my hat off.

"Oh?" He pauses. "Dead?"

A fly crawls out of a fold in the sheet. "And oozing like a ripe melon."

"Come around the back."

I flash the engineer's salute in the general direction of the blacksmith's sun shelter where we decided Raleigh would stand guard while Leagan climbs the water collection tower for a raptor view.

The line of warehouse thirteen leads to a section of weathered fence where a man in a gray uniform hauls the ill-fitting gate over a hump in the dirt. It's a small yard, still outside the larger one connecting the backsides of the warehouses.

"What's your name, bounty hunter?"

"Not relevant."

He hacks up the phlegm in his throat and spits it at a can near the table with halved oat barrels for chairs. "Have a seat. That's all the explanation I can expect?"

"Widow Sloan." I throw one leg across the other, knee spike in full view without my skirt. A bounty hunter is expected to be a vicious creature, we deal in bones and dead ends. "What really matters is I've got a rotting body to sell. Are you Japheth Ames?"

"No."

"And that's all the information you expect me to run with?" Safe behind my dark cascade of lace, I gaze down his sage-gray uniform, branded with the hand-tooled leather patch on his chest identifying him as Company property. "*Sol* to the Green Contract Company. It's a treat to see progress." Like getting a sliver in your ass.

"Who should I tell him you're bringing in?"

"Tesla the Widow Revere."

"Fool's gold." He whistles. "That name I do know, and that makes two of them if you're not shady. Don't go nowhere."

Unlike skirts, these high-waisted gentleman's trousers don't hide nervous tics such as a drumming heel, so I stand up and pace while I wait for him to return because that's better, isn't it? All I have to say is, Mother's body better not be hanging back there like a piece of meat, and it better not be on fucking display.

The gap in the wall is only a pinstripe, but I don't need to see much to smell the grain being milled back there or hear the decent amount grinding and clanging. His warehouse used to sit so quiet when he was dealing with smugglers like us. It's all evidence pointing to Green's blood money deal with the Von Kanes to bring law and order to the rails. His shop in Vantage, or even the governor's mansion he took control of there, isn't big enough to outfit the men needed for an undertaking like that. But this place is.

If allowed to succeed, these rail bullies will ruin the remaining shards of our business. This is *exactly* why I voted we go on Kane's Eden expedition last Season. Those who resist progress are surely crushed by it. I aim to adapt, just like a weed.

A male frame barely wide enough to cast a shadow turns a corner in the yard, elbows and knees jackknifing all over the place.

Oh, how shocking. I told Leagan Japheth Ames would be him, the bony beanpole.

St. Paul is the only man around here Green trusts enough to oversee a dirty job like this. His head's always been too far up Green's ass to smell any type of bribery. It's a calculated risk that he won't recognize me, and oh yes, the thrill is worth it.

I yank the body by her stiff ankles and let it slap onto the dirt as St. Paul comes out of the main yard.

"Unceremonious end," he says with a stuffed nose and a chuckle at my lace. "You bringing me the Widow. That's iconic."

"Ironic."

"Are you getting smart ass with me?"

Of course not, *Japheth*, dear. I don't say that. I want to, but it's exactly the kind of thing I *would* say. And right now, I'm dead. Shame.

St. Paul sucks the juice of whatever he's chewing back into his mouth as he squats down to untie her. "Sweet piss. Right through the eye."

I lift her hand and show him my ring on her cold, dead finger, as well as the lighter band of skin under it. Fine details. A fool like St. Paul might not appreciate them, but if Green is around, or asks, I've thought ahead of him.

"Widow Sloan, is it?" he asks. "Where'd you find her?"

"I staked out Hoyt Hotel in Vantage, one of their better-known protection contracts. I knew one of them would slip and make contact with someone they knew eventually. Turns out I was right. Unfortunately, she was alone, but one sixth of fifty thousand isn't a bastard's cut now, is it?"

"No, it ain't. The bitches are in pieces. We heard the half-breed was taken up north. Bet says she's been killed by now. Who knows, the others could already be bones somewhere, too."

"I'm going to keep looking. Money talks louder than rumors."

He finishes the thumb through his account book. I'd say reading, but I'm not convinced he does. "Well, it do appear we owes you something. The Widow, she's worth thirteen. Copper or gold standard?"

"Gold, it spends easier. If you don't mind, who beat me to the other Revere body?"

"The Jaxson Boys."

"And do they run town these days?"

"No boy." St. Paul pokes his chest out, a bony little rooster, rib ridges showing through the frayed weave of his child-size vest. "Descendants is clean as a virgin, courtesy of the Green Contract Company."

Fool's gold, that's too silly to not laugh at. "How long is that going to last? Descendants is a rabid animal. But alkaline luck to you and your *employer* with that. I'd like to see the other body."

"Why is that?"

"I heard it was the Raven. She was famous for having the sight. One of my contacts would buy her eyes and hand bones if your boss is interested in another deal."

Yes, I double down on this lie. Mother would understand.

St. Paul's joints click when he moves, clearly the bastard son of a centipede and a scavenger lizard. "Mr. Green's not sick to the head, unlike many others. He wouldn't keep a woman's body lying around like a curiosity display. We burned her a mighty few cycles back."

"You didn't keep anything?"

There's only room in his vest pockets to perch his fingertips. "No boy."

"Shame." My gambler's eye says he's not being entirely truthful. Walk away, my sense warns, but I tug the punch dagger out of my boot and offer it to him, handle first. Sun catches on the veins of black in the red jasper handle. "Still no ma'am?"

St. Paul's eyes eclipse, a cat with a prize. "Is that Cairosh jasper?" He reaches.

"Tov. At least ninety-one layers of steel." The first number I pull out of my ass. "Blacksmiths call this pattern starfall."

"Well…the body we burned, but Mr. Green did save the two rings she was wearing. Just sold one of them to a fellow from Hannah lasterday, maybe you can catch him before he leaves town."

"Can I buy the other?"

"Could, but Mr. Green took it with him to Vantage."

Of course, he did. Snake fucker.

"But in the case I remember the next time he comes by, I could be persevered to tell him you're interested."

Persuaded, you imbecile.

"I'll take my gold."

We cross Descendants as the sun finishes its downward spiral, like spiders on a web, the upper halves of buildings molten-red gold.

The lock holding the fence together falls to my pick in shame. The scrap yard holds empty boilers, spiral tube limbs sprout from the ground like mushrooms, waiting to be picked.

Leagan climbs over the piles instead, starting at the edge of them. Although we're close enough to the gnashing of a fight pit that I'm not too worried someone will hear the rasping metal.

She attempts to heft an iron pipe onto her shoulder and has to let it go. "Too heavy."

Raleigh goes through a box of fittings, sliding rings over his wrists and bolts into his pockets.

I glance around the ruddy corner, then at my pocket watch. "Three minutes."

"Alkaline." Leagan lifts a shorter pipe and turns.

Raleigh points back at her. Yes, that one.

The pile tries to slide as she climbs back over it. Raleigh catches the loose planks that collapse toward her.

"Careful," I hiss.

"You should have let them fall." She lays the pipe in the wheelbarrow with the soldering rods.

"Right." Raleigh picks out another flat metal scrap and flings the quilt over everything with a smirk. "I bet you hope there was nails in them too so you have something else to be mad about. I'm wearing you down."

"Did you get everything?" I ask.

"Yes." Both their answers come together, and Leagan rubs her middle finger against her nose on his side.

"Are you sure?"

"Yeah." It happens again.

"You're both adorable."

"I am *not*." Leagan stalks past me and out the gate, rust coating the front of her shirt and arms.

"Thank you." Raleigh hefts the wheelbarrow. "At least someone noticed."

ELEVEN
TESLA

THE ROOM IS STAGNANT WHEN I WAKE FOR AN UNSPECIFIED REASON. I DO notice right away that Leagan isn't here anymore, but it takes me a minute or two to see the note left on her pillow.

> *I couldn't sleep and I'm bored.*
>
> *If you find this, I went to the dice den two rows over, past the bunkhouse that has chickens living under it. The underground one with the green door and the roof that looks different.*

On the front side of the page, she drew a little armadillo and a heart pumping blood onto a rose garden.

I don't want to get up. I'm tired and this bed is so comfortable, unlike when I first laid down. Could I trust her pistol hand and let her come back when she's had enough fun?

No, that would be horribly irresponsible of me.

Farce. I kick the sheet away, reading the difference between the satin of my skirt and the lace weave of my veil by texture. I feel my age in the spike of worry driven through my chest, but Descendants isn't a place to wander alone, no matter who you are.

These gambling dens are controlled by the same sludge who run the flesh auctions. It's difficult to avoid being groped in tight spaces like that, harder to retaliate without hurting yourself, and I've seen ears ripped off in more than one fight.

"Raleigh." I knock on the thin wall between the alternation of yanking my boots over socks. "Get dressed."

Alkaline crystals leave no scent when they burn, but down here in the bowels, the air singes the back of my throat. It's roast chili, body odor, and the yellow, rotten-egg taint of bastard fire quartz. The lanterns drip sick green light over tables dripping with hands that kill, clear pine, and other fluids. It's the kind of place Mother would warn me not to enter. The kind with less than two exits.

Don't think I didn't notice the XX carved into the green door up top, marking this den property of the Jaxson Boys. Leagan, Leagan, my little Raptor, what have you gotten yourself into?

Brine sucks at the bottom of my shoes. That means it's soaking up into my skirt too, whatever it is.

"She shouldn't be too hard to find," Raleigh says. "Red hair, and it looks like the only woman here other than you."

"Don't be fooled."

"I know she's crafty."

"Careful, if she's drunk she might punch you."

"I'm hopeful if she's drunk she might forgive me."

"Care to put ten gold on that?"

Raleigh tilts his hat to a steeper angle on his forehead. "I don't like to gamble with my money, only my winning personality."

I chose my path intentionally. Not a slip along the outer wall to the deepest corner like a shadow, I make a damn entrance.

I'm still acting as Widow Sloan, the bounty hunter, but tonight she wears a dress of amber that east blood crystal barons would kill to keep by their side. The widow's lace, black as my hair, spills over my chest, and with it I cast a spell on them. All these murderers see me, feel me, smell me, want me. If only this lace wasn't brimming with bad luck, me so deadly under it.

With my steps, I sew a line through the thick of activity gathered at the gnarled tables by the longest route.

The edges are all drunk card games and dice, but the center is a wheel. Planks form channels to funnel scorpions into the center pen for battle races. I've seen snakes, raptors, roosters, scavenger lizards, spiders, and fire ants. As long as something bites while the other bleeds. People only want money and power. And if they can't have that, then it's blood.

Leagan's red twist buns perch like twin blooms on a prickly cactus girl among these fools chanting for their chosen fighters.

Oil and tobacco sweat consume me in the push between grimy elbows and fists clutching standards. Miners have shoulders like rocks. I lost Raleigh somewhere back there.

I place my hand on the back of Leagan's warm neck and lean to her ear. "What are you up to, ma'am?"

"Fuck off—" Leagan jolts, pistol out of her holster but catches her slip in time. "It's you."

"Indeed. So, what are you doing here in the middle of the night?"

The smirk rides Leagan's black lips so very well. "Playing this game."

"Sure, you are. Enjoying your first trip to Descendants."

"You don't know I never snuck off the train here before."

"Oh, trust me, I'd know. We would've smelled it on you."

She's quick and light-footed, but I don't think she's quite crafty enough to make sure to clean the shit stink off her clothes and boots before getting back on the *Absolution*. I'm not sure I would have considered that detail if Adelaide hadn't successfully pulled the trick, then described it to me later.

"Evangeline used to bare-knuckle box in Descendants," I say.

"I know." Leagan cranes her neck to see around the heads taller than her, a bird overstimulated by too much food on the ground. "Let's see if anyone's having a pepper-eating contest."

I hook her arm before she wanders off again in this dangerous place.

The three wranglers pull their fighters out of the flour sacks. A diamond-head backstabber scorpion, sensible brown. A southern menace, so pretty and deep blue. And a white devil. She appears an opaque green now, but in the full dark, they glow like angels.

"You want to play?" I draw gold from my secret money pocket and lift it to the light. "Eighty on the menace, gold standard, and devil to take the backstabber first. One hundred, the white devil will win."

"I see you." A bookmaker nods, penciling in my bets.

"The white devil…"

His accent falls in my ears like gold flung across a stone floor. Cairosh. You only hear that one grace the Rim once in a rare moon. And yes, I have heard it before. A whore gets to hear and meet many interesting things proper people never will.

"An interesting choice." The embroidery hugging the collar of his coat was done by an alkaline hand, but now the silk threads splinter. "I favor the backstabber."

"We'll see about that."

The wranglers let the scorpions slide off their gloved hands into their lanes. The white devil scampers over the wall into the diamond backstabber's channel on disturbingly agile legs and finishes him without even entering the arena.

I laugh to the Cairosh fool who doubted me. "I win."

And he's already gone. Shame.

My white devil creeps out to find the blue menace waiting for her. They ball up and roll together until the menace's longer tail impales her one too many times. I lose it all like that.

"And that's why you don't bet on animals," I say. "They're harder to cheat than people."

"Barton Jaxson." Leagan tilts her forehead to the fools lined up at the bar. The one in the middle of the cluster has a tattoo under his eye. A black water stain covers the wall behind him.

"Son of Boss Jaxson. You little devil."

"You're welcome."

"Watch my back." My gaze hooks into his padded neck as he uncorks a virgin bottle of Sun Fire. He's a young man hiding the fact under a thick, black beard. The yellow, arrowhead tail feather of a slip pokes from the band of his hat. I called Vesta my little slip since she was a baby. It was her favorite bird.

His gaze drops, avoiding my lace as I slide between him and another gun, wood still warm from the other asses who sat here before me. It's bad luck to look a fresh widow in the eye. Snake or woman. It's worse luck to fuck one as long as she's wearing the widow's band, she'll make your genitals go Tov white and drop off. Funny how these superstitions always implicate the woman.

"Barton Jaxson." I grab the bottle of Sun Fire below the hand he reaches for it. The black cascade of my widow's lace pools across the sticky bar.

"Hello."

"Fool's gold..." Jaxson watches me pass the bottle under the veil and taste it. "A fire drinker."

"Blessed are those who pass through the fire."

"Do you want something?"

"That's a fine way to get yourself a lady's attention. I want whoever runs town these days." I bet I'll get a different answer than the one I got from St. Paul yesterday.

"We do."

"Then despite being the ass of a bone picker, you *are* who I want." The skin under his eye is like velvet to my thumb, delicate and brimming with the ink of the family brand: XX.

"Are we talking about fucking or killing?"

"Aren't they the same? Acts of passion."

He chuckles. "Sometimes."

"Usually." No one will miss this sperm sack. "I'm looking for a new partner, due to my husband's unfortunate exit from this life. Someone with experience, I heard that could be you. Recognize this?" Mother's face on our bounty poster might be weathered thin, but the collection instructions remain the same.

I failed to give her a proper burial. She deserved that respect. But no, the Jaxsons sold her remains like meat instead. So tonight I'm going to kill a Jaxson boy in our name. Taste the ash and decay, for dust we remain, my friends.

"This is the Revere bounty." His sun-shot eyes skip the sheet like flirting flies. "No one's seen those bitches in cycles."

"That's because no one knew where to look."

"You?" He nearly laughs at me. "That's a nice *farce*."

"I haven't been a widow for very long," I say with my hand pressed to his inner thigh. I've found it to be most effective in keeping them interested in me while too distracted to hunt for the lie in what I say. "My husband and I hunted bounties all over the Rim. He was tried for murder back in Jezebel and shipped here before we met. But my father was a trapper, and he taught me all kinds of tricks for snaring prey. I just turned in the slipperiest Revere." The silver standard has been in my hand this whole time, but only now catches his attention as I bring it to the sour light. "Let me buy your drink, and make sure you don't ever underestimate a woman again, my dear."

"Maybe I shouldn't." He drags a finger down my arm. His hands don't tell me much, nothing but rough calluses and ghosts of past violence on my skin. Mother was always better at reading palms.

Was he there for the Fort Emmaline ambush, or here babysitting the bar while other Jaxson men brought my mother in?

Or did he help murder my lovely Vesta in Winchester?

Mother taught me to be mindful of signs. I take this one to heart and pluck the yellow slip feather from his hat and poke it into my hair. He assumes I'm flirting, but it couldn't be further than that. Something to remember my daughter by.

Navy said someone within the group turned on the others the night Vesta was killed. What would Barton Jaxson gain from treachery like that? The potential loss seems too high. He doesn't have the eyes of someone that reckless, he's a boy who needs instructions from his daddy.

Jaxson's hand closes around the Sun Fire bottle, hot over mine that still holds on. "We tracked the Revere bounty for a while. Lost a pocket of good men to those whores. I'd like to hear how you did it."

"You'll see my tracking abilities when we ride together."

"Split the reward." Jaxson keeps hold of my hand to bring the bottle to his lips. "I can cut you twenty-five percent."

The smile licks my lip like a wicked flame. "I think you can do better than that. I got the worst one."

"Which one did you get?"

Water begins to spill down the black stain, rivulets expanding and dividing across the planks. It must be raining outside, underground spaces an unwise choice during the *Solace* flash flood season.

I lean close enough for him to feel the heat of my breath past the lace, and I smell the fire on his. "The bitch who shot my husband."

I produce a rifle round this time, let its warm gleam coat his mouth with saliva and then witness how it disappears in my fist. "Interested?"

"Might be."

"I'm sure we can work out a deal, but not here. Those bitches might have ears places we don't expect." He lets me take his hand, but he's too blunt to perceive the hint. "Is there another room where we can go?"

Barton plants his legs on either side of the stool to stand. "Hang around."

Yeah, we'll see about that. I hook Leagan with a nod, Raleigh back with her from whatever hole he got sucked into.

They gather up behind me as Little Barton passes into the shadows, the door that shuts behind him barred by a man difficult to see the full outline of in this bastard quartz light.

"You're not considering..." Raleigh's shoulders drop. "Fuck it, you are."

"I came here for Raptor and Jaxson blood. I'm not leaving without either. Can I borrow this?" I whisk the handkerchief from Raleigh's breast pocket.

"You can have it now."

He knows us well.

Leagan crosses her arms, covering the hand already holding her pistol.

"Behold the work of a genius." I look to the Jaxson guard through my lace, the sharpened bodkin drops from my sleeve into my hand. "Can I talk to you? Where can I find the—"

As I said, murky places like this, it's difficult to see what's going on, and even harder to stop it once it's happened. I grab his shoulders and yank to where my knee meets his stomach and drives in. As he doubles forward, I stuff as much of Raleigh's kerchief into his mouth before the scream ends and he tries to bite my fingers off. A small strip of skin still peels away on his teeth even though I was careful. Water pooled around the door sloshes against my boots as he shoves. Raleigh catches his arm as it swings, and I stab the bodkin through his neck. Once he stops bubbling, we let him go.

No one even noticed.

I draw low against my skirt where the rest of the den won't see. "Whoever's in there... We kill them all."

"For the Raven." Leagan lifts her barrel.

"And the Slip." Raleigh grips the bolt latch with one hand and nods.

I sail through first, sweeping left, Leagan right behind me as Raleigh kicks the door shut. No one's getting out behind us.

Gunfire pops in the streets and hills outside Descendants as often as birds talk to each other. I don't worry too much that anyone outside will be alarmed by Leagan's double shots. The two slabs of meat standing by never have a chance to know something hit them.

Little Barton turns just in time to meet my barrel. At this distance the lead goes right through him. He tries to run for cover around the desk of payroll bags, but falls behind it.

Milk and glass shatter as Leagan fires one last time. The man —who I sincerely hope is Little Barton's wretched father— slumps in his armchair, gnarled and shitty and dead now.

I'll be shocked if any of the drunks on the other side of the door even looked up from their games.

"Ash to ash, for dust we remain." I draw the sign of Blessed Deliverance across my chest, a whisper recited purely out of habit. "That's for the Raven, you motherfuckers." I drive my boot into Barton Jaxson's stomach. "And that's for my daughter...I'm so sorry, my lovely. I should have been there with you."

I don't actually want Providence to have mercy on them, I hope they all go straight to hell with my regards.

Even the simplest memories, like seeing the color purple because it was Vesta's favorite, burn to hold. They're always at the surface, and as much they feel unbearable, I hope they always stay this close. It will hurt worse once I start to not feel them.

Blood drains into the milk seeping across the floor, reaching out for me with pink fingers, white beads clinging to Old Jaxson's shirt.

"You have your knife?" I ask Leagan.

"Of course."

"Foolish me. What kind of a question is that?" I throw the two payroll bags toward the door and sweep everything else onto the floor. "Draw me a snake, with its head cut off."

The Rim knows what that means. Blood and vengeance.

Raleigh kicks open the door with a heel. "We should go."

"Everyone grab a bag." It would be a sin to leave the Jaxsons's blood gold to rot.

"Go." I let Leagan and Raleigh get ahead of me before I grasp the arm of one of the bookmakers. "The den is flooding."

"*Sol*, widow," he says. "Everybody out!"

TWELVE
ADELAIDE

THE LANTERNS CHOKE UNDER ASH, SHADOWS THICKER ON THE LOW SIDE OF THE Slash than the hill where the Company businesses are.

I sit by the pit at the far edge of the soup camp, dimmed by shadows feeding on quartz light. Across the street lies the main mine.

The Stranger twitches with each voice that passes, the guards she counts in the dark over there. I scrape my heel through the dead ash skin until I find the cinnamon earth beneath, but the Stranger keeps picking at me. There has to be a way in.

A gray cat creeps from nowhere, winds herself through my ankles. Her pupils tighten as I reach with one finger. She sniffs but won't come any closer, frail like the bird skulls in Leagan's bone collection.

The elevator whistle screams.

The cat shoots under the meat shed, almost too fast for the Stranger to notice.

Eyes up.

The man hatch opens, a steel jaw in the hillside. Second-shift men, black dirt and fire quartz headlamps spill out, spread in groups of three and four. They pull off their deep-shaft respirator masks and form the line for ration tickets, but the Stranger watches the mine.

One minute, sixteen seconds. That's how long the elevators sit open between each load.

Six guards. At the elevator itself and the lookout towers, same as the rail yard. I'll get shot if I try to get in there.

The Stranger wants everything. But fire spreads. Maybe the one I start doesn't have to consume everything in Hannah at once, just enough for me to disappear behind. Enough that Hannah isn't worth rebuilding even if the deep parts of the mine remain.

Finish what you started.

Reluctantly, miners enter the soup camp, knees and elbows patched multiple times, bent from working under the weight of earth for so long. Most of them don't look at me. I'm not worth the white-bodice discount. The flesh being offered down the row isn't fox.

The Stranger rises, bristled like the cat. Two come toward me, nervous laughter wrapped around the scuff of feet.

A boy in miner's coveralls, hair shooting like straw from under his hat. The other such a tight shadow he steps on the back of his friend's heel. They're around Leagan's age. Seventeen, still outpaced by gangly limbs.

Leagan's age the last time I saw her. She's older now.

"He didn't listen, just kept digging and the water vein split open. Shaft nineteen is still flooded. Fool's gold, I've never seen that much water, even back east."

"How would you know?"

"I was born in Agnes County. That's east of Saint Laura, fool."

"Quit your bragging." The one with yellow hair yanks his accomplice by the suspender.

Get away.

There are four other fire pits. You don't need to sit by mine.

The boy resists before he gets pulled too close. "He said be careful."

"I am. I know what to do. Watch, picker." The yellow-haired one turns, backs the last three steps.

Never show your back to a stranger. Or walk by a pit of burning crystal without looking.

Little fools.

"Don't look her in the eye and she can't hurt you, that's how it's done. The fortune teller told me." Molasses gum pulls at his teeth, juice squelching in his jaw as he mouth breathes. He slips a crumpled paper from his belt, holds it at me.

I don't move.

"For you." He shakes his fingers. "Fox?"

Who's bothering me now, Saraline from the bathhouse again?

He senses me rise. "Shit..."

Three.

I pick the note from his fingers without touching. He shivers anyway, spitting fearful laughter.

"Oh fuck. Did you see that?"

To a Stranger.

The ink strokes are thick. Male. It crushes into my fist as I close it.

"Can you read?"

I slowly look back up at him, wordless eyes.

The yellow-haired friend cuffs the back of his head.

"Ow! What for, Jenkin?"

"I said don't look at her! You can't read. Of course, she can't, you fool." His voice drops below the first half of his whisper. *"Half-breed."*

"I was just asking. There's no harm in asking." He leans, staring where my mouth is behind the muzzle.

"She does bite." One of the soup women returns, wet things sliding out of her bucket into the pot. "Real hard."

The Stranger arcs through my skin like storm static. *Someone's out there.*

Beyond the sticks framing the camp and smoke like oil, the black outline of rooftops...just the dark.

I can't see them.

They're there.

"I want to see her pointy teeth."

"No, don't piss her. She'll eat you. Let's get out of here."

The Stranger ticks down each bone in my spine, dulls the ghost throb of the refinery, fills the void left by the absence of gunfire familiar as air across the rest of the Rim. Her beat is the one I know. *Look. Look. Look...*

The soup woman drags her long ladle around the pot. The smell that seeps over us isn't food cooking, it's the shit that comes out of people when they die.

I back into the shadows bloating against the firelight's ring.

Three.

The note peels like a clutched secret. Square, but folded in a pattern of five triangles.

I have something that belongs to you.
Hangman's yard. 5:00
Sol, sos Secuundas

A miner spits at the soup kettle as a group of them approach it. "I bet you a cigarette the boss eats fresh meat."

He does.

"Off the bone."

"Have you ever tasted human, fox?"

The words burn on my skin like his spit did on the pot. There are five of them. My head hurts, I'm not in the mood.

"I shared a cell with a war survivor back east," he says. "He told me the truth, you foxes raise your babies on blood, not milk. Cut your teeth gnawing on bone."

"She looks hungry."

"If she is, I'd be more careful," the soup woman says. "Leave her alone. She's not bothering anyone, and she's the mute I wish you were."

"She shouldn't be here." He scowls. "She'll rot the food."

"The food's already rotten." One turns away. "Worthless milk-bastard."

Without my family I might have believed him.

The woman swings her three-foot ladle out of the seething pot. "Get out of my sight or I'll boil you down and feed you to your friends tomorrow. I bet they'll come back for seconds too."

He glares down the ladle at her, fat drops shattering on dust.

They're not who I felt watching. They're too stupid. The Stranger can feel the difference.

Six.

He backs out of my way, crossing himself like Aunt Tess does. But she does it when she kills, not when she runs.

"You can stay." The soup woman says to me. "All people are rotten. You might be a fox but you aren't any worse than the rest of us. I saw that cat get friendly with you. Animals know if something would eat them." Her black eyes reflect back fire quartz orange. "Be careful out there. The ghost hasn't killed any women yet, but we know plenty of other things do. Don't give them the pleasure."

I offer her a gold standard, let the Stranger rise to the surface of my skin as she takes it. Paid loyalty is better than none.

The note drops from my hand, flakes away seconds after touching the pit quartz.

I won't. ⁻

THIRTEEN
TESLA

Leagan and I climb the water collection tower, and all morning we watch. The Green Contract Company comes and goes in the yard downwind. Manufacturing their own shitty ammunition from spent shells, unloading wagons of flour, rice, and beans, marching around in their little olive uniforms like good worker ants.

Why do men in uniforms all start to behave the same?

Is it literally because their clothes match and they become disoriented, or is something more sinister at work?

"Wanted, able-bodied men with a thirst for justice," I read, the fresh advertisement picked off the wall of the Express office this morning. "Military background encouraged by wage bonus, but not required. Fair pay. Inquire at the Green Contract Company. Stand with progress, join the Railroad Bullshit… I added that last part."

"Well, it should say that." Leagan finishes unhooking a piece of the sky barrel's sluice trough to get the two short support legs that will become her stovepipe's hand grips. She tucks them into her backpack along with the wrench. "Missed opportunity."

"I thought so. He should have hired me to write this."

And Green has found such men, thirsty for justice. I do wonder if they'll be as motivated once they're hungry.

"That's where you need to hit." I point out the newer warehouse where a push wagon of ammunition just disappeared into the black interior. Another one, rattling with jars of peaches and green tomatoes, right behind it. "If you only get one shot, it'll hurt worse if they'll lose all their food."

"I'll get two shots," Leagan says.

"If you don't, don't worry. Their repurposed ammo will sort them out for us. Green's been blowing thumbs off with that bastard shit for years."

"I said I'll get two shots."

"I like your confidence."

The sun suddenly isn't as sharp as it was a minute ago. It's not even noon.

The shade of a growing *Solace* storm cools the sky, wind that has a chill slapping me from the opposite direction. Its voice goes shrill as a human scream as it passes through the hollow rocks just west of here. I know it's science, not ghosts, but the hair on my neck doesn't recognize the distinction and stiffens all the same. Mother would take this storm as a sign that we should leave now. But I can't.

Leagan turns to me, catching the tail of her yawn with an elbow. "What are you thinking about?"

St. Paul is less trustworthy than we've ever been, and I wouldn't believe a word he says even if someone cut it out of him. If I don't find out for certain what happened to Mother's body, I will regret it forever, and that's just not something I'm interested in. Once I've made sure she's not being stored inside those warehouses, I'll feel less guilty.

I shove off my stomach, letting the binoculars go on the strap around my neck. "I'm thinking we should get off this tower before lightning turns us into bacon."

"But that's a delicious way to die."

The ladder is missing several rungs too short, the impact of dropping the last few feet jarring through my ankles. "What else do you need for the stovepipe?"

"Just a new stick of ghost quartz for the welder, but I can get that at the trader myself. Raleigh burnt mine out last night like a fool."

"Maybe you should stop being so hard on him. He's been our friend for a long time now. He's practically your brother."

"He deserves it. He's only here because he feels guilty."

We pass a man leading a donkey right as he belches, and Leagan belches back, louder.

"Impressive. You're still the queen."

"I can't believe I was never allowed off the train here before. People here are gross, and I love it."

I'm glad she has the luxury of thinking that. It means we did something right.

"I'll be back with the fun stuff in half an hour," I say before leaving her at the Lucky Sol trading post. "Don't get distracted on the way back, or we'll have to listen to Raleigh bitch about it all night. Don't talk to strangers."

She gives me a smile of sadness. "Only one."

"And don't burn the hotel down until I'm back to watch."

Thunder groans out past the edges of town as I head toward the rails where demolition items are locked up by the larger mining operations in the area. The fragrance of wet shit begins to rise from the ground like the dead come back to haunt us as the air gets clotted and warm again. You can see the rain coming for Descendants in a gray line.

A man who's been walking quite a few strides behind me takes an abrupt right turn as I do. He's likely no one, but we've all trained ourselves to notice things like that. I turn the opposite way, weaving between walls in a serpentine pattern as the rain cuts across me with a roar.

When I look back, he's still behind me.

The next corner gives me a sightline in a clear diagonal line. Quickly, I dump my hat and widow's lace into a pile of garbage and peel free of the men's suit jacket and vest that were my bounty hunter disguise. My cotton shirt adheres to my body in a second skin almost instantly.

The bundle gets caught on a nail the first time I try to kick it under the stilt foundation. *"Farce!"*

A surge of rain river gushes brown around my ankles and carries them off for me. There. Now, at first glance at least, I look like someone else. Maybe today is lucky, and my scarred face will be enough to fool anyone who doesn't know me very well, but I draw my pistol regardless.

The man comes through the last row exactly like I did, turning left and then right. Nice try, darling. I squeeze a double shot at him.

Someone grabs my hair from behind.

Fingernails peel skin off me, my head wrenching back at a disadvantaged angle as he yanks. I grab at the hand to keep more hair from ripping, but fire still burns in drag lines over my scalp.

I miss a direct hit on his groin, but my knee spike still gouges out a fat piece of his thigh.

He half-buckles, twisting my grip on my gun. I fire it one last time, partially in his hand, still partially in mine. Something in my wrist snaps, but my heart is pounding too fast to feel much beyond the vibration of the bone crack.

He drives a bootheel into my middle, knocking me out into the open. My stomach comes up, and my feet stick to the unstable mud. Real pain, wretched, hot pain, flares up my arm as I hit the ground, blinding me in black stars.

His weight lands on my stomach, pinning my hips to the rapidly thickening mud, peeling out my arms to either side of me. I dig my heels in and thrust up, throwing his weight off balance. He adjusts as I try to slip out, fighting my loose hands for control. It's a fist that connects with my nose, but it feels like pins that set my scar on fire and turn my scream of rage to sparks in my head.

"You almost blew my hand off, bitch."

"Well, I'll be sure to not miss again." The copper taste of blood coats the back of my throat. Past the rain, I look for a glimpse of the Jaxson Boys tattoo under his eye. It's not there, so it's not them.

Another one peels out of the rain curtain, stepping onto my unprotected forearms.

Fuck.

Rainwater fills up the hollow of my throat and slides all over my exposed face. I can't breathe without swallowing it. When I open my eyes, I'm blind, and my mouth, it pours in. I spit some back, but the man pushes my head down, embedding me eye-deep in the muck.

"Are you ready to drown in shit?"

"Are you, snake f—"

"Did you really think I'm a fucking fool?"

I only need one eye open to recognize St. Paul, soaked like the oily little rat he is.

"I did not," I sneer. "I know for a fact you're a fucking fool."

I swear his children's clothes have gotten even smaller now that he's wet.

"Well, the bullshit is on you Tesla Revere. I'm not a baby, born lasterday, no boy. You can't play me like that because you're not as smart as you think you are."

Of course, he picked today to grow a brain. "You should have let me see my mother's body, and I wouldn't have had to do anything to you."

"You're nothing but a liar."

"You're goddamn right. I am."

"Green burned her himself. Honor she didn't deserve, in my mind. Don't worry, we won't do the same to you. You can rot here as long as you like. Scavenger lizards and bugs crawling up inside you…"

I writhe harder, my face dipping below the waterline as I buck the man off my hips into the mud headfirst. Fool, I know how to change positions. I was only submerged for seconds but I come up with a gasp like it was a minute. "You're not drowning me in this shit."

The gathering mud water flows into my ears, over my lips and eyes again as I swing my legs overhead and slam into the man standing on my arms. I'm free.

Let me say, I'm *very* glad to not be wearing a skirt and fighting the weight of all that wet fabric at the moment.

Warm wet drags on my hair and the front of my shins as I stand. My pistol is long lost somewhere in this sludge. Good thing I brought two more.

The rope slips over my head before I have the chance to see it. The pain bites me in half, stunning and severing logic, instantly agony. Heat and pressure flood up into my eyes. My nails slash skin but skip off the rope, my dominant hand completely refusing to grip. Useless bitch.

A dull knife tears flesh, a rope rips it even slower. The street is a brown blur, my eyes about to burst.

Bastards, they're laughing at me.

I won't go like this. Oh no, not today. I stab my elbow into his ribs enough times it must break them. He has to let go of me soon. *Please.*

The rope gives as head snaps back, muzzle flash igniting behind me. Leagan. Leagan is the only person for miles capable of a headshot in weather like this.

My elbow catches on rough siding as I veer too close and collapse against the first solid object, air shrieking through my throat while my eyes bleed hot tears.

Shit, I think he broke my wrist.

Leagan breaches the sheet flooding off one of the angled overhangs to the song of repeating gunpowder flashes.

Further down, a dark shape drops from one of the roofs.

I yank my backup revolver from the holster with my weak hand.

Someone rises off the mud like a loaded spring. But I don't trust my eyes, or the distortion of the rain, not while a phantom rope still crushes my throat.

The dim figure spins, their skirt flares from the waist, a fan blade slicing water. The clipped end of a sword catches on a burst of lightning, an extension of their arm as they come around.

With a lunge step, he pins St. Paul to the wall, boot to neck like a stone beetle skewered to a specimen cushion. One short twist breaks St. Paul's arm from its socket, pink tongue spitting out a scream.

"Stop!" My voice barely stretches past the pulse of the storm. "He's *mine*."

"Mercy…" St. Paul withers as the swordman lets his languid arm go and shoves him this way.

The water slows him too much to run from me. I dig my hand into the back of his neck, nails first. "You want mercy?" We both go down but I wrap my legs around his body and bury him in the muddy water. "Her name was *Moira!*"

He takes long enough to drown, my arms and teeth shaking by the end of it.

Leagan stands over me, black lipstick is smeared up past her eyebrow, blood twisted in the rain running down her face, and flecks of mud unmoved by it. "They hurt you."

At the other end of the alley, the swordman watches us.

Leagan raises her pistol.

My blood slides off my upper lip into my mouth, warm as I pull back on my rampant breaths to adjust my slick, off-handed grip on my pistol. With the hand at the end of my broken wrist shaking, I gently cup the stinging gash in my throat and try my voice. "Finish it."

Farce, I sound like a lizard.

The swordman looks past the dark line of his brow, eyes black as souls underneath. It's him, the Cairoshman I spoke to in the Jaxsons' den last night, even with his topknot hammered flat, water riding off the ring of dark copper threading his nostrils.

"Go ahead." I drag out both arms, sleeves lead with muck and rain and everything wretched. "Kill me."

He can't.

The cackle bubbles out of me like blood from a deep wound. I'm alive. The mountain that swells through me doesn't stop. It climbs so high, it will be a bitch to fall off the other side and come back down, but I don't care. Maybe it's because I've felt dead inside for so long, but this is a rush better than sex.

The cough cuts off my breath, so violent I have to hang on to my knees.

Leagan doesn't flinch. She'll protect both of us. "Don't come any closer."

I holster my gun before I accidentally shoot a toe off.

"If death was what I wanted, we wouldn't be here right now," he says.

I'd tell him that's an old line I've used before, but I don't have enough breath.

He wears a black overskirt accented with turmeric lining. The threads embroidering the edges of his collar and sleeves have splintered. He's not fresh. A black glove buttons the length of one forearm, while the hand he uses to handle the sword is naked. And on the hip where a pistol usually rides, a silver teacup dangles beside an apothecary kit like the one Navy wears.

"Poisonneur." I get that word out without choking.

His black soul eyes can't match the emptiness of his voice. It swallows me from the core out. "I'm not a Poisonneur."

Oh really now? I know exactly zero men who twirl around with swords and wear overskirts, although it would really dress this place up if more of them did.

"Just a man, trying to survive in this hell, like you."

Mother told me about the rumor going through Lideon last Season, that a Poisonneur was hunting us. Before we went to visit Green for the last time, before the derailment. Neither of us believed it. Even now, it makes sense like a fever dream. If I was a legendary assassin, I wouldn't waste my time in a shit-hell like Descendants. But here we are.

Leagan looks to me. Kill him or no?

No, I shake my head. I want to know what's going on, why he's here, and if it's not to kill us, then what is he doing?

He plucks his hooded cowl up, a brown water veil sloughing past his face. "I'd get that neck cleaned out before it festers and leave this place tonight."

Thank you for the advice, sir, I wouldn't have thought of that otherwise.

I step after him. "What's my name?"

It's a test, obviously. The fact that he's here means he knows. Raleigh wasn't being a paranoid fool after all. Technically, I owe him an apology, but will I? Probably not.

"Tesla Revere," he says carefully, wise to ears that are ever present as the flies. "The Widow. Daughter of Moira Revere, the Raven. Engineer of the *Absolution*, name known to the Rim for ten Seasons. Origins unknown."

A shiver cuts through my bones. Not one made of fear, but possibility. It whispers at me through the keyhole like it did when I was a girl in my parents' house back east, dreaming of adventure. All of these events will mean something. Nothing is accidental, nothing is in vain. We prayed for a way into Cairo for Navy's eye operation, and here he is.

"What's yours?" Leagan asks.

"Not important." He twists the amber ring seated on his middle finger. His dark gaze connects with mine from under the deep hood. "If my name is your price, then you're cheaper than I expected. Otherwise, we deal in black gold."

"Say it to me again." *Farce*, this cough. I have to finish the thought with my hand. You're not a Poisonneur?

"We'll meet again when you're in a better condition to speak. *Sol sana*."

"Covenant." I get the word out before my raw throat spasms.

"No." It sounds like Leagan whispers.

"The church," I finish.

Gold sun punches through the bruised sky. I'm confident he heard me, even though he doesn't bother looking back.

Last raindrops strike my face, shoving needles through the scar on my dead cheek. Descendants reeks harder when it's wet, bodies often washed out of shallow graves.

"Fuck." My arms and legs weigh more than freight cars. I fall into a seat on a stoop above the waterline, the motion like a blow to my throbbing head. "How bad is it?"

"It's icky." Her fingertips sting my neck as they touch, hardly worth bragging about. Meanwhile, the pain in my arm is alive. "But it's not that deep." She slides her arms around me, but the warmth isn't enough to break past the shiver rattling my limbs.

"Are *you* hurt?" I ask.

"I'm mad. They only sent one guy after me." She kicks at a loose can floating by. "One. Bad for him I'm slippery like an eel."

My laugh becomes a gasp as the aches in my throat and wrist turn to stabs. "Stop that. Don't make me laugh."

"I don't remember what my mama looked like."

Well, I'm not laughing now.

"I used to look at her picture," Leagan says. "The one Grandma kept next to her bed. She didn't look the way she did in my mind. After a while I stopped trying to remember because it didn't help."

"She looked a lot like you." I burst one of the raindrop pearls clinging to her buns. "Blood-red hair, lots of freckles, but with Navy's chin."

"Was she spicy like me?"

"Not nearly as spicy as you."

"I don't want to forget Grandma like that."

"I don't either." As close as she still feels, things are already slipping from my mind too. I tell myself that doesn't make me a disloyal daughter, it's just...fucking life. It moves with or without us. "But you're older now, you got to know her longer than your mama. You won't forget what's important, that she loved you."

Leagan touches her head to my shoulder. She doesn't get mad this time when I kiss her.

"Come on, little eel. I need to get this shit off me." The mud is matted down to my scalp. It's going to take all night to get out of my hair with one hand, and I'm not looking forward to flushing out this neck wound with clear pine and morning salt, either.

Leagan goes through the pockets of the other dead while I check St. Paul. I'd hoped he was lying and still had Mother's rings, but all he holds is molasses gum and wet lint.

"Adelaide would not be disappointed in you—" I start.

"I dream."

"You what, ma'am?" Everything running through my mind halts with me, Leagan also starlight still. "For how long?"

She shrugs. "Always."

"But you never said anything?"

"Grandma understood her dreams. I don't... I don't want them. They scare me. And lately they've gotten worse."

"That's why you're so tired." I have noticed her recent insomnia, but I assumed it was a manifestation of grief.

"They're not as bad if I sleep during the day. I don't know why."

"What have you seen?"

"Hands, and hand bones. They come out of everything...or I get mine cut off."

I hold up my broken wrist, swollen like an overripe plum. "I think you can stop worrying now."

She swallows, some kind of memory stuck on her tongue. "Before Mama died, I dreamed about a town full of bodies, a church, with treasure buried under it. I could walk, but no one could see me, like I wasn't really there. It smelled so bad."

"Crow." Mother once told me her dreams of the flooded town leading up to Liza's death, the bodies in the water. I know the details because she described them to me with such clarity, I feel like I saw it myself. But Leagan's sight has a realistic quality, while Mother had to decipher the meaning behind hers.

"Every time I dream about death, it smells bad."

"Like this?" Nothing smells worse than warm, wet shit. Not even death.

"I saw Mama die."

"Oh, my love." The putrid air rattles in my chest as I reach for her. "You were so young."

"Three. And I still remember."

It's not something she'll ever forget.

"Grandma would tell us what she saw, and then it would happen. I thought saying them out loud was what made them come true."

"You were dreaming the same things, the whole time." Maybe this is why Mother always seemed overly protective of Leagan. I thought it was because she was Liza's last baby, but it's more likely she knew Leagan had her gift.

Her gaze darkens. "I've seen that bone picker before. The Cairoshman."

"When?"

"The week Vesta died. He cut off my hands with a hatchet."

"Fuck...I won't let him. We won't let him hurt any of us."

"You invited him to Covenant."

"But not Damascus." The sting of her accusation burns, although I didn't have the reason not to ask him at the time. "He appears to be a man, so I think it's a safe bet he doesn't know where the sanctuary is."

"Or Evangeline and I will have to shoot him."

"Does anyone else know about your gift?"

She hesitates. "Just Adelaide."

Yes, besides Mother, she is the obvious choice. "I thought so."

"She asks me about them occasionally, but I know she'd never tell without my permission."

"So, you think I will?"

"Yeah, you blabber."

This gives me such intense relief that Mother's gift is not gone. If you see what's coming, you can plan for it. Was Liza like this too and I just didn't know? I thought we didn't keep secrets from each other, but my sister could have been playing like her daughter here.

I pretend-punch her arm with my good hand. "Just give me a warning next time, you little rapscallion."

She grins crooked due to her smudged lipstick. "We're still going back to the warehouse, right? I was really looking forward to blowing some shit up."

"Absolutely. You worked too hard on that stovepipe, it would be a sin to waste such beauty. But we'd better go make sure Raleigh's still alive."

No nasty comment?

God of Mercy, she must be tired.

Mother would never forgive me if I let something happen to Leagan on her behalf. Or myself. But every once in a while, you have to give yourself to the madness and disobey your mother. That time is now.

FOURTEEN
TESLA

Wood scrapes wood as Raleigh moves the chair barring our door from the inside. "I heard shots—fucking Jezebel, did you take a bath in the flash flood?"

"We're fine." I step over their work, laid out across the floor on black taffy pitch coated canvas to protect the floor from the welding. The stovepipe is only missing its back end and the payload I was on my way to pick up when I was quite rudely interrupted.

"You liar." He points to the raw band sawed into my throat. "Fool's gold, I can see the layers in your neck! I'm starting to wonder if you have a death wish."

"Of course not. It wasn't our fault."

"I wanted the big scar." Leagan flashes her tongue, stained by something red she presumably ate at the trading post before she fled. "And now you have two. Hog."

I show my tongue back to her, fumbling my buttons left-handed to open my collar wider. "Yes, envy this."

"I do."

"I assume something you're wearing is responsible for that offensive smell." Raleigh gags as he pulls off the welding goggles.

"I left my trousers outside."

"Yes, I noticed."

"Well, I figured you wouldn't want to see me completely naked."

"I'll go downstairs and get you a drink, but please, bury those clothes somewhere very deep before I come back. Fool's gold, my eyes are burning."

"You don't want to help me wash the shit out of my hair?"

"I do not. I don't like you even close to that much."

"Wait." I hold up my wrist, purple and swollen to an ugly size. It really fucking hurts. "Could I trouble you to tie me a sling for this first?"

It's even harder to pry my boots off single-handed, and bending forward makes the extra blood pressure throb in my swollen face.

"Do you need help with that too?" Raleigh says. "Here, sit still. Let me take a truly wild guess. You still want to go through with the sabotage."

"Believe it." I dry-swallow a pain tablet while he unlaces my boots. Fuck it, I take three. "St. Paul doesn't get to maim me like this in Green's name for free. Scrawny little bastard."

Raleigh's grin becomes a cringe when his hand comes away greased in shit mud.

"However, I may need you to pick up the explosives. I didn't quite make it there, as you see."

"Excuse me, my job was supposed to be building the stovepipe with Leagan, which I've done. You told me we'd pose as Green Company men together to hide flash fire in the warehouses and open the doors from the inside." The pipes shake inside the wall as Raleigh pumps water over his hands and scrubs like he's about to give surgery. "Leagan's been helpful... you're the one who really hasn't done anything at all, and I feel taken advantage of. And now look at you, you can't go anywhere like this." He tears a long strip of cotton off the bedsheet. "You are lazy."

I appreciate his attempt to distract me, but the shock still makes my heel jump when my wrist settles into the sling a little too hard. *"Vacca voya!"* That's Tov for "fuck you." "And your bastard father too. Thank you."

"You're welcome. If I had even a shard of sense, I'd say no and leave you to dig your own grave."

"But you'll still do it, because you love me."

"Unfortunately. You know me too well. You know I'd take a bullet for you." He looks back at Leagan, stripped out of her dirty clothes and already in new ones. "Yes, even you."

"You're a sweet boy," I say.

"Yes, I am, so hear me now." He cuts me off before I can finish opening my mouth. "Tess, I know you hate it when I tell you what to do because of the organ I have growing between my legs. But I am not wrong."

"That's not specifically why I hate it." I just don't like being wrong, period.

"You need to disappear, you need to disappear fast, and it has to be for a long time. I will not bury you. Any of you. If you love me at all, please don't do that to me."

"Then I guess you have to die first," Leagan says.

"You know what? There." Raleigh jabs with the middle finger on his dainty pearl picker hand. "I was trying to have a moment of honesty, but you're determined to disregard that too. Go ahead, be a bitch child and hate me for the rest of your life. It won't stop me from caring about you. It's just going to make you bitter, and I will win."

"That's the most I've ever respected you," Leagan says. "I've just been waiting for you to actually get mad."

"Get over yourself. We have work to do."

Leagan steps into the closet containing the pump and begins to fill the washbasin. "Come in here when you're ready, Aunt Tess, and I'll salt you."

"You're going to need a barrel for her hair."

"You want honesty?" It still burns to speak with much force. "I want to retire someday, Raleigh. I want a place where we can be safe, I don't want to die in filth like I almost just did." I didn't want that for Vesta or Mother, either. "But if I wanted to sit around on my ass doing absolutely nothing, I would have gone back east and married a banker or a crystal baron before I got my face sliced up and I was still young enough to make that easy."

"All right." He draws a slow breath. "I understand. I know what this means to you, and I'm sorry."

"Help us finish what we started, and I'll tell you you're right. Mother would call us all fools for worrying about her body. It won't bring her back. So, we'll just burn the warehouses. Deal?"

He nods. "I can live with that."

"Then we'll go back to Damascus where Green can't get to us. We'll focus on getting Adelaide out of Hannah and Navy's science project. I promise you on a lady's honor."

"You fuck honor, as you love to remind me," Raleigh says. "I'll go get the explosives while you clean yourself up." The pain in his eyes is a reflection of mine, but it's the seeds that become resolve. "I'll expect better from you this time because I really would do anything for you. Except wash that shit out of your hair. Good luck, Raptor."

I'm not a crystal baron's wife. I'm not anybody's wife. I am going to *be* a crystal baron. *Sol sana* to anyone who tries to stop me.

Sweet Raleigh, I never said how long we'd wait, and now you don't need to know I invited the Poisonneur to meet us there.

Not as smart as I think I am?

St. Paul got lucky. And that's all I have to say about what happened here.

Nightfall surrounds Descendants, merciless and throat-deep. A ravenous beast like this town can't sleep, but the moon is noticeably absent from the vacant sky. I couldn't have picked a better night if I planned it myself. Oh wait, I did.

"I found a maintenance crew headed south that will let us ride along for the right price," Raleigh whispers. "As long as they keep their storm schedule, we can meet them in Junction."

"Alkaline." The bandage binding my throat reminds me of the rope every time I swallow. "Let's make Green cry."

"Can he?" Leagan says.

"Let's find out."

Simply breathing makes my bruised throat ache, so I stand back and hold the horses while Leagan creeps to the point of the roof across from the Green Company yard. The warehouse's main slide door hangs like a broken jaw, two men posted overnight to guard it.

It would take an act of Providence's mercy to stop us now. I pray that He doesn't, I really want this.

The snort of ignition rides ahead of a streak of silver smoke. That's a well-made stovepipe. A sharp boom turns the night blood orange. Flash fire to rapidly consume everything inside, a demo stick to spread the payload.

Leagan gets her two shots. The girl is reliable.

The second shell holds dynamite. That black taffy shell painted to hold fire out cracks like eggshell on a stone, and the walls of warehouses thirteen and eleven blow apart.

FIFTEEN
ADELAIDE

Sol, sos Secuundas. The Stranger turns the phrase in my mind, a coin. *Sol, daughter of Shadows.*

Does whoever sent this really think I'm foolish enough to fall for it?

The low side of Hannah slouches together, wood frames touching like bodies in a crowded room. I cross the channels of planks set up by other thieves like me. The second street, resting on the shoulders of its first.

Four fifty-six.

The flat roof of the Company bakery overlooks Hangman's Yard, the gate, the ticket booth, the corrugated walls too high to climb without help.

I'm not going to meet them. I'm going to watch.

On the gallows platform they ring the triangle bell. Five o' clock. The blood crowd gathers in the yard, death on the menu. A young scavenger lizard cuts across the ledge. It smells yesterday's flesh, knows there'll be more.

The air presses close, thick and windless. The Stranger feels them, looking for me again. But there are more people shoved together here than any other place I've known. Sometimes it's hard to pick out who the eyes she feels belong to.

Seventeen.

The stones poke as I press my ribs to the double chimneys. I brought one of my stolen revolvers, but it's the knife I draw from my belt. It kills quiet. I hold it in middle guard, breathe.

There.

A figure separates from the shadows.

He lacks a hard outline, but it's just the shifting veil of Hannah's fog, his loose black clothes. My eyes have moved in these shadows enough to see through them and find edges. He stands sideways, a thinner target profile.

Now I know how this started. I can choose how it ends.

"Wait." He drops the scarf under the well of his hood. Red sunlight catches on a ring threading the cartilage between his nostrils.

I stay where I am. Nothing.

"You have the instincts of a predator. They serve you well." His vowels snap off each other. Not the pretentious vowels of the east Kane tried so hard to dislodge. Not the chopped syllables from Eos like Markos.

He summons an envelope with a pickpocket's hand. "The Widow says hello, Stranger."

Farce.

I want to believe this. So bad my guts hurt, but the Stranger won't let me. Can't.

"She said you'd be difficult to convince."

The shadows hang off the chimneys, hold me like arms. I won't trust something that will hurt me.

"When you make it out of here, the Widow also said you will be doing her dishes for three weeks because she was right about the location of Lake Amnesty."

The hand around my knife is fine, but my empty one starts to shake. I force it to squeeze and open until it stops.

Aunt Tess and I made that bet so long ago. Before we left with Kane. Before Eden. Before Vesta and Grandma. We were at the engine, heat in the floor, wind in my hair, my copy of Kane's map shared between us. She, Vesta, and I were the only ones who knew about that conversation. He's telling the truth.

The Stranger thickens as I peel the shadows off myself. The smell of the *Absolution's* hot metal slips away.

In its place, it's all burnt gold.

Four.

"She was confident that information would turn you," he says. "It appears she was right."

A horse and lightning bolt—the patch of the Express Riders, stitched to the front of his shirt. He wears an overskirt, stocked with things the Stranger can't see but wants. Two pistols. On the ribcage, the hip. And a teacup. Cornflower blue, a twisted pattern lifted in gold.

Dr. Pike in Winchester had raised engravings on his set too. Each cup with a different pattern and subtly mismatched shape. Same leaf curl to the handle as this one, the second loop for the widow finger. Ones made back east aren't like this. He's Cairosh.

His gaze flicks down my arm to the knife lurking behind the seam of my skirt.

Observant.

The dangerous kind. I don't like it either.

"*Sol, Secuundas.*" He nods, a ghost smile flaring his mouth. "Cairo's pale cousins across the desert."

I'm not your cousin, you're not mine.

I put out my hand, his steps dust quiet to give the envelope.

It has weight, Aunt Tess's handwriting and her stamp in the dark wax seal. *TR.* Whatever news this holds, she has a lot to say.

His gaze travels over me again, and the Stranger rises to meet it.

There is something familiar here. Between us, in him. The Stranger tastes it. It's not ancestral bond—it's bitter. Death.

"Let's make an agreement tonight," he says. "I will make certain you get out of here alive, and in return you will never turn that Shiver I see lurking at me from your eyes on me. Fair?"

The Stranger coils, a wall between him and me he can't pass through.

I don't make promises.

And I'm not afraid to break them. "Yes."

"Then let it be, *so*. I leave in two days with the outgoing mail. I'm sure you have things to say to your family. I fixed a tin under the third step behind the air market where you sat yesterday."

Our small object method. Sit down, let it slip through the crack or pull out what was left for you while your skirt hides what you're doing.

"Leave your reply there and I'll take care of it."

"Why did the Widow trust you?"

Why should I?

I understand why they didn't send Raleigh. Why they can't come themselves. But who is he?

"Does she?" His head cocks.

Aunt Tess isn't wrong very often, but everyone can make a mistake.

"We have an understanding," he says. "Your family has accumulated powerful enemies. I have experience dealing with men like that and will exercise it on your behalf in exchange for information the Widow has."

"And the Raven?"

"You don't know…" He checks himself. "*Farce.*" The Tov word sounds like a new one, rocked by his Cairosh accent. But it means what I didn't want.

But you knew.

It was a fool's hope. The harder I hold on, the faster the things I want get ripped out of me.

Rafe didn't lie. Grandma is dead. I already lost my mother here. Now I have to let go of the woman who took her place. Someone I actually loved.

Don't cry.

But this ache doesn't obey me like the Stranger does. It fills up my chest, head like *Solace* floodwater. This isn't something I'm going to share with anyone, especially this man I don't know. Grandma would understand. This isn't who I am.

"Ah." He looks away, boot scraping roof plank. "You test me. A communal trait, I see. The Widow asked me to verify that you are still among the living and prove that I delivered her message to you untampered with."

All of us have lived here a long time. Express Riders take an oath to deliver their entrusted parcels to their one, true recipient. Moon weather, pickers, or death. An oath they're better known for breaking than honoring for the right amount of gold.

"If you think I upheld this service, I was instructed to ask your other name, the one given to you by Annabeth. Write it in the letter you send back."

Vengeance. A cat in our favorite children's story, black as the rare, moonless night. The name only Vesta used on me, and she was only Annabeth to me.

He draws his first two fingers down his forehead to his mouth. "We will meet again, lonely Shadow."

I wait until he leaves the rooftop. Until the Stranger's certain he's not coming back. Then I fall behind the chimney, tear open Aunt Tess's letter.

Four. One from Leagan. One from Navy. One written in a cipher Leagan and I created together, folded around a smuggler's tube of morning salt. And one that looks blank.

The sob I pinned down lunges back up my throat when I take my next breath.

I return to my room and activate the hidden ink with fire quartz, vinegar, and the salt. On the once-blank sheet is the cipher key.

After five lines, the Stranger doesn't need it to read the coded letter anymore. The pattern is clear.

Dear Adelaide,

The man who delivered this letter is Poisonneur Niall Montoya, in the future to be known as the Menace. (Although he still won't admit to being a Poisonneur, which he IS, but that's a story for another time.) I know you're extremely suspicious right now, but try not to kill him. He's going to be useful to us.

Montoya.

The name strikes cold as a crossing-bell through my chest.

Winchester.

The black throbs out of every free space in my head. I experience it all again, every wretched detail. The singe of spent gunpowder on top of juniper, and Vesta's rotting skin. The lace curtain moves inside Greta's upstairs window. A shadow gun sparks white flare and deep echo across falling dusk. One after the other, the gang of riders after our bounty fall off their horses.

He was there.

That's why he tastes familiar. The hand to the gun behind the muzzle flash.

Why?

I don't know. He was there. So was I. They knew his name. It proves nothing.

He looked me full in the eyes because he knew I didn't know. But did he think they wouldn't tell me? He's lucky this letter was in code and I waited until I was alone to read it.

Tears spill like blood from the void Vesta left in me. I read Aunt Tess's words again.

Try not to kill him? The Stranger resents everything.

Navy and Raleigh aren't here to hold me back like they were in Winchester. I don't know if I'm capable of stopping the Stranger on my own. She craves blood like water. And so do I.

He's agreed to help us get you out of there in exchange for Hannah. He thinks we're going to help him get it. (Of course.)

He also won't say WHY he left Cairo, but you noticed his clothes. He's obviously been here for a while and…marinated. Don't worry, I'm working on him. We will know the truth soon.

I have a plan, and it's quite alkaline. It does require you to stay in Hannah longer. I understand if you just want to come home. We won't do anything until we have your vote. If you want out now, we'll find another way.

Either way, Mother was right about Hannah. It needs to go, forever. And Rafe deserves to suffer for what he's done to us. We'll tell the Menace exactly what he wants to hear, we'll kill Rafe, and then we'll do what we do best.

Do you agree?

Below you'll find Navy's instructions for explosives. If you can hold out there a little while longer, your job will be planting them, and to help me decide where.

I've already got a head start on that.

In the meantime, I want to know everything you can give me about Hannah. Every. Last. Detail. If you can find out how often Rafe picks his nose, that would also be delightful.

I'm sure by now someone has told you about your grandma, and the Absolution. Please don't despair. Don't take the unnecessary risks, only necessary ones. Our time will come, and we WILL make all of these snake fuckers wish they'd never seen our faces. But right now, all we want is for you to take care of yourself and stay alive. Whatever it takes.

We love you, and want to see you again soon.

—Aunt Tess

My body shakes as I exhale, tears like flame down my face. As soon as I wipe them, new ones are born.

Navy and Raleigh did make it across the Rim. Leagan survived the derailing. The relief shatters me and the weight I've carried for cycles, the fear of not knowing who I'd have left to go back to.

I knew they wouldn't abandon me, but that doesn't mean doubt never whispered my name. It knows who I am. Where I am. It looks like my mother.

I have two days. That's enough time to draw Hannah for them.

I write my reply using mine and Leagan's cipher.

I don't want to stay here, I just want to go home. But we don't have one anymore. The *Absolution* is gone.

I've already started this. I might as well finish it.

I vote yes. I'll stay.
 Love,
 Vengeance

PART TWO
GHOSTS LIKE NIGHT

SIXTEEN
TESLA

Trader wagons line the main street of Covenant, flags of fabric remnants tied with bells that clap for the pink dawn, and stringed instruments warming to it. Evangeline steers the Sisters' wagon in line, loaded down with the baskets of yarn we all spent last Season preparing, dyes fresh and tight, ready for sale.

"Wake up." Leagan steps over Navy, curled in the bed she's made of the wagon. "The market people are waiting for us."

"You are too excitable in the morning," Navy mumbles.

"Be careful, don't get anything dirty," Della says.

My wrist aches as Evangeline and I draw the pins from the wagon's drop side, lowering it while Della rolls up the canvas window to display the baskets and the braided skeins hanging from the ribs. And now it's a yarn shop on wheels—how alkaline.

"Sorry, you have to get up now," Della says to Navy.

"Come on." Leagan shakes her foot. "Get up and we can go get breakfast."

"How's that arm today?" Evangeline asks.

"Still fragile." The splint I wore for two cycles came off yesterday, a thin cotton wrapping to take its place. My weak fingers don't want to do the tedious work of tethering the horses in the shade with the water trough. But I make them, it's good for you.

Down at the rail, wranglers sort animals in the auction pens, the finest ones marked with red chalk.

Dilly the vest-wearing goat prances his lead in a circle around Leagan's legs. As soon as she unwinds herself, he does it again.

"What do you want to eat?" she asks, our repeating rifle *Misfortune* slung across her back. It's still a little heavy for me to handle at the moment.

She's not the only one armed with a long-range weapon in addition to a sidearm. Cattle rustlers like the South Rim. It wouldn't be the first time they've burst into town to steal the fresh stock. The roads won't be safe tonight either. But we're all here pretending it's just a fair.

"Bring me whatever I can smell frying," I say. "Preferably with red meat." I've eaten enough beans and lentils in Damascus the last two cycles. "And some of that spiked melonade, please." It's not too early for a drink, I've had my eye on the barrels since we got here.

It's a fifteen-minute walk to the bluff where the church is. I go before fried food sits hard in my stomach.

The sun pierces the reformed glass and the holes in it as I enter, laying colors out on the stone floor. Black glass, sinner's blood, sunstone red for Providence's mercy, and the blue of skystone like things made new. The last preacher might have been starving, but the House of Mercy he tended is beautiful.

Pale dust and a scrap of tumbling weed sneak inside with me. The note I melted to the leftover altar wax hasn't moved, and the bell-arch lamp it says to light hasn't been touched, but Leagan said the Poisonneur was coming. I'll wait for him.

The reverent hush still hangs until another set of footsteps ring up the steps behind me.

Evangeline crosses herself before stepping inside, wind twisting the gray hairs falling from under her hat. The sun revives the leather fragrance of her trusty jacket—not old, but timeless.

"You followed me."

"What are you scheming?" Her voice carries across stone and wood with the clear tone of an engine bell.

"Oh, am I that obvious? Fool's gold, I thought I had a better liar's face."

"It's the smile. You've been wearing it a few days now. I'm glad to see it again. You haven't seemed quite yourself since you came back from Descendants."

No, Descendants was a hard blow, and I was already in a fragile state. At least the rope burn on my neck is fading, not going to be a permanent scar like the pale one on my face. I don't need a visible reminder that greasy little St. Paul got a trick in behind me for the rest of my life.

"Descendants proved you right." I brush the soft dust off the top of the candle altar as I circle. It finds a way to squeeze through the smallest gaps and sticks to everything like flour. "I do have more I could lose."

"Are you going to tell me what you're waiting for?"

I smile. "Not yet."

I can't say his name. Technically, I don't know it.

THE LAST DAYLIGHT SHIFTS FROM FIRE BLUE AND ORANGE TO STARRY PURPLE. Crystal burns brighter, and the fiddlers dancing with the dark play louder. I've spun around on enough arms, I smell like anyone you might want to meet.

A clear yellow light hangs in darkness that was empty seconds ago. Too low to be the moon, too wide and warm to be another star, but too high to be another campfire. My smile grows deep as the roots of a mountain. My words haven't lost their persuasive flavor to east luck or this hideous scar on my face. It can only be the church lamp.

Navy and Leagan have a dice game going with Evangeline behind the wagon. I set my hands on their shoulders and use my eyes to point. "Look who's here."

"Told you he would come." Leagan picks the highest die from her last roll and places it with her other two selections before she disentangles her legs from the bench.

"Who is that?" Evangeline asks.

"A new friend."

"This sounds dangerous."

"Aren't we all?" I nod to Leagan as she packs the last bites of her honey cake into her mouth. "Like we discussed."

She flips me the two-fingered engineer's salute, but returning it would make me a fraud because I'm not an engineer anymore.

"Friend?" Evangeline follows me to the back of the wagon to pull the shotgun from the bench hook. "Or a mistake you might regret?"

"It's not who you think."

He doesn't come this far south of the Salt Waste.

I snap the cut barrel shut once I've seen the double shells loaded inside.

"This won't take long. I'm just going to the church. But if you and Della don't want to wait, the girls and I can ride back together."

"We all stay. I won't leave you here drunk with strangers."

"I'm not drunk." The world is a little shinier than it usually is, but that's due to all the exercise. I'm in full control of myself and this situation.

The music and fire quartz fades beyond the blue lantern border, but not the heavy-handed warmth of roasted corn and meat. It stays with me well past the edge of Covenant. Sniffing my sleeve, I realize it's part of me now. Oh well, he might as well smell me coming.

"Who is he then?" Evangeline's gaze searches, my mother not my friend in this moment. "If you plan to desecrate the church with violence, I have to object."

"You're making assumptions, Evan. A church is just a building, it's people who give it power." Providence will meet with us anywhere, and the world is full of violence.

"Maybe I am, but I care for you. Don't punish yourself with someone who doesn't deserve you, if it is who I think."

"Don't preach to me." It's only because she loves me that I'm too good for anyone. I feel the same about her, but she has to accept this choice is mine. "I said it's just a friend."

"I'm aware you use that word interchangeably."

"Not about you though."

People make the mistake of assuming because of my past I'll fuck anything that moves. Sure, I'd fuck just about anyone for the right price, but that's business, not pleasure. I'm much more selfish with my free time. Unfortunately, my heart still belongs to someone who doesn't want it, and I haven't had the strength to take it back. Evan knows this.

"I know what I'm doing. Just trust me."

"Even so. I still have the letters you sent me after the other one you called friend wounded you. This back market plan of yours has me worried—"

"Evan." I squeeze her hands, then push them away. "Trust me."

She sighs, eyes closing as Navy and Leagan catch up with us. "Providence, God of Mercy, protect you."

"He will."

THE BELL ARCH RISES OUT OF THE SILVER GRASS, PALE SILK THREADS OF GREEN aura light eclipsed by its dark outline.

To the north, the Salt Waste radiates a pearl glow even with the sun fallen behind the hills, and the moon still low and creamy on the peaks. That's why I say it's entirely possible the constant moon is made of salt. Leagan can disagree if she likes, and she does.

Navy lets my hand go.

The church doors splay with almost no effort, the moonlight floods across the stone floor, throwing my shadow out ahead of my stride.

Churches always hold a sense of home to me. Though not the same kind as the *Absolution*, or even my parents' yellow house back east, but peaceful.

The red prayer candles burn against the head wall and side alcoves. Their gold light spills down the altar steps while shadows tremble up stone surfaces and the molten wax makes the air thick.

He comes from the void with prowling silence that should be impossible for someone his height, smooth as new glass and flowing ribbon.

Clarity settles over me, calm as the smooth walls. It's the same determination that took my hand in place of fear when I learned I was pregnant with Vesta. When I fucking hustled H.B. at cards in Hannah so she wouldn't be born a slave. When I saw the *Absolution* for the first time.

That sense of purpose shattered like an old bone when Navy returned from the West Rim without Vesta and Adelaide, and I'll admit now I was afraid I'd never have it again.

But I haven't lost the path, I'm still on it, and I'm supposed to be here.

"Hello, Poisonneur." My voice rolls across the stone and back over itself, shocking to the reverent stillness. "I've been waiting for you."

"I am still not a Poisonneur."

"Whatever you say." Fool's gold, he's really stuck to that lie. "Welcome to my church."

"You haven't been to Cairo. We thirst for drama and perfected the art of theater. This won't intimidate me."

"Well, well. Since you're so sure you're not a Poisonneur, you might as well tell me your real name before I have to make one up for you. And fair warning, it will be ugly."

"You can call me Ezrah." His gaze shifts with it too.

Oh please, do better.

"It's insulting to lie that bad to a professional."

"Well, perhaps I'm not lying so much as reserving certain information for myself. Why did you invite me here?"

"Why did you come?"

The white of his smile slips through the shadow collected under his hat and the dark ring threading his nostrils. "Because you asked."

My smile is a whip, fast and barbed. The right words cut secrets loose like prayers off dying lips, so watch me spill his.

"When we spoke in Descendants, you gave me the impression that you have something I might want." I twist my smile around the anticipation that rises in my throat. "You mentioned black gold. You know who we are —we deal in protection, arms, and transportation."

The overskirt flares around his legs with each padded step, holstered teacup riding his hip like a weapon. The liner rimming his eyes cuts down to meet the fall of his cheekbones, two long, black tear tracks preserved by it.

We cross paths and switch places, my skirt whispering tales to his and the steps that rise to the altar. Those same stones relay the whisper up to the beams supporting the loft.

"I need to get another thing off my conscience first," he says.

"Well, this is a church. You can confess to me, but I'm not actually a preacher or a Sister."

"You'll do."

"Oh, will I? Nothing like a backhanded compliment to make me wet—"

"Montoya." His voice drips low as the oldest candles that have to lick the wax from the bottoms of their saucers, and the syllables burn his tongue as they leave it.

I tilt an ear his way. Not because I didn't hear, but I want him to work a little harder.

"Montoya is my mother's family name. In Cairo, children are given the name of the family holding the prestige. Be that money or influence."

"Imagine that. Logic. Just because you leaked your weak seed and made a child doesn't mean your name deserves to live on. It's actually a rather common achievement."

"Yes, something your Republic could do better about."

Well, I resent that. This is the Rim. But I'll let it go this time because it's not all that important here.

Revere was not my father's name, either.

"Niall is my acquainted name, but we are not acquainted."

"Aren't we? Niall Montoya." It slips off my tongue like butter. Quite nice, actually. "Well, it is alkaline to meet you." I take the bench inside the prayer booth. Now Leagan's shot angle won't be disrupted by me and he isn't the wiser. "Confess."

"You have lost something of value."

Something being an absolute understatement. "That's not a confession."

"Your girl who was killed in Winchester. That was your daughter."

Fuck.

The wood screens splay the pattern of a thousand stars on my skin, gold from the candles, red from the lanterns, but they blur, my thumb popping from my own grip.

"Was it you?"

The stone and wood building up a church or the glass filling its eyes don't make it any holier than praying outside, but if he killed my Vesta, it would be my pleasure to send him to straight hell from one.

"It was not." Montoya's waiting to meet my gaze and holds it there. The truth then, ugly and wretched as it may be. "I could have, and at the time that was my intention. The deed could have been done several ways, and I was the best killer in town that night."

"Want to bet?"

"You have seen me because I've allowed you to see me."

"Please, *Niall*—"

"Am I already going to regret trusting you with that name?"

"Yes," I say. "And I'm not some virgin who finds that aggressive bullshit attractive."

"It's simply a statement of fact. You have not earned the right to use it."

"But I will, because this isn't Cairo and men have called me all kinds of names I didn't like before. Now it's your turn."

He scoffs. "Judge me by the works of others."

"You've been after us since last Season and you still haven't managed to collect the price," I say. "Yes, we did know about you."

"My reputation preceded me?" he says.

"Ours does too, remember? My mother was the best at what she did, she saw what fools like you try to hide. And anything she did miss, the rest of us were here to notice. So, if you are telling me the truth about Winchester, there must be a reason why you hesitated."

"I left two daughters behind in the Yellow City." He swallows. "And although it's unlikely I'll see them again in this lifetime, I would hunt anyone who hurt them to the ends of this earth."

"And haunt them from the afterlife." *Farce*, I feel sick. I grab a half-spent sage stick left as an offering and turn it through a flame until it smolders and the blue smoke spirals toward the blackened ceiling. "Then you have the vaguest concept of how I feel."

"Yes." He stares out at the far window that looks on the cemetery, the one missing its glass because the last preacher took it. "I am sorry for your loss."

Oh, you think I can't patronize too? "Had you never killed a young woman before?"

"I do not believe you're so naïve. Taking a life as a professional is not an act of violence or passion. Once you've let your first blood, you can reap five hundred more. Gender, age, circumstance, it shouldn't matter. Your honor is bound to the contract, life and death perpetuate each other. I kill because it's my job, and I support my family."

"Oh, like the rest of us."

"Yes, I studied your gang before setting my eye on Winchester. Disinterred some of your allies, your ways, what brought you to your present circumstances."

As any respectable hunter, thief, or conwoman does.

"I determined the order in which you must be killed to paralyze your operation." He briefly fixes his eyes on me again. "It wasn't your daughter I had in my sights."

"The Stranger." Please, Leagan, don't shoot him. Yet.

"The Tov. I watched her hold her dying sister." He lifts his arms, the reflection of what he witnessed, and in me it's only raw emptiness that nothing will fill. "Then I saw *it*... A Shiver is what we call this kind of ghost back home. One of darkness, a smoke you can breathe but not see except in the worst places. It can bend you, your mind, your will. I heard my daughter's voice, crying for me, out there, even though I knew she wasn't..."

Every last hair on my body stands up. We call her the Stranger. That's what he saw. Something more powerful than I originally believed, and a Shiver she does fit.

Montoya shakes himself as if to escape the sound only he hears. "A murderer feels emotion, or uses the kill as a conduit for the lack of it, a coward. I am not a murderer. But in that sphere of time, I felt like one, afraid like one. The one who kills a Shiver takes on their ghost forever. And it will drive you mad."

My chuckle fills the sanctuary like warm Mercy Day music.

"This is not funny."

My glory, we still have influence I was afraid was lost. "All I can say is you're a lucky bastard. Adelaide's Shiver is a particularly merciless one."

"There's power in pain," he says. "There's power in love, death, rage, and sorrow, and many forces in this world that the science has not yet learned the cause for. That was what I witnessed. Something we currently lack the mind to understand. But it saw me that night."

Good job, Adelaide.

"The last pieces of your puzzle only came together recently," he continues. "Hannah, many years ago. Now I understand why your god deems you live."

"Nothing snatches my slips from My mighty hand." And I have loads of unfinished business for such a tiny bird. "Tell me, if you were hunting with the Jaxsons in Winchester, wasn't Boss Jaxson suspicious when you came back to Descendants alone and empty-handed?"

"I met the Jaxsons on the road by chance, convinced them they could use another gun. Their boss was not aware of my involvement."

"Yes," I say. "Outsmarting the Jaxsons requires an extremely high level of infiltration."

"It was always my plan to kill them and claim the full bounty for myself. Either before or after I finished with you."

"Well, at least you're honest about that. I would have done the same thing. It's a nice coincidence, we've actually been looking for a friend with connections in Cairo."

"I can't be that for you," he says. "I'm interested in information you have, but if access to Cairo is what you want from me in return, you'll have to seek that alliance elsewhere."

"Because you still think you can convince me you're not a Poisonneur?"

"Because if I had access to Cairo, I wouldn't be here at all." The rear of his tongue lashes sudden as a widow snake bite, and I pocket the location of this nerve he just gave up. "I detest everyone I have met here."

"Until now," I say.

"The Rim is a poison pit of criminals and thieves the rest of the world wants to be rid of, and I despise what I've become among them."

"I don't. Don't be sorry, be better."

My mother's favorite saying. Graced with time's wisdom.

"Then you are where you belong." He hesitates. "I stayed in Winchester to watch over your daughter's grave until the new moon passed. It seemed the decent thing to do. No other fortune hunters came to steal her body in that time."

"If you're expecting me to thank you, the answer is no, I won't be doing that. Now what do you want from us?"

"I understand your story leads back to Hannah," he says. "And the boss currently residing there."

"It does. Am I right to assume it's Hannah's black gold you want?" I had assumed he was after the black gold on the West Rim like the rest of us, but this is much better. We already stand accused of stealing from Rafe with no way to clear our name. Might as well make it true.

"Not much but whispers escape the North Rim, but they speak of unrest among the workmen. Weakness we can exploit with my experience in politics, and your knowledge of Hannah's inner circle."

"Well, well, hasn't a fortunate moon smiled on both of us. We happen to already have a woman on the inside. Rook?"

The loose doors groan as the wind plays ghost games with them. Montoya looks that way as Navy turns the corner of the entrance where she's eavesdropped this whole time while Leagan haunts the long grass across the road, her rifle *Verdict* poised.

I've already taken Hannah once. There's no rule that says we can't do it again.

"Before we do anything else, we need you to deliver a message."

SEVENTEEN
ADELAIDE

A RETIRED RAIL CAR SERVES AS THE EXPRESS RIDER DROP OFFICE, STORM shutters welded over the windows. The stable for their horses shares the same wall as the bunkhouse. You could slide out the window onto the back of your horse if you wanted to.

The fastest legs on the Rim.

They have to be, transporting payroll to places the rails don't reach.

Twenty-eight.

The two horses at the water trough lift their heads. One is white and red, the other solid shadow. He turns his ears toward me, breath whispering on my hand as he searches for treats. Warm grain smells so much better than ash does.

Montoya leaves the bunkhouse, melts into one more body walking the air market. I wait until the Stranger is certain he's not immediately turning back.

Twelve.

The door is latched, not locked. Three bunkbeds, empty.

It's better to be sure you know who you're dealing with now rather than later. At least I got to teach Kane the same thing about me.

The beds hide nothing, the trunks bolted to the end of them, padlocked. Clothes. Spare ammunition. But Express Riders are known smugglers and thieves.

Ash sticks to the borders of two different cutouts in the wall planking. Fingerprints dark around the knothole used to pull them free while the Stranger pricks at the hair on my arms like storms do.

They're all empty. And I think Montoya is careful enough to not leave anything behind. That usually means you have something to hide.

Thirty-seven.

I miss Vesta.

She would have done this with me. The distraction.

I have to do the best I can without her now.

The air market has real food. Cabbage that isn't melting and going brown, meat that holds its shape, rice and peppers cooked on hot iron sheets. There're too many people, so busy and everywhere.

Montoya sits with a bowl and a fixed sneer for everyone his gaze crosses, overskirt a puddle of darkness around him. One last meal before he leaves Hannah. The Stranger picks apart the threads and buckles of his clothes, the angles of the pouch and teacup threaded to his belt. Skirts like that have things to hide. Mine does.

His gaze latches onto me as I cross open space, barbed like the flesh-tearing teeth of scavenger lizards. It stays on my back until I cross behind the other side of rug and canvas tents.

Forty-six.

My skirt spreads across the third stair where he hid the drop tin, blocked from easy view by the backside of the market. I let my letter fall through the plank gap.

And wait.

An hour passes before Montoya rounds the corner to collect.

He takes a lazy glance up and down the row before getting close. "The idea is that we are never seen together."

I don't move.

Not yet.

"You don't have to worry, I'll take good care of your words." He kneels between me and the rail to remove the tin, and that's when I slide out of his way.

Part of his overskirt drags with me, open just enough to get a hand inside.

"Next time I'm here, don't be waiting like this."

No, I'm not a fool.

I sit forward, arms wrapped around my knees and ankles. The short box that was his is in my hand as his skirt drags away.

The Stranger curls around the last corner of my letter as he inserts it through the top of his boot. Her dark tips scrape across the hilt of a push knife sheathed there as well. "Any words you'd like me to tell your family?"

It's all in there.

His chuckle brushes off my spine, but I don't know what's funny. "Then I'll see you sometime in the next moon cycle, lonely Shadow."

Sometimes pickpocket marks notice the missing weight as they walk away. He doesn't. But I get moving before letting myself study what I got, just in case he turns around. It feels like a cigarette case, but Montoya doesn't smell like tobacco.

Five-fifty.

The box is tarnished silver. Dark like night. An inch-long vial lies in a bed of yellow velvet. Black glass, dents where three others used to be.

The liquid glides, oil on the glass stopper, glassy yellow. Vapor bites into the back of my throat, hot in my eyes. I smother my cough. I bet one touch of this burns like flash fire without the flame.

Poison. It has to be.

The silver label is handwritten in Cairosh. *Farce.* Of course it is, but it's mine now, in the hidden pocket with my other dangerous things. I'm as explosive as Navy usually is.

Emptiness creeps over me slow. Now I have to wait for Montoya to ride all the way over to the South Rim. Then back. He might be on an Express horse, but that's as far as you can cross the map on a diagonal line.

And now I don't get to leave until everything is ready.

The part of me that isn't the Stranger already wishes I hadn't agreed to stay.

Now what?

You still have work to do.

The sun is going down. The Stranger's cold ash gaze fixes on the gray corners ahead of my soundless footsteps, leads me into blacker shadows pooled between buildings.

It's taken me a while to find him, this den where he sinks when not working for his boss on the hill.

Five eighty-nine.

I don't know his name. Kasey and Rafe's other guns never used it on the way here. I didn't give him one. He doesn't deserve it.

A ghost enters the gap between walls ahead, the slouched gait of a courage powder user.

Stale air becomes stagnant as I pass under the rug disguising the real entrance to the den.

Behind the next canvas sheet, crystal clicks. Blue-orange flame eats out the black, barely surviving off the last wax puddled in a cup.

I don't know for sure if he's in there, but he usually is at this time. If I'm wrong, no one will miss whoever is.

The Stranger beats at the edges of my skin, vinegar. The dry cotton twine resists the crystal spark I put to it, flame circling the blue edge of asphyxia.

Cotton smolders sudden as the bottle leaves my hand, drops of clear pine sloshed across the tent like piss. Blue becomes hot yellow, a spark like sunrise as flame tastes the clear pine and likes it.

They scream.

Thirteen.

I slip around the carpet, stop.

One floods past me, blood touched by courage powder too thick to burn, apparently. Two, caught by the fire.

Not him.

A third smoking shadow blasts through the carpet wall. I don't see his face clearly, the Stranger doesn't need to. He throbs familiar.

Eight.

I swing, knife out. The blade sinks past his ribs like water before his momentum rips it from my grasp with fire. He staggers around, worthless hand clutching the last body he'll ever touch. His.

He falls, blood in the dust, fingers locked in it. Like mine when he touched me.

They just wanted a body. Mine was available.

It's not hate that pours off his eyes as he looks up at me. It's fear. It always is, when men show us who they really are. Scared creatures who make the most noise.

Now the Stranger wants bodies, and his is available. It's not really all that different.

She slides across me like a razor. *Don't linger.* The things down here see better.

Fifteen.

I don't know exactly where it comes from. The knife. The impact of being hit across the ribs registers immediately, the tug as my shirt tears. The raw edge of a blade skips off the back of my hand as I swat it away, slides through my other palm on fire as I catch the next stab directly. It's the only way to stop it from going into my stomach.

The Stranger curls out of me. It takes two tries to get the stolen revolver from under my skirt. Two shots before the miner falls dead to the side of the alley.

I don't have to see the cuts burning across my hands and side to know they're bad. I smell the blood past the ash.

Farce.

Anybody could have heard that gunshot. And they won't stop to help me. They'll either try to finish the job or let me bleed all the way to the guns at the Company compound.

I leave the two bodies without looting them, blood sticking between my fingers. For the first time in my life, the Stranger doesn't protest.

EIGHTEEN
ADELAIDE

MY SHOULDER DISPLACES A TRAIL IN THE CONDENSATION WHERE I LEAN against the wall outside Thadie's door, face the room of gamblers sitting under their foggy bathwater. They don't stand up or even look at me anymore.

Voices rock back and forth on the other side of wood.

Steam plumes rise from the sunken tubs, collecting under the molded ceiling. A bead of condensation hits my forehead, too many others leaving trails down the walls. But the Stranger works on counting them anyway.

Sheer spots of blood the black plank. Mine. I can't see the cut on my back ribs, but it feels wet.

I peel the saturated hem of my skirt away from my hand. Fresh red spills to the point of my elbow, nothing to stop it. The cut doesn't go across the middle palm like I thought, it bends around the fleshy part of the widow finger side. Better, actually. I can squeeze the two sides together if I get something tied tight enough.

"Oh." Thadie halts as she opens her door. "You changed your seat."

I don't move for her customer, just let him push around me while the stairs tremble.

"Are you…is everything good?"

I make myself look her in the eye. Open my mouth. "Can I borrow some clear pine or morning salt?"

Her eyes spread. "Fool's gold."

Yes, I speak.

"Yeah, come in. Did you hurt yourself? We'll come back to the fact that you talk. Saraline said you did, but I didn't believe her—oh fuck, your back!"

Her gasp scares me. Probably makes the blood gush out of me a little faster too. Almost enough I don't want to look, see my intestines bulging out of my back or something. It can't be that bad though, getting my ribs broken by Kasey hurt so much worse.

Seventeen.

I avoid her nest of pillows and crocheted blankets, leave a trail of crimson toeprints on the naked floor.

"Can I look?" Thadie peels open the back of my wet shirt and gags. "*Farce.* Who did this to you?"

I twist at the spotted mirror above her little dressing table. My skin has never had this much color on it.

"Here." She passes me a braided hand towel to clot with. "I'm sorry, I don't do blood very well, but I know someone who can sew you up. He's not a real doctor, but he'll treat you, he doesn't care who you are. He gives stitches all the time."

"He's a man."

"Yes, is that a problem?"

Men don't get to touch me. Not even a half-doctor.

"I just need you to help me get a bandage tied tight enough." Then I'll wait and see what happens.

"You're past that now, you need a good stitch." She loops her wrist in a sewing motion. "You'll rot your lungs if you bind them up too tight. Don't worry, I know someone else. Saraline!" she yells off the top of the stairs. "I need you."

The floor vibrates as Saraline takes the steps two at a time. Her star-line tattoos distract the Stranger, only for a blink or two, long enough to let her get close to me. "What's the problem? *Oh.*"

Thadie nods, sits. "You see? Sorry, I'm feeling a little queasy."

"I thought she was your hired protection."

"She is."

"This didn't happen here," I say.

"Never get into a knife fight," Saraline scolds. "They're bad moons."

I know.

"Will you take her to Joelle? She doesn't want to see Geramiath and I told her she can't just wrap it up."

"Of course." Saraline puts out her hand. "Come on."

I notice she's not carrying any of her crochet projects, but that pistol is still under her armpit.

"I said *come on*. If you stay here bleeding and make Thadie throw up, I will find where you live and come put it on your pillow while you're asleep. Now move!"

I almost laugh.

Almost.

At least she doesn't try to hold my hand when I follow her.

Thirty-seven.

A chuckle slips out of Saraline, not as good as the way they used to bubble out of Vesta. "I hope you know, you're about to owe me the biggest, fattest favor."

Favors are always bad.

She skips up the steps of the building directly across the street. The eves hang low, wood lattice on top of the fly screens that starburst of pink light escape from. On the west side, beds of flowers, herbs doing their best to grow in choked light and falling ash. Pots of aloe and cactus hung all over the skeleton of an ironwood tree. It knows it doesn't belong here.

"This is our other business, the Pinings, tea house and apothecary. Hello…" she calls to the silent room.

The smell hits me back, stomach deep. The sweet, dried plants of Navy's lab. And sharper things, chemical things. They also remind me the *Absolution* is gone, that the last time I smelled Navy's lab was the last time. Maybe ever.

"You still haven't told me your real name."

The word sticks in my throat, reminds me of everyone I love, so far away.

Five…

The black floorboards squeak as I cross them, even barefoot. Glass lamps are what's turning the air pink, incense sticks and dried herbs smoldering on tables. Bones and bundles of rosemary and sage strung on the overhead beams, racks of copper pots and glass cups with them. So many shelves and bottles, spaces to lose things. The Stranger pulls in too many directions. Nowhere I turn satisfies her. She wants to possess it all.

"I said *hello!*" Saraline drives her heels deeper into the floor with each step. "Joelle, Soli!"

There's a basement.

She points out the table in the offset corner room, orange silk falling across the opening. "You can sit in there."

Beads clack as a woman parts the curtain covering the back room. Unfortunate for anyone trying to pass through silent and unnoticed. "I heard you the first time you yelled, Salty."

Her accent mimics Montoya's.

"Is Solstice downstairs?" Saraline tilts her head in my direction. "She'll want to meet her."

"I bet she will…" She—Joelle, I presume—takes her time with her gaze on me, like a sharpening stone, hair and eyes black as a moonless sky. "I'll get her."

"You might as well get your tools too. She's all cut up." Saraline pivots on a heel, back to me. "I'll make you some tea. You're going to need it."

The Stranger bends past the bell jars keeping dust off dried flowers, the corked bottles of tea leaves. She can't settle, but I make myself sit in the straight-backed chair.

A door claps somewhere in the back of the shop, rattling the floor.

She wears a hood. Head down, deep inside it until the blood orange silk closes over the doorframe, this windowless corner I let myself get pushed into.

I stiffen.

The hood drops. She looks like me. Sharp chin, white hair. Copper eyes. Two pistols stacked on her left ribcage, a person I don't know.

"Well, well. *Sol, so.*" *Daughter.* But the rest of the words continue their flow in a direction I don't follow. The Stranger picks across the vowel patterns. I let her, but I don't get too close to any of them that might become familiar.

She's older than the other Tov I've seen. Not quite Grandma, but older than Aunt Tess, time's lines fraying her eyes and mouth. Born on the bootheels of the war.

She reaches two hands toward my face. I lunge out of the chair, around the other side of the table before she can.

The Stranger resents the pity that flashes through her eyes.

"I'm not going to hurt you. It's good to remember our own ways."

I remember my mother. She used to touch me like that.

"Solstice *sos* Viola." She extends her hand instead.

Mine is coated in blood, cold, but I offer it back to her anyway. Wait to see if she'll pull away.

Her skin is dry. Paper.

Saraline creeps around the curtain again, watches from against the wall as the Cairosh woman returns with a wooden tray. Bandages, bottles, crystal.

"This is my partner, Joelle," Solstice says. "What's your name?"

"She's...I guess you could say a friend of Thadie's," Saraline answers. "The one I told you about actually. She won't tell me her acquainted name, Thadie just calls her the Stranger."

"*Adelaide*." Solstice narrows on me like a raptor. "*Xa?*"

I know that one too. "Yes."

"I heard a rumor you were here."

And? I cross my arms, remain standing this time. There's always more.

"That you were...different. Apart from the blood that makes you and me rare gemstones." Solstice nods slowly, as if, like Grandma, she can sense the Stranger's presence in me without permission. "What is your mother's name?"

Nothing.

"Do we frighten you or are you just rude?" Joelle asks. "Don't think you're getting an under-the-tablecloth trade on your Tov blood. Soli might try, but I won't let her. It's earn your own way or nothing. What do you have that I don't?"

That means they deal in favors, other things besides money. I hate favors over my head.

"I'll pay you. Gold standard."

"You can sell for us. I'm sure there's girls at your house that use. If you like the steady pay and we like you, you can even stay on."

"No."

Yes, I steal courage powder and turn sell it. Just enough to pay Charlene for my room and make sure I don't have to touch anyone. I'll do whatever I have to pay off this new favor, except sell their chemicals.

Working for them would make me dealer of the thing my mother chose over me. I can't.

"No? Do you have any other skills, or would you prefer to just continue to bleed?"

"Protection," I say.

"Protection from what? Knife fights?"

"That depends on what's bothering you." The Stranger pushes against her, outlines every item on the tray she holds and plans to use on me. Loud people tend to have brittle spines.

"That's what I was trying to tell you the other night," Saraline says. "You were too busy arguing to listen to me. She can take care of the other lab for us."

"Keep looking," a voice outside calls.

"Shush. What was that?" Joelle puts her arm across Solstice. Same as Kane did to me. "Stay here."

I was so focused on getting to Thadie's, I didn't bother to let Rafe's guns see me at least once before I disappeared into the bathhouse.

The door hisses across floor shaved thin by it, sticks to the warped boards behind the swing radius. Solstice pulls the drop hood back up over her hair.

"I'll deal with this." Joelle yanks the curtain to the wall once she's through it.

"You seen a fox?" Feet shake the floor as they circle the shop.

"Does this look like a chicken coop? No, I haven't seen anybody. What do you really want?"

"Just out seeing the sights. Company business."

"This is not Company property, and there are no *sights* to be seen around here without a smoke of redweed or courage powder. Would you like to buy some?"

"Do me a favor," he says. "If you ever see a fox lurking around, wearing a muzzle, remember it in case I ask you next time. There's only one here, it shouldn't be that hard for you to do."

They don't know about Solstice. Somehow I find that hard to believe.

"I'll keep my eyes open. Are you sure you don't want anything to drink, maybe a go-fuck-yourself tincture?"

"Keep it for yourself."

The door rakes wood to shut.

"And the soup does thicken." Joelle closes the curtain behind her. "Go watch the door, Salty. Tell me why Company bastards are looking for you, *Stranger*?"

However, the lines along her forehead and mouth have gone from stone to soap in harshness.

If Rafe's men don't know about Solstice, does anybody? Hannah is large and too full of people, but even I'm not good enough to go unseen indefinitely. Unless she never leaves this building.

Joelle exhales something in Cairosh. A curse probably. Aunt Tess would try to learn it. "How did you know I'm a soft pudding for a girl who brings trouble with them?"

"Then let's not make her suffer longer than she needs to." Solstice draws my arm onto the table, draws the cork out of a bottle of morning salt while Joelle picks a shard of ghost quartz. The hottest burn, the purest soul, they say.

"Sutures rip and still allow foreigners to enter the wound," Joelle says. "And no offense, you look like one who's going to have another fight. Cairo, we cauterize. You will scar, but you'll get to keep your hand. Do you consent to treatment?"

"Yes."

"Alkaline." A voice peels off the crystal's edge as she flays it up the striking stone, hangs in the air, a different ghost. My bones are cold, like the underground damp of the Eden mine, yet somehow my palms are still sweating.

"Alcohol actually brings blood back to the skin surface, so we do this raw beyond the numbing of the salt. Do you need to hold Soli's hand?"

"No." I lean forward, wrap my ankles around the chair legs, and grip the seat with my good hand. Solstice pins my arm down.

"I'll ask you again once I start. This is going to hurt. Breathe in…"

I hope it does.

NINETEEN
TESLA

I drift my thumb past Adelaide's Hannah map and the pages of footnotes. Her attention to detail is spectacular. Everything I hoped she'd give me is here, with details. Guard counts, shift changes, distances, windows, and who carries what type of gun. The dry moat and spikes are new since Rafe took over Hannah, as well as the steel wall and cannons behind it. Hannah's grown the past eighteen years, like the rest of us.

The wind pulls back only to come at us again, slicing at the church walls with rage when it can't get through.

Although I was fairly certain I knew what Adelaide's answer was going to be, it would have been wrong to assume. We always vote on the jobs we take.

The red circle of lamplight spills down the altar stones like blood, reflecting the scars on Navy's eyes that empty them of all color except silver and Leagan's hair to liquid fire.

The church itself holds its breath, the pews the folk of Covenant never visited coated in bat droppings and the same film of white salt-dust Montoya is.

"Are you satisfied?" he asks.

"Yes, I am, and you look excellent in that Express uniform."

"Your compliments are necessary."

"No, they're free. Take it and be glad."

"The Stranger is secretive," Navy says. "She didn't seem hurt, did she? She wouldn't tell even if she was."

"She's not a baby." Leagan rises off her heels, returning from the corner with her hands cupped around something, probably alive. "How did she look?"

"Pale. Difficult, and very, very talkative."

"So, like herself," I say.

"What?" Navy says. "That doesn't sound like her at all."

"It's a joke, darling."

"I'd put your focus into not getting ourselves caught at this before we're ready," he says. "It's better spent that way."

Leagan sucks on Mother's pipe only to blow bittersweet smoke. "You didn't answer the question."

"She appears to have all essential body parts attached," Montoya says. "Does that put your mind at ease?"

"I'm already five steps ahead of Rafe, but he'll only see three of them, so don't worry about my part." I tap my finger to Adelaide's information. "The Stranger is loyal to the bone marrow and exceptionally good at what she does. She'll get us everything we could possibly need to know about Hannah, plus extra, and you can take that to the payroll wagon, sir."

"How well do you trust her Shiver?"

"I helped raise it. You can trust me."

"Shivers are not tamed or trained."

"Because she's not an animal." Leagan opens her hand, the baby scorpion scuttling out and squeezing through a gap in the stonework.

"She's not human like you and I are."

This is all pointless if they fight, and I doubt Montoya will tolerate Leagan coming at his head as well as Raleigh does.

"Montoya, for someone so proud of their country's accomplished political arts I thought you'd have better table manners," I say. "Have a seat anytime, by the way. Stay a while."

Montoya crosses his arms. "If there were a table, I'd use them. And if there is a god here, he deserves none of my reverence."

"Why are you so interested in Hannah?" Navy asks.

"Rook, is it?" He turns, softening, the way most people do with her. Liza had that cool water effect on souls too. "The Chemist. Named for the alchemist from *Rook and Ladder* by Ezosia Fever, yes?"

"That's right," she says, startled.

"A fine read. One of my daughter Ellianna's favorites."

"You're not going to betray us, are you?" The things in Leagan's eyes speak louder to me than to him. They are the hands she's been dreaming about, severed in the dust or buried in jars, reaching and clawing. "*Rook and Ladder* was about betrayal."

He smiles, and that probably works on most people. It's a nice smile. "Well, I'd certainly be loud to admit it."

"Everybody has their price."

"But luckily for you, nobody around here can afford mine. And honor is just about all I have left."

"You didn't answer Rook's question either."

"I see nothing gets by you, Raptor." Montoya taps a finger, still wrapped up in that elbow-length glove. I believe he wants me to notice it, and I do hate a secret being flaunted at me.

"Why can't you go home?" Navy says.

Montoya looks at her with interest again. "Not yet."

"You might like Jezebel," Leagan says. "Everyone there's an asshole."

"Have I done something to her?" Montoya asks.

"You'll get used to it," I say. "We like her spicy."

Navy leans across the step to whisper at Leagan. "You've never been to Jezebel."

"I don't need to. I've never liked anyone from there, so what does that tell you?"

"I am tired, I'd like a bath but since I'm denied that, I'm going to sleep," Montoya says. "Does that disturb your day?"

"Of course not," I say. "We can talk about this tomorrow when everyone is rosemary fresh."

"Not too early, please," Navy says.

"Never."

"I know how to summon you, daughters of the Raven." He glances off the lantern up in the bell arch. "I will."

I tick up the corner of my smile at Leagan.

"Does Adelaide say where they keep the black gold?" she says. "That will be the best place to start the fire."

The ease of Montoya's posture pulls tight, that gloved hand becoming a fist.

Oh, Leagan…you do know how to deliver a punch.

I look him dead in the eye. "We're going to burn Hannah off the fucking map like a cigar."

The first half of his sentence ruptures in Cairosh. "I thought I'd made my goals clear."

"You heard me right. Boss Gerard Rafael owes everything he has in Hannah to me, and I'm going to charge him accordingly."

Believable lies are the ones laid so awfully close to the truth. When we change our mind, he'll think he's the one in control.

"And you decided annihilating the Rim's most valuable crystal mine was logical."

"Oh, Rafe deserves every last misery we have planned for him."

"He might, but your revenge doesn't have to require utter destruction. He could be displaced from that seat with finesse, which I possess."

I tent my fingers over my knees. "So *you* can sit there?"

"Wouldn't you rather have a friend in that position than nothing?"

"He has a point," Navy says.

Yes, he does. But he is not our friend, he's a tool.

The storm outside shudders, useless fury against the walls protecting us. The memories rolling in my mind are dark too. I not ready to call them regret just yet. They were practice.

"The Raven wanted to burn Hannah twenty years ago." How many times did she tell me her regrets about leaving the place still standing? What did I always say? That it was done. "She was right."

And I shouldn't be surprised at all. I did exactly what I had to in order to save my mother and sister. There's absolutely nothing I regret about that. Still, I should have believed her about this—I did in everything else.

"So before I slit Rafe's throat on her behalf, he can watch his world die."

Like I've watched mine.

"While I can't argue with your mother, I will promise that I won't become a tyrant," Montoya says.

"Said every tyrant before you." Smoke curls off Leagan's lip. "You both talk way too fucking much. We're getting the Stranger back. That's what matters."

"This is your final word?" Montoya's brow sits hard as wind-hewn stone, his inner lip sucked into his teeth. "Then our goals are too different, we cannot work together. I'm willing to give you any person residing there to slake your vengeance, but I require Hannah's mines intact and functioning. This is not negotiable. I will not lose this chance, and your family is not more important than mine. You can take the night to think it over, but once a decision is made, it will be final."

"Bye, then." Leagan waves to his backside, dropping fingers until only her middle remains upright.

I wait until he reaches the foundation stones surrounding the door, just to be absolutely sure he's serious, and that I don't sound too eager. Navy squeezes my hand so hard, I have to pull away from her. "Then change my mind."

TWENTY
ADELAIDE

COPPER HAS BEEN IN MY ROOM AGAIN. MY EXTRA PAIR OF SOCKS WERE LAID horizontally in the drawer. Now they're vertical.

A band of frail, yellow light separates Charlene's door from its frame. She always keeps it shut, and the girls like to talk about why she never leaves.

She could be dead.

The Stranger pushes me forward. My chance to look at what she might keep hidden.

Thirteen.

She slumps across her desk, the puddle of orange hair becoming one of blood on her open book. I don't have to get too close to see the points on her spine still lift with shallow breath. Piss so thick the air burns, her bucket about to spill over the brim.

The drawers. The other door behind the curtain. Open them.

Fresh blood strikes paper as Charlene coughs. She jerks upright, fire in her single eye, a cord of red saliva trailing off powder-gray lips. "Get out!"

Two.

She catches the blood tail on two fingers and sucks the rest back into her mouth. "Wait."

A bruise discolors her forehead where she rested on the desk. Her arm shakes as she uses it to help her stand. Half the buttons of her shirt hang undone. Instead of fixing them, she pulls a pair of lace gloves and parasol.

"Walk me down the row."

"Why?" Well, I can guess *why*, not why she wants me there.

"It doesn't matter, just do it."

I can't hold my breath any longer and have to taste another lungful of her piss before we make it outside. The ash air only feels fresh after being in her room.

"Were you looking for me?" She spreads her black parasol, tilting it against the eyes on the street. "Don't think of me as completely negligent."

Looking to see if she was still alive. Going to take everything of value if she wasn't. And probably just some of it if she was.

The Company gun assigned to watch me today easily picks up our trail. Across the street, it takes four more of Rafe's men to scrub out the red paint discoloring a first-shift boardinghouse: *Row Ghost, come kill these first-shift Bastards.*

The bubbled cauterization line burns like a spark each time the wind blows my shirt against it. The cloth bandaging my hand gets in the way, but at least it reminds me to be more careful.

Charlene's empty hand twitches every two or three steps. And every time, her crusty, velvet heels catch on the ground, sweat riding her gray lip. I keep a full step away so we don't brush.

"One of the green bodices usually buys for me. She didn't come home last night."

Does she not realize it's me she's talking to?

"It's not safe to walk alone." She wet coughs into the handkerchief tied to her wrist. "I know. Every woman who's ever walked this fool's gold earth knows. I'm not blind. I know what you're doing for work."

Do you?

"They're afraid of you." She glances back at the man following me. "The girls are afraid of me. It's the only advantage people like you and me ever get."

At first, I don't recognize the sound that tears out of her as laughter. It doesn't fit.

"I'll have the girls think of me as cruel, it keeps them from shade. You're not afraid of me. You have worse things to worry about."

Yes. And she couldn't hurt me even if she wanted to.

The beams supporting the bathhouse rot from the moisture inside, and it shows from the front. The entire face of the building has a downward curve, like a distended gut. But Charlene doesn't go in to buy from Saraline or someone else—she turns the corner. Deeper into miner's territory. Tents. Pieces of metal leaned against walls for roofs.

"Hey!" The whistle catches my ear like a fishhook. The Company gun takes double-length strides to catch up with us. "Yes, you."

The glance I waste over my shoulder is just to be sure he's not holding a weapon.

"Look at me when I'm talking, fox. Where were you yesterday?"

I don't have to answer.

"Every time you leave that shithouse you give us the slip and reappear the next day as if it never happened. I'm not going to the boss and telling him we lost you again. What are you doing?"

You could lie. Or maybe you just should be better at your job, not mad I'm better at mine.

Charlene almost rolls an ankle as she reels around. "What did you just say about my house?"

He puts a hand right up to her face, focuses on me. "If you were just giving out hand jobs like you're supposed to, you wouldn't need to act so shady."

And if I let the Stranger's instincts have full control, they'd never see me at all and half of Hannah would be dead already.

"Where were you?"

"Your hand smells like shit." Charlene slaps his arm away. "She's my girl, not yours."

"Then you keep garbage in your house." He backhands her, her weak legs finally collapsing as he follows her down, closed fist.

I eye the rock sitting in the dust, the Stranger already coiled around its jagged edges. Pick it.

Five.

The impact travels up my arm. Wet. One hit doesn't kill him instantly, the parts further down the body take a little bit to realize it's done. Limbs twitch. Air still rakes in and out of his lungs.

Charlene swipes the blood off her mouth, swallows the rest. "Garbage has its uses."

I shove my hand into his pocket as blood leaks out his ear. A little paper envelope, once sealed with wax but still powdery inside. Silver standards. A key. On his belt, a revolver and knife that can be resold.

I grab his ankles, drag him to the shadows deeper than the ones he fell in.

In my pocket is the vial of morning salt Solstice and Joelle gave me in case I needed to cleanse my shallow hand cuts that didn't need cauterizing again. I look at the dead gun, his glove.

Do it, the Stranger says.

If they fear my row ghost enough, maybe they'll leave me alone.

The leather is crusty, still warm to my hand. Charlene watches me grind the morning salt crystals to finer powder inside my gloved fist.

"Two of them did come around for you lasterday, you weren't there," she says. "I told them I sent you to a client with a fox preference."

"Why?"

"I've been paid to inform the boss on what you do, who you know."

Yes, I'm aware.

The sizzle of salt meeting his flesh is too soft to hear behind the deep hum of the refinery. The Stranger feels it tint the air. I don't. But I can imagine it as my touch is left in a red handprint seared into his face. They want to fear me for being different? Fine.

"I wondered if you were the evil they're gossiping about haunting the row. The rumors started walking around the same time you did." Charlene's gaze lingers on the body as well. "I don't care how you make your living as long as I get paid. I'm happy to continue telling the boss you're out whoring…I'll add the favors to your rent next cycle."

Or pay them off now. I offer her the courage powder.

"Or that." She taps a blot out on her hand, licks it off, fingers like weathered stems. "One of the other white bodices told me you collected from the man who broke her nose a few days ago. Thank you for doing my job for me."

Grandma, Aunt Tess, and Vesta did things like collect debts with words. I let the Stranger kill him, then took what he had. It was easier.

"Pleasure is a dangerous business, those on the outside don't appreciate what we do because we make it look easy." Charlene struggles to keep her eyes open as the chemicals bite into her.

My mother used to get the same droop. She'd sit in her chair and stare at whatever ghost the powder made her see.

I hand her the standards the man had been carrying. Just in case. "If anyone asks what you know about the thing that's killing men around here, tell them it was a ghost. She had a bone face."

"Ghost…" She accepts the money, a bent smile. "The weaker ones need you. But I won't put myself or the other girls in danger lying for you if the Company finds out the truth. If the time comes, I'll choose myself."

So will I. Survival isn't kind.

She starts to lean, but catches herself before I have to touch her.

"Don't, albino. Someone might mistake you for something with a soul."

I have a soul. It feels everything hers does, but they wouldn't believe me if I told them they were wrong, so I don't bother.

TWENTY-ONE
TESLA

THE WIND TRIES TO RIP THE DOOR FROM MY HANDS. THE APPROACHING STORM wipes light from the sky fast, burning with salt flayed off the surface of the Waste. The grain rake across the windows with voices like nails.

The air around Montoya is even saltier as I stalk to the hollow of the aisle that was probably meant to house a wind organ . He's on a knee, the glow off a pan of hot quartz harsh to the angles of his face. "Just in time. I had wondered if you'd make it before the storm. You are an evil kind of fortunate."

Or Providence is on our side rather than his.

"I have a knack for getting my way."

"I hope you didn't have to travel too far in this impending weather."

"Oh no, I only had to ride about twenty minutes." That's a lie, but none of us need him knowing about Damascus. I promised Leagan.

My overskirt drags on stone corners as I boost myself up to a seat on the altar. "I've thought about what you said last night."

"As have I."

"I'm willing to listen to your plan for Hannah."

"You can forgive the rise of my tone yesterday," he says. "I've been after this opportunity a long time, and the disappointment of having it slip away was painful."

"I said I'm willing to hear your side of things."

"However, I did not come here to beg for your assistance. Choose what you will on your own merit."

"You mean choose your way."

"It's not that complex. Economics. And if that doesn't quite prick your interest, personal insurance." He gives his pan of hot quartz a shake, brighter, captured sunlight escaping from the fire. Into the center he sets a weathered kettle, the old preacher's likely, but before that he smells the interior—bone-dry and iron.

He puts his nose to the water as he pours, then to the tea leaves before he adds them to the kettle. They aren't little sniffs for pleasure either. These are ritual, like you pray on your knees with your eyes closed.

"The spring outside is the first water that actually tastes clean," he says.

"That's why they built this church. But when you're thirsty enough, it all tastes the same."

"Not to me," he says.

"I should bottle it and charge you, then. A tonic to heal all ailments." Honey attracts more flies than piss or clear pine, but he doesn't laugh like most people would. My, my, the tension is downright sinuous.

Fools back east would buy a tonic from an exotic place like the Rim no matter what it promised. Not a bad idea, actually, but one project at a time now, darling.

That teacup he wears holstered on his belt has a cluster of yellow flowers painted along the interior. Montoya lifts it like a lover's hand, and yes, he smells it. I assumed the leather case next to it held medical supplies or ammunition, but no, it's a set of flatware he uses to scoop the tea.

He doesn't offer me any—rude, although I usually prefer coffee.

"Our dishes not good enough for you either?"

"You've never been to Cairo," he says. "If you had, you wouldn't have to ask. If you wish to avoid being poisoned at dinner, you bring your own utensils."

"I see. Like we say, you can't trust a gun you didn't load yourself. Unless someone poisons the food."

"That would be obvious. Poison that sits in food taints the flavor," he says. "Our poison tasters train longer than surgeons. If you want power and wealth in Cairo, that's what you become. You think you could get around one?"

"Absolutely."

"How?" he asks.

"I'd taint the back of someone's chair. When they pull it out to sit, their hands are contaminated."

"Again, too simple," he says. "Believe me, it's all been done before."

"Sometimes the best plans are the most obvious ones."

He only speaks about Cairo in the present tense. He still considers it home, the one he expects to go back to someday. When I talk about my old life back east, it's always the past. One that will always be part of who I am now, but not a cornerstone of the future I'm working to build.

Montoya laces his fingers together over a knee, drawing my attention to that bastard glove he always wears, and on the other hand, a lighter band of skin where a ring used to be. "The Rim is a dangerous place, but in the Yellow City, children learn the flavor of menace venom and lady decay in their milk. Danger is more straightforward here. You don't wrap it in silk before you serve it. It will stab you in the stomach over a bar tab."

I smirk deeper until he stops listening to himself and notices.

"Why do you smile like that?"

"You know an awful lot about poison, my dear friend Montoya. For someone who's not a Poisonneur."

I watch him stray fingers along the buttons of his single glove. Don't think I don't notice such an obvious tell.

"Maybe this lie is for my benefit, not yours."

"The worst ones usually are."

"I know what you're after." Montoya stares at me past his smoldering cup. "Why half of you went to the West Rim last Season with a gentleman from the east. The mass deposits of black gold out there make Hannah look like Wallis. Weak. Black gold isn't found anywhere else on the map that we know of. Only here in the Rim."

"I know."

"It constitutes ninety percent of the Republic of Delilah's trade with Cairo. We don't need your sunflower oil, your other quartzes or weapons. There is one bastard cousin deposit in northwest Cairo, known as lo pyrite. But it's a cheap substitute, like drinking the Rim's stale water when you could have white tea. Tell me what do you think would happen if that trade was to end? Abruptly."

The consequence has tickled my mind, but not so bad I haven't been able to flick it away like a fly. "I decided I didn't care. The problems back east don't usually bother us here. I might like to see the barons taste loss for once."

"I feel that this consequence is one you should care for. Its arm is long," he says. "The Tov controlled all of the Rim and its minerals for thousands of years without mining for export."

"They had better things to do."

"They did, but I like to believe that they did so mostly because they could. Their refusals to trade or treat was a display of power, until the Republic got a taste for black gold in Laithe."

"I know how the war started," I say. "The Laithe vein was depleted, the boom town died, and the Republic crawled west looking for more. I went to an alkaline school."

"The mighty Tov needed nothing of anyone, but therefore had no allies when the Republic came for their resources. Then their strength failed." His dark gaze searches mine. "Don't let that become you. No matter how powerful and bloodthirsty you are, destroying Hannah would create a crystal rush beyond what any eye has seen. By sheer numbers they would crush you and your chances to be anything more than good but ultimately forgettable thieves."

"Alkaline thieves, thank you. It's already begun. Mineral rights on the West Rim have been sold to crystal barons by the Von Kane Company, who backed that expedition to the West Rim you heard about. And women are not allowed to own land unless they inherit it through a will." Even then, things can go east. We tend to look like easy targets to claim vultures. "I'll have to get what I want by being cleverer than they are."

"Then why make your disadvantage worse?"

"I prefer to not dwell on what others see as disadvantage. It's unproductive." I do what I want in spite of it.

"If you annihilate Hannah, you'll have tens of thousands of desperate people plowing into your way, instead of just a few thousand…and you'll have made an enemy of me."

"Well, that would be unfortunate," I say.

"You mock."

"Absolutely. It means I like you." I twist his cup in its saucer. He doesn't stop me. "But you do make some valid points, sir, and I will consider them. *If* you consider maybe I want Hannah for myself? If I'd been ready for the responsibility the first time, maybe I would have become boss. Why should I give it to you now?"

"If you really wanted the title of boss, you would have had it by now. I can see that."

The wind moaning around the church walls like a grieving widow suddenly falls silent.

"Oh, listen to that. Sweet silence." I take the risk the storm isn't trying to fool us and go to the back door. Salt and sandstone particles grind under wood, sun dropping across me with violent abruptness.

Across the cemetery and the wide valley below, the glittering brink of the salt waste comes alive. The setting sun approaches the perfect slant for the granules to reflect the fire gold breaking through the sky.

"Hate the Rim as much as you want, but you can't tell me this isn't beautiful," I call.

Montoya reluctantly comes to join me "It is not bad, but it will never be home like Cairo."

"Whatever." I let shoulders fall with my sigh. "You're just determined to be unhappy. That's why you and Raptor won't ever get along."

"It's the truth."

"The truth..." The only truth worth knowing is that it's a different thing to everyone. "I owe my mother and daughter vengeance."

"Your mother would want you to do the best for your family."

"Yes, she would." *Farce*, he's an arrogant fool, and a double fool for thinking I don't already know that. Only I'm allowed to use my mother's name for personal gain. This *is* for the good of the family. "But say you are right—"

"I am."

"There's only one problem now."

"What could that be?"

"The Stranger. She's not going to like this."

Triumph slips into Montoya's mouth, binding itself over his eyes so thick he stops looking for warning signs as he steps in to clasp my forearm. "You'll tell her how it's going to be."

I don't tell him we don't work that way. "Or we don't tell her at all. Until it's too late."

"Whatever you think best, considering her disposition. I bow to your discretion in this instance."

How easily they must turn on each other in Cairo, even family. What a shame. He'll never know the support of true loyalty, real love. How strong it makes you.

I offer him my hand. "*Sol*, Poisonneur. We have a deal."

I've told a truth.

The truth as I want him to see it.

The truth for now.

TWENTY-TWO
ADELAIDE

SPOON AND GLASS CHIMES CLATTER IN THE RISING WIND. THEY'RE SUPPOSED TO ward off ghosts who don't like noise and I've noticed more of them lately.

They're not necessary. The refinery is a bad enough sound.

The setting blood sun is lost to the buildings and Hannah's permanent smoke sky. Fry grease taints the air, tent canvas clapping each time a gust moves through the air market.

The Stranger sees him before I do.

The uneven steps vibrate as he makes his way up the double turn to my balcony. There's not enough light for Montoya to cast a shadow on me. "*Sol*, lonely Shadow." He snaps fingers, flashes a pair of silver standards. Twice my street value. "Up."

Somewhere inside him, paper cracks.

I don't like the hand on my elbow, but he has to make it look real. Our skirts roll like this storm, black dust stinging my eyes.

Twenty-nine.

"You have two bastards on your tail again." He nods to the pair haunting the mouth of a fringed tent. "The boss doesn't trust you."

I wouldn't.

"So he isn't wrong." Montoya drops ten silver standards into the collection hat held by the owner of the hourly rooms.

No one will question why we're in here together. Not even Rafe's guns.

The corrugated tin roof vibrates under the wind, holds out some dust but not the steady creak of springs and grunts next door.

Inside his duster, the letter I've been waiting for. Waking up in the middle of the night thinking about.

The Stranger crawls up his single glove, but she can't get inside it without my help. What's he hiding under there? Weapon, wound, or skin disease?

I squeeze the curve above his gloved thumb as the letter trades hands. It's flesh.

He narrows eyes, pulling back. "And this, regards from the Raptor."

A seven-round revolver with the hammerless compact barrel of a five-shot. Black as the hour before dawn. *Reliable* etched into one side of the barrel, silver pin to release something hidden in the grip.

My heart pounds a little faster, Leagan's work solid in my hands. This chance to get out will crumble the second I let myself trust it. Everything else has.

Montoya doesn't leave, waits for me to break the wax and read. I have a standing seat against the outer wall. It hums with wind, like the roof. The Stranger doesn't like it, but I can wait too.

"Has the Raptor told you why she hates me so much?" Montoya's stare ripples, a sneer trying to change itself to a smile.

She's told me about her dream.

"You and I have much work to do." He nods his gaze to the envelope, my black-dust fingerprints scoring it. "Better get your instructions."

Not with you looking.

"Meet me at the soup camp in an hour."

Three.

I turn the latch pin. Montoya plants his gloved hand above mine. The Stranger rises up like hair prickled by storm static, her darkness at the corners of my eyes.

Not an inch closer.

"I seem to have misplaced an item of value," he says.

Farce. I hoped he wouldn't assume it was me.

"Although I always take great care with dangerous possessions." His slanted eyebrows shift as he studies the half of my face not enclosed by the muzzle.

I give nothing.

"It must have fallen out of my pocket the last time I was here. I only hope whoever is unfortunate enough to come across this composite doesn't seriously harm themselves. The heart of a deathflower called silent glove. Heartstopper. It goes by several names where I'm from, and was not meant to be used by untrained hands."

"How?"

"How does it kill? A deep cut works fastest. Poison similar to a copper cackler bite, but it takes longer to necrotize and stop a heart. I still have hope the item will finds its way back to me, and all is forgotten."

He's not going to accuse me directly, make me decide what he means by taking the scenic route. I hate people like that.

Montoya lets go of the door. "Curiosity is not an inherent crime. Sometimes we all make choices we later regret. I will see you in an hour."

I've never regretted anything I've taken.

Forty-four.

A miner staggers through a cooking stall like he didn't see it there. Hot crystal and grease splash across his skin, spilling smoke on the bare ground. I fade backward, shadows safe around me like blankets.

But he turns as he passes, as if something in him can see me despite the Stranger.

Red. The white part of his eye isn't white anymore, all flooded bright crimson.

That's called seeing blood.

My lungs lock. Vesta. A bitter fear passes through me, burns like the afterstrike of lightning. In my mind I see the deep west bone picker in the mine, infected with the pestilence, moving on hands and feet, twisted like spiders.

"Worms..." His lips crack, flaky, white. With his black nails he scratches open the crusted scabs on either side of his head.

The Stranger waits, flat and still as rock. He moves on, back the way he came, but I can't take a full breath. I'll never forget what the pestilence looks like. Not worms, worse.

I'll have to get too close to use a knife. I break open the chamber of my new revolver. Someone will hear, but this is still the safest way. I'm not getting any closer to him.

Wait.

He wrestles up one of the tent spikes, rams it into his own eye. It cracks. Through bone into brain.

CHAPTER
TWENTY-THREE

Dear Adelaide,

Our new friend the Menace thinks I've changed my mind about destroying Hannah. I have not.

Here is the plan:

He believes we're going to give him Hannah instead of ruining it, and that I'm not going to tell you beforehand.

Humor him, would you?

Leagan has a bad feeling he's going to betray us. Let's beat him to it. That's our thing, after all.

He will help you place explosives where he wants them. When he leaves to deliver your next letter, you can hide flash fire in the locations WE decided.

As far as why the Menace is here at all, he claims destroying the black gold will push the prospectors and barons west.

While he might not be wrong about that, it was only said to convince me to make him boss. He hasn't told me the full truth yet. He's hiding something about his past in Cairo, or why he left.

I'm willing to bet this quest for Hannah has something to do with it. If you find anything, let me know.

I know you've noticed that glove he wears. If you figure it out before I do, please tell me, I'm dying to know.

The Menace also thinks I'm willing to play you the way he's (likely) playing us. Won't that be a surprise later when he finds out he's so very wrong...

Assemble and load these guns Leagan sends (there should be two) and hide them with the spare ammo somewhere we'll be able to get to them later if needed.

Let us know the minute you're set, and the second you want to come home. We'll be ready.

Love,
Aunt Tess, Navy, Leagan

TWENTY-FOUR
ADELAIDE

THE SOUP CAMP SITS UNDER ITS BLANKET OF SMELLS, THICKER EVERY TIME ONE of the pots belches. Melted fat, sour intestines, partially digested by the other things in the mix.

Chickens peck at liquifying potato skins and cabbage leaves while my breath whispers into the muzzle covering the bottom half of my face.

A miner stops drinking to pick a stray tooth from his mouthful, white particles in his beard, then lifts the bowl to his mouth again.

Montoya presses a cloth to his nose as he approaches.

"I am not eating here."

I didn't ask him to.

"You read your letter?" he says.

Yes.

"When will you begin the burying process?"

I've already started. Explosives and flash fire sleep under several Company buildings. One of them is the ration and payroll dispensary right across the dirt track from here, the closest I've been able to get to the mine.

"Soon."

He clears ash buildup from his throat, dislodging whatever plots brought him here. "While vengeance for your grandmother is an honorable pursuit, what do you gain from the risks you take here? In my opinion, they are much higher than those your Widow and Rook are dealing with."

I'm already here. If make my suffering useful, I make it bearable.

"You are not blood family," he says. "You trust them far enough you're willing to pay the price to secure this mission? You're sure they would ask you to remain here if you were a blood daughter?"

You think I'm expendable because I'm a bastard?

I trust my sisters.

I trust Aunt Tess.

I trust myself.

You're the one I don't.

"The Widow thinks the fall of Hannah won't touch you out here, but she's wrong. I won't leave you in the dark to die for a senseless cause."

Blood has nothing to do with who we should believe in. My mother taught me that. If my family thought I was just a gun for taking, the Stranger would feel it and they would have fucked me over a long time ago. It's what we do.

"I wonder if you don't feel the same." His words knit together like thread, slow as a tiptoe so he doesn't trip on them. "Your intelligence doesn't hide itself behind a quiet demeanor. You are insidiously insightful, and I'm aware of that fact. Is this plan really what you want, or what you've been told by the Widow you need to do?"

I fold my arms, step aside so he can get around the firepit easier.

"She put you in charge of laying the explosives."

"Yes."

"Consider where they are placed. There are ways for a momentary crippling of Hannah's operations that would allow them to be resumed with a suitable replacement at the head, an ally, versus obliterating the black gold entirely. If this happens, the entire purpose of your journey to the West Rim is destroyed with it."

You think you can go behind Aunt Tess's back to me and I won't tell her?

Fool.

Black gold wasn't the only reason I went out west.

It's not the only reason I'm going back.

"You should make this decision for yourself," he says. "It's your life held ransom here. Bury the explosives where you like. Choose your own path, don't die in service to someone else's."

I will.

"The Widow will never know the difference."
Neither will you.

TWENTY-FIVE
ADELAIDE

I was going to ignore the favor I owe Solstice and Joelle for sealing my cuts. If I never go back to their tea house or work for Thadie so I don't see Saraline again, I could.

I wish.

The longer a debt sits under my skin, the more it burns. Not like getting that gash cauterized with quartz. Worse.

The air is wood warm, refinery noise a little softer inside the Pinings, but it's the dried herbs I like best. They smell safe. I hate Hannah more than I've hated anything else, but I feel less angry here.

Again, the place is empty. I like that too.

I open the porcelain hutch, count the teacups stacked inside so the Stranger will stop stretching me in two directions. They have as many colors as there are varieties of quartzes. Some plain, flowers and moon phases sprayed across others.

Thirty-two.

The gap in the curtain shifts as I breath against it. The shadow pair of Company guns drift the street like loose weeds where I slipped out from under them.

The beads across the back-room door click as Joelle appears. Black hair wrapped in a red ribbon, eyes of ink. "Ah. I see I need a better bell on the door. Or maybe you need one around your neck, like a little cat. You're not bleeding again, are you?"

I shake my head.

"Well, at least there's some good news. Soli, she's back."

"*Sol*, Stranger." Solstice, the moonbeam of white hair emanating from beneath her hood. I don't know if anyone has ever pronounced my name quite like she does.

The moist pressure of my mother's ghost breathes into my ear, but the Stranger pushes her back out like antivenom.

Eight.

I have a seat at the table angled away from the door. Draped in lace, crumbs that poke my arms as I fold my hands on it. "I owe you a favor."

"You owe nothing." Solstice turns away, hand up.

"She said a favor, not money." Joelle comes closer. "Let her get this debt off her back if she wants to." She shows me a powder envelope from her apron. "I'll make you the same offer as before, sell some of these and you can call yourself a debt-free woman. And if you're tired of the god-honest work of whoring and pushing Thadie's nonpaying customers down the stairs—"

It wasn't a push, I kicked him.

"You might like to become a permanent addition to our business."

This is why I've always hated favors. They come with threads attached and they've given me no good reason to change my mind.

"No." The word is Moon Season dry in my mouth. I can't get pulled into Hannah any deeper if I ever want to see my sisters again.

Joelle plucks a redweed stick from a silver case, sticks it in her lip to light it on the bowl of fire quartz pulsing gold on the worktable. Nutmeg, but twisted around a vegetable going sour. "Don't say I didn't offer, Soli."

The Stranger senses the ripple cross the room.

"I asked you not to involve her."

"Then you said I could handle it. A small problem." Joelle answers the question that obviously went through my eyes. "But one we'd rather not get dirty correcting ourselves."

"We disagree on how it should be handled. We're not the only courage powder still in Hannah anymore."

Were you here when I was born?

"But the others are trash," Joelle says. "Don't be nice, call it what it is.

It's a poor reflection, and that makes the situation worse. Those who don't know any better will taint our reputation, and we don't appreciate the disrespect."

I do understand that.

Joelle shakes her head to Solstice again. "I want to kill them. She doesn't."

"Violence is the easiest solution, but it doesn't last," Solstice says.

"A soft hand won't help them learn fast enough, Soli."

"I've stayed out of it," Saraline says from the doorway. She groans, going right for the kettle. "I don't even have to ask, I know what this is about. They never stop arguing about it."

"You too," Joelle says. "Soft as mud. We'll stop arguing once your friend here takes care of it."

"You were the first powder still?" I ask.

"Offhand," Solstice says while Joelle tries to hide a smirk behind a puff of smoke that turns pink from the lamp glass. "We acquired it from the original chemist."

"Bang, bang," Saraline says.

So they didn't poison my mother, but they're close enough to what did.

I stand.

"You stay out of this," Solstice says to me. "It's not right to hold a favor against someone who needs your help. You don't owe us anything."

"Fine." Joelle's lips tighten around the redweed stick, moving like an itch as she mutters. "I'll take care of it myself."

Solstice sends her a withering headshake. "You will not."

This wood-wrapped space whispered *safe* and lied to me with its herb smells. I almost tried fitting into it, but I don't.

Treacherous.

It reminds me I'm not a plant, not water, I don't have roots to sink in. I'm better off wandering.

Joelle comes between me and the door, breath haunted by onions and the tumble of fermented smoke. "Soli's right, this is not a company of prisoners like the *bastardos* who live up on the hill. You're free to walk away if the rest of our business doesn't interest you. Just know that I don't care if you are half Tov or half goat-sucking spider worm. The only thing you don't get to do is talk about what you've seen in here. Betray me, or the ones I love, and I'll put your hand through the quartz grinder until you weep for your mother."

I've never done that. Never will.

"*Joelle!*" Solstice snaps.

"I'm just telling her the truth. There's no benefit to lying, she can respect that." The ghost that passes between them is something I'll never understand. Love.

"You mean Solstice," I say. "They don't know about her. Do they?"

"See?" Saraline clicks her fingers. "I told you. She doesn't have to talk much, she's smart."

"That's what concerns me," Joelle says. "We don't know one thing about her besides her name. And I'm not convinced you told us the truth about that either. What kind of mother gives her daughter a name like that?"

The question asks itself by habit. Doubt that forever echoes like a storm.

Didn't my mother love me?

Now there's a new one.

What if the Stranger never finds what she's looking for? I used to have everything.

I remember Grandma teaching me how to braid hair. Aunt Tess letting me touch a gun for the first time. Leagan reading to me and Navy, doing all the characters with their own voices. The herb and spice hint of danger in Navy's lab, Vesta's laugh. Fool's gold, it hurts. My eyes, my throat, my bones, coats my lungs, a desperation I can't escape.

"Revere."

All of me burns. And all I want is to be with them again.

"Oh, shit." Joelle shuts her mouth on the redweed stick.

They've heard of us.

"Well..." Solstice says. "Here I thought your gang was just an overtold bone picker's tale. What brings you to the North Rim, Adelaide Revere?"

Red slashes through me, a double lightning hit. Maybe Vesta's death was preventable. I wish I'd never met Kane.

Solstice studies my face, gaze a mirror. The Stranger looks for treachery in hers, doesn't find it. "Tell me something, *Adelaide*. Did your mother really gift you that name? Or is that the one you chose for yourself?"

Does it matter?

She shrugs when I fail to answer. "So long as it fits. Don't listen to what

Joelle says. If you'd like to rest here, away from the world out there, I'm happy to let you. Anytime."

Women look out for one another. We have to. It's the main currency we trade with, our unspoken barter that even the Stranger knows better than to cross most of the time. I want to hold onto something safe so badly my chest hurts, take this chance to not be so alone. But I know better. People are only kind when they want something from you and think they have a chance to get it.

"My mother warned me never turn your back on a Stranger at your door." She smiles at Joelle. "Don't look at me like that. We can trust her. She won't tell anyone about me."

Unless it should become necessary.

THERE'S ONE DEEP VOID LEFT IN MY OTHERWISE COMPLETE MAP OF HANNAH.

Southeast. Old Hannah.

It's the last place my map lacks. One deep void in an otherwise complete picture. It stares back at me, sinister as that infected picker. An old gravel chute, headless water tower.

The refinery is here. I'll have to go in soon, place the explosives so I can leave. But my feet won't move, and I can't make them.

Far at the old end of the Slash, her ghost takes shape. Fingers of wind lift her gray dress, white hair. Always a body, head lost to the Seasons between us. She says my name.

I shut my ears, but she's inside.

The Stranger forgets nothing. I can look back at jobs we did ten Seasons ago and see who stood where, the clothes we were wearing, pages in books I've read, the notches on the deposit box keys Kane gave me before I threw them into the *Delta Sol* canyon so the men who captured me couldn't have them. The things those men did to me.

All this time I didn't ask why the Stranger never saved my mother's face. Didn't care, and maybe I've been glad.

I could draw the shape of each nose belonging to Kane's crew, even though we wore the respirator masks for most of the expedition. The direction of the cracked chin scar belonging to the boss of the gang we rode with when I was still a child.

Maybe it's me, making the choice to forget her. All this time.

If that's true, it makes her the worst thing that's ever happened to me. Still.

I'm afraid that if I look deep enough to find her face, it will be mine. And if I have her face, how many other pieces of her haunt my blood, waiting to poison me when I'm weak?

I turn my back.

What remains, what doesn't, none of that matters. It will all be ash soon.

CHAPTER
TWENTY-SIX

Dear Aunt Tess, Navy, and Leagan,

I haven't been able to get into the station yard or the refinery. There are too many people. Rafe has two standing guns mounted on the watchtowers there. They point at the rail tunnel.

Leagan, these are the scavenger lizard bones I found in the bone well. They're the biggest I've ever seen.

Navy, there was an infected bone picker here. I don't know how, or where he came from. But I thought you should know.

Kane split the rest of the payment he owed us for the expedition in two parts.

Wallis. Vantage.

Don't wait for me. Get it before someone else does. Here is a drawing of the keys. Box 13.

Love,
Adelaide

TWENTY-SEVEN
TESLA

VANTAGE HAS MATURED IN THE SEASON SINCE WE WERE LAST HERE. A FULL new street has widened off the back market, making it into the middle market, I suppose. The storefronts on the Avenue all have fresh coats of paint in dainty candy-shop colors, a third hotel planted, and of course, the new sheriff's office. Iron shutters aren't an unusual sight on windows, although they're usually to keep storms and bone pickers out. The east blood's first stop on the Rim is far too safe now that we're not here playing with it.

"Look at this place." I twist my parasol and breathe it in. That's fresh bread making the air sweet. "Fuck you, Green. It looks nice though, doesn't it?"

"It looks worse," Leagan says. "I just realized I don't care if I ever come back here again."

"I don't mind it. Now, what did we agree on? You're not going to quick draw with any east bloods today, and I will resist the urge to visit all of our old friends here and tell them we're not dead. We're here on Adelaide's business."

Although, it would be so satisfying to stroll into the Hoyt Hotel and make him drop the bottle he's pouring, all the table games falling to a silent gasp. Raleigh said Green was in Junction, but we don't want him to get wind of us before I say so.

"Fine." Leagan huffs.

The prayer booth faces the Avenue, stained with wax smoke and the husks of wildflowers plucked for the God of Mercy. I light fresh candles. For Mother and Vesta, then another for everyone I've already killed, and everyone I'm about to.

The gossip all over the street is the new ghost quartz strike near Windust and the expansion of the line. Everyone stepping off the last train was headed there. The West Rim is still officially closed, at least according to the survey maps tacked to the wall of the assay office. But I know that's not entirely true. It was bought by the Von Kanes.

What must that be like? Owning enough land, it could be considered its own country while some of us would be considered fortunate to have one acre to our name.

"Hey. Hey, girl." The prisoner raps on the perforated plate covering his cell window.

Leagan turns, hands clasped behind her pale, ruffled skirt, and drifts closer. She looks a lot like the doll Liza had back east. Except the pigment of the black lipstick I wouldn't let her wear today lingers in her skin, giving her lips permeant shadows. If she was a doll, she'd be one made in the image of death.

"Yeah, you." He presses his mouth up to one of the nailhead holes. "Buy me out of here. It's only fifty gold, but they won't let me out to get my money. I'm a good soul. Be a kind girl. Pretty girl. I'll owe you forever."

"What are you in jail for?" she asks.

"Nothing but a misunderstanding."

I spy the sheriff having a smoke with the owner of the boot shop across the street. He notices us standing too close to the jail and grinds his cigarette out before coming to talk to two ladies.

"Well, well, it's your lucky day, ma'am." I prod Leagan. "Your first time to see an officer of the law."

"Alkaline." She blows a raspberry with her tongue.

"He's a bastard." The man in the cell says. "You tell him I said that. Say it. Bastard."

"Fucker."

"Yes!" His faceless cackle bounces off the hollow walls.

"Morning, ladies." The badge pinned to his vest is nickel, etched with

Protecting Vantage over the sun emblem of the Republic. "What can I do for you?"

"She said fucker!" the prisoner yells.

The sheriff rounds us so that he blocks the window. "Don't associate yourselves with that man. He's a bone picker and will never be anything more."

The prisoner spits, impact echoing faintly off the iron plate.

"Are you new in town?"

"Yes." I hug an arm around Leagan. "This is my daughter, Lilith. We're looking for my husband. He was supposed to meet us here, but he's late."

"How late?"

"Well, he knew we were getting in this week, but I heard something about storm schedules affecting travel, so maybe he thought we'd be late."

"Moon Season hasn't hit us yet, but it's possible he got delayed."

Oh, he's too soft to tell a woman who isn't from around here the truth, that she's probably a widow now. I wonder, how long does false hope keep a bed warm?

He peels open a notebook, misshapen from being sat on. "I'll keep an ear open. Name?"

"John Sawyer."

"And you're staying at which hotel?"

"The Skystone Inn."

"I'll see what I can turn over. In the meantime, don't go wandering outside of town by yourselves. There's still plenty of unsavories out there in the hills."

"I was planning to ask around a few more places in town, if you think that's safe for us."

"That's fine, just don't go down in the rail yard." He grabs the top layer off a stack of pamphlets pinned down by a rock. "Take this and stay safe."

"Thank you, Sheriff." I smile, skin deep.

"My pleasure, ma'am."

My gaze trails him to the corner before we turn the other way. "Threat level?"

"I'd say…a three," Leagan says. "He looks lazy, and he's already got his job."

"I agree. Maybe a three and a half at the very most." I thumb the first page. "To the vigilant and informed traveler…well, well, this is new."

Be advised, the persons contained in this advert remain armed and at large in the Rim Territories. Exercise caution and pursue at own risk.
Bounties and collection information posted as follows.

—Published by The Jezebel Bureau of Information—

There are five names. Tedward "The Baptist" Seed and Reverend Alonzo Seed, wanted around Winchester for unknown crimes. The other three roadmen are accompanied by sketches I recognize from Descendants gangs. All unfortunately ugly bastards.

"We're not in here." I pass the pamphlet off to Leagan and her grabby hand. "That's a pile of *farce* and a shame. Apparently, we're no longer worth anyone's time without our train. We'll have to work harder, steal more things, murder a few more uninformed travelers. So much to do."

Of course, our lives will be so much more convenient if bounty hunters aren't actively tracking us. But still. One Season and the Rim's already forgotten about us. Rude.

"It's all right." The porch of the Express office still smells like its fresh coat of paint. "We have better things waiting for us at the moment."

"Like money."

"Exactly."

The clang of the bell signaling the shift of the switch track rings over the clap of wagons and feet. I still know the schedule in my heart. They're opening the eastbound line for the next twelve hours. I taste the *Absolution*'s hiss of pent-up steam. Someday, my friends.

"Wait outside for me now, my love." I fold down my parasol with a wink. "Don't wander off though. The sheriff says some men are dangerous."

"You made it just in time," the clerk says. "I'm about to close for lunch."

"Then don't let me keep you." I slide Raleigh's reproduction key under the mosaic slot window. "Box thirteen, please."

"Name?"

"Von Kane."

"Alkaline, give me one minute." The floor trembles as he travels down a set of stairs to the vault below.

Well, easy day. If he gives it to me without a fight, we don't have to break in or hide his body, and I'll have time to see what clothes the merchants have from back east.

"You don't happen to remember the first Von Kane crew who came through here," I call past the grate. "It would have been the Moon Season before this coming one."

"I do, actually." Part of his voice gets absorbed by layers of wood and stone before making it back to me. "Junior or Senior?"

"What was that?"

"The elder Mr. Von Kane visited the expansion of the line, but that was recently."

"Did he now?" Well, well. So, Millard Von Kane has gotten his east blood ass off his University chair and come to the Rim in the flesh. Sweet Jezebel.

"He travels light for an east blood." He returns with my deposit box. "Practical sort of gentleman, I assume. If you'll just sign here."

"And what about his son?" I ask.

"I haven't seen him since he made this deposit. I assumed you knew him."

"He's still here," I lie. "Railroad business, I'm his assistant. I had to go home for a few months to care for my ailing mother, but my daughter and I are on our way to meet back up with him now."

"Really? That's an odd job for a girl."

It's been a long time since I've been called a girl. I laugh it away. "It's the perfect job for a girl. I know how to pack luggage without losing anything, have lovely handwriting, and I'm much nicer to look at."

"Well, I can't argue with that." He laughs with me and slides the button-down pouch across the counter. "There you are. *Sol*, miss, I hope your mother's health stays gold, and good luck to your Von Kane as well. He seemed a decent fool."

He was.

LEAGAN DRAWS THE LOCKPICKS FROM HER TWIN BUNS AND CROUCHES EYE TO keyhole with the back door of the governor's mansion. Meanwhile, I keep watch on the stone garden. I do mean that. Nothing is growing back here but sun on rocks. One of the former occupants must have been a collector. I just can't see Green wasting his precious time on artistic expression.

Everyone assumes thieves break in at night. Green keeps one maid, and she just left. Let's hope Raleigh's information is right and Green took his hired guns to Junction with him.

We enter through the kitchen, the vacant stillness of the house at odds with the clatter outside. I trail my finger along the wainscotting. Sunlight pools through every dusty window, bleaching spots on the wool rugs.

Green's study is wallpapered dark like old forest. Potted palms and a vine with purple flowers that look too fragile to be here dangling from the ceiling.

Leagan twists her pick back around the lock from the inside. Just in case. I unshoulder the bag of dead widower snake and jar of blood.

"Take everything and read it later."

"I hope he has a diary." Leagan plops down in the cowhide chair and takes a spin before she picks the locked drawers.

"Oh yes, and full of dirty secrets."

The dead weight of the widower snake's body shudders as I dump her out on the desktop. Her black skin still holds the shine her eyes lack, gray tongue poking from her inkwell mouth. My knife slices her head off and leaves a gash through the polished wood in a single stroke. This would be a clear enough warning to anyone from the Rim, and I know Green hasn't forgotten the last time we spoke or the snake we left with him then. Still, next to the headless widow, I carve my name. Knife marks scar wood much like they do to skin.

Hello, Green. Regards – Tesla Revere

Ear to a listening scope, Leagan eavesdrops as the safe tumblers roll.

"Are you getting it?"

She puts a finger to her lip.

Mrs. Sawyer wore light blue to look for her poor missing husband this morning, but I wear black. It hides bloodstains.

"There we go." Leagan peels the safe door back.

The river flows red from my jar into the pale tuft cushions, stinking of iron. It spills across the floor and down Green's high-backed chair, a poisonous wine, while Leagan feeds the contents of the desk and safe to her backpack.

"Appointment book. Accounts, boring stuff. Ammunition…"

I plunk the company ledger out of her hands. "Let's see how the security business is these days." I flip pages until names catch my eye. "Hang on. What's this…"

"What now?" Leagan gets off the floor to join me.

"Green has the personal schedules of everyone involved in the railroad expansion." Millard Von Kane. Timothy Von Kane. Jonathaniel Swann… The pages fall back with thin paper voices, and I laugh. "I wonder if they know they're being spied on?"

"I doubt it."

"But it's in the name of security."

"Like that makes it okay." Leagan sets her hand in a puddle of blood, then tacks it along the wall, a trail of bloody palm prints until the moisture blots away.

"You're not wrong." I dust a fly off my arm. "Green's always been a slimy little voyeur."

Now we've left him some slimy little gifts to remember us by.

TWENTY-EIGHT
ADELAIDE

THE FORTUNE TELLER'S CANOPY IS MADE OF CARPET TO THICKEN THE DARKNESS. I like watching her spin the moon diviner, spilling the future out of it. The solar quartz glow calms the Stranger, the way looking at the night sky used to.

She uses ink to write fortunes, not wax like Grandma did.

Hot spices smolder in the wind, pots strung on wire under the air market tents cracking together.

"She's *farce*," Saraline says past her mouthful of fried rice. "That's what you're thinking right now."

Not exactly. I put away the memories building in me. They're mine, not for sharing.

The Stranger jumps through my skin as Saraline drums her spoon on the rim of her tin plate. "Tell me more about your family. I'm dying to know."

"Yes," Thadie gasps. "What's it like to ride a train?"

Unstoppable freedom. It's all I want right now. "Better than anything."

"Better than *anything*?" Thadie says. "Fool's gold...the best thing I've ever felt was the redweed Joelle mail-ordered from Eos. Do you remember that, Saraline?"

"Barely. And that's the point."

"But being a roadwoman could be exciting."

The Stranger pulls my gaze back to the glow of the diviner, the red tent fabric clapping to the thunder of the rising storm. Their voices fade into the Stranger. She's the black shadow, there in the blue diviner light.

The gallows bell clangs on the other side of the market. The wind carries the hangman's call. "See a ration thief hang at the beat of sundown... Stealing food steals from all of us..."

Thadie's looking at me, head cocked. Whatever she's wondering, she doesn't ask.

"Exactly," Saraline's saying. "They'll buy a product either way, so it might as well be ours."

Escaping down a powder hole doesn't solve your problems. It kills you faster.

I start for the edge of the market.

"You should come back to the tea house with us." Saraline deposits her plate in the wash bucket. "We can have a drink and smoke. All night if you want. I'll teach you how to crochet."

I almost wish I wanted that. But the Stranger won't let me drink anymore. And I don't want to be with voices and faces anymore—theirs, anybody's. I want to be alone.

"Do you ever want to leave?" The words leave my mouth, unexpected.

Saraline looks surprised too. "Hannah? No, this is my home."

"Have you ever been anywhere else?"

"Solstice and Joelle found me in Winchester when I was eight. My mother and brother had just died from hangman's fever. I'm glad I went with them. I probably would have died next, being on my own, or got picked up by some roadman and sold in Descendants."

Doesn't she miss the blue sky? Feel the pressure of the smoke's constant shadow, the monotone of living under the eternal dusk of the red sun.

"What would you do if Hannah wasn't here someday?" Nothing is permanent. The Rim erases all things eventually, either with storms or with people.

"I don't know," she says. "I've never thought about that. It's not going anywhere."

"If you could go anywhere."

"My whole life is here, all my friends. I'm not like you, I don't see any point in hating everything, especially the place where I am. That's such a waste of time."

How could I ever stop hating it?

My mother's breath moves warm on my forehead. Hollow eyes. Gray lips. It was her plan for both of us to die here. Grandma helped me cheat death. I lift my shoulder and the raised knife scar stretches on my ribcage. I'm still cheating it.

Saraline can disagree with me if she wants, but she's just lucky Hannah doesn't haunt her like this. Under the ash crust, the ground is the same. Bad.

"What about you?" Thadie asks. "Have you always lived on your train?"

The Stranger seeps up into my throat, plugging the truth like a cork.

"I was born here." Let them digest that statement.

"*Oh.*" Thadie goes stone still as if the black ground can listen to us. "*Farce.* You'd better be careful. They say if you return to the exact point of your birth, the Rim will suck the life back out of you."

"That's not true." Just a fool's tale.

"Still. Better cautious than foolish, right?"

"Can I read your moons, just to be sure?"

She's getting too close. Don't tell her anything else.

I glance up at the crown of the Company roof, just visible past the rest of them and the spinning smoke, shake my head.

They go silent beside me as we leave the market. It's never safe to draw attention to yourself, and it isn't safe to not be paying attention to who is paying attention to you.

And the sun has gone down.

Ninety-one.

The right side of the Slash, the Company side. That's where the other powder still they want me to take care of is. Right there on the edge of it.

"This way," Saraline calls in a whisper.

"It's that one, isn't it?" I point. The dark square, storm shutters blotting the core of the light inside, but not the outline of it.

"I thought Solstice told you that you didn't have to do this. She's the boss, not Joelle."

"What are you whispering about?" Thadie says.

It's not worth it.

Not this powder still, at least. It never did anything to me.

"Come on," Saraline tugs my arm. "The burning ghost could be waking up."

"It hasn't killed any girls." And Thadie glances at me. "I think if it was going to, it would have by now."

"Come back with us, we can all get drunk together."

"I'm teaching myself a new type of braid," Thadie adds. "I could practice it on you."

Is it loneliness pushing up against my throat and hurting, or is this still just rage? The Stranger doesn't answer.

Four...

"Okay, be safe," Saraline says.

I glance back and wave when Thadie does. "I'll see you tomorrow."

They want to be my friends. I could let them.

If I was somebody else, if I wasn't burying things to burn their home, that might get them killed. I let Kane become my friend, until that wasn't good enough for him.

I just want... That's where I stop.

I know what I want.

I've always known exactly what I want.

To be free.

TWENTY-NINE
ADELAIDE

I AM BLANK AS THE NEW MOON, HAIR AND FACE HIDDEN UNDER THE BONE shell of the mask, my scarf. Pointed fangs sharp as the predator they once belonged to.

Hannah is eerily dead for this single sliver of deep morning. The first shift isn't awake yet, the third hasn't been brought up from the mine belly. But it doesn't last long. And the refinery never stops churning.

The black dirt grinds as I scrape it out of my fingernails. I stop to dump the handful that found its way into my boot.

Only the refinery remains. Two last tubes of flash fire in my bag. Then this nightmare place will leave the map.

The refinery tower pokes a tunnel through the smoke, lost in the ash sky it's made. My stomach turns to sour milk. An ache I can't swallow.

Go on, the Stranger says. *Finish what you started.*

My eyes are so heavy, dry without sleep. I want to go to bed.

The refinery will be here tomorrow. And if it isn't, my problem is solved for me.

Seven fifty-one.

The door of Madam Charlene's house is just on the other side of the thin street, but not quite close enough.

Behind you.

I should have been more careful.

Montoya melts from shadows permanent as death. "You're out late, you must be exhausted."

Say what you mean.

"Getting started without me? I thought we were supposed to help each other lay the demolition sticks? Unless I'm mistaken." He slips around my step, faster, catches my wrist and pushes me into the seam between walls where the darkness is complete.

The Stranger shoots up into my head, but Montoya's leg snarls around the back of mine. By my next blink, I hit dust.

"Let's not do this." Montoya lets my arm go and holds his hands up, empty.

Yes, be careful, I'm carrying fire in my bag. I hope the fact he tried to manhandle me means he didn't see it.

"I need to know you and the Widow aren't plotting to betray me. Your cipher letters, this. It does not help."

"You opened my letters."

"Resetting a wax seal is basic subterfuge."

Breaking codes Leagan and I built isn't. She's too good with puzzles, and I haven't crossed a pattern the Stranger can't memorize. Good thing we kept using it.

"This is not a threat. It's a reminder not to forget the burning of alliances brought you here."

Fuck you.

The Stranger bars his gaze as it tries to pry me open. My ribs ache because she holds me so tight.

"The unpredictable ally is still dangerous," he says. "Let's discuss what we're both thinking, find understanding."

I brace myself against the wind rifling through my skirt. I did betray the last man whose ideas got in my way. And I actually liked him. Don't think I won't do it again, even if that is why I'm stuck here.

His voice softens, cheese left out in the sun. "Tell me, what would you give to see your sister and grandmother again?"

The pearl setting of Grandma's ring glides under my thumb, silk. My voice is just as smooth, even though I'm broken inside. "They're dead."

"My wife hates me for leaving her poor with a bad name. The last thing she said to me was, 'I hope it hurts when you burn down there in hell.' She got her wish. But I still ache to hold her. Her face is always the first thing in my mind."

I only have one thing to say to that.

Fool.

"You decided against taking matters into your own hands," Montoya says, "and still follow the Widow's plan for destroying Hannah."

Our plan.

"This is the only source of Cairo's black gold, you know," he says. "They willingly pay the Republic's ridiculous yet not unsurprising export tax. If I let your family cut off that supply, even temporarily, I get vengeance on my country. But if I save them from economic ruin, they might allow me to go home, or at the very least, restore honor to the family name so my daughters don't have to hide who they are."

Guilt. A dishonest emotion. One easily manipulated, and Aunt Tess is better at that than anyone I've ever met.

And if he thinks I'm going to be persuaded by a sad story about his pathetic family, everything he's observed about me is dead wrong. The only family I care about is mine.

"While I understand this place holds painful memories for you, I urge you one more time, look beyond yourself and what kind of power your family stands to gain if we liberate Hannah together."

I do. But this has nothing to do with liberation. He just admitted that.

I'll get black gold on the West Rim. I don't need Hannah.

But he does…

He coats his teeth in the poison that rides his tongue. "The Widow hasn't been entirely honest with you, but as I said, it's my belief a person risking their life should know the truth behind the request."

I know.

"The Widow and your sisters have already agreed saving Hannah is the better strategy. The Widow decided not to tell you. She still needed you to bury the explosives and believed it was the only way to get you to ride along with this new plan."

The Stranger splays heat through my chest.

I know.

"I tried to give you the opportunity to make the choice for yourself, not as a strategy board pawn."

Sure. This is a backup gun in case your game with Aunt Tess doesn't work out.

No one is wholly good, but I've definitely seen people go wholly bad. It's safer to assume they'll betray you. He should have realized we know this too.

And maybe Poisonneurs aren't as great at assassinations as they want everyone to believe.

Probably not.

I lift my chin and look hard into his black gold eyes. "I know."

He lifts two eyebrows. "What do you know?"

Aunt Tess likes playing. I don't.

"The Widow changed the plan."

"How do you know this?"

She told me. Like a family.

He's seen the Stranger before. Can he see her now? Flickering, a dark, thirsty flame.

Realization passes through his gaze, fed with the usual vein of fear. "I've heard men whispering your name. That a ghost devil stalks Hannah, burning those who displease her. The descriptions are quite fearsome, red eyes and unrealistically long teeth. But I don't know how they can be true since everyone who sees this *Stranger* dies."

I smile to myself. We've always left one alive to tell the tale.

"I wasn't aware this Shiver allowed you to divinate information hidden from you," he says, "but now I am corrected. Since you admit this, I assume we all reside on the same page?"

The lie comes out weightless as the others I've told. Most of them. "Yes."

He nods to the simple pulse of the word. He overthinks so much, he can't see the obvious. That lying to get your way is so easy.

He wasn't the one who killed Vesta. But seeing him only reminds me of that last night in Winchester. I lay bed every night with the echo of her last breaths in my head. Her blood hitting my face again and again, still warm. I hate that the last words I said to her were about Kane. I should have said anything else. No one else will ever know. But *I* do. And that's all that matters.

"I'm sorry for the doubts I've had about you," he says. "I am pleased all of us are finally aligned with one goal. However, should the moons change your mind again, you should know I care for my family with a depth an orphan like you will never know. Their blood flows in my veins, mine in theirs. So you be sure to tell that Shiver lurking at me from your eyes, do not cross me or there will be consequences... And they will be your last."

You just made yours.

A pale orange shadow flexes across Hannah's smoke sky. Not the moon, not aura lights—it's too early in the Season. The ash is too thick.

It spreads, a twisted beat of light and shadow.

Fire.

"What do you see?" Montoya turns, swears in Cairosh. "This isn't your doing. You've been here."

The Stranger has a guess.

Montoya follows. "Do not get too close."

We should know what it is.

Seven eighty-six.

Knives of flame consume the courage powder still on the Company side of the Slash. Wood cracks inside the heat, strong enough to touch my face from here. It's the brightest light I've seen in so long, pure and pulling like a compass.

I don't let myself get any closer, the flash fire in my bag more sensitive to heat than I am.

Across the grabbing shadows, the Stranger draws my gaze to Joelle, Saraline, scarves over their faces but I recognize their clothes, Saraline's ink. They pull away from the light as a crowd thickens toward it.

"Go back to your room, you'll be safe there." Montoya sprints across the Slash as the clang of one of the fire bells mounted on posts every other row breaks into my skull.

Go ahead, pretend like you care about lives, not saving Hannah's black gold.

I stay to watch something burn.

THIRTY
TESLA

I am woken hideously early in the morning. The constant moon rides low and silver on the blue horizon, still freckled with morning stars. It takes my tired brain a minute to recognize the sound of wood scraping stone.

I ignore the sound a while longer because the bed is warm and sharing this room with Leagan and Navy is actually very cozy, like our compartments in the *Absolution*'s sleeping car. But I'll have to call myself a fool if it's a picker breaking in to kill us, or if a scavenger lizard eats off my toes.

Only the top of Navy's head pokes from under her blankets, but Leagan's side of the bed is cool and empty.

Her bare toes grip the back of a chair and the dressing cabinet as she hangs a string of jarred animal bones from Adelaide and tiny shards of fire quartz between support beams.

I fold my arms against the morning chill. "Can I help you, ma'am?"

"No. I'm just decorating the area."

"Well, I had to make sure you weren't here to rob us. Don't fall."

The tap comes on my headboard once I'm back in my bed. I am not getting up again.

Leagan slips under the covers and folds her legs up next to mine.

"Excuse me, your feet are wretchedly cold."

She worms them deeper into the soft space at the back of my knee.

"Fuck off."

She snickers.

"Have you been awake all night?"

"I don't dream if I sleep during the day. I'll just become nocturnal."

"You can't run from this."

"I know."

"You have to sleep for more than three hours a day."

"I know."

"Do you know?" I comb my finger along the fringe of her copper hair while she picks at the seam of the top blanket, woven by Evangeline with Damascus wool. She keeps her eyes open even as I stroke my thumb up her forehead, the way I used to lull Vesta to sleep when she was little.

"What are you afraid of?" I don't know what it's like to see things and have them become truth. Mother never seemed to fear her gift, only what could come from ignoring it.

"If something happens to Adelaide, I don't want to see it. By the time we got to her, it would be too late."

Not seeing won't save her either. But that's not what Leagan needs to hear. "Grandma didn't always know how soon what she saw might happen. Has the dream changed?"

"Does your *friend* the trapper wear the yellow North Exodus ribbon?"

"Now how did you know about him?" Of course, that wouldn't have stopped Mother's sight, obviously not Leagan's either. "He does."

"I've seen his face."

"And what did you think?"

"Eh." She shrugs. "You can do better. In this dream I'm digging. I keep finding the bones, like I know exactly where they are. The dirt smells like blood. Right before I wake up, I smell something rotting. Almost like sun sulfur but…worse. I never find out what it is."

"What do you think it means?"

"I don't want to say and be wrong."

"Don't want to? Or you don't know?"

"Grandma said bodies in water is an omen of death, but I've read that a bad smell means betrayal."

"You stink of betrayal."

She almost laughs.

"Seems accurate." I brush my thumb across her cheek.

It's probably to do with Montoya. He's got something dirty hidden up that glove of his. Or it could mean Travis...the bastard. It's been a long time since I let him break my heart, but not long enough to forget what it felt like.

Across the valley's pale glow, Montoya's signal lantern flares, a single morning star hovering on the blue hillside.

MONTOYA WAITS IN THE COURTYARD OUTSIDE THE CHURCH, SIGNAL LANTERN now washed away by the full sun. He takes hold of my reins below the bridal and strokes the animal's glossy flank with kind flattery.

"You just couldn't wait to see me could you—"

He turns his gaze from the horse to me, and it's dark. "You lied to me."

"Oh, did I? That's an excellent way to get someone's attention. Accuse me of lying while my two feet are barely familiar with the ground."

"Put simply."

"Spill it, darling."

"The Stranger already spilt. The two of you have been whispering in your letters. You left me under the impression you weren't going to tell her you agreed to preserve Hannah."

Ah, so the Stranger is tired of playing the game. Well, I am not.

"Then you've won, Niall Montoya," I say. "You'll get your chance to hold a favor over your old bosses in Cairo and see your family again. Why piss in the water?"

"This deception feels unnecessary. Naturally I have to question what you're trying to hide behind it." The steel edge on his gaze doesn't let up, it hardens. "All you gained by this was to reveal your wholly duplicitous nature. Why should I believe this new word from your mouth is what's true?"

Because something that comes too easy is something you don't actually have, dear. He has to believe I've exhausted all my tricks and options. He has to see them fail.

"All those words just to ask me if I'm lying?" I wrap my hand above his and through the horse's bridal, but he's doesn't give up the reins. "I've let you keep your secrets, in case you haven't noticed. Like why you always keep that arm covered."

"The glove helps me grip my sword."

"Oh, I bet it does." My laugh skips off him with no visible effect. "The Stranger is a thief. She likes to work alone and things done in secret. You don't order someone like that around—you entice them with a prize and let them chase it. She liked the fact that you didn't know she knew, and she liked choosing when to give you the information. I didn't tell you because your behavior had to be real. Otherwise she'd notice."

"Cunning."

That's why they call me Widow. I finally get the reins from him with a wink. "I know my crew."

He trades me Adelaide's fresh letter. "Perhaps you would become someone in the Yellow City after all."

"You must be tired from riding all night. Go get some rest. I just heard our friend in Lideon was able to acquire the hand car. Your next ride to Hannah will be your last as an Express Rider. You'll get to give the Stranger the good news. I could say she might even start to like you, but that *would* be a lie."

THIRTY-ONE
ADELAIDE

I CROUCH AWAY FROM THE ROPE LANTERNS FAILING TO CUT INTO THE NIGHT, knees locked tight against my cold chest. My heart beats so fast I feel sick from it, the Stranger so strong in my bones, I might rip apart.

It's time.

I knew what this would cost me when I couldn't find the fifth man I rolled dice against on the *Delta Sol* since I've been here. Where he's been hiding.

Old Hannah. It stares back at me. The refinery so close I have to tilt my head back to see the two stacks vomiting the ash that's in our lungs and clothes.

The man I'm going to kill leaves the card den alone, bowler in his hand for the first five steps, takes the same turns he did yesterday. Deeper alleys.

Predictable.

Everything is changed. The laundry where I spent my days with Grandma, gone. The shed where my mother and I slept at night, her body like bone next to me. We didn't touch. Gap-toothed floors and walls replaced with taller, stronger buildings. There's nothing I recognize anymore, except her.

One-forty.

He steps through the brothel's curtain door, pink light spewing around him, black silhouette.

My mother's ghost runs down the back of my neck, stick fingers.

I open my mouth to breathe air I'm too tight for. Shit and sour leather. My jaw aches as I force it to unstick behind the bone mask.

I've been here almost a full Season, *Solace* and Moon. I'm tired of running from this. Of being so afraid of her.

I peel back the scab I've let grow over my mind for years and plunge myself face down in her memory. Sunlight swallows me whole. Her rough hands, too cold on my cheeks for the Season. Her eyes, rose-gold. She does look like me.

Pink light spills on the alley again, thinned out blood. He takes off down the row, whistling. I rise, fluid. He thinks he's going home to sleep now.

Forever.

The first step jolts my numb legs. Head down, eyes up, and give myself to the shadows.

We may share a face, but my mother and I are not the same.

Ninety-seven.

He climbs the exposed staircase to the boardinghouse's second level. Across the covered balcony, his room the third door.

The lock bends like grass under my picks.

Darker.

An iron pig stove for burning cold Ven quartz loafs in the corner, the first I've seen outside Rafe's compound and the Hannah Grand Hotel. He squats in front of the open grate, scraping at the leftover shards.

Curtains cross the two windows facing the street behind him. There's nothing reflective in front of him that he'll catch me in. The Stranger already looked.

He draws fresh crystal from the fuel box, rubs it off the striking stone. Blue, like Raleigh's eyes.

The breath I take feels clean.

His name is Jacoby. The one the Stranger pinned as most likely to slit my throat on the road here. The first to get his hands on me.

"She's no Shadow Warrior." He held my arms so they could beat me into submission. *"Finish up, she'll talk."*

There's no purpose in submission when the next stop is death. It won't save you. You might as well fight back, reach it faster.

The Stranger rides the line of my eyes. Blackness softer than the Rim's red dust, harder than the shadows clinging to this room. Storm copper. I taste it. The grip of the gun Leagan sent me conceals a punch knife. Saw-backed, sharp as a mountain peak.

He's not much bigger than I am. Aunt Tess says small men have something to prove. He did. That I was just a piece of meat, but so is he. A waste of water.

Five.

I grab his forehead, his skull and shoulders held against my front.

Blood fizzes on quartz, spewing into the cold fire.

A deal is a deal. Now pay.

His nails rake my arms, spine rearing. I stab the punch knife into his chest, hold on like a rail spike as his weight knocks me back on my ass. He gets one hand hooked into my mask. The dry bones snap, but the scarf I wired them to doesn't.

Weakness is more complicated than I used to believe. My mother and I are different more than we are similar. I have a family, a life outside Hannah, a future worth taking. She had nothing. Maybe her choice to leave me wasn't because she didn't care. She had no control over her life, so she took back what little she could and chose how she would die.

All my life I've been terrified of becoming her. I never considered maybe she was afraid of the same thing, that she gave me the only chance she could to avoid her end.

Moira Revere, and the Stranger.

His body releases gas as I let go, red fingerprints seared into his forehead by my salt glove.

What would I have become if I'd been left here with my mother? I'd have none of the things that I love. Might be everything that I hate.

Blood means nothing, Montoya. Loyalty is what makes a family. And I'd choose mine any day of the Season.

Red pulses through the hair of Jacoby's neck beard. Even though I know which one of them most likely has my crossgun, I look for it anyway.

Nine.

There were tears in my mother's rose-gold eyes the last time she looked at me, spoke my name with gray, stained lips. I don't think they were a lie. *"Goodbye, my Adelaide, my silent little fox. Be ferocious."*

She didn't choose me like I wanted. But she did want me to survive.

"Sol sana, my Moira. You deserve her. She deserves you."

I grind fresh morning salt into the glove and press down hard across Jacoby's mouth. When the men who eventually come looking find him, they'll know a fox did this.

Vengeance, the name my sister called me.

Five dead.

Only one more. The worst one.

THIRTY-TWO
ADELAIDE

THE FLYSCREEN AND BACK DOOR OF THE BATHHOUSE DANGLE ON THEIR HINGES, privacy sheets ripped off the rods, velvet and lace from Thadie's room drowning in the tubs. I freeze at the threshold, wood sharp and pale around the lock that snapped as it was kicked in.

"I was right." Joelle stops sweeping to tilt her broom vindictively at Solstice. The Cairosh tint on her vowels comes out stronger than usual. "I want you to admit that."

Lantern glass and loose objects snap under each step. Thadie's brass hairpins, wood splinters, ruined books, salt crystals, coating the floor like dust after a storm.

"Hey." Saraline rises off her heels, a bucket of fractured glass collected next to her. "You're just in time. We decided to redecorate."

Storms can wreak this kind of carnage if your shutters aren't tight, but we didn't have one last night.

"Where's Thadie?" I didn't expect my chest to get a little tighter not seeing her first, but it does.

"She's fine," Solstice says, disembodied by her deep hood. "She went outside to calm down. We had visitors."

"She has eyes." Joelle turns her back to sweep behind the counter. "We need to take care of this quick."

Solstice carries her full bucket toward the back door. "I'm not having this discussion."

"He *saw* you, Soli."

"That doesn't mean anything will happen. They ran when they saw me."

"Yes, they ran because of this." Joelle lifts the shotgun leaned against the support post, then looks to me. "You remember our competition in the powder market? Let's just say we, Salty and I, paid them a house call."

You obviously weren't careful enough.

I crouch to pick the glass from the wood shards like Saraline. It can be sold and reformed. And to see what else I find.

Under the tangle of mattress and sheets dumped over the banister, Thadie's moon diviner and star map lie hidden. Two little rabbits under a bush. Soft from fractured pipe water, but the ink is holding.

Redweed spikes the air as Joelle lights up.

"Nobody got hurt." Solstice returns, bucket empty. "It could be worse."

Joelle laughs like a hungry dog. "It could always be worse. Just wait, the rumors will get around now that they've seen who's making our product. We'll see how fast they turn then."

A cascade of holes in the wall allows rust-stained sunlight to seep in. It catches on Solstice's eyes, a spark in the shadows as she turns. "They know about Adelaide, and here she is."

"And none of them ever go out of their way to harass you, do they, Stranger?" Joelle asks. "I'm sure they make you wear that muzzle for a perfectly legitimate reason. Not to remind you what they think you are."

It's not how you win a fight that matters, it's that you win. The muzzle serves me now, not Rafe.

"Maybe I'm just a coward for hiding all these years," Solstice says. "Our mothers would be ashamed of me for wearing their shadows in fear."

"Your mothers would have praised your survival," Joelle says. "If they don't, they can reckon with me. You'd put your heart out for anyone, and I'd fight anyone who disrespects you."

"I already know." She takes hold of Joelle's face, hands shaking. "You don't have to prove something to me. I love you. To the ends of this world. Maybe we can't live in a better one, but we'll never know unless we try."

It sounds like exactly something Aunt Tess and Grandma would say. So far, we've all been wrong.

Joelle's head becomes a blur of redweed smoke as she blows. It's a sigh everyone's familiar with at some point. Defeat, anger. Fear. "Letting them fuck you does nothing either."

"No man gets to do that with me."

"Don't try to get funny right now. You can't win against a mob gone blind and stupid—you know this better than most. We earned the life we have here, and I'm putting these snakes in a hole for good."

"Please don't do this. You'll only make this worse."

She has no idea that's exactly what we're going to do when the rest of my family shows up.

Thirty-one.

Thadie sits by the barrel growing herbs out front. Elbows to her knees, braiding a strand of wilted mint into a ring. "I thought I heard your voice." She laughs a little. "It's very distinct now that I know it exists."

"These are yours."

She gasps, making a basket of her arms and hands for the moon diviner and wet star map. "Where was it? How did you find it so fast?"

"I'm good at looking for things."

"You're very sweet. Not in the regular sort of way, your own way." She turns my palm over. "Here. Your reward."

The mint ring, weightless in my hand. Green.

"You'll be happy again someday. There are good things in your next moons," she says. "I can feel it."

The shudder moves through me. But it's not safe to acknowledge that longing here.

A thorny lizard pokes out of the gap below the porch. I try to place the ring on its head before it hurries off—almost, but miss.

Thadie laughs. "Aw, he almost had a little crown."

Sudden, charged needles stab into my skin. The Stranger, wary of watching eyes.

Copper emerges from the air market hive. Gaze dark as black gold, smirk on her mouth twisted as the colors in it as she waves to me. She turns the other way when I stand.

"Who is that?"

"A bitch."

I wish Copper didn't see me here, and I should leave before she gets too curious.

MADAM CHARLENE'S HOUSE CREAKS EVERY TIME A DOOR OPENS, ESPECIALLY the front, walls brittle as anything that echoes off them.

"Oh." Copper's voice stalls. I close the book Thadie borrowed me on one finger, listen. "What do you want?"

"Is Adelaide here?"

Solstice.

"She never has visitors. Who are you?"

"Just a friend."

Copper laughs. "Yeah, that's likely." The stairs shake as they come up. "You can take your coat off. Why don't you?"

"I'm fine, thank you."

"Suit yourself. As long as you know there's no business done in the house. This is a safe place." My door rattles as Copper wrenches the handle, finds it locked, and kicks it. "Sweet Jezebel, fox, locking your door *again*. What do you think is going to happen?"

This.

Three.

I use my body as a wedge to keep her from throwing the door completely open the second I turn the pick. It's a struggle. She's bigger than I am. "What?"

"Why don't you pull that stick out of your ass already. There's someone here to see you."

Solstice palms her a dropper vial of dark oil. The pressure on the door releases. "For your beauty and wellness. I was never here."

"If you say so." Copper radiates a smirk, slashing air and part of the wall with her skirt overlay as she goes.

I lock the door behind Solstice, lean against it, book still in my hand.

Why are you here?

This isn't a safe place for either of us. Copper has big ears and a giant mouth. She wants me to think she went away, but she stopped on the eighth stair.

"Thadie told me where you lived." Solstice walks the three steps across my room, peels back her hood. Her voice barely breaks beyond a whisper. At least I don't have to tell her that, even if she was foolish enough to come here. Does Joelle know? Probably not.

"I'm obviously disturbing your evening, so I'll make this quick. We're sorry about the way we might have appeared hostile toward you earlier. That was misdirected frustration."

"Joelle sent you to apologize, or was this your idea?" Say it yourself or don't bother. This doesn't count.

"She thought you'd listen to me."

Wrong.

"Joelle has big feelings and can't hide them. I'll likely be playing her peacemaker until the day I die."

But you don't mind, you love her.

"She's like you in many ways," she says. "Suspicious from the start, slow to trust. A hard upbringing will do that to you. However, I have found those who don't give out their loyalty so easily are the ones who stick around the longest once they do."

I've never given my loyalty to anyone but my family and Raleigh. Kane was the closest I've let someone get outside them, and there was still something for me to gain from it. I'm not sure it counts.

"Do you know the origin of your name?" Solstice asks.

"Yes."

"I thought so. You have an air of acceptance around yourself. I admire your independence, you're not hiding who you are. I wish I had your courage, but it wouldn't serve our business, and it might put Joelle and Saraline in danger."

I wasn't raised with shame or to apologize for things that aren't my fault. But there are still days I avoid the eyes too.

"I hope to prove that I am worthy of your loyalty."

I nod. I'd be willing to give her a chance, but not Joelle, not their powder business. The Stranger's will to survive and move on is too strong. Always there, like a heartbeat. If I pull this trigger and regret it later, then that's the way it is.

"Who do you owe here?" she asks.

"They owe me."

"I assumed you were indentured in some way."

You could say that. But you can always claim a debt the other way around.

Montoya will be here any day. Hopefully, this time he'll have word that

Raleigh has transportation ready, and how many days behind him Aunt Tess and my sisters are.

"Do you have any widow snake venom at the shop?" I ask.

"Ah." Solstice is careful with her smile. "I'm afraid not... Who is the unlucky bastard?"

"The man who brought me here."

The one who stole my crossgun. Who went through my bag and found the black gold I brought from Eden, reeking of strawberry candy. The one who didn't listen to the others and kill me when he had the chance.

Now his friends are dead.

I don't know if those men were ever his friends, but he's still Rafe's right hand.

Dathan Kasey.

"Give me a little time," Solstice says. "I'll see what I can do."

I may not have that, but she doesn't need to know.

"After you collect what he owes you, I assume you'll be going back to your family..." Her center brow twists, and she reaches for my face, unsteady. "May I?"

This time I let her.

My mother's ghost doesn't cut so deep today. It reminds me of Grandma.

"You're the last Tov I might ever see." She swallows tears that I don't see, only feel them tremble in her fingertips. "That may not mean much to you because you're young, but it breaks my heart."

It doesn't.

Eventually all of us will be gone. And I feel...nothing. But I cup her face with my hands anyway. For her.

Skin, dusty warm.

One tear slips as Solstice's eyes flutter shut. Down her chin, fast as memory, only to shatter on her shirt like glass. For a breath, the Stranger doesn't move either. Something does settle then, only in me. The last bone of what I could have been, laid to rest next to my mother's unmarked grave.

"*Sol...*" She breathes. "Will you tell Thadie—or Saraline—goodbye before you go?"

No. It wouldn't be safe.

Solstice wipes the last shimmer off her cheek. "Then if our paths never cross, may our mother's courage protect you and your future children if your blasphemous name doesn't, Adelaide Revere, *sos rohvonen*."

Adelaide Revere, daughter of no one.

THIRTY-THREE
TESLA

THE PROTECTIVE APRON HANGS TO MY KNEES, CROSSES BOTH SIDES OF MY BODY and buttons up my throat. Under her blackout goggles, Navy looks like she's been swallowed by hers.

Morning salt crystals grow up their glass chimneys, Navy's notes tacked to the walls behind them in columns, scavenged glass instruments lined in rows because Leagan's been helping with the project.

Their prize: a surgeon's glass ordered fresh from Jezebel with a complete set of magnification lenses. Their original one, lost with the *Absolution*, was scavenged and only had half. I look at a yellow grub sleeping inside the dish beneath the glass, made large as my hand by the lens. A hole breathes in its ribbed belly, white projections like roots sprouting through the black rot. It looks like a second mouth.

Leagan sets another thin dish to the center of the space between us and shutters the lamp attached to the surgeon's glass. Dark liquid forms a coin on the glass. Blood, Vesta's. In the absence of the light held out by Damascus's stone walls and covered windows, it shines black like Vesta's hair and the hole in my heart where she still resides, the dark space between stars.

"Ready?" Navy passes a vial of milky liquid over the dish.

Fragile light rises from motes in the fluid. The closer she brings the tube, the harder the newborn bud glow works to expand, solidifying into something real.

"Fucking Jezebel." My breath hits my respirator and comes back as I breathe out. "You did it."

Farce, she's brilliant. Liza would be so proud.

I am glad Vesta didn't have to suffer the long, living decomposition of the pestilence like the worm under the glass. But the space she occupies in my mind is still raw. I don't believe it will ever be easy for me to think about her death, but at least this is a chance for her loss to mean something, the way she meant everything.

"Yes." Navy's sigh is relief. "The incident Adelaide wrote us about, the picker killing himself in Hannah, it fits my hotspot theory. If the pestilence was spreading, she would have seen more of them by now. He must have gotten contaminated somewhere else, then traveled to Hannah."

"Makes sense to me. Now, we take the night off. What do you want to do?"

"I still have a lot of work. It's not perfect yet."

"But it is the best that's been made so far. Bask in your achievement, Rook, you made this happen."

"All I did was help pour," Leagan says.

"Say it."

"Okay…" A flush fills Navy's voice. "Yes, I am an alkaline scientist."

"Ladies, we just became more powerful than Von Kanes, Hannah, and Green combined." I let that sink into my chest a moment. Fool's gold, it feels good.

"I did it so all of you would be safe," Navy says. "I wasn't letting you go back out there otherwise."

"And thanks to you, we now hold the railroad expansion by the balls."

"I'd prefer to hold them by the hand, or the sleeve or something," Navy says.

With this divining tool to read contamination by the pestilence, we can bargain with anyone, control where the work crews go or don't, the price of safety set by us.

"As they say, the one who controls the water holds God's hand to man."

They can't erase us if we cut so deep into the Rim's history, we find blood.

THIRTY-FOUR
ADELAIDE

THE WIND BLOWS ASH INTO MY EYES, BUT IT MASKS THE SCRAPE OF MY BODY AS I slide under The Pinings's foundation stilts, any vibrations on wood that might be felt inside.

The ground slopes hard, ending in stone burrowed into the earth that you don't see standing up outside. I was right. Joelle and Solstice's courage powder kitchen is down there.

From my bag I draw the last demo stick, bound up in cloth to cushion its greasy smell.

Am I wrong?

The doubt clashes against the wax weight in my hand, an unexpected visitor. Which I hate. Right behind it, the Stranger.

Survive. Any cost.

The promise I made Vesta. Myself.

Make them sorry.

Even if it wasn't Joelle and Solstice who did the dealing back then, this still cooked the powder that poisoned my mother. It's one more thing I don't need around.

I set the stick to the dirt at the base of stone, grind in.

As long as Hannah exists, the ghost of my mother is forced to remain alive here too. Without a place to haunt, she becomes nothing. Free.

Something creeps against my temple. A spider, cobweb, or my own hair.

No. The Stranger flashes black as I flinch away. *They'll hear you.*

If we destroy Hannah, am I doing the same thing to Thadie and Solstice that Green did to us? Do they really deserve it?

The Stranger narrows around me at the thought, hard and fast, a punch to the stomach. Montoya can't be right about this. I'll be sick.

He isn't.

I force the space into my chest for a breath. One day I'll snap from being stretched too far in two directions.

I dig my heels in and drag myself back, leave the demo stick, but no fuse. If it detonates when the rest of Hannah goes, fine. If it doesn't, then the powder still wasn't ever meant to burn.

It's okay to not have this choice on me.

The feeling of dirt crawling down the back of my shirt lingers even after I sit up.

The hazard lantern punctures the watchtower up the hill by the main shaft elevator. Yellow. The Stranger hardens around me.

I rise halfway off my heels.

Three flashes. Pause. Then the pattern continues. No bell alarm, no spreading light. Not another fire, just a warning. Maybe poison earth gas. Maybe a collapse.

Or my explosives were found on the hill above the mine yard.

I stow my last vial of flash fire up in the rafters of the floorboards. It can't be found on me. I will be ready, whatever Montoya brings with him.

I LET THE STRANGER CHOOSE HIM.

She settles around the shoulders of a miner leaving a gambler's den alone, an embrace made of smoke. Cotton patches protect his knees and elbows, worn through several layers deep, a permanent crease circling his face where his respirator digs in every day while he does the same.

Nineteen.

The blade tip glides through flesh, the poison I stole from Montoya oiling its bite as we cross paths. He feels air, me glance past him, but I doubt he felt it cut.

I press into the shadows. He drops to his knees in the mouth of the next row, blood spilling down fingers from the top of his hand. He clutches his left arm, not the cut.

The mine's warning light still flashes yellow. Up there against the dust.

The Stranger beats along with my heart. He flinches, buckles forward, retching black bubbles from his nose and mouth at the same time. He curls into himself. I wait until I'm sure.

Ten.

Gold standards, he must have won his card game.

Bloody bile pools along pits in the dirt. All over his beard, spilling into his ear.

I stuff an empty bottle of clear pine between his neck and shoulder, nothing left but vapor.

From my inside pocket I draw the leather envelope branded with the *Hannah Mining* seal, shove it into the band of his pants.

Ready.

THIRTY-FIVE
ADELAIDE

Sitting on the flat roof of the bakery watching the Slash gate doesn't make time go by faster. It only makes me more anxious.

I hang my spoon chime at the head of the alley, a mouth funneling to the broken bathhouse. I might as well sell the last of my stolen knives, salt, and butter. It gives me something to do, focus and not pace, the Stranger wound tight as a spool of wire.

Wooden soap crates tip across each other, barrel of used towels collecting ash while they wait for Saraline or Joelle to boil them. I stack three crates and sit against the bathhouse wall to wait for someone to come buy.

The wind cuts down the alley, rattling chimes up and down the Slash. So many of them now.

Against the gnarled sky, thicker midnight smoke rises to the south. Closer. The train I saw smudge the sky earlier is still coming. Crystal barons, not my family.

A train came the day we left Hannah the first time. Aunt Tess was on it. So was Rafe. Which is why we couldn't use the same plan twice.

The slap of a loose holster draws the Stranger, cigarette-lipped mutters and boots creaking with each step. Something about them she doesn't like.

I work my glove on, release the punch knife, and put the rest of the revolver away in the band of my skirt. Easy reach.

I'm the colors of Hannah. Gray ash and dirty white like the wall behind me, pale fox eyes above the black scarf covering my muzzled face and head.

Two, three…they file out of the gap between buildings. Foremen. One in the long, gray science coat of the refinery bosses, others the blue coveralls of the mines. Miners in full respirators with a shovel. I've united enemies.

Six of them.

"Ain't that something," one sings, whistling low. "Providence, God of Mercy. Just like the newspaper drawings."

They flare away from each other, come at me from opposing angles. The only ways out of here are through blood or the bathhouse door behind the sheet.

Don't move, the Stranger says. *Wait.*

"Use caution." The refinery boss stops well out of my reach. His too. "It looks real to me."

It. As if stripping me of human qualities makes me less dangerous. People are the worst thing there is.

The man he looked to nods. Balding, fingernails also too clean and even to be a miner. "We're told you deal in certain items that can be difficult to come by, fox."

They're not here to buy anything from me.

A knife bounces off the pitted dirt as he tosses. Green wood handle, I sold it to another white bodice five cycles back.

"We're claiming your portion of the powder market today, fox."

They think I'm who they saw the other day. Unfortunate, for them. I'm not Solstice.

Something shatters inside the bathhouse, the wall at my back quivering. One of the last lanterns that wasn't already broken. Behind it a failed scream.

Wait.

Thadie and Saraline will have to fend for themselves.

One of the miners adjusts his grip on the shovel, checks me with a slow grin. He sees my skirt, my hips with no holster, gray quartz eyes. The grin stays easy. He doesn't see the Stranger, the poisonous punch knife locked in my right hand, or the gun in my backband.

I'll use the knife as long as possible. Gunshots draw attention here.

The flare of cheap pipe tobacco follows a quartz flint to lips.

"Step down from there." The hairless refiner beckons to me. "*Stranger…* You owe me a drink, boss. It is a female."

"Ghosts don't have gender."

"We can check." The mine foreman draws a brass pipe from his belt, not the pistol. "Fool's gold, the fucking stories they're telling about you. You're a ghost. You're a devil. Your breath is poison…so are your parts."

The Stranger lets him come in.

I've done this kind of reverse robbery a hundred times, but I always have Leagan or Vesta with me. Alone, it's going to get messy.

"One of my best crewmen was found dead in his room by no cause other than the unnatural. He was otherwise healthy, cut to death with a handprint burned into his face, the door still locked from the inside. Something evil slipped in through the cracks like dirt. I'm not so sure what to believe anymore." He sets the pipe against my knee. "But what I do know for certain, you're about to be the sorriest piece of ass in hell today."

The Stranger explodes. I throw my leg over the pipe, trapping it as he pulls me and the crates over. The knife point slips across his knuckles, but the pipe stays in his hand. It has a voice as he swings.

My shoulder absorbs the full blow. A loose bucket catches on my leg as I stagger into the weeds tangling the alley's other side, arm numb. Only my fingers threaded around the bar-grip of the punch knife kept it in my hand.

"No need to be afraid, boys." He chuckles, choking up on his grip as I circle out of his way. "That arm was real as mine, and I bet you I can make her scream when I snap it."

He misses my head, but not the swipe to my upper leg coming back across. He grabs as I cross behind him again, keep distance between me and that pipe. I lunge. The blind swing grazes the elbow I throw up to protect my head, and my knife plunges all the way up into his armpit.

Already dead.

I shove with my glove hand, blade ripping through his shirt on the way out. An instant red flood down his side like a cracked water barrel. You can thank Leagan and her anatomy books for me knowing the location of that artery.

A gasp breaks free of the foreman. The pipe drops so he can clutch his arm instead, blood spitting across the ground every time his heart pumps. Legs buckle, fall.

The revolver is an extension of my arm as I round on the next ones, shoot three times. Leagan's touch etched down the barrel. *Reliable.* Gunpowder. I breathe deep. *Farce,* it's been a long time.

The others' wind-chapped lips go still on a collective breath.

Now run.

There are still two ways out of this corner. The alley that has three enemies standing in front of it. The door to my left that leads into the bathhouse, whatever is going on in there that I can't see.

Seven—

The shovel catches the front of my shin from behind, impact splitting through my bone as I fall. My vision sears to endless black. Weight on top of me, hands ripping into my clothes, hair. The gun breaks out of my grasp. I plant my gloved hand directly on his face. He screams, both hands clamped over the salt burn, and I punch with the knife.

The holes that I put in him weep. Red like the sun lurks in the smoke sky. Red as the Season Moon out there somewhere.

My back slams into the wall, a forearm up under my chin, reeking mine-belly dust. It presses the air out of my throat, acidic tears seeping from my eyes.

The visceral urge to curl inward pulls me down as they spread my arms. The Stranger rolls like a blast of wind, but I'm not physically strong enough to break their grip.

"Don't make this too easy now, milk bastard. You have a reputation. They paid us in powder to put an end to you." He peels up my little finger. A bright red snap flares through my hand, but I hold onto the knife. "I'll keep going as long as you do." He grabs at my widow finger next. "A bone for every man you killed."

The other hefts the shovel, lays the point to my throat. "Move your arm."

"That's too fast. Take her arms and legs off first. Let her bleed."

My head throbs deep black. Only a slipping telescope of sight remains —beyond that, only the Stranger, the dark wind she's made of.

The door into the bathhouse creaks as it gives in.

I know a Jezebel bodyguard when I see one. They all have an oiled danger, like a factory-fresh gun. There are two, dressed in solid black, shoving another refinery man out ahead of them, scratches on his face. Saraline steps out behind them. Hand held to her throat, tears mixed with blood dripping off her chin, pink.

"What's going on out here?" He wears a long, black duster, green-tinted lenses, a blade-tipped nightstick in his stacked belts. The other carries the same weapon under his arm, both fists wrapped in knuckle dusters. Street-fighting weapons, common in Jezebel I've heard. I prefer a gun. But they have those too. Three each. Crystal barons can afford the pistol tax.

"I said, what's going on here?"

Blood runs over my lip, itching. Silence bleeds over all of us.

"Fine shit." He steps over a dead arm, disgust in his mouth. "We had arranged to deal with this young lady, only to find you pickers with your hands up in her pockets. I can only assume you have your own offer for me."

The refiner shows off a handful of Saraline's wax packets. "We have other things to worry about so I'll gladly unload this cheap. One thousand five, copper standard."

The other Jezebel guard touches the copper ring piercing his ear. "I believe the word you just used was cheap." Eos accent.

"That is cheap."

"Quite a racket. Prices just went up today, didn't they? There's Jezebel money in town. All you snakes can smell it, can't you?"

"We don't make the rules. That's just the way it is."

The Eosin bodyguard crosses his arms around his nightstick. "Did I hear a gun go off a minute ago?" He taps his counterpart's arm. "Let's make a complaint at the hotel."

"He was a foreman of the first shift, he was allowed a weapon." The refiner stoops to collect my revolver from between the bodies. "The shady bitch fired the gun."

"You're nothing but a fucking thief." Saraline spits at him. "You'll be sorry."

"Stay over there, snake," the refiner snaps. "You're driving up the value on our sludge with your chemical shit."

"Have you tried it? It's a dream you won't want to wake up from."

"I have pickers trying to steal from the waste pit now."

"Do you think I'm stupid?" Saraline sneers. "I know who you are.

You're picking from your own waste pit to supply your chemicals, and that's why your product is third-shift shit."

"I should beat you when we finish with the milk-bastard."

The Stranger coils over him, a whisper, remembered. The hands holding my arms back slacken a little.

"Listen," the bodyguard says, "we didn't come down here to pay copper to sludge. Give us a better deal, or we'll let the appropriate parties know what you've done to Miss Salty. Her boss is in good standing with many of the barons, and their chemical services in high demand. You'd be wise not to anger them."

"One thousand, *gold* standard," the refiner says. "Cheap enough?"

I lunge against the one holding me, poison knife sliding through shoulder meat.

He hits me so hard I go blank.

Detail comes back, broken into slices.

The gray dirt is very close to my face. It smells like rust.

Dark.

The bodyguard handles a roll of standards.

Dark.

"Walk back the way you came in and wait ten minutes. I'll throw you whatever's left of the fox, no charge. She'll stay warm enough for about an hour."

Not this time.

"You have a sickness," the Eosin bodyguard scoffs. "My God. We've clearly interrupted something, and I do not care to know what. Just the powder will do enough damage."

I get my arms under me.

A boot hits me in the stomach. Steel toes.

"You can't kill her. She's Company property," Saraline says.

"She's been murdering Company property. The boss'll thank us for getting rid of this troublemaker and hang you when we tell him who committed the arson at our still."

A jar of dirt shatters against the ground behind him.

"The Stranger will suck the soul out of your body like a river clam," Thadie yells from her window upstairs. "You think she needs that body? A ghost can't die."

Someone grabs the band of my skirt.

Go for the throat.

Like wind, I slash him. Saraline grabs the shovel as he drops it, clutches the shaft in front of her, even though she has a pistol in her holster.

The bodyguard drives the blunt end of his nightstick into the refiner's gut. Overhead, down, air whistling from the cut.

"You don't steal from someone who has friends in higher places than you." He polishes off any scalp clinging to his nightstick on the back of the refiner's shirt, then takes a sniff of the powder packet.

The one from Eos picks the rolled standards back out of the man's loose hand, passes them to Saraline. "You should take better care from now on, Miss Salty."

I find my revolver in the mess of limbs.

"Hold it." He levels the nightstick at me, blade out. "That does belong to you, fox?"

"She works for me," Thadie says from the bathhouse doorway, cold as Ven quartz. "Like you work for your baron, and he pays your pistol tax."

He glances across the corpses I made. "I can see why you made that choice...*Sol*, Salty. Our boss appreciates you."

"Likewise." Saraline stabs the shovel tip into the dirt, finally wipes the blood off her chin. "Sorry about all this. Come again."

Now my leg hurts. My ribs, my shoulder, my head. The muzzle was ripped off my face somewhere in the middle of that. Fuck it.

"That was way too close." Thadie's breath floods my neck through the scarf. The first hug she's ever given me. "How bad did they hurt you?"

I don't want to know. "I'm still alive." That's what matters.

I can tell she doesn't buy it. She gives me her handkerchief for my bloody nose. The Stranger strays to the gun sitting cozy in Saraline's ribcage holster.

She sees where my gaze is, lays a hand over the end of the grip.

"I have to tell you the truth." The truth shakes in her. "This gun, I've never actually fired it. It's more of a...deterrent, you know?"

Like my muzzle.

"I would have used it if I had to. I wouldn't have just stood there and let them kill you. Don't judge me, lady outlaw."

I believe she means that. Would it have actually happened? Fear twists off your shell, strips you down to what you really are.

"There are other ways to get what you want," I say, and Thadie nods with me. Those Jezebel bodyguards knew who she was and did what she said without bartering. "My sister was like you. She knew how to get her way just by talking to people. They always liked her."

"You're charming in your own way," Saraline says. "Stabbing everyone the first chance you get."

"We made a good team." Vesta and I. The words leave me behind and empty.

"We have to warn Soli and Joelle." She pulls at Thadie. "Come on."

"You don't have to come with me, Stranger," Thadie says.

It feels like I should.

THEY PROWL THE STREET OUTSIDE THE TEA HOUSE. BLACK SHAPES TWISTED BY lanterns, wild dogs after dark. Piss taints the air. They laugh while taking turns aiming at the steps, the entrails of snakes slick on the wood. Cigarettes shine bright on lips, but they don't dare set the place on fire. Technically, that's still a hanging crime.

The Stranger finds the faint rust line of real dirt torn through the ash where something was dragged.

I hold back.

Someone, dragged.

A man in a long chemical smock like Navy wears slits the rope attached to a horse, a body on the other end of it. Joelle, bloody as sunset.

Dead.

"No!" Saraline shrieks. "You fucking bastards!"

I catch her shirt, lose it a second later.

"Don't!" Thadie hisses, empty air in her grasp as well.

Saraline trips trying to correct her own momentum. Too late. They turn.

"Run. Not the bathhouse." I push Thadie back the way we came. Somewhere else they don't associate with Solstice and Joelle's business. She'll have to figure that out. She's smart enough.

Wind slashes through chimes, Saraline swatting a set out of her way, tangling the strings. The air is too hard on my bruised ribs, each step a pulse in my broken finger.

We break through the curtains cloaking the alley.

Thirty-three.

"Go around!" one of them yells. "I saw the fox."

"She was down in the cellar. *Farce.*" Saraline catches the sob in her teeth, chokes it back down her throat. "Solstice, I mean."

"She's good at hiding," Thadie murmurs to her. "I bet she got away."

"Probably," I say, since they're still hunting me. "They think she and I are the same person."

Fools.

"I'm going to the Company marshal," Saraline says. "They owe me a few favors."

They're less likely to do her those favors if I'm there.

I wrap my grip around the punch knife again, *Reliable* the revolver in my second hand, back to the wall.

"You're staying here?" Thadie asks.

I can only nod to her, my bruised side stabbing with every breath. Go with Saraline.

She smiles like death, bones only. "Be careful. You don't die today."

Not today.

Not here.

They slip beyond gray laundry and shadows. The Stranger fills up more dark space in my body than seconds ago, but I am here too.

The boots send echoes tumbling the wrong way up the close walls. This is why I don't do favors. Why the Stranger knew I shouldn't get involved in this powder business. I've sunk so deep in this shit that isn't even mine, it's a wonder I can breathe.

Wait...twenty-one...twenty-four. His stride is longer than mine.

Shoot.

He never even saw me.

The stick captures my neck from behind. He drags me back three steps, pinned against his body. "Looks like the ones we sent for you missed."

The pressure hurts so fast, bleeds out my eyes. The knife falls from my hand, cold stone, point down.

It doesn't last long, the Stranger's black fills me up to the brim, loose from my body in the void. I grab the revolver off his left hip. He doesn't notice until I squeeze the trigger and the bullet goes through his foot.

My palms and knees skin in dust. My throat peels open, black dissolving in a cough that burns my lungs.

A different hammer clicks. "Stop."

Montoya.

"Just stop." He holds his revolver at the man's temple. "Let her go."

My legs shake as I rise.

"She yours?"

"Don't concern yourself with her." Montoya holsters his gun. The hooked tongue of a blade knife pokes from under his gloved thumb. I'm sure the refiner doesn't see it like I do. "Move along."

"This is war. We'll make an example of you all." The dealer crosses his torso to Providence like Aunt Tess does after she kills. "Give me the gun, milk-bastard, before you hurt yourself."

I break open the cylinder, dump the ten rounds into my hand, and toss the empty weapon down the street for him to chase, a dog after a scrap of food. He said the gun.

Montoya steps in behind his limp gait, feeding the hook blade into the man's back. "Sleep now, friend."

Twenty-one.

He turns back. "Let's go."

Not yet. I've been waiting for you all week. You can wait for me to loot their dead pockets. My swollen finger tries to get in the way, but I have practiced this so many times it's still easy. Two rolls of gold standards, a copper ring.

"You should be more careful," he says. "Things are getting tense around here."

My lip is bleeding, not yours.

"We need to get out of sight."

I step behind the motheaten curtain of an outhouse just to see if he'll follow me in there.

The smell is too bad.

Eight.

The next corner has a chicken shed that's unlocked. The hens cluck, disgusted by our intrusion. I would be.

"Look at me." He tries to grab my face, false concern. "You'll be all right?"

Yes, I will.

And you will too, as long as you don't touch me.

For now.

"That will have to be reset." Montoya takes hold of my hand, my little finger sticking out like an elbow. "Will you allow me?"

I nod, look at the hay and shit packed into the floor.

"Breathe in."

A single, involuntary gasp leaves me, sharp as the vibration that shot up my arm when it broke.

He finishes the rip started in the hem of my skirt and uses the cotton strip to bind my little finger to its neighbor. "You're a tough girl."

I've had worse. Than he knows or ever will.

My arm aches bone-deep. Already black from the shoulder down, fingerprints purple on my forearms. Just reloading the punch knife into *Reliable* and tucking it in my waistband makes me heavy.

I'm going to steal some pain tablets from someone in Charlene's house, go back to my room and be alone.

"The news is good." Montoya checks the sky through the gapped slats. "You could use that. The Widow's snare is set. I leave again tonight if you're ready, then we'll be back with the new moon and all will be well."

Fourteen days. I can make it.

"Try to avoid getting cornered like that again. It would be a shame to get yourself killed when you're so close. Let's get you back to your room."

"I can go by myself."

"As you like." He touches his forehead, lips. "*Sol sana, sos Secuundas.*"

Good luck, daughter of Shadows.

I take a full breath, test the pain in my ribs, and let myself be heavy against the soot-coated wall for a moment. I sink lower, rest my pounding head on my bruised knees.

The Stranger jars against my skin.

Get up.

For that flicker I did doubt myself. Wonder if burning Hannah was the wrong thing to do.

It's not.

THE NARROW WALLS OF CHARLENE'S HOUSE OFFER BRITTLE SAFETY. I FORCE OUT the breath I'm carrying and prepare for the pain that's coming as I inhale another.

Five.

Leather and sweat. Not mine.

The Stranger flares, the sick yellow of the bastard quartz lamps turning black. A silhouette detaches from the stairs, Company gun. *Farce.*

"In the kitchen," he says.

It's too late to run. This is my mistake, letting my guard down now because nothing has followed me in here yet.

Thirteen.

Kasey sits at the three-leaf table, breathing over the cup of tea in front of him. Rafe's right hand, the last thing I'm going to kill before I go.

Another one stands over Madam Charlene, hand on her shoulder to keep her there.

"The fox does have a presence, doesn't she?" Kasey raises himself with a sigh. "Something not quite alive, but not really dead yet."

I stare him through the eyes.

"It's been a while, shady. Your madam has been telling us quite the story about you. Hexing men with a killing curse, justice for the working girl, among a few more outlandish rumors alive on the Slash. It looks like some of them fought back." He matches his fingers to the thumbprint bruises on my arm, then brings his nose in to mine, spent sugar in his breath. "You still think your balls are bigger than mine. I know for a fact they're not."

My lead gaze holds. It unnerves him when I stare.

He looks away first. He always does.

"The barons are in town so there's new faces, the kind of distraction someone like you might use were you planning trouble."

Planning? You're cycles too late to stop me.

He takes out his packet of striped candy. "The flies around here like to gossip. One of them led us to an explosive little package over by the refinery last night. You wouldn't know anything about that, would you?"

Would Montoya really stupid enough to cross now, or did they just get lucky?

"Then there's the fire last cycle they say was arson and the slaughter this afternoon." His hand plants against my back where *Reliable* rests, pushing long enough for the metal to dig into my bruises. "You've been a very busy girl. I know you won't waste your breath denying that. You're wearing all the evidence right here." He pulls the gun. The second gift from Leagan he's taken from me. Irony is sick, and I'm going to step on its head someday. "This is a quality weapon. *Reliable…* You interested in paying the pistol tax? I'm the man in charge of that. You can have this back if you tell me how you did it. Who smuggled this in to you?"

I show him my middle finger. I am a smuggler, fool.

"I know…" He chuckles, squats down to search me. "You'd be dangerous with a toothpick, shady. You and I were both there on the *Delta Sol*, I watched you bludgeon that bastard to death with your hands tied together."

He doesn't make any sudden moves. Neither do I. Slowly, his hands push up under my skirt, around my hips. Down my legs, inside, between, up my torso.

"That's enough," Charlene says. "If you want to touch her, you can pay me. If not—"

"The boss already pays you. You don't own this house or these girls. I could touch you right now if I wanted. But the Company thanks you for running things so well here. She feels healthy."

The Stranger runs into his ear.

You'll feel something else soon.

Beneath Charlene's callousness of years, I glimpse the bead of empathy, crouched like a rabbit behind her single eye. It only survives because she hides it.

Kasey's going to find the poison as soon as he stops handling my skin and goes through my pockets.

I want it. Definitely don't want him to have it.

He pinches the skin on the inside of my thigh.

I reach around him, start picking bullets off his belt, slow, deliberate. Two…three…they clink as they fill my hand.

"I see that, fox," the other gun snaps. "Kasey, check her hand."

He peels my fingers open and laughs again. "You…I won't fault you for not trying." His wretched smile cools as he feeds the three bullets back to his belt and slips a pair of cuffs from his pocket. "It's a six-day trip to a mine cell for the pistol infraction, and a full cycle wage fine. Of course, you'll only have to worry about that if no one puts a pickax through your skull. But you have an appointment at the Company office first."

Of course.

"I won't spoil the beans, but the boss has his own questions for you."

The Stranger tightens around me as the steel cuffs bite down. I will get out of here. But each time I let them take me up the hill like this, she starts to believe me a little less.

"After you." Kasey's wisely never let me walk behind him. I hate him for everything, even that. He tips his hat to Charlene. "Thank you for your hospitality, Madam."

Charlene looks at me, not him. Sour-orange lipstick caked around her gray mouth, and that one good eye that could almost look sorry. But I'm not worth the risk of pissing off Rafe and the Company. She did warn me this would happen if she had to choose.

"You can rent the fox's room out at your leisure. She won't be back again."

THIRTY-SIX
ADELAIDE

Rafe frowns at Kasey when he sees me. "Fool's gold, you couldn't have given her five minutes to clean herself up?"

"Not worth the risk of her trying anything shady."

"No one wants to walk around wearing another man's fluids." Rafe sniffs as he circles me. "However, it does appear the bloodbath I heard about was not exaggerated. You killed a foreman—"

"Two." Kasey holds up fingers.

"*Two*. What's this about, Revere? Under ordinary circumstances, I wouldn't concern Company resources over a dispute between chemical dealers. Those types of people tend to sort themselves out. But these are not ordinary times. Are these chemical dealers stirring the fire under the workmen and organizing a takeover? Or is something darker at work?"

His gaze follows me to the window, heavy as my limbs are right now. There's no disguising my limp.

Nine: the number of cupboards and drawers in his office that I've never been able to look in, crawling just under my skin. Below the distortion of reformed glass, Hannah is brewing under the sun's fading red light, all the windows orange eyes gorging on darkness.

Rafe joins me, copper jaw hard under his beard as he stares down on what he's made like some sort of god. Gods don't bleed, but he will. "I set you up with a place to live, a madam to make sure you'd have work and care. I didn't want you having to turn to other sources like the dealers."

No, you wanted to know who I was with.

"Tell me what happened. The truth."

"I got caught in the middle of whatever problem the chemical dealers are having." It's not a lie.

"So, you were simply minding your business when the wrong people showed up. How very unlucky."

"Apothecaries provide certain things women need."

"Ah." He diverts his eyes exceptionally quick. "Well, lack of adequate care is the reason we're all here. They didn't...take anything out of you recently, did they?"

"No."

"There's some good news, at least. You aren't in female recovery." He lifts my arm, tries to tilt my head to examine the scale of my injuries. "This is somewhat of an issue." He sighs as I avoid his touch. "It looks painful. Do you need a shot of whiskey, or the doctor?"

I could have used a day alone in bed.

"Let me show you the bathroom." Rafe points out the door in the west corner of the office, wood brimming with polish oil. "Take your time. I'll have someone hunt down clean clothes."

Thirteen.

The bathroom shines with copper tile. The ceiling too.

My broken finger has my whole hand swollen stiff. I try to keep the wrapping dry as I sluice water over my bloody hands, get them clean before touching the washrag.

Blood freckles my face and neck, sharp against my colorless skin. It's crusted around one nostril and my split lip, dust streaking my arms deep gray. I push up my undershirt, my whole right side is purple.

There's nothing to do about the stain sprawling down the front of my bodice and skirt. It's visible over the cycles of black ash, already set thick brown.

Rafe's medicine cabinet gives me nothing. Beard oil, no razors. Brush for his teeth that aren't made of copper. Nothing I actually want, but I steal a spare bar of soap anyway. Lemon.

The door out the other side of the bathroom is locked. By the murderous red light seeping through the windows, I see the shape of his bedroom through the keyhole. It faces west and south.

Rafe waits with two amber glasses when I come out. He sets mine on the tea table. "You've had a rough day."

Fuck you.

I could have murdered them both with the poison punch knife if I hadn't bothered to put it back in the gun Kasey took from me. But that would still leave me with no way out of here except running. I didn't do all that work burying explosives and flash fire just because I like digging in the dirt and exploring underneath buildings. I do, but that's not the point.

Hannah is the rotten core of a wasteland. The *Io Rift*, or the Northern Plains as they're now known. Two hundred miles of meaningless grass in any direction worth going. Escape isn't just about slipping Rafe's men and the wall with the standing gun. It hinges on being able to disappear quickly after you've done it. I know the inside of Hannah too well, what's outside not enough, just that the North Rim offers nowhere convenient to hide. The rail in is long. The way out, no shortcuts.

I need a storm to disappear, but there isn't one brewing tonight. And I had to spend all my energy fighting chemical pickers.

Moths cling to the window, drawn by the light inside.

Kasey's gun hand taps aimlessly on the backrest of the velvet couch, the full-length bookshelves behind him.

Rafe lights himself a cigar, gaze lingering momentarily on the drink I didn't taste. "Do you smoke, Revere? Tobacco...redweed? Really, no vices? It starts to make sense why people say your kind isn't human, and why you always look so angry." He clears the black lung from his throat, woody cigar clotting with the ash taste on the air. "Well, I thank you for gracing me with your dim presence, regardless of whether you ever intend to speak. You do remember Jonathaniel Swann." He waits, cigar pinned between two fingers by the ash plate, but I never respond. It wasn't a real question.

"He's coming in for the shaft lease auction, and he's asked for a repeat of your company."

My stare is flat, nothing, like the colorless plains outside the wall. Rafe's gaze doesn't break like Kasey's does. He's not afraid of me.

Not yet.

"I hate to give you to him looking like a bruised pear, nothing to be done about that now. However, considering the events of today, I'm going to keep you here until he arrives. That trouble that found you today won't find you here."

Trouble is my first and last name.

"But injuries aside, I bear unfortunate news."

He wouldn't summon me if he had good news.

His exhale is deep, clouded by smoke. Bitter. "Your aunt sent a spy."

I know. I killed him on that street for you to find.

Still, my pulse puts pressure in my stomach. The fear they're hoping to see me betray myself with stays locked behind the Stranger. She twists in me, ready as the configurations of Aunt Tess's plan align.

"She doesn't trust me. Although, the feeling's mutual." Rafe stabs out the cigar on the plate behind him, barely tasted. "I am offended that she sent a lousy one, got himself knifed outside a game den lasterday night. Such obvious lack of respect for my intellect."

"He wasn't ours," I say, and like Aunt Tess wants, they know it's a lie. "We do our own dirty work."

"So, you won't object if we hang him on the gate as a warning to others?"

Go ahead, I shrug.

"You want to see him?" Kasey asks. "Just to be sure? He looked kind of like your "brother", the one I met in Descendants."

No, he didn't.

"If he wasn't yours, then you don't know anything about this?" Rafe peels open the crumpled paper from the leather envelope I planted, blood sticking to the edges. "You've spent enough time on the low end of the Slash to know the other pickers. This was on his person. A copy of last cycle's rail schedules. Names of my men."

Decoys. Like the bullets I intentionally failed to steal off Kasey. You're in the Widow's den, drunk on her poison. The walls are narrowing around you, but all you feel is the need to taste more.

"I don't fault you for trying," Rafe says. "I would try. I worry. For whatever it is she's about to do. We both know her."

I know her better.

"She's cooking something...the question is what." He studies me. "The love of a family is so hard to break. You obviously have that. The purest loyalty, and you are a creature determined to survive. But your moons brought you here, to me."

We've all wasted enough time pretending he was ever going to let me go. Even if the full ransom was paid. This was the risk the Stranger and I both accepted when I first came here, when I stayed.

"I warned you, fox," Kasey says. "I'd have put you out of your misery a Season ago if you'd asked, but you made me bring you here. Don't you forget that."

I'm aware. And I'm sure it would have been an easy, painless death too. Not a drop of humiliation. But Aunt Tess is the best gambler I know. She hates losing more than anything, and I'm so glad she's on my side.

"I'm no fool, Revere," Rafe says. "I see the hate in your eyes every time we meet. You want me dead. It may come as a surprise that I don't hate you, and I don't relish what I'm about to do. I'm just sorry this is what we all came to. I'll tell your family you died well."

I'm not sorry. Grandma and Vesta are dead because Green tried to ruin us and Rafe fell for it. I won't ever be sorry for hitting them back.

"I remember you, you know." Rafe's pewter eyes pass through me, to a memory. "You were just a little girl when you left here, and I was a younger man…"

Nine.

The desk is a disarray of letters and mineral survey charts, a merchant scale with a black gold sample in the tray, a plate with a half-eaten sandwich. I look for anything that wasn't here before, anything I might have missed.

"But you're not a little girl anymore." Rafe picks another bloodstained letter from his gray vest. "Your spy was also supposed to be delivering this, I presume, before he met his untimely end."

I've seen it too.

My dearest Gerard Rafael:
The son of an honorable man.

Congratulations. We have collected the remainder of the sixty thousand ransom agreed upon your behalf by your right-hand man, Mr. Dathan Kasey. We will gladly pay you the full amount, plus a generous twenty percent interest in exchange for immediate release of the Stranger to us. She must be alive and unharmed.

Fair enough? I think so.

I will also apologize to you in person. I wasn't sorry at first. I thought I was the smartest person on the Rim. I was wrong, and I am sorry now.

We will meet you on the track two miles south of Hannah. The first day of Moon Season, 9:30 am.

As much as we both hate violence, let's solemnly swear in advance that we won't kill each other, in honor of your mother and mine.

Until we meet, I'm yours forever in mercy.

Sol,
Tesla Revere

It was hard to read past the fuck-you mouth-breathing between her sarcasm.

"I could choke on the sentiment, but I know she's mocking me. My father was a dishonorable man, like yours no doubt." But Rafe's smile is so obviously smug. The apology is what he wants most. Aunt Tess knows this.

I reach, my hand telling the lie that I haven't read every word she wrote.

Rafe crushes the page small. "Shame...I really would have liked to see what she had planned. I'm sure it was complicated."

He's not taking the bait.

Kasey cracks the knuckles on one fist, then the other.

Fuck.

One—

Rafe grabs for my elbow. I slap that hand away but miss his second grasp as my broken finger catches something solid. That's all it takes to tip a fight out of your favor. He yanks me by the wrist to meet his other fist with my stomach.

"Your family will come for you, and I'll be here waiting."

I hit the desk front facing down, Kasey's hand full of my braid and other arm. The Stranger rears, my breath gone.

Fool. But she's talking to me. *You knew this was too easy.*

Paper slips and the lamp shatters against the floor, hot crystal chewing into the wool rug while the edges of my vision sear.

Kasey struggles to hold me down, losing control of the one arm he had. The desk shaves floor as his leg jabs the back of mine, buckling it. "I told you to leave the cuffs on her."

"Careful of her face," Rafe says. "I can't give her to Swann with a second black eye. Something tells me he'd find that offensive. Hold her still."

Kasey lets go of my hair and finishes folding both my arms back.

"Here's the final deal, Revere." Rafe removes his cufflinks, rolls his first sleeve up, fold by fold. "You're going to fuck Mr. Swann as many times as he wants, however he wants. When he's done with you, you're going to hang. Your aunt can promise me the moons, but you've become a dangerous liability. And as much as I find you an intriguing character, intrigue simply isn't worth the risk anymore. I sincerely hope whatever scheme Tesla has cooking died with her spy, but I can't trust that. I see no other choice beyond this."

Kasey presses into my back, all his weight laying into bruises deep enough to touch bone. The back of my head briefly connects with something hard in his face.

Rafe coils my braid around his hand twice, draws my head back.

Farce.

I hear the desperate gasp of all the throats I've slit open, but this time it's mine. He just said he's going to hang me, but steel kisses leather. There are other things he can do to me first.

"I said don't let her go."

"She's not a rabbit, she's got some muscle."

"Go fuck each other." Spit flies off my words.

A tear burns its way out of my eye. Salt rage. It might as well be blood.

"Trust me when I say it's nothing personal, Revere. I would have done the same to any of you."

Vacca voya.

The Stranger burns like iron left in the sun, black consumes light, and slowly, like unsticking a dull blade, Rafe saws through my hair.

The sound is silver. It's not over in one slice. It takes four. I dig into Kasey's flesh, peeling his skin as the Stranger coils. She can knot herself into whatever shape she likes, she can't escape my body. By the time the final strands snap, the room is gone.

They must have let me up. I don't feel my arms or legs, only heat where they should be.

Black spots burn on the rug. Black spots in my head, a silent gasp.

Kasey shakes my touch off his arm as blood seeps from deep scratches. Hand on his gun, should he need it, between me and Rafe. Loyal dog.

Wait.

The Stranger's bloodlust is strong, but right now it's just me that's so blindly enraged.

You don't want to die here.

I will if I have to. And not with a rope around my neck. We can all die here in this room, together.

No.

There are plenty of things to bleed on in here. The glass of the broken lamp, the bronze letter opener. They made me wear that muzzle so I couldn't bite anyone. Now I will.

Wait. Make him suffer.

She's right.

I don't want to see my hair, in Rafe's hand, no longer part of me. Another memory I'll live with forever. But it would be a foolish thing to die for.

I turn my gaze on him.

"You're angry," Rafe says. "Understandably so."

My nose bleeds again, the first real thing I feel in my body. Then my cheeks itch as two fresh tears follow the path the others made. I tighten on myself again.

Did this thing that should have been small finally break me?

But it's not small to me. I've never cut my hair.

I still haven't.

Them seeing me like this doesn't cancel out my rage or make me any less myself. My wet stare still bores into him like it would dry, and burns. Doesn't flicker like other flames touched by water.

You don't know what's coming, Gerard Rafael. A woman will be the last thing you see. Even if it's not me, her name will be Revere.

"For your family." He holds up my severed braid and dumps it into an empty cigar box, wiping the stray white strands off his palm onto the floor. "Less gruesome than sending an eye, a hand, or your head. I'm not interested in traumatizing anyone, just sending a message. They can mourn you in whatever way seems best to them."

He's lying. It's a trap.

The Stranger is right. She's always right. I've set enough of my own traps to know.

Rafe knows we are vengeful, and I'm the bait. I have to survive so I can warn them.

Kasey doesn't stop watching me even to blink. At least I left gouges in his arm.

Leagan. Navy. I want to see them again. They're the only things stopping me now. I have to want them more than I want revenge. Always.

"Still nothing to say?" Rafe kicks the spilled fire quartz into an ashtray, grinds out the smoldering fibers of his rug. "Then I will. You are brave beyond words. Many lesser souls would have cracked by now. When this is over, I won't let anyone call you a traitor or a rabbit. There is no love purer than sacrifice, and you have honored yours. Behave yourself with Swann, and I'll do you the courtesy of hanging you privately. No one pays to watch."

We tried to do this Aunt Tess's way. Our bet was that I'd have more time. I don't.

Now I'll finish it mine.

"I won't be needing anything else from you." Rafe pulls on the service chain, then continues to fix the destruction of his desk. "If you've somehow managed to communicate with your family, and my gut tells me that you have, however unlikely that seems, tell them not to come for you. I've heard your train is now part of the Boneyard, but I'll be inspecting the track for sabotage, and a standing gun is loaded at the tunnel. If that's not enough to deter any mischief, I'll have a surprise waiting for them."

What did I miss?

The Stranger ricochets off the suggestion like spit on hot iron. *We didn't.*

It must be a lie then?

It doesn't feel like it.

Female footsteps ring down the hall, sweeping open the door with a gust of spoiled perfume. Copper, madam's high-waisted slacks and tailed waistcoat in place of her overskirt.

"Surprise, fox." She smirks. "You had no idea I was Company payroll too, did you?"

Please. She's not smart enough to spy on me with her own plan in mind.

"Thank you for arriving so swiftly, Madam," Rafe says. "You will find our shady friend something appropriate to wear in the Hannah Grand. Ask for her here when Mr. Swann arrives."

"Yes, sir." Copper stalks around me, scraping my arm with the beak of her ivory walking cane. "How long did it take you to realize I was spying on you?"

"If you were trying to keep it a secret, you should have been more careful going through my stuff."

"Maybe I wanted you to know."

Because people like her can't live with secrets. It suffocates them.

"Mr. Kasey." Rafe turns.

"Boss?"

"Lock her in one of the spare rooms with access to a tub. Have someone bolt the storm shutters down, and put a man on the door. Make it clear there are no circumstances below the moons that he's allowed to go in unless he wishes to die. If she doesn't kill him, I will. That door opens for no reason until Swann gets here. Feed her through the dumbwaiter, and if she tries to leave, shoot her."

Well, fuck.

"I advise you bathe yourself before Swann, fox. It certainly wouldn't shorten your lifespan."

THIRTY-SEVEN
TESLA

RALEIGH RETURNS TO THE TABLE WITH A PLATTER OF ROASTED SAUSAGE, potatoes, eggs, and peppers, still steaming from the cast iron he cooked it all in.

"Have I ever told you how much I appreciate a man who cooks?" I say. "It's a very attractive quality. I don't like my coffee on an empty stomach."

"I approve of the handcar you got for us," Leagan says from behind her book. "It's beefy, not the bastard one rolling around with the maintenance crew in Damascus."

"Well, sweet Jezebel." Raleigh sits back. "Lady Nasty is in a good mood this morning too. Mark the calendar."

"Oh, you know what the secret route to her heart is," I say.

"Death." Leagan turns another page.

"Food," I whisper.

"You know I wouldn't get something less than alkaline for you," Raleigh says. "Steam-powered, lady. Nobody wants to pump or pedal a handcar all night."

"You're both wrong," Leagan says. "The only reason I'm happy is because we're going to get Adelaide back. Then I'm finally going to see the West Rim."

"Sooner rather than later, my dear."

"Well, neither of you are going to guess what stunning piece of information I came by this cycle," Raleigh says. "Would you like to hear it now or wait for Navy?"

"Now." I glance at my pocket watch. "It's only seven. She won't be awake for a few more hours." And I don't want to wait.

Raleigh flicks his tongue across his lip, light flaring through his blue eyes.

"Oh." I lean forward. "This is juicy."

Leagan finally lowers her book.

"Yes, it is. You will kiss me. Not you though." He wrinkles his nose at Leagan's black lipstick. "I have it on good authority an *Exodus Ironclad* is coming to the Rim."

It rises slowly, my laugh, desire blooming like *Solace* flowers as Raleigh's grin stretches.

"Told you."

"You'd better not be lying to me, because it's far too early in the day for rude jokes, sir."

"Oh, I'd never joke about Exodus products. It's against my religion."

The last time an *Ironclad* came through must have been...well, shit, a long time ago, because I can't remember.

"On a scale of Green to my mother, how reliable is this authority?"

"It's my contact within the Exodus shipping line. The man behind every bullet you ever hauled for me. We've been doing business together six Seasons. It would be a tremendously odd moon for him to lie to me now."

I don't want to get too excited over a *farce* rumor. But too late, I'm all fluttery inside. Fool's gold, if we took an *Ironclad*...

"I will kiss you." I stand to plant one on his upturned cheek. "When is she coming, and where is she headed?"

"It's a private order, not stock going up for auction."

"I can think of only one operation with enough melded resources to afford that. I bet I can guess."

"I bet you can."

I bump Leagan under the table. "I told you I'd get another train."

She smiles back. "I like it."

"Along with the other thing we discovered, we're going to be some very busy women."

"Other thing?" Raleigh says.

"Green has kindly been keeping track of all his business partners coming and going. There's a secret meeting between the intangible yet mighty Millard Von Kane and the other railroad investors happening soon. This private order of munitions says to me things aren't going so well for them out west."

"Call the sheriff," Leagan says.

"They'll be meeting in Oath when the investors arrive. When we're done with Hannah, I'm going to make sure they have to linger in Oath a little while longer." Leagan dreamed of Travis, and his home camp has been Oath as long as I've known him. That's a good enough correlation to convince me. "I think it's about time Papa Von Kane met a Revere."

Hard boots pound up the Lideon staircase to the front of the shop, the glass panes rattling under an aggressive fist. "Rider with the Express."

Raleigh plucks the napkin from his collar. "Coming."

Montoya's Cairosh accent follows the unbolting of the door, vowels that melt like sugar on a wet tongue. "You must be the friend in town I've heard them brag about."

"Raleigh, the man."

"Your shop is at odds with the stench outside."

"Thank you. The two best smells in the world, freshly oiled barrels and coffee. If you'll follow me, I can show you more of it. Just out of curiosity, what do assassins drink? It's the resolution to an unanswered question with a dear friend of mine."

"The blood of beautiful enemies, the tears of lovers, and occasionally, cream tea."

"Now I can rest in peace." Raleigh halts as I meet them coming through the door to the back of the shop. "Ah, here is one of the people you're actually here to see."

Montoya draws the pack off his shoulders, producing a brown parcel. "I'm afraid I come bearing news questionable in nature. This was brought to the Express office by a man belonging to Boss Rafael."

It doesn't weigh too much.

"Oh, Rafe sent me a present, how thoughtful." My knife slits through the string holding the package together, paper shell dropping from a cigar box. "Oh fuck." I'm stunned into recoil by the shrillness of my own gasp as much as what's inside. "Fuck. Fuck."

White hair. Adelaide's hair.

My heels meet my backside as I sink, and Leagan begins to sob. What have I done?

THIRTY-EIGHT
ADELAIDE

Copper leads me up the service staircase in the backside of the Hannah Grand Hotel. Outside windows tall as cliffs, the sun's red eye burns hot despite the black ash cloak.

Forty-five.

I plant my hands against the oiled railing of the upper floor, high above the crystal barons and girls stirring across white and black floor. Vesta would have known how to charm the secrets out of all of them.

The copper chandelier burns black gold in eight glass chambers, warming wire coils, bright false suns. The crystals glow from the heart, a dark green heat. I didn't expect that the first time I saw them burn. The hole created when Vesta was torn out of this world aches within me, all these things I'll never get to share with her or Grandma again. For a moment the spaces between the gold bands of the wallpaper bleed.

Vesta would have loved the fanciness of this place.

I hate it on her behalf.

Copper circles, judging the gray stripe skirt gathered at the waist and riding above my knees, long stockings, and steel bone corset to keep me from being too flexible and pressure on my bruises. "Good enough."

Her hands take similar command of the rail as mine, clouding my nose with her rose powder. "Look at them. Can't you just see the crystal fortunes, *oozing*? It's the only good kind of ooze."

They all look the same. Silk vests, jackets with all their buttons. Jezebel men. I bet a few of them know the Von Kanes.

Outwardly I am still, holding my tight jaw in place while the Stranger slowly boils.

I'd be lying if I said I'm not afraid. But that's not enough to make me freeze, to wait to die by Rafe's noose. It's harder to take a hangman down with you. I'd rather die in blood, a free woman.

Maybe Aunt Tess and Rafe both overthought this situation and that's the problem. My approach has always been more straightforward. A good plan doesn't have to be complicated or clever. It only has to work.

"Mr. Swann is waiting for you in the billiard room." Copper's gaze outlines the bruise flowering just under the surface of my shoulder. "You obviously can't remember what I tried to teach you—thanks for wasting my breath. At least I don't have to deal with you trying to charge him an injury tax afterward. I can only imagine why he'd ask for you. But then again, the richer the man, the deeper the vices."

"You've never met Jonathaniel." And you'll never be anything better than this.

"Oh, *first* name. Maybe you're not the dumb bucket of rock you seem."

Jonathaniel is a fool's gold tourist. He comes to the Rim for the thrill. Not to hunt black gold, he has a fortune in that. He wants a similar thing to what Kane did, an experience. Not Adelaide Revere the Stranger. A fox. Something all the money in the Republic can't easily buy because most of us are dead. A story to scandalize his rich friends back home.

This time, I'm going to put a gun to Jonathaniel Swann and make him take me with him when he leaves Hannah.

"Come along then." Copper worms her sticky fingers through mine. "You and I get to welcome these fine gentlemen to the Rim. Now you say, 'Yes, Madam Copper.'"

No.

She's got what she wants, girls like her usually do. Her life is meaningless beyond this job, but here she is, still alive, and my sister isn't. I hope these things she thinks matter turn on her.

Ven quartz the size of logs burn cold in the monstrous fireplace, alive with the first cracks of a storm. This tile floor is unnaturally slick under my boots, the chilled air sliding across it funneling up my skirt as the Stranger picks every shred of movement reflected in it. And them.

Forty-two.

"That hanging today…sick spectacle—" The baron steps aside as I pass, quickly knocking his gaze away.

The next doesn't bother. "They're letting the animals wander inside now, I see?"

Fifty-one.

A sapphire-bodice girl I sold knives and sugar to passes a soft wave from the circle surrounding the blue fire.

The baron whose armrest she perches on lifts his drink, whiskey hissing around teeth. "*Shady.*"

"Through that door, to your right." Copper points ahead, then closes a hand around the front of her throat like the noose they have planned for me. Smile nothing but mean. "See you later, fox."

You'll see me when Hannah burns.

The lamps make the windowless billiard room feel submerged. Brass-toned light, not gold.

The Stranger counts the men. Then the men with guns. *Eight.* Five of them hired, weathered by the Rim. Three barons packing their own lead. And one sitting in the corner probably has a sword inside his walking cane.

Past the glint of copper standards on the game tables, the Stranger singles out Jonathaniel's handlebar moustache, the deep part in his hair. He slaps the bar, laughing with the others around him.

I close the parts of me I don't want to feel.

Twenty-one.

"That's what I told him—there she is!" Jonathaniel abandons his drink and pipe to open both arms to me. "My lucky strike! It's been too long since I've seen the moon on such a fine night." Clove smoke grips me as his arms do. Too tight, my ribs are full of weak spots. "How have you been keeping—" His black coffee gaze fixes on my chin-length hair, then the deep blue shadow running down my cheek. "What is this?" Before it's obvious I don't answer, he finds the seam of bruises crossing my body, makes me turn in a circle. "My God of Mercy. What fiend did this to you?"

The cost of doing business. It's higher when you're alone. And the worst of them are under my clothes.

"They better not have put you to work in the mine. That's no place for you, love. Sweet Jezebel's bones." Jonathaniel brings my knuckles to his mouth, voice lowering. "You would tell me if someone mistreated you. I'd have them brought to justice."

I could laugh. I'm aware that most people would consider this kindness. Tell me I should be glad he doesn't plan to hit me tonight. This is the Rim. We're in Hannah, and I'm a woman.

I could also spit. Justice is *farce*.

He's renting me, like a horse. And I'll never forget that. If the choice was mine, he'd never be allowed to touch me. Kindness doesn't scrub that out. The Stranger and I have killed for less. He's lucky I intend to use him, otherwise the Stranger would meet him tonight. I've run out of patience for mind games and things to lose.

He passes his hand down my arm, back up, soft as milk. "I have missed you. Such powerful silence."

The baron seated at the bar behind him shakes his head, suit pale gray. Rabbits and cactus-nesting doves. "A ghost can't keep your bed warm, Jonny boy."

"Is that so? Maybe you need to broaden your horizons, Lewis." Jonathaniel lifts his voice to include the barons clustered around the billiard table like succulents on rock. "Gentlemen, you haven't truly tasted the Rim until you've been with a Tov, rulers of the west."

You fool.

"Keep your perversions, Jon. I'm a God-fearing man."

"You'll be begging for my wisdom after the auction. Even the rocks give up their prizes to me. Remember shaft thirty-five?"

"A lucky guess."

"Exactly."

"I'll remember to ask you again when she kills you in your sleep," Lewis says.

"Then I'll have lived a full life." Jonathaniel sighs. "The truth is, I'd be the happiest man alive if I could leave all this drudgery behind and stake a west claim, live with the sun on my back for the rest of my days. But alas, such are the bonds of responsibility."

"Well, at least you won't die by a picker's ax."

"No, I'll die of boredom."

The graying baron with rolled sleeves leans over the billiard table to make his shot with a scoff. "I hope you enjoy the taste of your own blood as much as the taste of her."

"Right," another says. "If I wanted to pay for something dirty, I'd go down to the Fen Street house in Jezebel and wait for the barge to come in."

"So says ignorance." Jonathaniel laughs. "The truth is, none of you are man enough to ride a Shadow."

"She's looking a little wasted." The gray one comes around the billiard table, polishing the end of his cue stick as he looks down on me. "Been a while since you've had a lover to eat, milk-bastard? Which part of our friend Jonathaniel looks the most succulent? His brain, or maybe the fat he's starting to collect around his middle?"

The fool called Lewis cracks into a walnut from the dish and a smile when I don't answer. "You like the quiet ones, eh, Jon? If I'm going to pay for professional companionship, I prefer someone who at least appears interesting. Of course, you wouldn't be paying for intelligent conversation with that."

You wouldn't survive a day on the open Rim. I'd rob you, not waste my time talking.

"Quite the contrary." Jonathaniel slips a hand around my side, squeezes. I hold in the flinch, barely acknowledge pain this time. "Adelaide and I have quite the intellectual exchange. In fact, she can read."

"Bullshit." Lewis laughs. "You're off your rail, Jon. Off your rail. A cold day on the Rim might come when my moons turn, and maybe then I'll need the wisdom of Jonathaniel the great, but until then..." He plucks his drink, moves on. "They have better prospects in the foyer."

Go ahead. Laugh. If only Rafe was foolish enough to underestimate us like east bloods do.

"Well, it seems this is good night to you then, sir," Jonathaniel calls. "Come along, my love, let's leave these buffoons to smoke their lives away. Should any of you wish to socialize before the auction, you know where to find me. But in the meantime, I shall say good luck, gentlemen. You'll need it."

Sol sana.

THIRTY-NINE
ADELAIDE

I DREAM I'M BACK IN EDEN. IN THE MINE WITH KANE. THE MALFORMED, DEEP west bone pickers come scrambling out of dark pockets like scorpions, ripping at my hair and skin.

I've shot upright before I'm actually awake. My breaths roll down my bruised back, locked in silent shudders as I hug my legs.

The furniture takes up too much space, rough shapes lurking in the dark. The smell of leather upholstery piled on top of dusk roses, mint sachets and yesterday's garlic.

Jonathaniel's hotel room.

It's not my first dream about being underground. It won't be the last. But I'll be going back to Eden someday. It's better if I get the fear of that deep dark out of my body now.

I shove what's left of my hair back and blink the red sting out of my eyes.

Grandma and Leagan's dreams mean something. Mine have only ever been storms. Come without warning and leave no traceable pattern once they've gone. The Stranger makes me look at memories when I'm awake.

Kane could be out there right now, redoing the work I gave so much to undermine.

Or he could be dust and bones.

When I make it back to Eden, I suppose I'll find out.

I enjoyed being out there. Riding in the sun, drawing the rock formations and flowers every day, collecting information for my map while Kane made his. It was a taste of everything the Stranger's always longed to do.

Horror is other people. We were safer on the West Rim than Grandma, Aunt Tess, and Leagan back on the train.

Maybe Vesta would have been killed in the *Absolution*'s derailment or by a different bounty hunter's gun. I didn't ask her to come with me. She always wanted to go where I went, ever since we were little. Maybe no choice I made would have saved her.

I slide from under the spare blanket. Jonathaniel stays a quiet log buried in sheets on the other side of the room.

Five.

Last Season, I got to leave when he was done with me, went back to my room at Madam Charlene's. I didn't expect that this time, but I didn't think he'd actually trust me in the bed next to him. And I didn't expect the Stranger to let me fall asleep anywhere in this room. Fool's gold, even this couch was more comfortable than my bed at Madam Charlene's house. The sour chalk of refinery smoke held out by better walls.

Jonathaniel didn't feel me slip away once his sleeping tablets sank their teeth in.

The brass gears of the mantel clock mesh together one click at a time. Three-fifteen. Not as late or as early as I thought, depending whether Leagan or Navy. Hannah clatters away outside. It never rests.

Through the hollow eye of the keyhole, Rafe's pair of guns still walk the hall, too close to get around. Even me. Their silver pot of coffee breathes steam, and the ashtray is only half-full.

Seventeen.

The long drapes welcome me as I slip between the damask and lace layers. The glass is wide as a door, seamless and impossible to walk through. The pre-dawn presses over chimneys, thicker than usual, a red fog that creeps like evening, or maybe drowning. This storm is going to rain. *Solace* should be over, but it doesn't want to let go of us quite yet.

My hand leaves a ghost outline on the glass.

Jonathaniel's things have been unpacked, arranged in the bathroom cupboards and armoire. I look for weapons, look at everything.

His daily appointment book lies open on the chair by the dead fire.

Black leather, embossed with his initials in copper. I bring it to my nose. Not the potent saddle leather of Kane's journal, wind and dust crisping the pages. Ink and cloves, business done over pipe tobacco in velvet rooms.

A slab of letters falls from between thumb-tumbled pages. Jonathaniel is not organized like me, or artistic like Kane. He has notes for his tailor about sleeves being uncomfortable in between production estimates, meetings crossed out on the next page. But I was taught the value of information, and the Stranger was designed to hunt it.

I only get one chance to escape. My strike has to be flawless.

I find today's date. *In Hannah—how grand,* written at the top of the week.

> *Montgomery, 7:00 am.*
> *(Boring company dulls the mind!)*
> *Procure new sleeping tablets. These ones smell like feet. Good gracious gold!*
> *Auction?*

Tomorrow.

> *Clark & Stokes, 11:45 am.*
> *Auction? Such suspense!*
> *Play cards with Lewis and show him all kinds of disrespect!*

Jonathaniel hasn't moved, breathing evenly.
I flip ahead.

> *Buy a new hat.*
> *Auction?*

Five days.

> *Depart Hannah? Oh, sad day. I might not feel like it.*
> *Send letter to J.A. and brag about my good luck at the auction.*

Six.

Depart?
Don't forget Montgomery—as much as I might like to.
Send word to MVK confirming meeting in Oath.

MVK... The Stranger circles the letters.

Five or six days. Good enough to find the right moment to put a gun to Jonathaniel.

Now you need to get one.

I slot the letters back into the center of the book as I read them, lay everything back the way it was.

Five or six days to live. That's not good enough for me.

Aunt Tess needs to know the plan is dead but I'm not. That Rafe has laid a trap, and I'm giving my escape to the Stranger.

My family can't come here. Even if my new plan fails.

I check that Jonathaniel's eyes are still closed, then take a pencil and paper from the desk. For some reason, I struggle to write the last words. I don't want to die. But I've always known it would be red.

Like Hannah's sun.

What if this is my bloody end?

I love you.

The pencil scrapes so loud.

They won't be your last, the Stranger says.

Still. I won't let my last words be something to regret ever again.

THE FLOOR CREAKS UNDER FEET MOVING QUICK THROUGH THE HALL. SIX O' clock. Someone new, not the Company guards.

"For Mr. Swann." The tap is hard against the walnut door, meant to wake, boy's voice jumbled by the wall between us. An envelope skims across the foot-worn boards from under the door.

Nine.
The Hannah Mining Co.

Jonathaniel turns over, reaches for me, but I'm not there. "That had better be breakfast. Damnation, it's Thursday, isn't it?" He searches the bedding, collecting his robe and slippers. "I have to meet my friend Montgomery."

I hold out the letter.

"Ah. Thank you." His face brightens, ripping the envelope unevenly. The Stranger pricks against edges, hungry for a look at what's inside. "Sweet Jezebel, it's denser than wool in here. Would you light that fire, my dearest?"

The fireplace's gold-veined tiles bear the warmth of the room, equal in temperature to my skin. The old embers crumble under the iron poker, blue like sky and fractured to slivers. I pull two fresh sticks of Ven quartz from the firebox.

Jonathaniel slaps the letter across the back of his hand. "Excellent! You know what this means? Those fools downstairs can eat their bowlers for breakfast. Lewis first." He clears his throat. "'To the honorable Mr. J.T. Swann. Please note the shaft lease auction will take place in the Hannah Grand Hall on the fiftieth day of *End-Solace*.' Why, man? Just say Saturday morning."

Because the day of the week doesn't matter as much as what Season it is around here.

"'As usual, you will be summoned half an hour prior to start time the morning of—' This is how it goes every year. Mr. Rafael has got it in his head one of us might try to bribe someone inside if we know too much about when the auction will be, so he likes to spring it on us. Got to keep every man trustworthy. The suspense does make things exciting, though, doesn't it?"

Rafe has other problems in his head this Season besides keeping the crystal barons from fucking him over. Me.

I strike one Ven against the other, shearing a white-blue hole in warm shadows.

It's probably better this way. Less time for something else to go east before I make my move. But now I really need to get this letter out of my corset and into the hands of an Express Rider without anyone knowing. *Farce*, the one time Montoya could have been useful.

I blow onto the crystal, and the cold burn sharpens.

Solstice told me the ancient Tov came from a nameless land of rain and snow. Gray seas and white sharper than the sun. Serpents as long as trains tunneled in the ice, and sailors were speared out of their ships by whales with horns.

They longed for a home where they didn't have to fight the cold. The dark fogs that could linger for cycles, soaking to the core, the howl of sea dogs driving you mad. They found the Rim. A red sun paradise all their own.

It's the kind of story mothers tell their children to help them sleep when it's stormy. Grandma would read us the story of Vengeance and Annabeth, cat sisters. Or the one about Mother Raven and her treasure tree.

It's possible someone else along my bloodline felt the Rim pulling their compass, the way it pulls on me.

The flames rise cold on my face.

I'm not a child. The Stranger will never let me stop wandering, even if I found a place worth staying in.

Jonathaniel stands over me, partially dressed now. "And you don't care, do you?" He sits on his appointment book to put his spats on. "I can see you're not captivated by my business affairs." He pauses to look at me again, one boot cover still unbuttoned in hand. "I hope I didn't offend you last night. That was all just foolish men's talk downstairs."

Foolish men's talk. Foolish men should talk less.

"I, for one, know you're not a cannibal, and I enjoyed your company more than anything else here. I loathe sleeping alone."

Flattery. I wasn't in your bed. But what you believe becomes truth. I know fools when I see them, the Stranger sees intelligence. Jonathaniel is somehow both.

"You're quiet," he says. "Well, you're always quiet, but I can tell you have something on your mind."

I smile sedately. I'll never be as good as Grandma, or Vesta, or Aunt Tess, but contrary to what Copper thinks, I have learned.

"You won't tell me." Jonathaniel sighs. "Damnation. Keeping your secrets close to the vest, are you? Well, what could I do to earn one?"

A man with money can have anything he wants here. Even me. My words are the one thing I don't have to give him.

"Sadly, I must go." Jonathaniel finishes arranging his black throat scarf at the standing mirror, securing it with a pin cast in the shape of a beetle. "As much as I'd rather stay here with you, I have a breakfast meeting with a business partner."

Montgomery.

"He's an old man, gets up frightfully early. I do hate him for it. He is also mind-numbingly dull. Wouldn't need anesthetic for tooth surgery with that man around. You haven't said one word to me today, and sweet Jezebel, you are far pleasurable company. Tell me this, what would impress you, my love? Now is your prime chance to ask a favor. Would you like something from one of the shops?"

I rise off my heels. "How do you know the alkaline shafts better than Lewis?"

"Ah, so you *are* interested in what I do. I haven't misjudged you then." Jonathaniel winks. "I rarely do. It's no secret. I was born lucky."

And I was born in the worst place on the Rim. Luck runs out. Usually faster than water.

"The real secret, however, is that luck is playing your opponent. And damnation, have I played Lewis for the feeble-minded fool he is!"

Fool's gold, he's the male version of Aunt Tess.

"There." Jonathaniel points at me. "That look. The others may read you as a blank slate. I'll admit, I first bought your time thinking you might be a fun curiosity, but then I saw that look, and I knew…you're a creature of implausible depth."

The Stranger closes over me. I go to my boots, tucked under the lip of the bed.

Eleven.

Jonathaniel drifts. "Where are you now?"

In the sun. On the *Absolution.* Riding a horse I own toward towering hills, wind loose through my hair. I smell Grandma's tobacco perfume, roses. Hear my sister's laughter, see Leagan's alkaline red hair and her black lipstick grin. The empty ache in my stomach rises to meet the hard one in my jaw.

"I've had my fair share of fortune-hungry women try to seduce me, but my God above, look at you." Jonathaniel's fingers push through my chin-length hair. "You're not flattering me, so I'll pay you more, or worse, marry you. You seem tolerant of my company but not legitimately thirsty for it.

Therefore, the only explanation as to why you're here is you're after something other than my money."

You *bought* me. That's why I'm here. Is it really possible to be deluded enough he doesn't see that reality, and still smart enough to get under my motives?

The Stranger stabs deep in my core, black in my eyes, warning him not to look any deeper. My hand turns into a barrier between us. Ready to shove him as far as I can.

His thumbs spread, out across my jaw. "You are not a very good whore. And I mean that as the sincerest of compliments."

Survival is dirty work men like him will never know.

I straighten out the copper beetle pinning the scarf to his collar. Don't be late.

"It is exceedingly refreshing to be with someone so…stoic and sure of herself. Your secrets keep you interesting, be sure. But by Jezebel, someday I will know that mind of yours."

You won't get the chance. Next Season I'll either be gone or dead. And so will you.

"I expect to continue this fine conversation when I return." Jonathaniel brandishes his appointment book on the way to the closet. "It would be my utter delight to discuss the art of crystal mining with you later this evening. If I survive Montgomery, that is." He sets his burgundy overcoat straight with a snap. "If I could ask one favor of you, my love, I'm in dire need of some better sleeping tablets. Where might I purchase some? Of course, there are boy servants around here who do that sort of thing, but I like to get out and see the sights myself."

"The Pinings Tea House," I say. "It's on the miner's side of the Slash."

"Oh, the fun side."

"The owners have apothecary training. They can make you something."

If any of them are still alive and the place hasn't been pissed over by the other chemical dealers.

The smile bursts out of him easily, nothing attached underneath. "How did I know you'd have the insight I needed?" He nods to the green pill bottle on his night table. "Those are the leading brand of poison back east, and believe me, that *B* on the label is for bile."

He almost gets my laugh. "Tell them I sent you." At least they'll know I'm alive.

"You are a peach. Now, if you promise not to miss me too much while I'm gone, I will try to do the same. Farewell."

I sit down on the floor, sigh. It feels like I've spent the last half hour walking against a strong wind.

FORTY
TESLA

I TRIED. I REALLY, REALLY TRIED, BUT FUCKING JEZEBEL.

Wind moves through the grass by the Lideon tracks, lost to the reckless noise of the *Sol*'s green current. It ruffles Adelaide's letter in my hand and tugs apart my hair while the sun cooks us. Again, Leagan's rifle goes off downwind from the canyon backstop, pounding through rounds like lead is the cheapest thing here.

It's one of them.

Navy strokes my shoulder. It's hard to see what her face is doing under the veil covering her from head to waist.

Rafe didn't see through my plan because he's smarter than me. He just got lucky. My heel knocks against the rivets of the steam-powered handcar. Now what will we do with this beautiful little beast and its double copper boilers?

"Do you think she burned the whole place down?" Navy asks.

"Probably," Raleigh says.

"I could scream." This headache crawling behind my eyes keeps squeezing out all my better thoughts.

"Do it, if that's what you want," Navy says.

"It won't do us any good." I try to crush the headache to the back with both hands. "Thank God, Rafe didn't kill her."

"I know," Navy murmurs.

"I'm so glad we wasted all this time on a damn fine plan."

Raleigh leans over and pats my other shoulder. "There, there."

"It wasn't a waste," Navy says. "It was practice."

"What about Montoya?" Raleigh says.

"What about him?" I ask.

"What happens with him if Hannah is now a smoldering pile of ashes and bone?"

"Adelaide didn't say she was going to set Hannah on fire behind her." But we all know that doesn't mean she didn't. "I told him from the beginning he could have what was left when we were done there. We might be done there."

"Vague truths are so convenient."

"It won't kill him to wait and find out naturally."

"I dare you to tell him something like that."

"I will."

"Don't," Navy says.

Raleigh picks at the pearl buttons running up his sleeve. "What could possibly go wrong with this plan?"

Navy scoffs beneath her veil. "He could find out and kill us."

"Yes, all of that was sarcasm."

If that second Express Rider hadn't arrived with Adelaide's letter an hour behind Montoya, we'd be halfway to Hannah by now. Whatever happened there is already done.

"Do you think Montoya could have told Rafe about our plan?" Navy asks.

"Valid question," Raleigh says.

"I wouldn't be surprised by anything at this point," I say. "Let's be safe and assume he has already done something under the table. He's always bragging about how smart with machinations they are in the Yellow City."

Leagan comes up the slope, gunpowder in her wake. The traces of the tears she cried earlier are gone. "Well? I gave you time to think. What now?"

My mind won't stop splitting into multiple veins. Adelaide, the *Exodus Ironclad*, the railroad meeting in Oath. I take a deep breath and let the others go. It's time to pick one, the most important, and do it right.

"Adelaide was very clear she doesn't want our help." Her exact words: *Rafe set a trap for us, and I'm the bait. Do not come here.* "Her borrowed ride,

Jonathaniel Swann, was on Green's list of railroad investors. They're meeting in Oath." Not the kind of name that slips out of your head, but I checked to be sure I wasn't mistaken. I was not. "She says she'll meet us there, so we are going to trust her. Just to be prepared, though, someone should stay here in case any more letters come or her plans change."

"I'm going," Leagan crosses her arms. "I'm not being left behind this time. You can't tell me no."

"I didn't say you."

"By someone, you mean me," Raleigh says.

"I wasn't going to make you, but since you offered... A good friend shouldn't take advantage of loyalty."

"Montoya doesn't know what you're working on," Raleigh asks Navy. "Does he?"

"Absolutely not," I say. "He'd try to get it for himself." It's too valuable to tell anyone about yet. All of our futures depend on it.

"Are you going to tell him where you're going or just disappear in the night?"

"No, that would look suspicious. I'll talk to him myself."

FORTY-ONE
ADELAIDE

Of course, the spare guns I hid aren't in this room. Not even in the hotel. I open the door leading into the hall, nine steps padded by the thick carpet runner before the Company gun notices.

"Hold it, fox." He comes tramping back my way, hand to his pistol. "Where do you think you're going?"

"Mr. Swann asked me to get him some sleeping pills."

"Well, that's too bad, isn't it? You're not allowed to leave the hotel."

"I haven't left the hotel."

The consequences roll over in his mind. "You can go downstairs and ask for something from the house doctor." His gaze drips down my body. "Swann seems to have a taste for rotten milk already. If he's interested, Miss Salty, the chemical dealer, is visiting a few other barons with some sweet hallelujah this morning."

"He might."

"If your ass isn't back up here in ten minutes, I'll come looking. And when I find you, I'll throw you back down those stairs and tell everyone you attacked me. They'll take my word against yours."

I know.

One-seventy-nine.

Saraline sits by the palms filling the corner of the breakfast parlor, pipe to her lips, sunset shadows around her eyes. A hollowed, green horticulture book angles at the rest of the room, ready to flick open and pass powder to the next baron who gives her copper.

The squeak from her chair splays across the tile floor up to the arched ceiling, a whisper is still loud in a vacant room.

She starts to come to me, but I lead her behind the palms.

"I've been looking for you for two days, you motherfucker," she says. It's not anger, it's fear. Two things that like to bleed together. "Solstice has smoked herself blind on redweed every day since...and lasterday she made me go to the four o' clock hanging because she was convinced it was you."

I'm sorry about Joelle. The words almost make it out of me, then don't. If someone told me they were sorry about Grandma and Vesta, I'd know it was a lie. You're never actually sorry something bad happened to someone else. You're glad it didn't happen to you. Grief crushes you from the inside out, then leaves you alive to bleed slow. There is nothing to say to that.

Saraline digs into her pocket. "Solstice gave me this, just in case I found you."

The vial is deep blue. *Widow Venom.*

She didn't forget, even though she just lost Joelle. Even though she didn't owe me help.

I reach for the part of me that's honest, closed so tight and careful. "Tell her thank you."

"That's what friends do."

My lifestyle doesn't exactly attract friendships. I don't either. Only business partners and those who owe us favors. Kane was one of the first real friends I've ever had, then he took that from me because it wasn't enough for him. Now I can't miss his company without resenting him— and myself for ignoring the Stranger's better judgment.

I tried to hold Saraline and Thadie away too because I knew this would end, make things harder than they have to be.

"What are you doing up here?" she asks. "Going to rob some helpless crystal barons naked?"

"I already did." No one's watching. This is my chance. I pull the letter from my corset, slot it into her hand. "Will you take this to the Express office and pay them whatever it takes to leave now?"

"You're not going to tell me why?" She looks at me through narrow eyes. "If you tell me it's too dangerous, I will hit you."

"This is me buying your gun, and a packet of powder."

For when Rafe's gun upstairs asks to see it. He will.

"*Oh.*" She blinks at the roll of gold standards I put into her open book, taken from Jonathaniel's coat pocket this morning. "I'll take that instead." She points out Grandma's black pearl ring on my first finger.

I harden inside my skin. "No…check behind the loose brick on the roof of the bakery. You can have everything I left in there."

That should make us close to even.

"How about this. I will give you this powder for free if you tell me what this is all about someday."

"Yes."

A lie.

"Like I said." She draws the revolver, offers it grip first. "That's what friends do."

FORTY-TWO
TESLA

MONTOYA SITS ON A SPIT OF ROCK ELBOWING OVER THE *SOL*, PAST THE FERRY dock and the deep pools of fat, lazy current where the pearl divers swim. His eyes stay closed, his head tilted up at the sky as I approach.

"It might be polite of me to wait for you to finish praying," I say. "But there's a life at stake. Providence will understand."

"I don't pray," he says. "I never have. But I suppose it's a credit to your character that you could lose so much and still do."

"Maybe not as often as I should, but I don't think that's the point." My skirt spreads across the bread-smooth rock, hot with sun. I catch the bead of sweat that runs behind my tinted glasses. The green water of the *Sol* washes it away as I push my hand under. I can see to the bottom despite the depth, sun spots quivering on the submerged rocks. Cooler water lurks beneath the piss-warm top layer, and so do eels that look like shadows and twist like smoke.

"I'm sorry this alliance did not work out in our favors," Montoya says. "Considering the changes in circumstance, I can no longer believe our interests are aligned. I wish you well, so long as we don't cross paths in Hannah."

"You think we're going to abandon you and our deal now? I don't quit that easily, even if you do."

"I've spent years studying the art of people. Judging their strengths, faults, fears. Adelaide is a sharp sword wielded by an undisciplined hand, and you're far too used to being the smartest person in the room. Your main source of strength and failure is an absorbent amount of pride. It tells you no one else can possibly be better than you, and then you're wrong."

You fucker. But Adelaide is not the tool he sees her as, and I am not that callous.

"My dear, Poisonneur, you don't know us at all. We didn't get here by being afraid of failure."

"Now that the Stranger is either loose to the wind or dead, you've lost your incentive to need me. I'm not talking about failure, it's your opportunity to seize the upper hand and cut me out that I worry about. I know you see it."

"That doesn't mean I would ever act on it. Adelaide is my daughter's sister. I would never gamble with her life without knowing exactly what the outcome would be."

But that's exactly what I did, didn't I? Was I blinded by something I couldn't even see? This scares me. If it snuck up on me once, it could just as easily happen again. Evangeline did try to warn me. Adelaide agreed to stay in Hannah so we could strip the bolts from the inside. But did I take advantage of her willingness to sacrifice just to get my way?

"We take care of each other." I take his gloved hand, look deep into his shadowed eyes, and squeeze. The skin hugs bone, so very normal. "And that now includes you. It's everyone else that's fair game. Besides, if you do manage to get back into Cairo's good graces, we still need a friend beyond that border."

He doesn't hesitate the way I expected him to. "We've come too far to be enemies now."

I draw the cards from my skirt. It's a standard deck, red and black, moon cycles and starscapes in thirteen faces I know as well as my own. "Play me. If I win, you'll tell me what you're hiding under this sleeve."

"You will cheat," he says.

I can cheat with any deck, but this one is special. The house always has an advantage after all, darling. The face values and cycle symbols glow on the card backs like real stars, Navy's translucent ink visible only through these tainted black lenses I wear.

"That's the real game. The cards are the distraction. If you can catch me at it, I'll tell you something personal about my past. If you can't..." I lift his arm. I can only presume it has something to do with why he's here on the Rim, expelled from Cairo and the Poisonneur's Order. But I want to know if I'm right.

He picks up the smile staining my lips. "I accept the risk."

I cut the deck and lace the cards. That thrum of embossed paper is so immensely satisfying.

Montoya catches my wrist as I pivot to cut again. "I'll shuffle."

"If that makes you feel better." The two full moons I keep placed on top peel away in my hand, and he fails to see it. He's off to a wretched start, exactly how I hoped this would go. "Do you know Cycle's Thirteen? *Secuundas*, Devil's Angle…it goes by many names, played in many variations."

"At the end of the hand trade, you give your estimate of the total value of moon faces on the table. If your count exceeds the table deal, you lose."

"Black moons lower the count by face value. Red Season Moons raise it. We'll play a bare-bones stick round of three trades. *Sol*, my dear, Montoya."

He lowers his hat to his brows so his eyes vanish below the brim. I don't need them. His game is poison, and I'm sure he played it well back home. But this game is *mine*. I won my life with it.

He draws his fist of cards first, then deals the first of three to the center house. It's a red seventh-quarter moon. I peel my hand of three, then the second toll I'm supposed to turn over for the house. But instead of the red card drawn, I lay the black full moon I drew with it.

In his hand he holds a total value of eighteen, all black.

In my hand, I have the red full moon, unseen by his eyes.

Montoya lays the third house card on the baked rock. The dealer pile slips as he tries to thumb a double peel like I did.

"I see that." With a finger I turn his hand and flick the card out of it. "Amateur."

"I let you have this one," he says. "I am a gentleman."

"Sure. Now take your glove off."

With a repulsed sigh, Montoya slips the buttons on his cuff and begins to roll. As soon as the top of the glove peels free of his elbow, my face scar tingles. I hold in any sound, but my stomach sinks. The scar is purple, a melted-fresh canyon-scape of cracks and pits. He stops rolling his sleeve at the elbow, the glove at the wrist, but the wound keeps traveling in both directions.

"How high does this go?" I ask.

"To the shoulder, down the ribcage."

"Salt-acid?"

"Venom." He turns his arm in the sunlight. Through the marbled damage, hints of black tattoo ink linger, the ghosts of the exalted murderer he was. "When you are excommunicated, you take nothing with you other than a painful reminder of what you've done. Being resourceful, I did set aside a few rare ingredients that would be difficult, if not impossible, to procure elsewhere."

"Like your sword."

He dared to question me about betrayal, *several* times, by the way. But I'm not the one with a traitor's mutilation on my arm.

"That looks painful." My scar still hurts when the weather changes, and it doesn't look as bad as that, thankfully because it's on my fucking face. "So, who did you betray?"

He takes care rolling the sleeve back down, but I have experience with Adelaide. Patience will get you answers.

"A contract holder." His voice is quiet, blunt, leaden shame. "Politics in the Yellow City are complicated. It's known for them. But the etiquette of a proper poison order is straightforward. Don't kill your clients, or sure as the moon rises, you will soon have none and find no friends to welcome you when the night comes."

"My, my. How many times did they make you recite that doctrine as a child?"

"The contract is trust. Trust you'll get the job done, obviously, but foremost, you're selling someone safety. You won't kill them for a higher price."

"At least until the contract is done."

"No. Never. Without that trust the organization would be worthless."

"I suppose, if you ran out of rich people to kill."

He can make it sound as sophisticated as he wants, but it's not so different from how we run our business. Money buys protection and power, those are the rules regardless of where you are.

Montoya pauses as a pearl diver surfaces from the deep pools, sunlight slashing off the wet helmet. He can't hear us, he's too far away with the river talking in his ear.

"A merchant from a high-blooded family came to us. Well-known. It was said he held contracts with every member, barring the apprentices. I had done his work before, but this job was on behalf of his son. The targets were two young siblings who had made…we'll say, troubling accusations against this only son. The mother and her husband were to be left alive and find their children dead. Now there are ways to poison painlessly, but these deaths were political in nature. A tool to frighten. And his death by my hand was frightening." Montoya looks down at that empty hand that once held murder for money.

"I say you did the right thing. He deserved it. Did you kill his son too? I would have."

"Have you ever had to make an impossible choice?"

"Yes, I had to leave my mother's body to be collected by bounty hunters, or else Leagan and I would have died with her."

"At least she was dead at that point. My wife said I ruined our lives, but the ruination had already been spilled over us. Had I served the contract as I was asked, I would have still become something to loathe, and she would have been right to feel so. No matter what I did, someone would suffer."

I wonder if Mother thought something similar about my father. "Does she know why you did it?"

"I agreed to several conditions to secure a solo expulsion and spare my family this exile. One of them was my silence. They invited my wife to the final sentencing. She asked me why. I can still see it in her eyes, the pain. I had to look at her and endure the agony of not being able to tell her the truth, or even that I loved her."

"She's your wife. She should know you well enough to trust you had a damn good reason." If it was my husband, I would have gone with him. I would only hate him for not giving me the opportunity to choose for myself. "You could have told her and let her make her own decision." Like an equal, instead of leaving her behind like she didn't matter as much as his male pride.

"It was my choice to betray the contract."

"Did you both choose to marry each other? Or are women in Cairo told by their relatives so their families can stay rich like they do here?"

"They wanted her to despise me, and I'm sure they sent out whispers that cut apart the image she once held of me. Death is merciful. If you betray the Poison Order, you will suffer. They make that certain. And I have."

"And now you want to go back to these people?"

"They're my family."

A family takes care of each other.

"You can doubt me if you like, Tesla Revere, but this desert is desolate."

"That's what makes it beautiful."

"The city I was born to is beautiful. I mourn that place, its life and art. I had hoped to see my children have children, and when I die, leave a grave for them to visit."

Farce. I once thought Travis loved me with that kind of devotion, a foolish time in my life.

Vesta would talk about the two daughters she wanted to have someday to name Olive and Viola. A piece of my legacy died with her. But I've realized those shattered dreams aren't the end of my life. I can create new ones as long as I still live.

I press my hand over the top of his gloved one. "Thank you for sharing."

"Testimony under coercion."

"No one put a gun to your head… Sometimes getting to say a thing out loud makes it easier to live with."

"I appreciate the effort, but you're not the person I need to make this right with."

"What if you never get that chance?" This delusion of his is nothing but a heat mirage, shifting silver and always just out of reach. I know from experience. Not to mention, the people he just described sound so full of kindness and mercy.

"I will."

FORTY-THREE
ADELAIDE

Jonathaniel doesn't notice me enter the smoke lounge. He stands in one of the private alcoves, pipe in one hand, amplifying glass in the other. He leans over the table, running it over the veins of a map.

Thirty.

I step around the embroidered privacy screen to join him at the table.

"Oh…hello, Adelaide. I didn't expect you to find me here, but welcome. One of your friends at the tea house gave me a fascinating hypnosis treatment. She said I'll sleep like a cat in a sunbeam tonight, and I do say, I'm inclined to believe her."

The map is what I assumed, a survey of Hannah's mineral deposits. It's not keyed, only marked with numbers, but I could make an educated guess about the colors of the layers.

"A last bit of research for the auction." Jonathaniel puts a finger to his lip with a wink. "These are the shafts I intend to bid on." He drags fingers down two clusters, three shafts each. They split into smaller veins that will never touch the surface. Although the ones that do will never know sunlight either. "I hold this lot currently. There was a big bastard solar quartz strike here about two months past." He taps the blue shading on the lower left shafts. "I'm trying to keep that hush hush, but I know I can trust you not to say anything. You know what that means?"

"Bastard solar quartz is usually what you find right before a black gold strike," I say, my gaze on the map. The Stranger picks over every detail, drawing it in me forever.

"Excellent! Like the pretty blue eggshell before you crack into the real prize." Jonathaniel grins. "And this orange layer here, dirt that is rich in iron. That's also an indicator of high alkaline. You wanted to know how I pick my bids so well. Part of it is luck, the rest is investing in the right information. My surveyors are better than Lewis's."

I decide to ask. "Do you know the Von Kanes?"

"I do, indeed." Jonathaniel sets his pipe down in the green and gold ash dish. "Millard Von Kane is a member of my gentleman's club back home. He holds the pistol-dueling trophy three years running. My question is, how do you?"

"Everyone knows them."

"Everyone who's anyone, and I am someone." Jonathaniel regards me with rekindled interest. "And clearly, so are you. I admit I took the liberty of asking around today, but no one seems to know anything about you."

Good. Holding him hostage will be easier if his guard is down.

"I suspect laziness on their part. Everyone comes from somewhere. The man at the front door had a ghastly tale to tell, but I know he's just pulling my moustache because my southern parts did not drop off in the night and your breath did not kill me. Your father is not the devil. However, the hotel madam did mention your mother was a fortune teller."

"Grandmother."

"Ah. Well, that's something more than I knew about you two minutes ago." Jonathaniel glances furtively at the barons across the room with no interest in us, only their water pipes. "It is odd you should mention the Von Kanes at this moment. You've heard the news about the railroad expansion, I assume."

Time didn't stop because I've been trapped here. I feel the Rim shrinking like a shadow in the sun. Everything I want slipping, panic momentarily closing jaws around my head.

"When I'm done with the auction here, I'll tour one of my solar quartz mines in Oath before I head back to Jezebel. But before that, I'm tempted to go see the progress on the new line."

"How far west are they?"

"Here." Jonathaniel grabs his appointment book on the chair behind him, pulls a letter from the bundle inside that wasn't part of it this morning. "This is the latest progress report."

The Stranger soaks up the map like the ink is still wet. I find Winchester first, trace that line west to Outpost 20, then check the scale. Two hundred and fifteen miles. Not close enough to spit on Eden, but not slow enough to stop them from getting there before I do.

"That's the lead camp. They have a steam hammer to set the spikes, and they say you can feel the vibration in the ground from ten miles away. Just imagine. What a moment to be part of. Someday, they'll teach this as history, but we get to live it."

I know.

"But I digress."

"How much time does it take to mine those shafts?" I ask.

"Oh. You're not considering going into the mineral business, are you?"

"Yes."

He laughs. "You had me there."

Go ahead, believe I'm joking. I do my best to read him, see his tells. It's not so simple. Does he know about the Eden survey? Has Kane been talking to people in Jezebel? I can't decide.

"Where is the railroad expansion going?"

Of course, I know. The Stranger has known it since the first time I saw Kane's map. All of us are only going one direction.

"Westward, my love. Always west." Jonathaniel kisses my forehead.

He's not as easy to pry information out of as Kane was. I'm not good enough at it.

"What is it you desire, Adelaide?"

Was my face that obvious? Or is he that insightful? I hate both.

"Desire is the well of all our actions. That is how I stay on fortune's pretty side. I put luck and goodwill out into the world, and it manifests back to me." He regards me with a smile I can't trust. The intelligent kind. "Our desires tell so much more about us than trivial anecdotes and sky charts. So, what is yours?"

Vengeance.

My sisters. The Stranger echoes Vesta's name like a promise. It's a blood ache, desperate like hunger. Relentless as sundown.

"I want to see the moons." The sky, to smell hot sage and the pines that grow up in the high hills, not burnt ore.

If I could have the Rim all to myself and never have to worry about it becoming someone else's, that would make me happy. I don't want it to rule or build. I just want to keep it the way it is, wander in it forever. That's my curse. I will always want a thing that can't be owned. Something impossible. Somewhere to drift. Everything to discover.

But most vicious today, I just don't want to die here under Hannah's black fog.

"You're not being entirely truthful. I take that as a challenge." Jonathaniel folds the survey map with care. "I'm starting to feel empty. Join me for an early dinner, and I'll tell you about the moon on the water when I visited Eos. You'll sit with me in the Grand dining hall, and I don't care how many of these old frogs stare at us. In fact, I hope we make all of them lose their dinners."

It feels good to be someone's entertainment.

At least I'll get to eat.

FORTY-FOUR
TESLA

Our house on Navy Lane in east Saint Laura County was yellow. I would listen to my parents through the speaking tubes after Liza and I went to bed. Usually, it was to decide whether they were in the parlor and likely to notice me slipping out the spare room window and down the trellis to the garden.

Back then I was seeing a boy named Willy Marston. He promised to marry me in another year once he was eighteen. That we'd head out west and he'd strike crystal. I would laugh and say not if I struck it first.

Willy would bring me cranberry lemon tarts from the bakery, and I'd steal the housekeeper's liquor or ply it from the neighbor lady who ran a still. Then we'd meet under the ancient oaks that bent by the river. A romance of rebellion, the best my fifteen-year-old heart could conjure. We were such children. But our love was pure, untainted by experience or heartbreak.

Most nights Mother would offer occasional polite talk to Father while the typical reply from him was the crinkled flipping of newspaper pages, or the Bible. But that night they argued.

"I wish you had at least mentioned the offer to me," Mother said. "I warned you it was a bad investment. Now what are we going to do?"

"I don't want to hear about those witchcraft dreams of yours," Father said. "I've told you."

"I don't care about the house. Sell it and pay him off."

"This is my problem. I'll deal with it myself, it's not your place—"

"It is my place. I'm the one who got rid of his collection man who came today. I won't allow the girls to stay in debtor's square with you..." Or worse, her pause whispered. "We're going back to Jezebel to live with my cousin while you pay for this."

"You will not."

"My Uncle Faulkner might be able to bail you out, but if you want us to stay here, you'd better talk to Lazar in the morning and come to an agreement about this debt."

"Don't tell me what to do, Moira."

"You should have consulted me first, *Abner*. That was my family money."

"It became mine when you married me."

"I never asked to marry you. We both did what was expected of us."

"Don't act like your life has been a hardship," Father said. "You've never lacked the necessities and then some."

"Don't act like I dishonored you. I've tried to be a good wife—"

"Because that's what a good woman does."

"Because I was told. My family money for your good family name. Same as every other woman in this wretched town—"

There was a sharp, fleshy slap. I knew he hit her, not just because of that sound, but because of the sour pit that split open in my stomach like a cherry.

"Don't curse in my house."

I slapped the sunflower-shaped cap over my father's voice and dug the day bag out of my closet. I would do it this time, convince Willy to go to the Rim with me. I'd forever miss Mother and Liza, but at least I wouldn't have to be married and unhappy like a good woman. I could be free. In my house, I'd curse as much as I wanted. I'd learn to curse in other languages too.

And now, darlings, I can say *fuck* in five different languages. Beat that.

While I packed, I whispered every foul word I knew. They made me smile. They gave me courage.

The sheriff and two deputies found me and Willy holed up in the second story of an abandoned paddleboat house two days later. I assumed they'd bring me back to our lazy brick street, and even lazier yellow three-story. That I'd have to face my parents, a lecture on fornication, and explain to Liza why I'd tried to abandon her. But the wagon rolled over the tracks, past the drab brown sheds to the fence behind the granary. I'd never see our yellow house or east Saint Laura County again.

I used to wonder about the *other* world, the one behind that fence. It was sinful fun, safe across the tall, blue grass on my way home from school. The preacher warned us weekly about the wicked sinners who practiced there. Fox dens of gamblers, thieves, and prostitutes, corrosion of body and soul, he said.

Once, my friends dared me to steal a lantern off the gatehouse windowsill. I walked slowly, fear in my stomach and palms. It was thrilling. No one tried to grab me from inside to drag me under the dirt to hell, and I didn't immediately drop dead from the sin. If I was corroding, it wasn't happening fast enough to worry about. I strutted even slower on the way back, swinging the lantern like a county fair prize.

Inside the fence was a maze of brown buildings. I quickly lost myself. The wagon stopped, and I didn't know how deep inside I'd been taken. In the gathering dark, the only thing I could see for sure was how ridiculously shiny the deputy's boots had been polished. The walls weren't rotting with the devil at all—these were simple warehouses that smelled of grain and sunflower oil. The preacher didn't know what the fuck he was talking about. If he'd never been inside the sinner's lair, after all, how could he? Now I had. I could tell him he was wrong.

"You worked very hard on polishing those shoes," I said. "Why do grown-ups always turn so boring? When I—"

"You don't need to talk." The deputy motioned me to get up and follow him. A globe of blue glass flickered over the door, and the man who stood under it wore a sad velvet suit, white threads worming from the seams.

"What's this?" he asked.

"The other Sawyer girl," the deputy said.

"The *elder* Sawyer girl," I corrected him.

The man I didn't know passed the deputy an envelope and opened the door for me, closing it behind us.

Inside were my mother and sister.

Mother didn't cry when she saw me. It wasn't her way. She rose, everything a proper lady should be, and calmly put her arms around me.

But I had been missing for two days. As a mother, of course she was feeling things.

My concept of viable danger was low—I was still a child. I knew I'd just witnessed the sheriff's deputy accept a bribe, but I didn't know enough about the world to anticipate what was really happening to us. I'd only had innocent dreams, read too many adventure books, sheltered by my parents' rules. Good and evil are subjective, except in east Saint Laura County. There, they were water and iron.

My mother knew. I recognize it now. She didn't let me out of that hug. As soon as she did, my perspective on life was going to change, the price for being a woman waiting like a snare under grass.

Lamps hung from the beams, burning bastard quartz that only lit the main spaces while the corners crawled with shadows and spiders. And probably some rats.

Two men, both in responsible gray tweed, shivered under the dirty yellow light. Wet when nobody else was, why? I was being braver than they were, not crying like a baby. Those guarding us didn't explain a thing either. They must have all taken the vow of silence before I arrived. Well, it didn't apply to me, since I wasn't there to agree.

"What are we doing here?" I said to Mother. "I'm hungry, when can we go home?" I'd much rather get my punishment over with.

She put a finger to her lips. "I'll explain this to you later."

"Don't you want to know where I was?"

"Yes, Tesla, I do." But she was looking at a far door as she said it.

Through that door, they dragged my father. The starched collar he always wore was ripped off, blood running from his nose, mouth, even his eyes—I didn't know eyes could bleed. Now I've made them bleed myself.

Liza turned away, her face pressed into Mother's shoulder while Mother held onto both of us.

The man who followed came heavily, silk sleeves rolled past his elbows, gunmetal knuckles grinning on his fists. He was the poor kind of fancy. His clothes didn't quite fit. They were made for someone else, and he acquired them later.

They dumped Father on the floor and kicked his ribs. The two wet rats shuddered. They were next, and they knew it.

"Williamson, Dekklos." That fancy, poor man, the boss of this, nodded to them in turn. "Take notes, worms."

I had only just started to open my mouth to say "yes, sir" very flippantly, but Mother put her hand over my jaw and shoved it closed.

"Mighty pretty family you've got here, Abner. Must be thanks to your wife's good looks. Certainly not yours. Goddamn."

"Lazar." Mother's tone tested the air, the one she used on me when I was testing her. "Please."

"Not now, Mrs. Sawyer. It's your husband I want to hear."

I flinched as Lazar brought his heel down. Father screamed, hand pinned while he tried to recoil like a half-crushed spider. I swear my teeth felt those bones crack.

Mother's arms clamped tighter, squashing Liza and I together. "Don't look, girls."

But I did.

Air shook in his throat as Father tried to speak, tried to sit up enough to be on his knees. He was so weak, the stern sense he once had squished out of him like a bent rose stem. "The house deed and the horses—that's all I have left."

"Not *all*." Lazar leaned over him, deep pressure like a steaming engine. "I told you the rules when you borrowed the money, fifteen percent interest. You signed, and I am hellbound on helping you keep that word, you fucking son of a bitch. Providence hates a liar." Lazar looked to Williamson and Dekklos. "Are you paying attention, dogs?"

"I'll pay," Williamson whimpered. "I'll pay you tonight, I swear."

"You definitely will. Your son's growing into a strong young man. I see he outruns all the other boys in the schoolyard races."

"Don't hurt him."

"I don't have to. Those strong, fast legs of his will stay as they are. As long as you pay."

"Our house is worth ninety thousand, copper standard," Mother said. "I'll stay and help settle this. But please, let my daughters go home—"

"Your husband owes me a hundred and eighteen," Lazar said.

"Good God, Abner." Mother covered her mouth. "Why didn't you tell me?"

Father didn't look at her. I don't think he could, his eyes swelled shut, broken teeth stuck in his lips.

I wasn't a complete fool. Mother, Liza, and I were here for some purpose, same as Williamson and Dekklos. Our presence wasn't an accident, and my mind worked to decode what it was. But I was still a fifteen-year-old girl from Saint Laura. Orphans and boys from poor families sometimes sold themselves to the Rim work trains, not girls. Or so I thought. Although I also thought I knew quite a lot about sex, thanks to Willy, my experience with men was still limited to the honest safety of my narrow world. Lazar wasn't going to break our legs to frighten Father into paying money he didn't have. We were worth something else to him.

A little tremor shot through me as one of Lazar's men took hold of my jaw, turning my head side to side like one examines bone porcelain for defects. I'd never been looked at as an object before. Trust me, it becomes familiar, but you remember the first time.

"No," Mother snapped, nostrils flaring. "You do not get to touch her."

I held my chin high, even as my skin crawled, as the fat tongue he flicked over his lips made me cold. I didn't want Liza to be more afraid, so I told myself I wasn't either. I could be strong like our mother, brave for my sister.

"How old is this one?" he asked.

"Did you not hear me?" Mother said. "When I said take your hands off my daughter, I meant *now*, not when you feel good and—"

"And her?" He pointed to Liza.

I gave him my best equally degrading look. "Old enough to know your father should have pulled out."

Mother's jaw fell, eyebrows all the way up, *horrified* that something so vile had just come out of a mouth she'd raised. But where we were going, none of that mattered. The shock drained out of her face like blood, and she let my insult stand. I think we both decided then. We would become something our stiff neighbors would never recognize again. Something that survives. And then, when our teeth were strong enough, something that fights back.

The truth is, I was always going to end up here on the Rim. Some fates are like that, straight as the rails.

"Sassy." He let go of me, laughing. "Wasn't expecting that from a Navy Lane girl. What else can you do with that mouth, pretty girl?"

I don't remember what I said, because Lazar wheeled around to punch Father in the head and that man left me to watch.

Lazar waited for the shock to fade, the pain of that blow to dig in, and Father to try to collect himself out from under it. Long enough to make a man think that was the worst of it. Then Lazar hit him again. And then he didn't stop. The knuckle dusters on his raised fist flashed like wet teeth in the lamplight every time he struck. Flesh makes a distinct, wet sound as it splits. Kicks are punctuated by jagged gasps. Awful until the sounds began to fade into the fog my bravery had surrounded me with, and my father's blood was just rain hitting the floor. After all these Seasons, I've lost what angles his face bore, but I'll never forget that sound.

The wet man called Dekklos turned away and vomited.

Liza cried. I didn't in the moment, but later, once the shock wore off, yes. He was my father. I have a soul.

"Get up," Liza whispered to Father's wilted body. "You have to. Get up."

He didn't have to do anything anymore. He was dead. He couldn't protect us now, and he never had. I put my hand around Liza's little ice fingers. It was always Mother.

Lazar shook out his shoulders, prying the bloody knuckles away from his own and wiping his hands with a rag that didn't look to clean itself. "Someone scrape this meat up."

In Descendants they would have hung him with a pig hook off the water tower as a warning to others. I imagine they just buried him in the woods somewhere.

Dekklos may have been the one to vomit, but Williamson, who had the fast son, clung to the shelving, unable to stand upright. I'm fairly certain he pissed himself. I smelled something past the wet wool.

"This is what happens to those who don't pay up in a timely manner. Or worse, come with excuses. Think of your wives and daughters." Lazar cast one short glance at us. "Put them upstairs for the night, bring some food. Don't cry, girls, you're too pretty for that. You get to live. No one's going to hurt you."

Men tell the same lies to cows about to be slaughtered so they don't panic in the holding pen.

"Widow Sawyer, you and I will talk in an hour about the rest of that debt."

We were sold in Descendants two weeks later. No one there cares if the merchandise is slightly bruised. But none of them touched me or Liza the three days we spent locked in that warehouse, or on the train west. Mother admitted nothing, but I know I have her to thank for that small mercy. She was the kind of brave I someday hope to be.

I'm not angry at my father for doing this to us anymore. It wasn't on purpose. He was just a fool who didn't know anything at all.

In the end, I won the freedom I craved so desperately, and I will never give it back. Not to Green, not to the Von Kanes, not even to someone who loves me like Evangeline. No one. My life is mine.

"Widow Sawyer." One of them took hold of Mother's arm. "Girls, this way."

I watched her take three deep breaths. Like beautiful sorcery, all tremors in her hands cleared.

"Call me Moira," she said, even steel. "Moira Revere."

FORTY-FIVE
ADELAIDE

Another flash rainstorm floods Hannah the morning of the auction. A black *Sol* that courses down the Slash, carrying souls away.

Not enough of them.

It's wetter on the North Rim than I knew. In the Core, rain only comes the first three cycles of *Solace*. *End-Solace* is usually dry, but not so volatile as Moon Season.

This wet storm will probably be the last. I hold the stolen compass at the window, level on my palm, and the needle shudders. The Season Moon rises, out there behind Hannah's black smoke.

The auction lasted five hours last Season.

The Stranger ticks with my trigger finger to the pulse of the clock on the mantel. Five hours. Six. Six and a half...

You won't die here.

If I do, does the Stranger die with me, or will she be free?

Approaching footsteps stab straight through my stomach. Fresh air barrels into me as Jonathaniel sweeps in, plum flavored smoke in his wake.

"Hello, hello, my dear." He plants two hands on my chair, and his mouth almost catches mine.

I don't flinch, get away in time. But it takes everything I have not to heel-shove him into the Ven fire.

"I'm sorry," he says. "I know that breaks whore's protocol, but you, my love, are a fist of good fortune. I mopped the auction floor with those fools. Sweet Jezebel."

That's what he said last Season, but he wasn't nearly this giddy. Didn't add the "sweet Jezebel."

The Stranger catches his tongue crossing his lip where it just touched me.

Do you taste my rage, Jonathaniel Swann?

"I have to admit I've also kept distance between myself and others," he says. "I'm a man of deep passion, and I knew our time together would end. I didn't want to spoil the memory with yearning. However, I realized something today. Providence blessed me with fortune so I'd never have to be without the things I want."

You're going to be disappointed.

My body may be temporarily for sale, but my forgiveness and my loyalty are not. That's all I am to Jonathaniel. A fast distraction and a body because he's afraid to sleep in this vast bed alone. Some cavern deep inside him has to know it's *farce*.

He wrestles out of his overcoat and tie. But his gaze goes to the pearl clock on the mantel one too many times. Mine follows, dread of a different kind seeping up my throat like bile. A dead giveaway he's waiting for something. Whatever it is won't be good for me.

Thankfully, this won't take long.

I reach back, Saraline's gun in the backband of my skirt, and rise.

He stops my other hand before I get there, holds it. "I've been burned by intimacy in the past. But you are different." He fingers a strand of my white hair. "Beautiful..."

Kane used that one on me too.

Beauty is only the thing they think we need to be to feel worth. Out of fear, a lot of us have perpetuated our own lie. Intelligence is a threat, and strength wears too many faces to pin down. Skinned clean, physical desirability is an empty gun. All but worthless.

He doesn't get to touch you again.

None of this touches me. I've already lived the most wretched day of my life. Nothing will ever be worse than the way Vesta's body shuddered and gurgled as she left it. I went too long so scared that Hannah would rot my soul like it did to my mother, but none of this ever had a chance to break me. It already happened.

Try me.

The Stranger's cold presence forces him back, the side of the magnet that repels.

"God above, I am famished. Let's eat, shall we?"

Seven.

I drift, keep an eye on him through the unclosed bathroom door. "How was the auction?"

"My love, you are looking at the proud owner of shafts eighteen through twenty-four, as well as the coveted number five." Jonathaniel exchanges a fresh shirt, dropping the old one as he returns to the parlor to tug the gold service cord. "Plus, something extra for myself. My broker will have a fit when I get back to town, but he'll soon forget come the first returns."

"Congratulations." The word is lifeless.

"I wish you could have been there. I thought that bullfrog Lewis was going to shit himself. Now that would have been a sight. You would have appreciated it. Where is that waiter?" He gives the cord a second ring. "Don't they realize doing business stokes the appetite in a man?"

I curl my knees up on the couch by the parlor fireplace, the outline of Saraline's gun pressing into my spine. "When are you leaving?"

"Tomorrow morning."

Good, I'm tired of dreading.

The cutting edge of tobacco spills into the air as Jonathaniel fills his pipe from the box on the armchair's attached table. A smile begins to creep around the corners of his moustache. "I have a gift for you, but you have to wait until after dinner."

"I don't like surprises."

"You'll like this one." Jonathaniel shoves himself out of the chair in the same breath that his ass touches it. "Damnation, this won't do! I was going to make you wait, but sweet Jezebel's bones, this will kill me."

The Stranger counts as he paces in front of me.

"The past few days I have struggled to pick out the little bug that's been nagging me. And up until this afternoon, it's had me absolutely bamboozled. Do you know what conclusion I finally came to?"

You are trapped, Jonathaniel Swann. There's no way out without me.

"You."

Wait.

I lift my chin.

"There was another Tov smoking redweed in your tea house when I visited. She offered to read my sky chart, a black gold opportunity one could hardly pass up. My moon fell in the house of The Stranger. A friend in need, or cursed enemy."

Solstice. She really does care. What I question...is it because she thinks I'm going to reproduce and keep the Tov bloodline alive, or does she actually care about me?

"She recited me a delightful poem titled *The Stranger* and said I will continue to have good luck if I offer myself to someone in need."

Grandma used to tell me the same poem, told to her by my mother.

"I learned something about you from this fortune teller." Jonathaniel takes the seat next to me, grinning like a fool. "I know what your name means."

Do you?

"*Adelaide* translates to 'the Stranger' in Tov. While I did know Tov and Cairosh are sister tongues, the girl who sold me the sleeping tonic confirmed it."

If Jonathaniel was just a hair more suspicious, he would question this coincidence. But he's from the east. Solstice and Thadie played him like Grandma used to do to our marks, even though I didn't ask.

"I also learned I've been mispronouncing your name all this time. My love, why didn't you say anything?"

Because it was hardly important. It kept distance.

"Anyway, as a thank you for your exquisite company, as well as the good fortune you brought me today, I'm going to buy your work contract from Rafael."

The breath stops midway out of my lungs.

"Aha." Jonathaniel's grin deepens. "This does make you happy. And that makes me happy. I don't want to leave you here."

I assumed my exit would be bloody. Was prepared to die trying. I've always known that someday that's how I'll end—a savage, red death. The Stranger accepts that fate, but I'm not ready for it yet. I'd be a fool not to take an easier way out.

"You are wild." He wraps a dry hand over mine. "Oh dear, you're cold. And no wild thing can live inside a cage. All those bruises and cuts you have concern me. You may not want to tell me where they came from, but don't take me for a fool. I know they're no accident, and whatever hands made them will never be held accountable like they should."

No. *I* already made sure they paid. They're dead now.

"This place is killing you slowly, Adelaide. I can see it in your bones. I can *see* your bones, and that's not a Tov joke. Allow me to help you."

Chances like these break the second you dare to believe in them. Nothing in my life has ever come this easy. But I breathe desire into this glinting ember anyway, and it lights.

I make no promises this works. You can't trust him.

"Two smiles in a row. My love, all you had to do was ask."

I'm not one to do that. Usually at my own expense.

"I have a meeting scheduled with Rafael to finalize the details in…" Jonathaniel examines the clock again. "A little more than an hour. But after all the money I just poured into him, he owes me a favor or two. And I've never known a man who could refuse me."

Rafe might be the first. Jonathaniel doesn't know who I am, or what Rafe thinks my family and I have done. I just hope his greed is stronger than his wrath.

Either way, he hasn't met mine.

FORTY-SIX
ADELAIDE

Shoe polish and coffee grease the air of the Company parlor. But the steam rising from the copper kettle dies while we wait, unmoved.

Jonathaniel takes another lemon candy from the dish.

I stopped listening to his story when we walked in here. The drawer pulls from the side table with the effortless glide of warm butter. A silver ashtray and a pack of cards. One domino.

"To that I said, 'Lewis, you—'" Jonathaniel finally realizes I'm not next to him anymore. "What are you doing over there? Are you nervous? There's no need."

Beneath the wall shelves open two latching cupboards. One with a dusty mousetrap, the other empty.

"You know my coat looks fine on you," Jonathaniel says. "But it's not the right cut. We'll stop by the dress shop once we're done here, then get you fitted into some nicer things in Vantage, or possibly Oath. No more of this plain white or gray, cheap cotton business. I see you in afternoon blue, like spring grass in Jezebel. Do you prefer Eos linen or taffeta?"

I prefer black.

The stairwell door opens, and Kasey enters Rafe's guest parlor the same way we did. I rise off my heels, hands at my sides, don't reach to feel the bulk of Saraline's gun under the duster like a fool. It didn't go anywhere.

Kasey touches the dark spot on his hat. "This is an evening surprise, Mr. Swann, Miss Revere. You here to see the boss?"

Now I have a real name. He's smart enough not to call me "shady" or even "fox" in front of Jonathaniel.

"Fine evening indeed." Jonathaniel twists in his chair. "But I'd be enjoying it more if we didn't spend all night sitting around here. I have plenty of things to do."

"I'm sure."

"If you could pass that along, my good man, I'd be delighted. Thank you, that will be all."

Kasey's jaw flexes under his ash-tone beard. He would open anyone else a new asshole for talking down to him like that. "And what are you smirking about, shady lady?"

That was short-lived respect.

"If I recall, and I do, you have nothing to look so pleased about."

We'll see about that.

His steps ring down the black planks into my feet as he proceeds to knock on Rafe's office. "Boss. Swann is waiting. Impatiently." He opens and shuts that door behind him, Rafe's voice bloated on the other side.

Jonathaniel leans my way. "Revere, is it? That's an excellent surname."

"Alkaline," I say.

"Pardon?"

"Alkaline means excellent."

"As with crystal." The smile even lifts the corners of his moustache. "I do love how worlds and words collide here."

The gun who brought us up here steps out of Rafe's office, holds the reinforced door for us. "Go on in, Mr. Swann."

"Finally." Jonathaniel waits to take my arm.

I let him. Wear him, the way Aunt Tess would. As a weapon.

Twenty-one.

The Stranger knows these dark red walls down to the black swirls around the knotholes, the marrow marks of once-trees.

"Mr. Swann." Rafe rises from the desk to shake Jonathaniel's hand. "I do apologize for making you wait. I hope it wasn't too much of an inconvenience. And Miss Revere." He picks my left hand, on purpose. Squeezes my broken finger, pain vibrant and crimson, whiskers like wires scraping my knuckles. "Always a striking sight."

"Isn't she?" Jonathaniel says. "Mind yourself though. I paid for her attention, and I'm afraid I don't like to share."

"Why should you?" Rafe treads across the four black moons burned in the wool rug the last time I visited, plucks his favored whiskey bottle from a shelf on the third bookcase. His back never fully turns on me. "I understand the auction scales tipped heavily in your favor today."

"Indeed, they did." Jonathaniel beams.

"Then let me offer you a drink, and my congratulations."

Kasey is the one the Stranger watches, framed against the ash-frosted windows. She wraps dread around his shoulders, his neck like a noose, pulls into his nostrils to drain out his mouth like breathed smoke. Despite how close she is, he never flinches because he doesn't know she's there like I do.

"*Sol.*" Rafe passes one glass off to Jonathaniel. "Now, to what do I owe this pleasure? I would have thought today would find you celebrating your new investments with your companion here."

This really is the worst he's been able to come up with to make me as small as his mind.

"My train doesn't leave until after lunch tomorrow," Jonathaniel says. "And it won't go anywhere without me. Plenty of time to divert the mind and enjoy Hannah's last indulgences before I have to return to drudgery."

"Alkaline." Rafe turns the smile on me, poisonous.

"Excellent," Jonathaniel says quick, so proud of himself.

Rafe thinks he's safe. He probably plans to burn my body in the refinery furnaces like the rest. Or maybe he'd bury it in a shallow grave outside the fence so the coyotes and scavenger lizards could dig me up. One last act of vengeance.

"I'm here to thank you for the magnificent debauchery." Jonathaniel tilts the whiskey glass. "In fact, I so loathe to see it end that I have one final offer to make you, my good man."

Rafe chuckles. "I'm afraid my time isn't for sale."

"Oh, you dog. No, no, I had someone else in mind."

Rafe is still smirking as he accepts Jonathaniel's envelope. It takes a full minute for the self-satisfied curve of his false jaw to go hard, match the lines between his wire eyebrows. That thick vein knots up his forehead, solid as a root. "What is this?"

"My offer. For my lucky strike. A highly generous one, I might add."

"I can read."

"Well good, I should hope so. I'd hate to embarrass you."

"She's not for sale."

"Oh no, my dear sir, you told me yourself the very first time I came here, everything in Hannah is for sale. One just has to name the right price. I did not forget," Jonathaniel says. "I've grown awfully fond of her."

"As have I." Rafe looks through a lidded gaze. "I'm afraid the answer is no."

I stare into him. The Stranger is a will inside me, not just a shadow, a heart and a pulse. A hunger. He has to feel her. I taste her. Blood. Salt. Vinegar. Fire. All the things that burn on the tongue.

Kasey puts a hand on Rafe's shoulder, speaks to his ear.

"No." Rafe's stare doesn't break with mine. "She's still a Revere. It doesn't matter who's telling the truth anymore."

"I'm not sure what to make of that accusation," Jonathaniel says. "But I'm afraid I've never learned to take no for an answer."

"This is a lot of gold for a milk-bastard. She can't be that good to fuck, and I know for a fact she's worse at conversation."

"Value is set by the heart," Jonathaniel says. "It's a tricky thing to measure against a life."

We've been here before. My gaze, Rafe's, both holding tight, burning each other like coffee and Sun Fire in an empty stomach. He's finally getting a taste of what I've felt. Cornered. But I've never been the prey. He's the rat, I am a fox. He just failed to see it.

His iron lips twist.

"Fuck it." He lets the paper go on his desk, downing the last of his whiskey. "You really are a man who gets his way, Mr. Swann."

"Indeed."

"And you..." Rafe steps in, deep-earth gaze to mine once again. "This is the luckiest day of your life, Revere. Don't you ever forget that." The thumb he rubs across my cheek barely scrapes skin, the Stranger reading the shudder that crosses his palm. He'd rather slap the spit out of me. It's all he can bear to hold the rage back. "I won't forget you."

The Stranger is a bare blade, cold like silver on my tongue. "*Sol.*"

She won't forget you. I won't forget. When your unlucky path crosses mine again, you die. "If anyone asks what happened to your crystal last

Moon Season, tell them Mr. Green, the governor of Vantage, snake-fucked—"

"You kept that mouth shut for cycles, fox. You wire it together another two minutes or so help me Jezebel, you'll wish you had." Rafe finishes scrawling his name on the purchase agreement, casts the pen back at the ink tray. Misses. "There. Allow me to say goodbye."

I angle my knee for a straight upshot into his groin as he grasps my arms with both of his. Copper teeth click against my ear.

"Say one more word about stolen crystal in front of him and I'll fuck you with this letter opener for all the times I didn't. Then I'll give you to Kasey and let him slit your throat. It'll be well worth repaying Swann for the damage done to you. This is not over."

No, it's not.

"Now get out of my sight before something happens we all regret."

I make sure to look him in the eye. The Stranger's dawn-cold presence scrapes bone. "*Vacca voya.*"

He knows what I mean even if he's never heard those words before.

Rafe yanks a crease out of his vest. "Don't let her murder you, Mr. Swann."

"Oh, if she was going to murder me, she would have done it already. I don't believe that the Tov were as bloodthirsty as we were all led to think. I suspect most of them were harmless as kittens as long as they were well fed, same as the rest of us."

"Not this one."

"I'll take my chances." Paper crackles as the deed disappears into Jonathaniel's breast pocket.

"I'll see you next Season, Swann...hopefully." The windowpanes shudder as Rafe exits through the bathroom.

Eight.

"You know I had a little side bet going with Nelson and Jacoby," Kasey says. "How long it would take you to get yourself killed in here. I was the only one who said you wouldn't. It's a shame they're not alive to see it."

"Why, thank you, my man." Jonathaniel sweeps ahead as Kasey grabs the door from me.

"Word of advice, Swann? If you're ever in a gambling den, don't bet on her, she's a terrible dice player."

Dice is only luck, fool.

Luck dies.

"Are you now?" Jonathaniel retrieves his hat from the coat tree. If he knew what Kasey's actually talking about, he wouldn't be laughing.

My face must be telling part-truth. His smile fades out.

"I do believe it's time we were going. Come along, Adelaide, I'm suddenly ready for dessert."

Kasey nods to me. "I told the boss you're not the thief."

You think that matters now?

"You would have bargained with him if you had anything to give, not waited this long. You weren't lying."

I pass my slow gaze down his body. It's only meat and bone. Not believing me is the least of your concerns. I let him see for one blink. The Stranger a beat along the outline of my body and his, heavy black smoke.

The skin of his throat flickers.

Jonathaniel wraps an arm through mine. "Farewell, sir."

Thirty-eight.

Down in the stairwell beaded with quartz-fed coil lamps, it's darker. But out of Kasey's sight, the Stranger doesn't climb so far up the walls. It feels brighter.

"I did not like the way he just spoke to you up there," Jonathaniel says. "Whatever he did to you, I'll make sure it never happens again."

"I need to say goodbye to a friend before I go back to the hotel."

"Of course, I don't mind at all. Now that I don't have to say goodbye to you, we have all the time we want. I already planned to play cards, probably egregiously late tonight. Don't feel the need to wait up."

I won't.

FORTY-SEVEN
ADELAIDE

I FIND THADIE IN HER REAL ROOM, HER BEDROOM IN THE HOUSE A FEW ROWS down from Madam Charlene's.

"Did you still want to read my moons?"

"You're saying goodbye." Honesty rises though her mask of easily given smiles. The person she is underneath is insightful, fortune tellers have to be. She hides it the way I hide the Stranger. "It's okay, I knew it was coming. The moons tell me all kinds of things."

"It would be rude not to."

"That's what you'd do to anyone else."

She's not wrong.

Thadie draws her moon diviner from inside a spare pillowcase, lays it on the floor between us. "I'd love to."

I feel very far away as she makes the globe spin over a blank sheet of cotton.

"This is just for fun." Her voice jars though me, the crackle of paper once wet and dried as she pins her star map over the cloth at the corners, holds both up to the diviner's lavender glow. The dark stars spilled from ink bloom from the light passing underneath. "You and I know it doesn't mean anything, but everyone likes it. Isn't it pretty? You can keep it, and think of me." Her smile turns. "What I see under your bad moon, you're wearing a lot of blood. I'm not trying to scare you, but some of it's yours, not all of it."

"I'm not afraid of blood."

As long as I don't die here.

"Have you ever betrayed someone?"

I laugh, a bare, dry thing. Montoya. Kane...just the most recent.

Thadie joins along with mine, hers unsure. "I'll say *he*, that seems the most likely. I don't see a face, but he's not out of your life. I can't say if that's under your good or bad moon, they're in an eclipse. But your good moon is bigger. You're going to get something you've wanted a long time."

I hope she's not wrong. Fortunes are only specific enough to make you ask more questions, fill in the gaps with your own life. I did this for her, not for me.

"I understand why you need to go, but I'll always be your friend," she says. "No matter where we are."

There are things that could make her turn on me. They are going to happen.

The Stranger rips against her own desires and what we both recognize is something good for me.

"You should leave too," I say.

There are so many better places out there. She's too smart to get stuck here, a waste that won't be around much longer.

"I've thought about it." Thadie squeezes my good hand. "Wherever you go, please be careful."

"You too."

I'm glad I met her.

THE SASH HISSES WARNINGS THE DARK IGNORES AS IT SLIDES, MY SHAPE nothing to the deepest part of the night.

Jonathaniel sleeps back at the hotel. First and second shifts sleep, the third chipping away the bowels of the earth. Even girls who work at night are home. It's the hour of ghosts and other wretched things.

I drop the black scarf covering my head, the bone face of the Stranger the same cutting white as my hair.

Eight.

The door is locked from this side. I don't have to worry about someone walking in.

Shadows cast by light can't fall in darkness, but the Stranger isn't one of them. She spills over the bed, a lawless one, tethered to nothing but me.

Kasey sleeps on his back like a dog, chest sinking under the weight of his snore.

Like I hoped, Rafe withdrew his guns guarding the hotel hall. I'm Jonathaniel's problem now.

I uncap the glass tube Saraline gave me. The needle sinks deep, soft neck no resistance. Kasey's steady breath cuts off mid-snort. His leg kicks the sheet before all of him goes rigid as a day-old corpse. Widow snake venom.

The Stranger uncurls around me, mattress dripping black as I step onto the bed. There are no moons in Hannah, eyes are accustomed to darkness. I know he can see me inside the vague shadows.

Two.

I sink onto his chest, my weight pressing down on his already heavy lungs. The Stranger vibrates as he blinks, his neck stretched into taffy cords, hands dug into the blankets and paralyzed that way.

He always sleeps with a knife. I reach under the pillow, find the walnut handle.

The memory spawns with the sudden bite of a cramp. Kasey's body is still a defenseless bulk under me. But I see him and the others the evening they caught me, their camp, bloody with firelight. Me, just bloody.

"Look at that," Kasey said as my crossgun unfolded in his hands. "Now here's a fascinating treasure."

I set the clip point to the hollow of Kasey's throat. His weapon.

"Give it here," Jacoby said.

"Wait your turn, vulture, seeing as I didn't get one." The one without a name lifted my crossgun from Kasey's grasp before Jacoby could get it, rubbing the stock as he prowled toward me. "Wouldn't that be fitting, fox?"

My barrel was tainted with the scent of gunpowder as he shoved it up under my throat.

I push the blade in. Slow.

"I kill you with your own gun."

"You'll get twelve years bad luck for that." But Kasey laughed along with the rest of them.

To twelve years bad luck.

Kasey doesn't flinch. He can't. Widow snake venom turns your body to stone around you. They say you still feel it as you die. I hope so. What I see in his eyes tells me he does.

The blade sinks deep, to spine. I lean until the tip pops through the mattress on the other side of him. Air spills up his throat, wind escaping through the gaps in an old house. The same noise Vesta made as her life unraveled in front of me. I smell iron, but taste copper.

When you get to hell, tell them the Stranger sent you.

I rise.

Two rifles hang on the rack by the door. Soundlessly, I pull each drawer of his dresser, top to bottom, the medicine cabinet, the trunk under his bed.

Blood weaves new patterns through the sheets, black as the widower snake who gave its venom for this. The river finds its way to the floor in drops.

A familiar shape haunts the larger trunk in the closet. My crossgun.

The smile punches through my storm.

The barrel is silk, wood stock sleek as a cat's tail. Fool's gold. Leagan made this for me with love and craftiness, equal parts. I've missed its weight on my back like an amputated limb.

I open the break barrel, then eject the bolt cartridge. Both are empty. That would have been too easy. Still in the pocket of the coat he wore five days ago is Leagan's latest gift to me. The revolver, *Reliable* down the barrel.

I turn.

The Stranger reaches toward the bed. Stillness. He's bled out into the darkness. Meat.

From my belt I draw on a new morning salt glove. Between the hair on his neck and the hair poking out of his chest, the shape of my hand seared into him like judgment.

FORTY-EIGHT
ADELAIDE

J<small>ONATHANIEL'S TRAIN GLITTERS</small>. T<small>HE</small> E<small>MERALD</small> C<small>ONSTELLATION</small>.

Carpet absorbs my steps, the smell complicated. Leather upholstery, varnish, and heating metal. The memory of the *Absolution* strikes like lightning. She smelled like home. This doesn't.

Forty-eight.

The velvet drapery scrapes my fingertips against the grain. The storm shutters, fixed below the windows and wind up, not down. This isn't our train. The Stranger and I both know it.

Fifty-seven.

Four guns. Playing cards, smoking, staring out the window into the gray. Four men to protect thirteen cars. There were six of us to the six cars of the *Absolution*.

No one ever stood guard at his door like the other barons in the Hannah Grand besides Rafe's men, paid to watch me. They don't belong to Jonathaniel.

Hannah may be a safe place for rich men, but now we're going to cross hundreds of miles of the open Rim. The *Emerald Constellation* is a target worth the risk. I would know.

I hope she's fast.

"Captain Montgomery!" Jonathaniel calls down the living car. "You are looking very ill this morning. Don't tell me the whiskey's gone bad."

Montgomery glowers under his gray mutton chops, trailing me with sallow eyes. "You've lost your mind, Jon."

"And enjoying every minute of it. Insanity is an acquired taste, but once you do acquire it, you'd never go back. Ordinary life is exceedingly dull."

I tail Jonathaniel to his private car like a reflection in glass. My new skirt flares around each step, catching on its own length and weight. Soft blue. But I like skirts. The way they shape, how air and fabric brush my legs at the same time. This one is too long and dense for quick motion, but it hides many deaths so I forgive it. Grandma always said skirts were invented by women to hide weapons. She's not wrong.

Below the double-plated windows, the station yard shifts with bodies in motion, the cascading smoke cutting through them like ghosts. Sighs of the engine's slow boil disturb the early air. A slow smile warms my face, and I pull the first drawer of the mirrored display cabinet. Ours held weapons and spare ammo. These have porcelain and actual silverware, things an east blood would expect. The cabinet shelves books, an obsidian strategy board, a collection of pipes and flavored tobacco, licorice and candied fruit.

Other suits hang in his closet, a palate rising gray to crisp-brown, not the ones he wore at the hotel. Cologne bottles shaped like roses and vials of shave oil arranged on a mirrored tray in the bathroom.

"While we have the rest of our lives to get fully acquainted, I just have one question now." Pressure comes against my crossgun where Jonathaniel places his hand to my back, the bulk under my coat. "Why?"

So, his eye is sharp to some things.

"This is the Rim."

"Indeed, but you are with me now."

"Have you spent much time here?"

"Oh yes. You don't need to be afraid. No one is going to hurt you anymore."

So many things here will hurt you given the smallest chance.

Jonathaniel flips open the copper speaking tube in the wall. "I have arrived, you may start moving whenever it's convenient." Then he lifts the fresh bottle of liquor from the fig and cheese platter with a sigh. "God of Mercy, I am quite parched."

"Why don't you travel with bodyguards?"

Jonathaniel blows the notion off his lips like a fly. "Waste of money, love. They'd only get in my way, and I don't have time to be tripping over anyone who isn't good-looking. Besides, I've never been unlucky a day in my life. Why would I want to tempt Fate's evil eye on me now?"

You'd regret that if I'd had to threaten you.

The engine takes a full breath. I want to be up there, touch the valves and dials, see the track stretched out in front of me.

"Finish acquainting yourself," he says. "If you're hungry, I can call the staff."

We lurch. The Stranger pulls me to the windows.

Five.

Steady the vibration of the wheels fills me up. The red and flat black of Hannah slides off the windows. Down the pitch throat of the tunnel. Faster.

The walls fall away. Pale gray grassland. The sour fist up in my throat unclenches two of its fingers, less fear of this getting ripped away from me.

Red lightning spears the blank skyline in front of us. Somewhere out there is the sun. I can't wait to feel it burn.

Jonathaniel comes to my side, two goblets of the sticky pear rum with him. "I know it's still early, but why not." He tips his glass to mine. "To adventures on the Rim, and elsewhere."

"How many settlements have you been to?"

"So many. I own mines in Windust and Oath. Vantage, of course. I've passed through Descendants and Junction, all over."

"You are lucky." If he wasn't, he'd already be dead.

"I told you so. Never met a man fool enough to kill me. So don't worry, you'll be perfectly safe with me."

It took half a day to cross the waste-scape into Hannah. I stay on the catwalk or at the windows. When the smoke staining the sky clears, I will be there.

It happens suddenly. Light punches through to landscape that was gray one breath ago. Shadows still writhe on the ground, but the clotting overhead melts like a healing bruise. Colors. The bloodshot sunlight burns my eyes. And nothing has ever been so beautiful.

The *Emerald Constellation* knifes over red dirt and green shrubs, the smell of sage, sweet cactus flower limitless. My arm fills with the weight of the wind as I reach out, hand glowing with sunlight.

I have two shadows.

One is cast by the sun and moons, fire and lamps.

The other is the Stranger.

My mother didn't curse and abandon me. She gave me the chance to become whatever I wanted.

I choose Revere.

FORTY-NINE
TESLA

It takes five days to reach Oath on horseback from Lideon. But I am a smuggler. Men and mining gear are slow, noisy, and obvious targets for bone pickers. We Reveres know how to move things, stealthy and efficient. It was our business after all.

The girls and I ride the steam handcar across the south *Sol* on a smuggler's bridge. It shudders desperately, and I stare down at the churning green water and wonder how bad it would feel to hit it. But the rusted iron and planks hold, cutting us over to the main line, and we reach Oath in just under three days.

Oath looks deceptively like an eastern town. Pastels coat warpable wood siding, and flower baskets hang from eaves. Anyone who forgets fortune is the only god here can turn north. They'll see its mighty altar, the ore elevator rising off the striped gold-and-copper hillside.

They mine Ven and ghost quartz here, the rest of the land belongs to the trappers.

I steer my horse along the vegetated path of the *Sol* after breakfast, alone. The scrub trees fill the natural hollows and flood the backside of a homestead with their own irrigation trenches. It reminds me of the all the green in east Saint Laura County.

I wouldn't go back there for all the crystal on the Rim, but sometimes it's nice to breathe something green and remember an innocent time. A life as someone's wife would have been my personal hell. And worse for whatever fool had the misfortune of choosing me, I assure you.

I dismount alongside the tannery in grass up to my knees, the *Sol* tight up on the bank and whispering about it. The stacks of traps and water barrels soaking hides behind the cabin are things to avoid. Animal smells stick to clothes faster than human ones.

A hundred scraps of yellow fabric flutter on the line between lantern posts, as well as the pole in front of the cabin. This is a North Exodus Trading post. Free agents and the pickers from the Smythe and Matthan-Atlas Fur Company better know where they're stepping and not. Trappers, such territorial bastards.

I can't say the lazy braid actually tames Travis's black-walnut hair, more yellow ribbon and fur tails hanging off his belt. If anyone finds his dead body, don't they dare mistake him for a fool's gold Matthan-Atlas man and bury him. Let the wild claim his bones.

Damnation, I feel like I swallowed a few of those ribbons.

I was the one to do the right thing, the *smart* thing and cut myself off, but not because I wanted to. These miseries give us texture, or some other *farce* like that, that Evangeline would say and be right about. I still think about him at night.

The things you love are the ones that know how to break your heart.

His back faces me, arms laid bare as he scrapes the pelt stretched across the frame behind the cabin. The lush, shimmer-tipped fur basks in the sunlight.

"Mountain cat." I stop before the vats, in the shade of the rough trees.

He goes still, my heart knocking into my ribs as he straightens up, shoulders spreading. "Jezebel be damned."

"Damned to the dust," I say. "Tell me I'm right though. That's a mountain cat."

His turn is deliberate, meant to draw out my reaction time, and still flight. He's used to handling wild game. "Come a little closer and find out."

Fuck, I remember all the time we've spent together. The warm shiver under my skirt tells me my body does too.

"I don't think so," I say. "This is a new skirt, and I know this is a messy business."

"You live for messy business—" He squints, probably at my scar. Even fully healed it's the first thing about my face I see. Unfortunately, everyone else does too.

"It looks good on me, doesn't it." I beat him to the trigger, but I know he'll have something to say about it. Men always do.

"It does, actually. The trains around here are getting careless because no one's been held up in so long. I was starting to think you'd abandoned this life for the next. Or was that all part of your plan?"

"We've been a little busy elsewhere."

"You're not here for the usual reason?"

I remove my duster. "Unless you're not interested."

He snorts.

Montoya hasn't tried to fuck me, which I was suspicious of until he told me that story about being faithful to his wife. I was beginning to wonder if this scar had made me a little too rough. Silly me.

I put up a hand before Travis makes it around the last tanning vat. "The least you can do is wash your hands before you touch me."

And fool's gold, I want him to touch me.

His smile is equally lupine, but he plunges his arms deep in the standing tub of water, scrubbing until the surface boils. His gaze never separates from mine, water rushing off his hands as he yanks them free and lifts me at the waist. I set my forehead against his, run my fingers through the wire of his beard. His skin smell—*Vacca voya*, I could sob.

"Do you want something to eat or drink first, or should we just get down to business?" he asks.

"You're a terrible cook."

"Jakob and Eben don't care."

"Just fuck me."

He kisses me once, deep and hungry, then drags my head back to go for my neck. He pushes away the collar of my shirt, tilting my skin against the light.

"Did you find something more interesting than me?" The contact burn of the rope left a lighter patch of skin inside a darker rim. But it's already faded so I don't expect it to last forever like the one on my face.

He drags a thumb down the thickest part of my cheek scar, but the skin tingles in the wrong half of my face, the injured side dead to the touch. "What happened to you?"

"Not now." I unbuckle his tool belt and let it fall, sliding my hand down his pants. "Did you miss me?"

He leans into me with a groan. "Like the wicked man misses sin."

"Prove it."

Coffee rides his tongue, animal musk embedded in his skin so deep, it's part of what he is now, the smell my mind and body both remember. We get only half our clothes hauled off before he pushes me back on the table, splaying my legs.

"*Fuck.*" My toes curl, back arching. There are so many aches locked inside of me, so much violent rage. This helps.

"Fuck!" I let my head fall back and yell it.

Oath sits off on the other side of the *Sol*, blinded by a mask of green trees while the sun peels the paint off the walls. They won't hear me, and I don't care if they do. Not when his beard is scraping my skin and his tongue is down between my legs.

My end comes sudden, like a handful of stars shattering in my head.

He comes up gradually, kissing the sweat on my thighs and stomach, hands like fire on my skin.

My salt is still on his tongue when I kiss him, inhaling so hard I can't breathe past the blood thrashing in my ears.

"You're shaking." Travis pulls me against him.

"That's your fault."

"I'm going to fuck you so hard you forget the name of everyone you've ever fucked before."

That would be quite the list. Not that I've ever known all of their names.

The first few strokes into me are silent, his grip pinching my legs and his teeth digging into my shoulder, too much lust fuming in both of us. I bite him back, his breaths building up a tower stacked higher and higher to reach the gasp that brings him crashing down.

His beard catches on my thumbs as I cradle his face, while the skin under his eyes is rose-petal soft. "I've missed you too."

He holds onto me, still inside. "What makes you think I'll let you go this time?"

"What makes you think it's your choice?"

There it is. That pang of sad affection in his eyes that keeps me coming back even though he breaks me every time.

"You know why."

"I know."

It hurts to smile, but not as bad as it would to never see his face again. "I don't want you to get bored of me."

"I wouldn't. It would be nice to have someone to come home to."

"I know." Cold floods into his place as his hands fall away from my chest, and I gather my pants. "I'm one of the most interesting people you'll ever meet."

"And humble to boot."

"Of course, it's part of my charm."

It's not wrong to want someone to hold, to love, and to love you back. Having him in my arms feels *right*. Damn him for this ache and every other time he's made me long for a future that won't ever exist.

"I haven't seen you in two Seasons," Travis says. "What brings you back now?"

"You haven't heard?" I draw my overskirt up my hips. This is going to be a longer conversation than I hoped. "You have been out on the open Rim too long and haven't kept up with the news, sir."

I'm not against the idea of choosing a life partner, but never someone who would expect me to stay behind, protecting the homestead and waiting with the children while they got to live. He goes trapping in the wilderness for cycles at a time, and I prefer having a bed and a bathroom to smelling like an animal and using a bush. I won't play second-best to a job unless it was one we did together.

He's made it abundantly clear he has no interest in my chosen way of life.

I loved my train. I loved my Vesta even more, but she was rare as a blue river pearl. A joy I didn't ask for and wouldn't have chosen if I'd been offered one. Providence gave her to me special, and no future child could ever replace her.

Travis can deny these realities all he wants—and he has—but I'm right, even if he never sees the truth. That's what our life together would be—a compromise. Mine.

"The news never changes. You'll fill me in on the important stuff." He opens the portable stove, stirring up the quartz inside. "Want some coffee?"

"Please." I turn the chair so I can face him as he works. "How's the fur business these days?"

"Lucrative." He glances across his vats soaking with accumulated wealth off the porch.

"Alkaline. Have you ever trapped up north?"

"How far north?"

"Hannah."

"Ah," he grunts. "I haven't been that far for three Seasons."

"Would you like to?"

"There's almost no game in the area. The refinery puts out so much smoke, the sky turns black, like the biggest storm you've ever seen, but it doesn't move. Even the animals know that land is petrified. Most of the men stay south of the *Io Rift*, or the Northern Plains as the east bloods would say. The Matthan-Atlas pickers hold the balls on North Shore, all the best bear and otter spots."

"You should just kill them."

"We've tried. The company just sends more. No, they can keep their bear, I've got more than ten times your weight in fox and cat pelts in here."

"Good on you."

"What do you need this time?" He rubs a hand up the inside of my leg. *"Farce..."*

I get very close so that his only assumption can be I'm about to kiss him. "Your help."

The sigh is familiar. "You only come south when you do."

"How do you feel about knocking out a rail with me? A baron train is coming from Hannah. I need to make sure they don't slip out of my reach before I get the chance to meet with them." I give his arm a squeeze. "You have all this muscle, let's put it to good use."

"Fucking with the rails fucks with my profits." He looks at me sideways. "And yours, I thought."

"Times have changed." I spy dirt under my thumbnail. It hurts to admit the *Absolution*'s loss out loud. I never took to smoking like Mother and now Leagan, but right now I almost wish I had something to huff just for the distraction.

"So you said."

"We were derailed, last Moon Season."

His face twists, winding through several variations of pity and vicarious anger. "Fuck…I know what that engine meant to you."

"It gets worse."

Breath escapes him with a hiss. He removes the percolator from the bed of breathing quartz, returning to the log table with two tin cups and a dusty bottle of Sun Fire.

"You saved this for me?" I pull the cork and inhale bright cinnamon and hellfire.

"Never know when you might come around…I told you your lifestyle was dangerous."

And there it is. The heat from the coffee and spices dulls next to what's in my chest. "Don't fucking start this with me. I didn't come here to fight."

"All right. All I'll say is what I said before: I'm making a life here. We could share it. But I can't be what you are. I want an honest living. I can't watch you get killed by some other roadman."

"And I've said this before too: all life is risk." I got my face flayed like a fish, but he still hurt me so much worse. "Honest living isn't all they want you to think it is."

"You'll never know unless you try it."

Now I wish I hadn't come just to get this wound reopened all over the place. It seems we're both still determined to have our own way. So be it. Leagan's dreams showed him to her for a reason. I'm here to collect him for whatever that might be, so allow me to swallow my pride like a mature adult. It tastes like burnt bread, by the way. With no jam.

"I can promise you this job will be worth the losses," I say. "You'll get more sex and gain an alkaline story to impress all your friends when you get back."

"About which, the sex or the robbing?"

"That's up to you. Please be my accomplice this one time because you also care about me as a friend, not just someone for fucking."

"You've never been just someone to fuck. Have I been part of this plan for a while, or was this just convenient for you?"

"I'm not here because you're my last choice, but I know how you feel about our business. I'm trying to be more respectful of other people's wishes." I'll admit I was momentarily scattered when my first plan crumbled. But I found myself again, and now I believe I'm glad Rafe escaped me the first time.

He nods. "I appreciate knowing where I stand."

"I know… And you should know I'll always think about you."

He doesn't say anything to that.

FIFTY
ADELAIDE

THE FIRST SUNBURN TIGHTENS MY FOREARMS BY NOON. THE HOURS I'VE SPENT on the catwalk while the red slopes rush by are to blame. Worth it.

I look west, and the Stranger's desperate ache fills me. She reaches for that forever line, for more. It fits like my crossgun, a thing I know as well as my skin. Sometimes better.

Jonathaniel joins me at the railing, and the wind rips the card-game smoke off him.

"I can already see the change in you. You do have some color after all. The sun looks good on you. Come join me for early dinner. Let's get fat together."

The Stranger catches on the distant blue humps, pulls as I turn away. Now that I've glimpsed a crescent of what's out there, she will never let me stop.

Forty-two.

Meat simmered with sage fills Jonathaniel's private car. I uncover the porcelain tureen, releasing the steam rolling off the green onion soup inside, inhale.

Jonathaniel sits and immediately begins salting his potatoes. "Tell me, do you speak Tov?" He stops and stares at me until I can't ignore the question.

"*Sol.*"

"Come now." He laughs. The salting begins again, the soup this time. "Everybody who's ever put a toenail on the Rim knows that. I want a new one. I heard you say something to Mr. Rafael before we left."

Those words I learned from Aunt Tess. Ones to curse with.

"*Roh.*" The word forms delicately, as if it might break apart on my tongue. "Means ghost."

Many ride here.

"*Roh,*" Jonathaniel says, but he stresses the vowel too hard, and the word becomes the manipulation of a boat. "Is that what people call you, like the Stranger?"

Sometimes. But they would be wrong.

"Well, I disagree. Other fools can say what they like. But that's not a good name for you."

My name means something entirely different.

Jonathaniel shoves a bite in. "Another."

"*Delta.*"

"As in *Delta Sol*? And what does that mean?"

"Sister."

"Ah! River, and sister river. It all makes sense now. How delightful! Now what did you say to Rafael? I must know."

I fill up with the Stranger's smile, cold as first dawn. "*Vacca voya.*"

"Which is?"

"Fuck you."

His laugh startles me, the spoon in my hand hitting plate. "You bold little devil. Oh, the things the fools back east miss—"

The sharp screech of brakes cuts him off at the throat. Our dishes surge sideways along with my stomach, but only my water goblet loses contact with the linen-clad table and flies.

Five.

"Careful now!" Jonathaniel grabs for my arm but I elude him, make it to my boots.

We continue to drag, speed rapidly dropping away. I stomp my second boot on and grab hold of the safety rail running along the top half of the wall, sink at the knees and brace. I know what's coming.

We hit a full stop, and everything slams back the way it came. My loose goblet cracks against the forward wall. Shouts, not definable words, fly outside. Calls for cover in the car next door.

I grab my crossgun from where I hid it in the bench seat. Kasey had plenty of shells to steal. Too bad I only had room in my pockets for sixteen.

Fourteen.

Jonathaniel recovers his balance, but still grips the table as he rounds it. "Where are you going?"

"Stay here."

"I'm sure everything is fine. Please come back, sit down."

If everything was fine, we wouldn't have stopped, fool.

I close my back to the wall and unlatch the sliding compartment door that covers the real one. Heat buckles in my face, the steel-plated car crossing hot enough to boil blood.

Two horses gallop past, the lead rider firing into the air under the wallop of the black flag trailing his saddle. Bone pickers. Glass breaks as the hired guns start shooting back. The engine is visible, four cars ahead of a bend of the track. Sunlight catches on railroad stripe as the engineer pitches off the deck to the hollow ring of a gunshot. He hits the ground in fresh puff of dust and is shot again.

I was wrong. These aren't bone pickers. This gang is organized. If I was running this holdup, I'd send someone in from behind. The riders are a distraction.

I unbolt the back door.

"What are you doing—" Jonathaniel scrambles after me, every breath the opposite of quiet. "You shouldn't go out there."

I snap a finger to my lips.

Silence.

The pistol he clutches is smaller than his palm, too fragile for standard caliber ammunition. Problematic. The kind a gentleman probably slips in his pocket in Jezebel when he wants to feel dangerous at a poker game but has never actually needed to fire. Navy keeps the same snub-nosed variety in her boot. At least hers has a grip spike and fires tear vapor instead of bullets.

"Stay here." If he doesn't listen to me this time, dying will be his problem.

Stay out of my way.

Glass splinters behind me as I keep low through the next car, another bedroom and parlor. No external doors.

The yell comes from outside. "All of you, pick a car."

The crew passage runs like an intestine through two freight cars of food and water storage to the kitchen before the crossings aren't enclosed anymore. Open to the air like the *Absolution*'s were. Alkaline.

The brush cackles with a thousand creatures. Air like boiler fire where it touches my skin and the metal of the maintenance ladder hotter still.

Five...

The long screech of a raptor wheeling overhead slices in between bursts of gunfire. She knows what that sound means. Fresh meat about to rot.

I boost myself off the last rung to the roof, flat on my stomach. The metal cladding sears right through my clothes as if they don't exist. But the longer I keep still, the worse it hurts, so I tuck my hands into my sleeves and crawl.

By the time I reach the gap between the final two cars, I've stopped feeling.

Wait.

Boots strike the metal coupling. "Don't fall behind!"

The roadman steps up, ripping open a door. His breaths heave through a scarf as he crosses under me. Silver and dishes clash with floor, the crack of bone against an unforgiving solid.

The door doesn't fully close.

I use my skirt to bag my crossgun and slide over the edge. My toes touch down first, knees absorbing sound my weight might throw. Eyes up. I stay below the windowsill, no shadows. The roadmen continue picking the car apart, they don't notice me.

With my left hand I catch the wafting door.

Crew quarters. Bunk beds and a shared bathroom, still shiny with the same emerald velvet and copper trim as Jonathaniel's car. A dead hand sprawls in front of me, blood and glass glistening in his palm lines.

Clouds of white stuffing spill from slashed mattresses. A roadman on his hands and knees claws spare bedding and clothes from the underbed compartments.

The second taps his pistol to the crystal dewdrops clinging to the lamp, prying the cork from a bottle with his teeth. "You think that's real ruby?"

"Could be."

My opening shots gore through the closest man's back, bottle dropping from his grasp. I pull back, and the returning fire embeds in the car's metal framework, shockwaves ringing through my spine. I snap my reloaded barrel shut.

Fourteen shells left.

He retreats into the bathroom. The Stranger rakes the room for suitable cover. None exists.

A third roadman rounds the corner from the front end of the car. I take both shell shots again, just in case. I don't want him getting up again when my back turns.

"That's four shots," the one in the bathroom calls. "How much lead are you packing, fool?"

Enough. I turn the corner, inside.

"I'll wait you out. I'm not afraid to kill a woman."

You've probably done it before.

The patterned rug bristles with glass. I stay to the wall of bunks, out of the bathroom's line of sight.

That wood is thin. The door folds back with a slap as I shoot into it. Again, through his chest. His unguided legs stagger a few feet before weight buckles them. Know the difference between the discharge of a pistol and a shotgun.

Seven.

I go for his ammo. Then his wallet.

The burns on my arms and stomach sting. I could leave now. Let Jonathaniel live or die by his own *farce* luck. We're only five hours from Winchester, but that's by rail.

A stray hat lies in the spread of belongings spewed across the car. Black. Property of a head that can probably no longer wear one. It'll keep the sun out of my eyes, extra fragile from being in Hannah's dark so long.

"Hey!"

I lunge into the enclosed shade of the bunks. But the whistle wasn't for me.

They approach from the front of the train, revolvers aimed at the roof. "Get down from there, baron. Yeah, you."

It's been interesting knowing you, Jonathaniel.

We need him.

Why?

Of course, she doesn't answer. She tried to get me to kill Kane, but now she wants to save Jonathaniel? I tuck the hem of my skirt into the band and shove it deep, legroom. Fine.

Thirteen.

Out the opposing door, into the final car, leave it open.

"Give me that gun."

"Let's not be rash," Jonathaniel says.

The roadman cuffs the back of Jonathaniel's head with the baby pistol as the other pulls him from the ladder and shoves him into the crew car.

"Sweet Jezebel…" Jonathaniel looks more concerned about the destruction around his feet than the man about to execute him.

"You see anyone else?"

"You mean the bastard who did this?" the other says. "No."

He stalks across broken glass, every step crunchy. "I'll find him."

"No, no," Jonathaniel says. "You're making a big mistake."

"Doubt it." The roadman shoves him onto his knees.

The other pauses at the disheveled bunkbed curtains, takes a step toward the bathroom. Then he turns around.

I lift my crossgun.

Closer…

He kicks the loose door out of his way. I wait behind it for him to come inside.

The gun smoke clears fast.

Ten shells.

My skirt drags over his legs, catches on a boot buckle.

Five.

"Whatever wealth you see here, let us go and I'll double it," Jonathaniel says, right in the backdrop of where my shotgun spray will fly. "Do you know who I am?"

"I don't care if you're boss of all the fucking east bloods. This is the Rim. Only one thing matters here. Now why don't you let us in on where you've stashed all your valuables."

I pull my knife.

Eight.

"I'm afraid I can't tell you where I've stashed *all* my valuables because, you see, I'm horribly wealthy and I didn't have room to bring them all with me."

The roadman's laugh bites like a dog does. "Then tell me how you'd like to dine with Providence tonight. Red-breasted or with a piece of lead through your eye?"

"I prefer rum, actually."

"Shut up." He swings at Jonathaniel again, doesn't catch my outline. Not in time.

Thirteen.

My blade rips through fabric, flesh. Red crescent. Shit and piss.

"God of Mercy!" Jonathaniel crumples to the glassy carpet.

The pulsing spray hits my hands, and I see Vesta. Fatigue in my limbs from so many days spent running locked up in my jaw. It's her blood I feel.

But it's not. She's gone.

I swallow the hot lead blocking up my throat. Some things you become numb to, but *that* you just don't. As the black throbbing between my ears recedes, I see Jonathaniel where he should be, not Vesta's ghost, anointed in red. It's running out of his split nose, beads of it in his moustache.

He stares up at me, mouth and eyes wide as moons. "Who are you?"

What are you? the tremble in his throat says.

I stare for so long, I almost don't bother with the answer. Like Kane back in the Eden mine, he's seeing me for the first time. "The Stranger."

"I don't understand."

Then you won't. And it doesn't matter.

I pry the belted holster off the dead roadman and wrap it around my hips, empty his gun. *Reliable* slots deep, weight that settles like a promise. The gunfire up front has stopped. I hope that means the guns bought by the old baron, Montgomery, did their job, but I won't take my chances. I have twenty-five rounds from the belt now. That's better.

"Sweet Jezebel." Jonathaniel stands, one weak leg at a time. His knees are bleeding. He tries to put on his smile, but it's too fragile to wear. "Providence must have a plan for me after all. I told you I was lucky."

"This is why your rich friends travel with bodyguards."

"I will from now on. You wouldn't happen to be interested in the job, would you?"

No.

People may not see the Stranger without my permission, but the animal instincts that make us afraid of the dark always sense her. The reason he found me so appealing was that deep down, he's always known I'm deadly.

"Mr. Swann," the call rings from ahead of us.

I hug the wall between windows, but it's one of Montgomery's guns.

"Swann, you alive?"

"Indeed!" Jonathaniel calls, struggling to step around the dead on his way to the door. "Alive to tell the tale. Unless I am a ghost. But if that's the case, I wouldn't necessarily know the difference, would I?"

"We have a problem. Follow me."

I go with them.

Three-fifty.

A lineup of six dead roadmen and four engine crew lie in the dust by the nose of the debris breaker, face down. What's left of the kitchen crew circle around them.

The itch creeps up my hand for the first time. My fingers dust away crusted blood from my knuckle. When that happened, how it happened, I didn't notice.

"Better get back inside in case there's more of them, sir," the cook says to Jonathaniel. "The engineers are dead."

And the spotter, binoculars cinched in a noose around his neck. But there should be a fire seat engineer too. To feed the furnace, or in case something like this happens, take over.

The debris wedge on this engine is sharp, curved like an ax, thick enough to split another car in half without tipping.

Three…

One of the hired guns throws out a hand to stop me. "Don't go up there."

I'm not afraid.

The fire seat engineer is impaled on the wedge, railroad stripe cotton turned red, a new rib of metal splitting him at the seams.

"Can't one of you run this thing?" Jonathaniel says. "I have appointments to keep. It's very important that we get moving."

They shake their heads.

"I believe you'll be more comfortable inside, sir," the waiter says. "It's not safe. Best thing to do will be for two of these boys to ride ahead and grab some help. I'm told Winchester is about a day's ride, round trip. They can pick up some spare hands there."

The sound of that name twists the knot at the top of my spine. Winchester is the one place I haven't missed. Home of the view I used to love, now I'll be happy if I never see it again. But I'll keep my promise. I owe Vesta that, even if I'm dreading the sight of her ghost.

"None of you knows the basics of an engine?" Jonathaniel says. "Nobody even wants to try? Seriously, Boris, I'll double your usual wage."

"Not a good idea, sir."

"Where's your sense of adventure?"

Farce. I can't have them with me in Winchester.

One of the guns spits past the tobacco he just tucked in the pocket of his lip. "It's not as easy as it looks, friend. But you're welcome to give it a go. It likely won't blow up and burn your pretty face off."

Those pickers had horses.

The Stranger didn't let me leave Jonathaniel for dead eight minutes ago. What does that mean?

She doesn't like that I point that out.

"Don't be ridiculous, I'm wasted on mechanical," Jonathaniel says. "Come on, men. It's just forward momentum and a stop at the end... Not one of you can engineer?"

I give them all plenty of opportunity to speak. This isn't involvement I wanted, but this will still be faster than riding.

The Stranger sighs as I cross my arms. "I can."

FIFTY-ONE
ADELAIDE

I smell it first. You always do. Wood smoke layered under juniper. Winchester.

The town passes like a shadow, but I feel it like a broken bone. I keep the turn windows open, let the night wind come screaming through the engine to blot out my thoughts, the memories of my last days with Vesta. But all it does is tangle my hair. That smell pulls a trigger that's too powerful to ignore.

I hate that the last thing I said to her was about Kane. Vesta knew that I loved her, but I still should have told her that instead.

The track stretches on, shadow and silver in moonlight. I keep my attention on the pressure gauge, the Stanger's on the horizon, and add more quartz to the firebox once an hour. The *Emerald Constellation* runs closer to seventy miles an hour than Aunt Tess has ever pushed an engine, but I feel myself standing still.

My eyes and jaw ache as we approach Junction with the morning.

The engine door slides, and I turn to face Jonathaniel with one of Montgomery's hired guns.

"Pardon," Jonathaniel says. "I don't mean question your judgment, but it appears we're slowing up, Mr. Ezraos here says that means you intend to stop."

"Junction." I nod ahead. The five spurs of track aren't visible behind the early heat mirage, but the dark outline of the signal lamp is, and it's blue. Our rail is open. Six miles out.

"Why Junction?" Ezraos asks through his Eos accent. "Not that I'm ungrateful you got us moving, Miss. But my boss has got his balls all twisted up because you're engineering. He sent me up here to make sure you're not jacking the train."

I could have left him on the track to burn.

"Crusty old fool." Jonathaniel rolls his eyes with a huff. "He and I are on the same schedule, and we will get there when we get there. If we're late, our partners will simply have to wait, and that's just the way it is."

"All lines going east pass through Junction," I say. "So do the Express Riders and independent stagecoaches. You can find another engineer."

"You don't want the job?" Jonathaniel says. "You do seem to know your way around this beast. I assumed you'd get us all the way to Oath."

No, I have my own schedule to keep, and I've already had to waste enough time with him.

"I'll pass Montgomery your intentions." Ezraos tips me a nod. "*Sol.*"

"Tell him shame on you. He should be thanking Miss Revere for getting us out of this brine," Jonathaniel calls. "Tell him I said that!"

I check the pressure gauge again and close the third and fourth valves. The weight of the cars behind us begin to push against the couplings. Jonathaniel watches me wind my way through the remaining six valves. Eventually, the weight that was pushing back accepts its fate and becomes drag, and the *Emerald* settles into its long stop.

"You are quite the ever-revolving mystery." Jonathaniel touches the empty engineer's seat. I prefer to stand. "Where did you learn all this?"

"My aunt."

"Well, she must be a rare lady."

She is.

"I must follow up that question with, why did you learn all this?"

Can't you just be glad I did?

The top of Junction separates from the silver heat distortion.

Jonathaniel swallows the silence sitting on his tongue. "You mean to go your own way. I can see that."

At least I don't have to explain that to him.

"Have no fear, I wouldn't try to stop you."

You wouldn't get too far if you did.

The main rails and switch tracks web out of Junction's core like cactus arms. The fort with gaping wounds from the war, circled by a wheel of detached cars that have found new lives as homes and trading stations.

Then there's the Boneyard. Miles of train wreckage and the machine heads who do engine repairs with the salvage steel that finds its way here with the maintenance crews.

I set the main brake, then the backup. The ghost roar of the wheels still haunts my ears, they don't realize they're now empty.

Eleven.

Sun pricks my skin as soon as I step out of the engine. The white flag of the Republic shudders atop the platform pole, tattered by the relentless winds that cut the valley. It takes my full weight to drag down the long arm of the signal shutter, changing the open track indicator from blue to hot orange.

Dust blows thick and malt brown against my legs. Each breath dries me from the inside out, grit sticking to my tongue until I wind my scarf over my nose. Just over the next hills peeks a red crescent, shallow in the pale sky. Moon Season is here.

Jonathaniel climbs down the engine steps with the duster I borrowed from him. "I thought you might want this to keep the sun off your back. Keep it. Until I see you again."

I'll keep it until I get something else that didn't belong to him. I am going to keep these goggles I found in the engineer's locker. The lenses are new, black amber and unscathed.

The duster settles, shade and weight over my shoulders.

"I don't suppose anything I say will change your mind," Jonathaniel says. "You're a good driver."

No. This shouldn't have to be said, but here it does. And I need to be the one. "You don't own me."

"I know." He smiles, pain making his eyes squint. It's just the sun. "Only a fool would think that, and I never have. Even if that holdup never happened, I would have let you go if you'd asked. I simply couldn't live with myself if I left you in Hannah to get hurt again. I only ever wanted someone to keep company with. When you're fortunate like me, you forget how to make friends the natural way."

Or do you just become lazy and give up?

Fifteen.

"At least let me make sure you're settled. I'd still like to call myself a gentleman. You'll protect me if we get robbed here, won't you?"

I'll protect myself. That might extend to him if he's standing close enough.

The Boneyard bristles with the snap of welding rods. The hum of the well turbine catching my ear between hammer strikes.

I approach the attendant picking apart a roast chicken beneath the sign. *Clean Beds for Silver Standard. No Indoor Spitting.* The arrow points down. The Buried Hotel, a whole other layer of train cars entombed underground.

"I'm not taking any guests before breakfast." Sweat grays the borders and pits of his cotton undershirt, vest and scarf dangling off the post behind him. Two black flies crawl across the carcass, too greedy to worry about his fingers. "Come back in an hour."

Farce, I'm hungry. The Stranger almost lunges out and grabs the bird from him.

His gaze finally lifts, split by one lazy eye that lags behind. It's made of stone, painted. "For two?"

My stare doesn't change. "One."

"I suppose you want your own room, not a bunk in the common space."

"I want a door. And a lock. That works."

"High demands. Fifty for the day or two hundred for the week, gold standard. No meal included."

"That seems awfully steep for a single bed," Jonathaniel says. "The sign says silver."

"A clean bed," the man points out. "No snakes or scorpions or other shady pickers in your pants. I'll have to wash the bedding twice after a fox sleeps there. So, I charge her for that. It's a good deal, so don't argue with me."

"Does it come with a working fan?" Jonathaniel asks.

"You can open the air pipe. Can't promise nothing won't climb in. But you'll be underground, out of the heat." The man motions at me to pay up, pawns off a key in my palm once I've given the fifty to him.

I wipe the grease off my hand and turn away.

The smell of grilled potatoes grabs me. My head aches, and the tremble in my hands might become visible. It's my fault for not wanting to slow down the engine to eat.

"Well, he was most obnoxious," Jonathaniel says. "Are you routinely overcharged for simple things?"

That depends on the moons, their mood, and sometimes if I speak or not.

Thirty-three.

"What will you do now?"

I'm finally going home. To whatever that is now. I thought I'd feel more relieved being out of Hannah, but I'm still being crushed on the inside.

"I am sorry our time together has to end, but I'd feel a little better hearing that you have somewhere to go... Is there someone waiting for you?"

The woman dicing peppers into the potato and eggs smiles at me from inside the framework of a passenger car. Extra pots hang off the walls around her, lanterns on chains, the scents so rich I could vomit. There's nothing inside me to give up.

"Allow me." Jonathaniel steps around me, ejecting a gold standard from the copper-plated money tube. It feels like charity. I don't like that.

I remember when we were nothing, pickers living out of a single room after fleeing Hannah the first time. Vesta and I learned quickly she could distract our targets, usually by singing or telling a story while I stole from them. Most of all I remember how good it felt to eat that first time we weren't so poor.

"I want you to know, I consider us even," Jonathaniel says as I accept the tin plate from the woman. I almost choke on the heat of the first bite.

"*Sol,*" I tell her, swallowing even though it burns.

I'm not a beggar. I haven't been one for a long time.

"For saving my life," he continues. "I was in shock and I never thanked you. I will forever count myself lucky for having you along. You owe me nothing."

What a gentleman.

Rafe and Charlene were the ones who got paid so my body and I could be his entertainment. My reward was going to be hanging without an audience. Gentle as he was, Jonathaniel still did things I never would have allowed if my survival hadn't hinged on it.

I don't hate myself for doing what I had to survive. Anyone who does has never had to look their own death in the face, and they can go to hell.

Jonathaniel's just lucky *I'm* not interested in collecting any debt.

"That fortune teller in the tea shop sure knew what she was talking about. Just think, if I'd left you in Hannah, I'd be a dead man now."

That's the thing about fortunes. Advice told without specifics will always be true because truth isn't an object or an absolute. It will twist itself into whatever you desire it to be. Grandma's words.

His gaze brushes over me, but like a freshly sharpened blade. He knows better than to run a hand down me. "Will I ever see you again?"

Doubtful.

"I have a fortunate feeling about it. I would say good luck, but something tells me you don't need it."

I almost smile, narrow as the first-quarter moon. I've been waiting for this so long. "Stay alive."

"That's all part of the plan." His smile is bright, and fool's gold, not disguised by his overweight moustache. "It turns out that damn Lewis was right about you. A ghost can't keep your bed warm. Well, I regret nothing. It's been a pleasure, Adelaide the Stranger Revere."

In my hand hides his tube of gold standards as I turn away. It falls on the three pearl ascot pins, copper ring, and survey map I stole from his luggage already in my pocket.

I regret nothing either.

Let it be bloody.

Red as the Season Moon.

Red, the color of revenge.

FIFTY-TWO
ADELAIDE

"*I heard a knock at the door on a moonless night.*"

Grandma used to tell me the Tov poem when I was young. The one my name comes from. At night when we'd look at the stars.

"*A Stranger waited outside. I offered them shelter from storms so they would know kindness of me, food so they would not take my children.*"

I never told her I hated it because she'd learned it from my mother. I couldn't break Grandma's heart like that. I just did my best not to pay attention, let her recite it because I know she loved her.

"*This Stranger rode back to where they came. They told our enemies where our walls were weak.*"

Winchester doesn't notice me as I ride into town, a black shadow on a black horse.

"*That Season the Stranger came riding, an army like poison in their wake. Before winds, my city fell.*"

In books, ghosts always appear glowing white, long teeth and sunken pits for eyes, because that's what scares children. But I think ghosts are the color of the shadows that hide them. Soft. Formless, and that's why we don't see them.

"*But for the kindness of shelter, I alone survived and became a Stranger myself.*"

There will be no shelter in Winchester tonight.

Only blood.

One thousand, eight hundred and three.

The grass whispers to the backsides of porches and walls. The weathered planking of the street where Vesta took her last breath, Dr. Pike's office where we spent our last days watching her rot. Those memories overlap and stich themselves into the one I'm making now, forever locked together like mismatched quilt squares.

I knew smelling the juniper would hurt, but I didn't expect to hear Vesta's voice. It explodes in my head, clear as the sky.

I don't look out at the canyon. I'm not ready for what I'll see there.

"*Roh,*" I whisper to my horse before I leave him to the shadows. *Ghost.* That's his name now.

My feet go numb when I touch the steps into the hotel's heat-cured breezeway. I am dust, the rest of this sharp as two storms colliding.

Six.

Head down, eyes up. Any stray noise of mine is blurred by the scrape of spoons on bowls and the dozen voices wielding them.

The Stranger twists a dark flame through the air around me, the black pants I stole off a line in Junction, the duster that once belonged to Jonathaniel. My short hair hides easy under my hat's wide brim, the deep scarf swallowing up my neck, jaw, and the toothed bone mask of the Stranger. My face is someone else, and no one eating stew at the elongated breezeway tables wastes a glance to notice.

It's all like the last time I was here. Markos sat at that table right there, writing in his pocket journal before we left for the West Rim. I'm the thing that's changed.

Twenty-five.

I take a seat against the west wall.

She's here. Behind the bar, ladling out beer while her hired help collects empty dishes.

Greta.

I thought about her when I lost the dice toss to Kasey and two others that first night on the *Delta Sol.* I held her name in my mind until they were done with me. Picked through all the things I could do to ruin her until I found the one I liked best.

The rose tone of the quartz light holds off the impending night. But it can't stop an enemy. I'm already here.

Bald spaces widen as the two long tables empty. Greta tucks away strands of honey hair behind each ear, the rest of it braided in a twist. Her lace collar rises to meet her earlobes, and her gingham skirt kisses the floor with every sweep of her broom. A respectable woman.

Traitor.

Silence has always been part of who I am, but patience is a smaller glove that's never fit as well. As I wait for the last two men to leave their dinner and the hired girl to take the dishes out back, it squeezes.

Greta only notices me once the breezeway is empty. "Something I can help you with?" She leans the broom against the wall. "Dinner's over."

Navy and Raleigh aren't here to stop me this time. The Stranger tastes like cast iron, counts Greta's steps like mine.

"Excuse me. Did you not hear, or are you dumb? This ain't a dance hall. If you want to loiter, do it outside on your own time."

The brim of my hat keeps my eyes from meeting hers, and she doesn't seem to know my voice. "Sit."

Greta lets out a sigh. "You're a woman. That's a relief." She gathers her skirt to straddle the bench across from me. "I wasn't sure with you dressed like that. You have no meat on your chest."

Her shoulders go stiff as I place *Reliable* on the table between us. My finger lays alongside the trigger, pointing down the barrel to her.

"How much do you want?" she asks, low.

I told her to run the last time she saw me. I meant it. It's her fault she didn't listen.

"Who are you?"

Slowly, I bring up my chin. Vengeance, the name Vesta called me.

"*Stranger*—" The breath skips as it leaves her, again when she sees the coyote fangs wired to the scavenger lizard jawbone of the Stranger's mask, a dream warped wrong.

Tears bead out the corners of her traitor eyes. She clutches for her Ven crystal hanging around her neck, empty of good luck as a promise.

Bitch.

It's not enough that she betrayed Grandma's trust? She had no idea Vesta was already dying. She didn't know Navy and Raleigh would escape. But she knows exactly what bloodhungry men are capable of. We all do.

Of all the things I've done, I've never handed a woman over to be raped and killed by her enemies. Now she has the guts to cry as if that will make me merciful. I remember the taste of my own blood.

If you betray someone, you finish it. Don't cry when they come back to finish you.

"I'm sorry." She grips the Ven closer. "I heard you were dead."

You wish.

She was in such a hurry to scrub the bounty-hunter blood off of her porch that night, she forgot my family name, the money she paid to hide under it for years. The cousin who tried to claim this wretched hotel out from under her when her husband died, and the day we made that cousin disappear into the *Delta Sol*. I bet that fool's gold husband didn't die in her arms, his face split open, the way Vesta did in mine.

Did she look when it was over? At Vesta's blood in the street, Navy's eyes swollen from crying?

It doesn't matter if the bounty hunters pried our whereabouts out of her with knives while we were still on the West Rim, or if they paid her for it and she gave us up willingly. This betrayal proves she never really believed in what we might do to our collective enemies.

If I was cruel, I'd sell her in Descendants. Let her suffer like me. If I wanted to see tears, I could pour morning salt in her eyes, but I'm too rigid with rage and the Stranger locked inside my skin. There's her mercy.

"I told you this would happen if you kept antagonizing the Rim," she hisses. "I told you not to go out there on the West Territory. Those bad spirits followed you—"

I plant my other hand against the grease-pocked tabletop, lift the gun. The shot is not silent, but the wild roar in my head falls away. No one can take this from me now.

This has nothing to do with the West Rim. This was all her choice. All Green's plan. All a fucking mistake.

I walk over the bench and table to reach the lantern as I go. From my coat I pull the tube of flash fire Kasey took from me last Season. He kept it.

For this.

Greta's body lies slumped across the table like a drunk. The blood hasn't pooled and spread enough to be noticed from here. The glass vial of flash fire slides free of the metal smuggler's tube, into my hand with the lantern and I throw them both. Glass shatters, and a burst of blood orange heat flash floods into the room.

Vacca voya.

Hey!" A prospector comes stumbling down the alcove stairs, still working to get his suspenders up. "You. Arsonist—" The gasp stops mid-air when his gaze reaches my bone face.

I shoot him once, don't stop. Out the backside of the breezeway, down into the yard. The table drips with flames, Greta engulfed by them.

"Fire!" The yell comes from the front side of the street.

I don't run. Rabbits run. Guilty people run. The people rushing to put out my fire run as the fire bell hanging beneath the water tower clangs. I'm a deep shadow, the Stranger. Bone. Ghost. Dead. Unrecognizable under this face I've given her, made of nothing and daughter of no one.

The planked street is flooded full of copper, gold light creeping fingers over back porches and moonlit grass. Silhouettes dash to the blaze, away for more water. But my flames own the first floor. They soon lunge like foxes through upper windows, chased by sparks. It will burn in my mind forever, and I'll look at this memory whenever I feel low.

My horse waits at the edge of Winchester, eating the bush where I left him. Together we leave for the cool of the canyon cliffs.

I have one more ghost to face before I leave town.

The grasses have grown up around her, but I know the place. It's burned into me, and my pulse drags me there.

We left her with a simple, wooden stake. Someday Aunt Tess or Navy will come back to give her a permanent stone, one that casts a long shadow in the moonlight.

I drop to my knees, and everything inside me splits open. I didn't let myself cry for her in Hannah. It wasn't the time, it wasn't safe. Now I sob. Pain that I resisted bleeding wretched and deep until my jaw aches and everything below it does too.

The love I have for each sister is unique. I will never love anyone the way I've loved Vesta.

The press of footsteps on grass jars my head like a gunshot. The Stranger shoots out of the recess she slipped into, and I'm up, grabbing my gun before I'm fully aware. I turn on the fool interrupting my moment, but no one is here. Only me. The Stranger, my horse, and the hungry little rabbit darting away. Gradually, my chest stops heaving.

I wipe my nose on my sleeve.

The mark of solar quartz I left on Vesta's grave is long lost. Blown away in the first storm, probably. But I kept my promise here, and I'll keep the rest of it wherever I go. Green, Rafe, anyone else who crossed us will pay like Greta just did.

I read Vesta's name one more time, touch my forehead to it, feel the clouded pulse in my ears and the wind blowing through all the cracks that sit open inside me.

"Vesta..." My wrung voice gets swallowed up by the emptiness of night. But the night isn't really empty. It's full of scurrying feet and crickets, wind and stars, shadows and ghosts.

"I'm sorry you couldn't be here..." *Farce*, it still hurts. More than anything ever has, bad enough I don't know how it hasn't killed me. "I might not ever come back...but that doesn't mean I didn't love you."

It means I did.

PART THREE

PISTOLS AT DAWN

FIFTY-THREE
TESLA

THE TRAIN GLIDES TOWARD OATH UNDER A BANNER OF MIDNIGHT-BLUE STEAM, the mark of an engine burning the purest fuel: black gold. I take the scope from my waist bag and get a closer look at her. "The *Emerald Constellation*...my, my, with green copper trim to match. Double stacks. That is an alkaline lady."

Leagan grips the support post, adjusting the zoom of her goggles' sniper lens.

"Is it them?" Navy asks.

"Looks right," she says, heel drumming.

They slow at the red arms leveled across the track, warning engineers of impassable blockage ahead. Our doing, thank you, Travis. The passenger platform lies out across the yellow grass field, but I can taste the heat ripening her metal from here.

Some of the windows are shot through, others boarded up.

"What have they done to her?" I say. "Look at that disgrace."

"*What?*" Navy gasps.

"The train," I add quickly. "Not your sister."

"Who cares about the fucking train?" Leagan drops off the porch. "It's just a piece of metal. Let's go."

"Calm down, ma'am. Let's not run over there and scare the little rabbits off."

Gray and white suits of Jezebel trickle out and begin the hike through the waist-high grass.

"Barons, what luck." I smile, collapsing the scope. "I do believe our plan worked."

Navy uses the rail to exit the wide porch of the trading post. I take her arm to help her along as the ground gets uneven.

"We'd better hurry up before Leagan gets too far ahead and is unsupervised for too long. She's a troublemaker." But she doesn't hear me, already down the slope where the road narrows.

Yellow grass tangled up with oregano, wild as unkempt hair, lines the road to the rail platform. I break off a sprig just to smell it, then twist it between my hands in case Travis left any animal piss on me. That's a turn-off to the rich.

"I don't see her," Leagan says.

"Me neither. And they look too calm to be hostages." I quickly put a hand to Leagan's shoulder before she panics. "Let me talk to them. You go search the train."

"I can make it back by myself." Navy taps her newly chosen walking stick on the packed dirt—an attempt to hide the flutter in her voice, I think.

"Are you sure?"

"Yes. I'll be at the tea house."

"I'll meet you there. Don't worry, we'll find her." I unpin the widow's lace from my hat and drop it like a curtain over my scar.

By the time the new arrivals leave the dirt track for the cleared road, the fatherlier of the two barons pants like a dog in heat, while the hired gun holding the silk parasol over him looks absolutely delighted with his life choices.

"Hello, gentlemen," I call, casting my prettiest smile from behind my widow's lace. "You must be the crystal barons I've heard my father talking about. Oath, the valley of alkalinity and prosperity, is so pleased to welcome you."

"Glad to hear it, good lady." His dense, gray moustache and mutton chops tremble as he breathes, dust already trapped in the sweat on his forehead. "I'd like to know what the meaning of this blockade is, but you can't possibly be privy to that trouble. Where might we find some reprieve from this damnable heat?"

"The tea house is serving cold-pressed mint and root across the street, or the saloon is just a few steps down if spirits favor your taste." I slip my hand between the two rolls of flesh bulging from the crook of his arm. "My father runs the trading post. I'd be happy to show you around."

"Tea sounds lovely, thank you." He pats my hand, stepping to my lead. "Captain Montgomery. And my condolences for your loss."

"Thank you." My smile lies for me, like the widow's lace. "May I call you Captain?"

"Only if you will join me for tea."

"Only if you'll call me Tess."

"It would be my pleasure, Miss Tess."

The other baron sits much closer to my age. He wears a mahogany velvet waistcoat and his brown hair combed heavily to one side, sleek as an otter, the only one of these sweaty bastards who's abandoned his overcoat. What bravery.

Jonathaniel Swann? I think so.

"Look at this!" He stops to stare at the anthill we just passed, calling to no one. It is an impressive one, almost three feet high. "Magnificent work these little bastards are doing."

"Keep up men, but don't step on me." Montgomery turns to check on his guards and realizes his friend isn't behind him anymore. "Swann! Don't stand there gawking like a street vendor, you'll be shot."

Well. This *is* the Jonathaniel Swann I've heard of, but I still don't see Adelaide. What happened? Or did she change her plan entirely? She would do something like that, and if that's the case, I'll have to curse her with damp socks for a Season for making us worry again.

"No one will be shot here," I say. "Oath is a civilized sanctuary in these Providence-forsaken lands."

Not really, but Oath isn't as bad as Descendants. I know which side of the two roads is safe.

I point out the stone church. "See? Providence protects."

"And may His mercy shine on us all." Montgomery has to hitch one leg around at a time, as if they can't bend in the middle anymore, and sounds about as sincere in his beliefs as the pastor of the church I went to growing up. Most religion is just a different type of protection people like to buy and others sell.

"We went through hell to get here," he says. "I would say Mr. Swann is still in shock, but he's been making fool's decisions since we got to the Rim

Territory. I'm afraid he's just a born buffoon, and there's nothing to be done about that."

"You were held up?"

"Yes, but I won't alarm a lady such as yourself with the retelling." He thumbs an itch on his flabby nose, purple with burst capillaries. "Tell me, which company does your father do business with?"

I make a quick study of him before I answer. I smell ancient money. "Smythe and Matthan-Atlas. The free agents will ruin fur trade forever."

Montgomery cracks a gray-toothed smile, a few copper replacements scattered between the rest. "That's my girl."

"Have you traveled far?" This trap is already long sprung, boys, but now I will take all the information you have, thank you.

"Too far. Ordinarily, I only visit the North Rim for the Hannah auctions. I've never been this far south."

"Just you and Mr. Swann?"

"No, no, there are many investors invited to the auction. Too many. The man who is boss there has gotten greedy, and the auction is an affair for younger men. This will be the last year I attend, thankfully. My grandson will be taking over the legwork of the business. The Rim is nothing but a cesspool for blood and violence. And disease. But I and several acquaintances have been optioned to invest in the railroad. I deemed it prudent to not pass up the opportunity, so here I find myself on this tour of hell. I will say, however, I am pleased to have found one bright spot, Miss Tess."

"Why, thank you, Captain."

The tea house storm shutters sit wide, hot, slow wind breathing against the lace tacked up to keep flies out. I give a secret nod to Navy, then touch her shoulder as I pass in case she didn't see it.

"Here we are." The table by the pig stove, radiant Ven quartz blue behind the belly grate because Captain Montgomery is so sweaty. The dark wood ceiling gives the illusion of forest cool, even though the clang of the mine is close enough you have to talk over it.

Montgomery draws the chair for me before seating himself—such gentlemanly behavior. Where's Travis? He could use a lesson in table manners and in return teach Montgomery a thing or two about ladies first. I seriously doubt he's ever bothered himself with that.

Jonathaniel grabs the door before it closes on him, stamping out the remains of his pipe in the ash bowl. "Hear this news!" He grasps the chair from the adjacent place setting, angling it to ignore his table and face ours.

Montgomery growls, his chalk-blue eyes rolling up to white. "What is it now? There is a limit to the shenanigans that are healthy for a person."

"If that's so, I haven't found it yet. No, my man, there's been a fire in Winchester. Imagine the timing! Two more days' delay, and poof. My lucky stars continue to hold. You're welcome." Jonathaniel tosses a sheet of light green letter paper at Montgomery with an afterthought. "This was waiting for us at the Express office. This rail trouble is worse than we thought. The eastbound line won't be passable for fourteen to twenty-five days."

"There are worse towns to be stranded in," I say. See? I was merciful in my choice.

"That's simply too long. Unacceptable," Montgomery says. "Those crews will have to be faster. I want a foreman."

"The missive did not sound optimistic."

"That's because you don't know how to negotiate with the working man. Your language is too flowery."

"I beg your pardon. No amount of negotiating will conjure bodies that aren't there. We're in bare bones territory here, isn't that right?" he says to me. "The maintenance crews are stretched far too thin. Apparently, the westbound tracks are also experiencing a 'surge of violence' is what the Express man said. Although crime back east must be down—hence, the lack of prisoners arriving for track work."

"No, they've been diverted to Hannah for some time now," Montgomery says. "Although at present, they're being sent to the line expansion."

And our dear, delusional Montoya still thinks he can tame a place like that? I smell bullshit.

"But the good news is, the Von Kanes are behind schedule as well," Jonathaniel says. "Our time is our own until they arrive. And this does seem a pleasant enough place."

Montgomery sighs.

"You know what this means?"

"I don't want to hear it."

Jonathaniel's grin is absolutely radiant. As long as he hasn't somehow murdered Adelaide, I think I like him. "It's our copper chance to ride out and see the expansion firsthand."

"Good God, Swann!" Montgomery almost spits up his tea. "There's not enough whiskey or black gold in this world to make me consider that."

"Ah, see, now that's where your priorities are wrong, my good man."

I *do* like him. People with the zest for life are the most fun, and he is snapping with it.

"We need numerical reports, yes," Jonathaniel says. "But the stories are what actually keep the other investors interested."

"He's right," I say. "Presents help too."

"I warned you, he's a blathering fool. Do not listen to a word he says."

"I have half a mind to head out there anyway, without you," Jonathaniel says. "All I need is a gentle push. Murders be damned."

"Murders?" My, my, things have taken a turn for the worse at the line expansion camp. Maybe why the Von Kane Company ordered an entire *Ironclad* shipment of Exodus guns Raleigh heard those rumors about... These other parts of the picture typically become clear if you know how to keep your eyes and ears open.

"No one said anything about murders." Montgomery pats my hand, his eyes giving sharp orders for Jonathaniel to shut up. "Please, be sensible for once in your life, man."

"I'll give you a push," I say. "I'd love to see how the line is built. If you go, would you take me with you?"

"No, you wouldn't," Montgomery says, and now he sounds like my father. "I've let you act a child this long and didn't say a word, Jon, but I'm not going to risk my life so you can have a story to tell at the Wednesday Club. Now, see what kind of nonsense you're putting in this poor girl's head?"

"You've said more than a word. I remember two or three." Jonathaniel flashes a clean and complete smile at me. It's hard not to appreciate a set of honest-to-bone teeth after more than fifteen years on the Rim. The wooden replacements are the most unfortunate.

Montgomery unfurls his napkin in Jonathaniel's general direction. "Away with you, Swann."

"No, no, I'm at a loss for company these days, so I'll be joining you at every occasion it suits me, Montgomery, and you can just deal with it. You are *my* guest, after all."

"I fail to see how that is my concern." Montgomery leans close to spoon more sugar into his tea. "You should consider yourself fortunate to have gotten away with your intestines where they belong, not roasting on a spit. Go wallow about someplace else."

"That's offensive."

I can tell Navy is listening, her head angled to one side. Leagan would be getting impatient enough to kick somebody in the shin right about now, which is why I sent her off to do something else.

I've done what I can with Montgomery, he doesn't know much. It's time to wring Jonathaniel.

"You say you need company, but I admire anyone who can drink alone," I say. "It shows you're not afraid of who you are."

"Then anoint me the patron saint of bravery." Jonathaniel ignores the tea on his table and pours himself a cup from our chilled pot. "*Sol*."

"Tess." I offer my hand. He expects a lady's gentle clasp, moving to kiss my knuckles, but I shake hard. Unfortunately for me, his touch is sweaty and I have to clean it off on my skirt. "I've gotten to know your friend the Captain, now it's your turn. Tell me about yourself Jonathaniel Swann."

"Delighted, well read. A lucky man in search of fascinations, life is full of them. You'll tell me the truth, Tess, I can feel it. Why are women cruel?"

"Why are widower snakes venomous, and the yolks of prairie chickens green?"

"A riddle? How charming... Oh, I don't know."

"Because we are born that way." I pat his knee. "Saddle up, darling. You'll feel better by the next full moon. But if you're desperate, you can try the house with the green door at the end of the street. Ask for Clair, she's only cruel if you ask her to be."

"Oh, if you only knew." Jonathaniel sighs. "The friend poor Clair would have to replace is something vicious."

"You came by way of Junction then?"

"Indeed," Montgomery says. "My last stop will be Vantage, and it can't come soon enough. Say a prayer for me tonight that the debris crew can get that track cleared tomorrow."

"Actually, we came by way of Hannah," Jonathaniel says. "And once we make it back to Vantage, old Montgomery here will be able to boast he made the red circle. I myself, this will be my third time."

It's a wicked smile that splits across my face. I can taste it. Sweet on the tongue and deliciously sour along my jawbone. "Oh, Mr. Swann, I'm afraid you've barely scratched the surface. Once you leave the circle is when the Rim really becomes interesting."

"You know, Tess...I'm inclined to believe you. Don't tempt me any further or I may never get back on that train. I did plan to tour my mine here, but that will only take an afternoon. What would you suggest I do with this spontaneous gift of time? Actually, do you know where I might find some scavenger lizards?"

"My niece could get one for you."

"Truly? Is she here? I'd love to have one. It's been a dream of mine."

"A dream since yesterday." Montgomery passes a dismissive wave. "You've never been anything but full of tomfoolery, Jon."

I pass my cup under my widow's lace to drink. "Tell me about Hannah. I've never been that far north. What does one do up there?"

Where is she, Jonathaniel?

The longer I look, the easier it is to find the cracks in his smile, slip the right words into and pry. I am my fortune-telling mother's daughter, after all, and she taught me well.

"It's everything Descendants wanted to be," Jonathaniel says. "Darker, filthier, magnificent."

"Damnation! That's no talk for the afternoon." Montgomery reaches to shield me from the sting of hearing such talk. "You'll have to excuse him, dear girl. You see, Jonathaniel is a deviant."

"Oh?" I lift my eyebrows together. "You can't mean that. Surely a gentleman can't be all bad."

Gentlemen are full of shit is what I really mean. Ladies are bitches, anyone can be bad, and most of us are both.

"The worst kind, I'm afraid," Montgomery says. "There will be no salvation for his like."

"I am damned." Jonathaniel lifts his glass. "Cursed by a Shadow the color of the constant moon."

I plant my hand hard on the table to make sure Montgomery is watching as I draw the X of Providential protection across myself. False, feminine-based shock is what he expects, so I give it to him. "Mercy me. Where is she now, this wicked Shadow?"

Jonathaniel shakes his head, draining the remains of his glass as he stands. "Tess, although it's been a pleasure, I have to collect my thoughts before our other business partners arrive, and I believe to do that I'm in need of a walk, or perhaps something stronger than tea."

"Well, good luck to you." I nod.

"Always appreciated. *Sol*, I believe you would say."

Dead or alive, Adelaide, we'll find you. And, Jonathaniel, don't say I never gave you a chance. Now I have to bring in Leagan, and Raleigh doesn't call her Lady Nasty for no good reason.

"He's a *fox* lover," Montgomery says with a most grave whisper once Jonathaniel has gone. "Hired a Tov girl's company back in Hannah, if you know what I mean. A milk-bastard, actually. Took her right in his bed like she was a fine, east-bred companion girl and now he's moping about over a— I'm sorry, I shouldn't be speaking of such things in front of a respectable woman such as yourself. I do beg your pardon."

"No, please, don't be sorry. Vigilance is the enemy of sin, as my late husband used to say, Providence's mercy be with him."

"Yes, deeply sorry." Montgomery looks to the widow's band on my little finger because I give it a twist. "There was a time when his sort of behavior was considered treason. During the war, three men in my battalion were hanged for... colluding with the enemy. Men had better sense back then."

I doubt that, considering the behavior warranted such a severe punishment. He's also forgetting it takes one of each to make a half-breed. I'm sure Adelaide's father wasn't forced into Nia's bed at gunpoint, weeping over his sin.

Leagan taps the window from the other side.

I cross one hand behind my chair and raise my little finger at her. *One minute.*

"Well, I'm glad you were here to warn me about him, Captain. My propriety still intact."

"Indeed. Jonathaniel is otherwise harmless, but it wouldn't fit to see the reputation of a young lady as kind as you sullied by such filth."

Kind. That's not often a word I use to describe myself. My mother and sister were kind, Navy is kind. I see opportunity. And sometimes, kindness does fertilize it, like now. I have the opportunity to track down Jonathaniel and kindly ask him what's going wrong with the railroad, and what the fuck happened to Adelaide.

Leagan's boots leave no floorboard mice sleeping as she stalks to

Navy's table. They speak to each other briefly, then Leagan clears her throat, aiming a lump of cheese scone at me. "Time is *wasting*, Widow."

Ah, here she is: Raptor, the Lady Nasty in the flesh.

"You'll excuse me, Captain." The silver jingles as I stand. "I have to go. I left my niece with the scavenger lizards, and I have to make sure they didn't eat her."

LEAGAN SLAPS THE SALOON DOORS OUT OF HER WAY, LEADING NAVY BY THE hand on a one-way mission, but I take the time to sweep all the faces as I enter. Jonathaniel plays the upright grand piano...no, he's not playing. *Brooding*, he's brooding over the piano, practically bleeding over it. He flexes and bends with every note, more drama than Leagan running over those keys.

He doesn't realize I'm here until I drag a fingernail across his throat the same way I'd use a knife, and his song ends mid-chord.

"What a lament." I pluck his drink from the instrument's ledge. "I just killed you there, without a fight. You'd better start paying more attention if you want to survive the Rim."

"Funny, I was recently told something similar." He aims that smile up at me. "I didn't expect to meet you again, Tess. You have to indulge me. I have a flair for the dramatic."

"So do I." I sink onto the bench opposite him. "But, alas, I don't play, unless it's cards."

"I do." Leagan reaches from his other side and licks her fingers across the keys in a rise and fall sequence, then slams the lid shut. "There you go."

"Most impressive," Jonathaniel says. "Thank you for not taking my fingers off. That's a bold look you have going there, with those death lips. Who are you?"

"My nieces." I down what's left of his drink. Golden rum my ass. He would.

"Ah, you must be the one who can find me a scavenger lizard." He leans out to get a better look at Navy. "And you were in the tea house, weren't you—"

I pass my hand along the inside of his leg. Meanwhile, he doesn't notice my other one siphoning the standards out of his pocket. If I were a man hiding my weapon, the best placement would be on the ribcage under the jacket, but he's not wearing one. So up a sleeve or inside a breast pocket in his vest it is. Or possibly in his hat, if he had that. Male clothing is very unforgiving without skirts—so few places to hide a significant bulge.

Jonathaniel clears his throat, shifting from under my touch. "Tess, although you are a lovely conversationalist with a smile to light up a room, I'm sure, I'm afraid I just can't…you're wearing the widow's lace—"

"Oh, I'm not getting fresh. I'm just checking you for weapons." I pat the lump of a baby pistol in his vest pocket. "Cross draw is slow, dear, although maybe you're left-handed."

"I am, actually."

"We're looking for someone, and you are the last person we know who saw her."

Leagan presents him with the two white hairs she found stuck to the velvet in the suite car. Jonathaniel squints to identify them.

"Where is she?" I ask. "Adelaide Revere. We know she was traveling with you."

"I'm afraid I don't know—"

"The Widow would like to see you upstairs." I come around him with one arm, grabbing hold of his vest and forcing him to stand along with me.

"You didn't let me finish. I'm not lying to you, we parted ways back in Junction."

"You're a rabbit," Leagan sneers. "How are you still alive?"

"I do know rabbit's an insult, young lady. This isn't my first time on the Rim, as you know."

I don't let him pass as he tries to step around me. He's short for a man, but not fat like most short, rich men are. It doesn't take much strength to move him toward the stairs.

"One can only assume Adelaide didn't kill me because she likes me," he says.

"She doesn't like anyone." Leagan glares.

The upstairs rooms are silenced by frayed rugs that only disguise half of the noise inside, prices listed on each door. I dig for the gold I just stole off Jonathaniel and pass it to the madam controlling the top hall before she makes one of her girls get up. "We only want to borrow the room for some peace and quiet. There shouldn't be a mess."

The rings on her knuckles shine as she grips the roll of standards. "Take as much time as you want."

The hanging lamp casts tired pink light across walls paneled in solid wood, no windows, and a single-space bed. Efficiency and quantity of customer are the money in a place like this, my friends.

"Oh, how kind. Refreshments." Jonathaniel plucks the bottle of Clear Pine abandoned on the feeble night table by some previous occupant. Liquid splashes against the sides as he upends the bottle to take a short drag.

I slide the door's pin latch and wait for the inevitable choke to follow.

"Sweet piss." Still coughing and crimson, he looks for the distillery label, but there is none. "That will bite you back."

I'm on him in a swift stride. The nightstand knocks against the wall, bottle clattering away as my forearm forces him to take a seat on top. "Welcome to the Rim." Leagan takes his pistol from me as I step back and peel off my lace-draped hat. "Consider yourself honored, Mr. Swann. We also need you alive."

Jonathaniel's throat dips in a sharp nod while his raven eyes glance down to the scar on my face. "The Widow, I presume."

"Named for the snake, not the deceased. But I'm glad to see you're observant. Now, with that out of the way, I really hope we can be friends, Jonathaniel. *Farce*, I do enjoy saying your name."

"I am rather fond of it. And I do believe it's better to have a dangerous friend than a dangerous enemy."

"Absolutely. Now, Adelaide told us she was leaving Hannah with you, but you say she ditched you in Junction. Why?"

"I couldn't say. She is an enigma, and she wouldn't tell me where she was going beyond there either."

"No, she wouldn't." That's just like her, secretive little bastard. "And Junction is the last place you stopped?"

"That is correct."

"All right, I believe you."

His shoulders betray surprise. "I'm relieved."

"But just in case, you'll tell me the tale of your dealings with Adelaide.

Start to finish, and don't spare me the details, Jonathaniel. I'm no lady despite what your friend Montgomery thinks, and neither are these two."

"Yes…" He shifts his collar. "I'm becoming aware of that."

"The Rim is no place for a lady."

FIFTY-FOUR
ADELAIDE

I SAVE MYSELF A NINE-DAY RIDE AND HITCH ONE WITH A BONEYARD HANDCAR crew leaving Junction. They tell me the pass is out northeast of Oath, which typically means there's been a derailment and metal for picking.

I keep my scarf up as a precaution as I arrive in Oath. Suddenly, my hands won't stop sweating, my stomach jagged and nauseous from intrusive thoughts. What if they're not here or they didn't get my letter? A warning won't save you if you're already dead.

Stop, the Stranger says. There's no reason to assume something went east, but Winchester left me raw. I can't help it.

The *Emerald Constellation* sits idle on the eastbound track. I don't want to see Jonathaniel. Aunt Tess's trapper *friend* Travis has a cabin south of town, but I'll check the boarding houses first.

Oath's main street is rust dirt, packed so tight it appears stone. Wagons rattle and voices smear together, join with the pulse in my head.

Three twenty-one.

Red hair. Sharp as a spark. Leagan sits on the far wraparound porch, rocking to the pace of the book in her hand. My throat seizes. I'd know her any Season.

Auburn hair. Rich like copper and threaded with gold veins. She wears thick goggles, one lens of solid metal, the other black glass, knitting needles crossing between her fingers. Navy.

My speed builds with each step, the savage desperation climbing up through my middle into my lungs and throat.

The door flies open, and Aunt Tess swipes the book from Leagan's hands. She lunges out of the chair.

I let go and run.

Thirty-four—

My stride breaks as we collide.

She's warm, solid, our bodies pressed together like the cover on a book. She has the measurements for a weapon design inked on the back of one hand, smudged. Black lipstick, still the only makeup she ever wears. *"So people will be afraid to kiss me."*

Rose tobacco laces through the gunpowder that always haunts Leagan's clothes. Grandma's ghost cuts through me. Vibrant as a lightning strike and bitter like chalkroot, the comfort of her voice. It's smell I was afraid I'd never taste again. But it's not lost—now it's my sister.

Leagan shakes as she holds onto me, breath pouring through clothing layers to my shoulder. "Never leave me again."

"I won't."

Aunt Tess releases Navy's hand the step before they both crash into me. Cotton and lavender oil and skin.

"You're crushing me!" Leagan yells.

"Good." Aunt Tess squeezes harder.

I love them so much. They're mine, and the space I have is full.

Aunt Tess clears her throat. "By the way, you owe me three days of dishes, ma'am. I guessed the correct location of Lake Amnesty."

A laugh bubbles out of me, then suddenly it's a sob. I don't know why. The fear that weighs so much comes off, meanwhile my body gets heavier. My knees find the packed ground, the heat in it.

Navy rests her head on me. Leagan touches my chin-length hair, but she's not going to say anything about it. She doesn't have to—that's why we get along.

Aunt Tess dusts off my wet cheek, swallowing the tremble the Stranger just caught on her lip. "Welcome home. We sure missed you."

FIFTY-FIVE
TESLA

RUMORS SPREAD LIKE BLOOD, AND EVERYONE IS TALKING ABOUT THE FIRE IN Winchester. Over half the town burned beyond recollection. Arson, they say. Set by an angry ghost, murdered and never laid to rest.

Adelaide stands in the open door of the boarding house widow's walk, facing the moons as they rise over the desert.

I stack our used plates on the serving tray and join her. The slopes are still pink, heat trapped in every rock, the land's shadows falling between them purple. "It is a lovely view…"

Her stare is deep, reaching further into her mind than I can guess.

"Are you here right now? Or somewhere out there?"

Adelaide's gaze doesn't leave the blue horizon, but for a flicker something brushes my skin, immaterial as wind, yet real enough to tighten the tiny hairs on my body. The shadows her hair cast on her face and the contour of her cheekbone seem thicker.

And then it's gone.

"I promised myself I wouldn't die without seeing the sky again."

"There won't be anyone dying anytime soon. We have too much work to do, and there's not enough time on the schedule. I checked."

We have to address what's happened. It's eating up the air, and if I don't say it first, she never will.

"I don't expect you to tell me what happened in Hannah," I say.

"Unless you want to of course. That's your choice. I'm always here and willing to listen. There's just one thing I want you to know." I touch her arm. "Look at me."

She does.

"What happened to Vesta wasn't your fault." Any more than it's mine, Mother's, or Navy's.

The muscles of her neck go taught as she crosses her arms, locking in any rogue emotion that might escape her seams. "I know."

"So long as we both understand that—" A black pearl ring perches on her center finger. I swear my heart stops, as dramatic as that sounds. "Is that…"

"Grandma's." She touches the setting that made words drop off my tongue and mind. "Rafe had it. I took it back. He doesn't deserve it."

With a pliable laugh, I show her Mother's moonstone gracing my hand. "He absolutely doesn't. I'm so happy right now. You don't even know."

When the pearl wasn't in Green's safe, I tried to console myself that it was lost to the Rim, not in a picker's pocket. It didn't work so well.

"Annabeth." She touches the moonstone on my ring, the pearl on her own. "Vengeance."

The whisper doesn't feel real, but I know I heard it.

"She never would have admitted it, but you always had a special place in her heart," I say. "I think her intent was to not have you feel different from your sisters, but you were her third daughter. She loved you the way she loved me. She'd want us to have these."

Adelaide nods, resolve in her mournful smile.

"Which brings me to my second point. How did Winchester smell, engulfed in flames?"

She side-eyes me.

"Oh yes. You can keep your secrets, ma'am, but don't think I didn't put the clues together."

The smart-ass flinch of her lip says, *Not all of them.*

"It explains why you were late."

"It was something I had to do. Alone. Navy would have tried to stop me."

The same heartbreak runs a fault line through my chest. We've both lost our mothers, our sisters, but within those ashes lies fire. And between the four of us, we can burn through whoever stands in our way. The future is bright because we are not alone.

"I'm going to ask you this once, and as long as you don't lie, I won't have to bother you about it again. If you do lie, well, I'll still hold you to your answer because you chose to not tell the truth... Are you all right?" I watch her face, wait to see which direction her eyes shift, for how long. But like a reflection in glass, they don't. "The jobs we have coming aren't easy. We all need to be our best. We all got time and peace to heal from what happened. You didn't. If you need that, you should take it. Evangeline has a room for you in Damascus. Navy says she'd stay with you and would love to have your company while she works on her project." There's sadness in her face that didn't used to be there. Not right at the surface, like some people wear for everyone they meet to see, but rather held under her tongue, like a pill she refuses to swallow. "You've sacrificed more than any of us to make sure Rafe pays for what he's done. I won't ask you to do anything else you're not ready for."

My ambition comes at high costs. I am trying to do better about not demanding that others pay them.

"Leagan won't go without me."

"Remind me to tell you the story of how she beat up Raleigh. You'll appreciate it."

She takes a closed breath. "Everything that happened is done. I am not a victim. I'm ready to move on."

That phantom ripple passes across my skin again, gone behind a blink. Copper storm static stings the back of my throat, but the sky is clear. "Alkaline."

"You saved me."

She catches me off-guard with that. "How's that?"

"Do you remember what you told me before we left on Kane's expedition?"

"Remind me."

"'Make him trust you.' It was good advice," she says. "I wouldn't have survived without it."

"I doubt that. But I'm glad I could help."

Her eyes narrow again. "Where's Montoya?"

"That is a good question. I sent him to harass Green's men along the westbound tracks. From the rumors, it sounds as if he's obeying me. But we shall see. As long as he stays away from Navy's project, nothing is a devastating loss."

"They're never going to give his family back."

"No, but that fool's gold hope is all he has. I won't be the one to take that from him and shatter his poor bastard soul."

"He's going to turn on us."

"Of course. He's from the Yellow City, as he *loves* to remind me."

"Someone told Rafe about the explosives by the mine. He didn't find them on his own. You need to listen to Leagan."

"I will, but if it was Montoya who tattled, it's important to let him and Rafe think we don't know what's going on yet. Don't worry, we'll flip him like a reverse robbery before we outlive our usefulness."

A thin line of dust lifts from the fast-fading horizon, not there for long as night tightens its grip on the sky. Just long enough to reveal that someone rides this way. With any luck, our old friend from the east and his distinguished general of a father.

I give Adelaide a quick kiss and toss a glance at the dirty dishes. "Those are for you, ma'am. Good night."

FIFTY-SIX
TESLA

THE PAPERS FLUTTER AT THE CORNERS LIKE THE LEAVES ACROSS THE FENCE IN the vegetable garden, pinned to the table by rocks and teacups. Kane stands on one end of the boarding house veranda, dressed in responsible tan pants and an undyed cotton work shirt. And from what I've read in Green's spy notes and in the familiar chin, one can assume the cannon-sized man in the gray suit with him must be his father, Millard Von Kane, the cunning bastard who bought the West Rim.

I resent not having the idea before him.

Dust smudges the window and my view. I wipe, but it's on the outside.

Even with my binoculars, I'm not particularly adept at lip reading. That was Vesta's skill. I spent too much time learning how to pick pockets and count cards.

"It looks like they're staying out of the path of the chickens..." I nudge the lens dial, trying for a little more clarity. "And they have a map. It looks like the West Rim to me. What do you see?"

"They have charts on the grade," Adelaide says. "Time schedules and how much labor they need."

"How does Kane look?"

"Alive." Gears click as Leagan adjusts her scope.

"And still pretty?"

Adelaide doesn't twitch.

"Did you kiss him?"

"Why would I do that?" she says.

"No, no, the question is why wouldn't you? Have you looked at him? I'm looking at him now, my glory."

"He was very kind," Navy says. "I'm sure he still is. He did like you, I could tell."

I can't help but laugh as Adelaide remains silent. "Oh, I've missed teasing you."

"I have not." But she smiles.

"Did you think he was dead?"

She rolls the answer past her teeth several times. "I considered it."

"And how did you feel?"

"Glad?" Leagan says.

She shakes her head slow. "Nothing."

"You lie." I poke an elbow into her. "You have feelings, darling Stranger, same as the rest of us. And that doesn't make you weak, it makes you the opposite. Feelings give life texture and flavor." They make us everything we are, and everything we have meaningful. "Go talk to him."

"No."

"Yes. Yes, yes." I catch her arm before she can walk away. "Get back here, ma'am."

"I'm not doing that—"

"You're the one he spent the most time with, and the one he might be least likely to forgive. But I doubt that very much."

"I wouldn't."

"I bet he doesn't even remember me," Leagan says.

"I be he does," Adelaide says. "He was observant."

"Well, he didn't strike me as the vengeful type," I say. "But we still need to know exactly how pissed off he is, and what he's told his father about us. Then we'll decide if it's better not to have Kane in the room when we introduce ourselves."

Kane mentions one more thing to his father, then grabs his hat off the hook by the back door.

"Oh, look, an errand. Perfect timing for you to go, my dear. What do you want to bet me he'll be happy to see you?"

Adelaide removes her goggles' scope and yanks her hat down to her scowl. "Five hundred gold."

"Overconfident, are we?" And I'll laugh again when I take her money.

"I stole three cycles of his life. Would you forgive me?"

"No, but I have no interest in fucking you. And I *am* the vengeful type."

"If that's the only reason, do you think he wants to know what my gun feels like up his ass too?"

"Ah, the lingering feelings of a lady carefully hidden under resentment." She wouldn't be this riled otherwise. They spent three cycles riding the West Rim together, the perfect plot for one of those romance novels Liza loved, if only this wasn't Adelaide I'm talking to. "Maybe. There are some sick bastards out there."

"If he's not sorry he met me—"

"Then he's a fool," Leagan finishes for her.

"Don't put your gun anywhere, you leave it in the holster, ma'am," I call after them. "We need him alive."

Someday I'll get the truth out of her.

FIFTY-SEVEN
ADELAIDE

Kane walks south through Oath, past the blacksmith, the smell of horses and fresh metal, white heat seeping off the forges.

Two fifty.

I'm stuck to him like a shadow. I've known this ever since the West Rim. I don't care what Aunt Tess says, I'm furious with myself for letting him past the Stranger. She knew I'd regret it. The texture and flavor of this is rancid. Any chance I had to walk away from him without consequences is dead because he isn't.

This will be easier if he does hate me. I'm used to that. I was going to avoid him for the rest of our lives, but here I am again.

Stop.

A stagecoach lurches around the corner, top-heavy as it rumbles toward the end of Oath. Once the chalk dust rolls by, I force a full breath into my tight lungs and fix my gaze on Kane again. I'm not here for me, it's for my family. Just another job to do.

He enters the mill and gives the foreman a letter, a handshake.

This is your chance, the Stranger says. I could walk away, and he'd never even know I was here. If I chose to be his second shadow, I can choose when to grow long or melt away. Gone like one at sundown.

But I'm no coward. And I'm not sorry.

I stand my ground as he turns.

Farce.

A wagon of grain rattles up the street between us, churning up a new dust devil from the one the stagecoach left behind. I don't see Kane take his first steps, only him splitting the dust, halfway across the street already.

He seemed too proper to hit a woman, at least too good in his own eyes. But it's possible after what I've done, he doesn't see me that way anymore. Now I'm just a threat.

The Stranger counts his steps as he comes. *Eight.* He reaches my side of the street and slows. *Eleven…*

"Adelaide…"

I don't resist fast enough. He hugs me.

Pitiful.

Memories cut me like gunshots, accompanied by the scents attached to them. Leather and skin soaked in sun, the damp trails through the mine, his sour tongue rubbing against mine, hot sage and the hours we spent drawing rocks. The hug is tight, desperate even, but I'm a rigid core inside of it.

What happened to him after I left?

"I hoped I'd see you again," he says.

Why?

Aunt Tess might not think he's the type to go after vengeance, but the Stranger doesn't discriminate. An enemy is an enemy, and I've made myself that to Kane.

I work my shoulders free, hands empty because I found nothing in his pockets except lint.

"No more trains are coming through until the track is repaired," he says. "I didn't notice yours in the yard. When did you get here?"

"I've been around."

He half-smiles. "You haven't changed."

No, I really haven't.

"I wouldn't want you to." He looks at the sun's three o' clock position above the horizon.

I look at the Season Moon behind him, waxing just above the buckled cliffs. Red. Like a smile or a cut in the blue sky.

"Do you have time to take a walk with me?"

I nod.

Six.

I let him lead. Only fools walk ahead of someone they've crossed. And I don't stray close enough for him to hug me again either.

He takes a cattle path down to a *Solace* flood creek. The water is nearly gone, but a dull current still passes through orange and yellow rocks.

"I'm not angry for what you did." The words have the sudden, explosive edge of something he's been waiting a long time to say. "I was. I told Markos I hoped I never saw your face again. But the more time passed, I started to accept his conclusion that you must've had some purpose for stealing from me like that, even if your motive is in direct opposition to mine. I may not know you as well as I'd like, but I've never seen you do anything arbitrary."

Not this, at least.

"You were better off getting out of Eden when you did," Kane says. "Maybe you knew that...Markos told me about Horne." He picks a rock, squeezes it in his hand before tossing it away. "I know you two had bad blood already running between you, but you did try to warn us he'd get infected."

He'll never know I lied to Markos about why I shot Horne. He didn't have the pestilence. The Stranger decided to kill him cycles before we ever got to Eden. A bastard waste of water who would have easily done the same to me if I showed him a weak side, so I made sure I got to him first.

"What happened?" I ask.

After I left.

I'm going to make him tell me what became of Randy. Vesta's death was wretched and violent. One those horrible ends she didn't deserve but was doomed to meet because she chose to stay with him instead of visiting the Wells's gravesite with us. I need to hear the word *dead*.

The haunt in Kane's eyes is something familiar. I've seen it in my own. There's darkness out there, and we looked into it. The Stranger felt it look back.

"We were ten days west of Winchester...I thought the worst was over, we were all getting out. Well, not all, but...you know what I mean. Randy dumped all of our water in the middle of the night and smashed the reclaimers. After that he only got worse. At first, we thought we could restrain him and get him to a doctor, but...like I said, it only got worse."

"Did you kill him?"

"It seemed like the merciful thing to do."

What passes for mercy on the Rim looks different everywhere else. And Randy was only a hired gun, not a sister.

"After that, I didn't know if you and Navy and Vesta were even alive. Even though I couldn't think about you without anger, I did worry. Nobody deserves to die like that."

I can think of a few.

"What about Markos?"

"He's back in Eos now," Kane says. "He developed some sort of rash after we got back to Jezebel and had his leg amputated at the knee as a precaution. You know how he is. But I had a letter from him a month ago. He got fitted for a replacement limb, and he's happy to be home."

I know the feeling.

"He'll be glad to know you're still alive. He always spoke well of you, even after you left."

Which bothered you?

A lizard scurries out of the brush on the other side of the stream. I squat down to watch it lick water out of the pool trapped between rocks. It's the little brown kind with the red spot just behind the eye, a teardrop of blood.

It runs away when Kane takes in a heavy breath. "How long were you planning to betray me?"

I see no purpose in letting the Stranger lie.

"That long." He nods, unfortunately still better with insight than most people. "All right, well, that answers my follow-up question. There wasn't an event that made you turn on me."

Was he angrier that I stole his work or that I rejected him personally? It doesn't interest me enough to ask, and I'm not giving him any ideas ever again.

I rise back off my heels. "I said no the first time you asked to hire our train. Remember? You didn't wonder why we suddenly changed our mind?"

"Not long enough. Your grandmother is very persuasive."

A hot needle stabs into my throat. I walk to the next break in the slipping water.

He doesn't know Grandma's gone, but I still want to hurt him for acting like he knew her at all.

But she wouldn't like that. I choose to honor her.

This time.

I breathe in slowly, and the Stranger coats the back of my throat like lead. "What did your father and the University say when you came back to them with nothing?"

"I…well, I told them Randy got to my notes in one of his fits of madness. I told my father I was lucky to have made it out alive, and everyone believed me. At that point I didn't know why I was protecting you. It just happened, and I let it."

Ask, the Stranger whispers, black fringes that bend like grass at the edge of me.

I already know the answer. The map is back there at the boarding house, on the table between him and his father. Lake Amnesty. Perspective, the Wells's gravesite. *Sol Darius,* the ghost river. Eden. The West Rim and all the places we visited, laid out in ink forever. But I will make him admit it. He made me be so honest when I didn't want to. He might be fool enough to forgive me, but I do not forgive him for being part of the future coming to take ours.

"Have you been back to Eden?"

"Yes."

The Stranger flickers, cold.

Even when I did it, I knew stealing his work would only be a temporary setback. I'm going back, and he's determined like me. In a lot of ways, we may be each other's worst enemies. I hoped I'd stolen myself more time than what I actually got, but I try to resist the bitterness of disappointment in myself. It's not my fault that Green's bounty and Hannah got in my way for so long.

"The main focus has been the new line," he says. "But we've started stocking a supply cache ahead of the first prospecting crew."

So it's already started.

"What about you?" Kane asks. "I'm sure you've done all kinds of interesting things since then."

Nothing you're getting to hear about.

I have the answer Aunt Tess wants. Unfortunately, he doesn't hate me, and I won't be starting something I'm not willing to finish this time.

My gaze finds Kane's once again, and now I hold on.

"Apologize to him," Aunt Tess told me. *"You don't have to mean it. Just say it."*

I don't mean it.

Never.

"I'm sorry."

Kane nods. Slow, methodical, evaluating the quality of my honesty like Raleigh does with pearls. "Thank you. I know you didn't have to come and talk to me. You didn't have to let me see you here at all. I know that means something coming from you."

He's not as good at reading me as Raleigh is pearls. At least not right now. Other times, he saw too much.

He thinks Grandma was persuasive. He doesn't know Aunt Tess at all.

Farce, now I owe her five hundred gold. I'll try to lie my way out of it, but really, I need to stop making these bets against her. I know better.

I angle my way out of the creek bed. The scrape of my boots on loose rock displaces the silence that's suddenly grown too thick for its own good.

Kane makes no move to follow me once we're out of the gully and on the dirt path we came down. Either he can tell I want to be away from him or he doesn't want to be with me anymore.

Fifteen.

"I would ask you to stop by again," he calls. "But maybe that's not a good idea."

It's not.

I offer him the engineer's salute. It's all I'm comfortable with.

Unfortunate as it's been for both of us, we're here to stay in each other's paths until one of us is dead.

FIFTY-EIGHT
TESLA

Leagan steadies the trellis as Adelaide climbs to the roof of the boarding house veranda.

My midnight-blue skirt swells and contracts around my legs as the wind picks up, orange aura ribbons snaking across the stars. I wait until Adelaide clears the eave before pulling the bell cord. The corner of a lace curtain in the bank of windows shifts. I wave to the woman behind it. "She's coming. Better move it."

Leagan scurries back to Navy and I before the door opens.

"Widow." The housekeeper bites her lip before she attempts the smile. "I heard you were back from the dead."

"Hello, Jessa. We need speak to your guests."

"Mr. Floyd just brought these carpets in new from Jezebel. I waited since last Season for them. Couldn't you wait until the men go out tomorrow?"

"Oh no, we're not here to kill anyone. I swear on my wind-burned lips." I steal a look past her, the hall empty, but voices move inside. "I just need to see Von Kane, that's all."

"They're finishing their meal."

"Thank you." I don't care if that was an invitation or not, I pass her a roll of copper standards and push my way through. "Oh yes, these carpets are alkaline. It's like stepping on a sheep. Don't worry, I'll be kind to them."

"Just wait," Jessa fusses. "I'll announce you."

"How sophisticated."

A gray cat shakes its bell collar and darts to the back staircase where the quartz sconces aren't burning bright enough to reach him. Jessa's skirt catches on mine as she rushes to beat us to the double doors at the head of the hall. The male voices fill in when she opens them.

"Excuse me, gentlemen, you have a visitor."

Millard Von Kane, our Kane, Jonathaniel Swann, Captain Montgomery, and a man I don't know. The railroad expansion heads and their higher calling to bring peace and prosperity to the Rim, in the flesh. They sure look like regular east blood meat to me. They're no better than us, just walking in different ways.

They take in my naked face, no widow's lace hiding me or the scar in it tonight, revolvers filling both sides of my shoulder harness and a necklace cutting a copper line down the front of my chest. Leagan wears her cleanest gentleman's town pants and hip holster, Navy out of her veil and goggles since it's nighttime, a pair of amber-tinted wire frames to hide the silver scars on her eyes instead.

"Hello, Von Kane." I nod to him first. The boss always sits at the head of the table, and Montgomery has taken the foot, Jonathaniel below our Kane. So kind of them to make their power dynamic so easy to read. "Kane. Swann. Captain." And the one I don't know with the shifty eyes. "Sir."

"This is most irregular." Montgomery twists his swollen body to look at the double door, but Jessa has closed it. She knows me, but I meant what I said. No killing on the new carpet. "Who are you?"

"You don't recognize her?" Jonathaniel's smile twinkles conspiracy. "Typical. You met her last week."

"I most certainly did not."

He certainly has a type. Women who are murderous. But if you don't want to fear someone, it is easiest to be on their side. He's not the fool Montgomery takes him for—he's a player of a longer game, like me.

Millard Von Kane blinks back at me with dubious blue eyes. "Hello... madam. Have we met?"

"Not you and I. But now we will. My name is Tesla Revere."

I drag out one velvet chair for Navy and another for myself. "My nieces. Navy, the chemist, and Leagan, weapons designer."

She lifts a finger, mouth already stuffed with cheese biscuit.

Kane says nothing, so I smile at him. "It's nice to see you again, Timothy Von Kane."

Millard turns to his son. "You know this woman?"

Now the truth will come out. Is this plan of mine a fool's dream like Montoya's, over before it begins, or did Kane lie to his father about us like he claimed?

"Her associate saved our backsides on the way here." Jonathaniel picks through the rosemary and roasted tomatoes garnishing the game hen platter. "You remember my friend Adelaide, Montgomery, or have you forgotten her, too—"

"Sister," Leagan says, mouth still clotted with bread.

"Pardon?"

Here we go.

Leagan swallows. "Adelaide *Revere*. She's my sister, not an associate."

"Oh, how nice. Well, she was looking forward to seeing you."

"I know." Leagan stabs her finger into an olive. "And she was looking forward to getting away from you."

"Now I am confused," Montgomery says. "Were these women invited here?"

Jonathaniel reaches for the tea decanter bleeding beads of condensation. "The question is, old friend, have you ever *not* been confused?"

"I'm not confused, but I would like an explanation," Millard says. Of course, a general, former Jezebel governor, and University man would never admit to being confused. At least Montgomery has honest courage dear Millard does not. "Son?"

"We spoke about the Reveres, Father." Kane's gaze remains on my face. "They were our transportation and guidance on the first survey expedition."

"An ill-fated affair...but—" Millard parts his hands. "—some things cannot be helped. Risk is part of discovery. You industrious ladies are part of the Rim's history now. My son spoke amicably of you and your services when he returned, and for that return his mother and I thank you."

Not highly enough for Millard to remember our name, but I'll take it considering Kane could have told him the truth.

"I'd be very interested to hear your side of the story...some other time, when we have more of it." The teeth prickling Millard's gaze sink into mine, demanding I read between those words and shut my fucking mouth if I know what's good for me.

Well, lucky for him, I am astute. Unlucky, I am more than that. It seems he's still keeping things from his investors, and probably his son. For example, the still very present siege of the pestilence. Possibly his purchase of the West Rim. He may be able to fool his friends at this table, friends being a loose term like I employ it. But I read your coded letters to Horne, you slippery bastard. You're sending hundreds of people west to dig for black gold and die on land you've so graciously rented to them.

Think of us as a thing of history if that helps you sleep tonight, Von Kane. You have no idea you're going to need the cure Navy's creating before this is over, and oh so badly.

"I'd love to hear this story," Jonathaniel says.

"Of course you would." Montgomery sighs like an exhausted engine farting petrified fuel. "Especially if there's something foul about it."

"How are you, Navy?" Kane asks.

"Alkaline, thank you."

"Have you been doing much science?"

"All the science."

He's piecing us together. He knows something's not right, but he's too well-mannered to come right out and ask what.

"You surely didn't come here to reminisce old times," Millard says.

"Of course not," I say. "We came here to meet you. Your son also spoke highly of his father. I heard through a mutual friend you'd be in town."

"Well, that is...too kind." Millard turns a hand to the man with the shifty eyes. He's a skeleton inside a gray suit, with forehead lines of serious displeasure. "May I also introduce Dr. DuPonte."

"Oh, this is good news. The Rim is in dire need of more doctors." Especially one who looks like he eats human kidneys with salt.

"I agree," Montgomery mutters.

"You're also a railroad investor, I presume?"

DuPonte nods once and turns back to his bread pudding, his beak nose almost bent enough to touch the spoon. Shifty *and* sour.

Millard's gaze crosses over us again, attempting to cut and weigh like one does with quartz. I do have to admire him. He's not just someone accustomed to being in control—he's someone born for it. A fate so set in iron he couldn't possibly have become anything else, like me, like Adelaide.

"There's one more person involved in that ill-fated expedition who I am curious about. My son said his survey guide was half Tov. Is she also here with you in Oath? I'd like to meet her."

Oh, I bet you would. A vulture, picking at the carcass of the Shadow Nation under the protection of scholarly pursuits. It's no accident Adelaide is the one family member absent from this meeting. Yes, she needed the opportunity to break in upstairs, but she also knew Millard would want to see her, and she decided to deny him, no prize.

"I understand you're having trouble out at the railroad camp," I say.

Millard's gaze stays level with mine. Good. I can't respect a man who won't look me in the eye. "Rumors."

"That's not what we heard..." Leagan says. "You need better guns? I can make you better guns. I do customizations and test them all myself, nothing bastard. Nothing *Green*."

"And some competent people to use them." I flick him with a smile. "Our family has been providing protection to the Rim's business owners and travelers for the last ten years. We are the best. Ask your son."

Millard doesn't waste one glance at Kane. "With all due respect, Miss Revere, I can't accept your offer. We have an existing security contract and a budget to keep."

"With all due respect, I've also been an engineer for ten full Seasons, and it's been eight since I've seen this many line holdups. If I was paying the Green Company to keep bone pickers off the rails, I'd expect better results by now."

"How did you come by this information?"

"You don't become the best at anything by accident. We know the Rim by experience, Mr. Von Kane. Front to back. And none of those sides have scared us away."

"By this experience you think you can do better than our current partner?"

"Absolutely."

"I have to agree with her, your Mr. Green has given poor results," Montgomery says. "We were almost killed getting here. You can't call the rails clean if there's still vermin crawling around shooting people."

"Although it was terribly exciting," Jonathaniel says.

Leagan whispers something to Navy that makes her laugh and blush. Probably something rude.

"One can hardly expect over fifty years' worth of violence and depravation to disappear overnight," Millard says. "The Rim was where the Republic used to export violent criminals."

"Used to?" I say. "This must be a very recent change. I heard they've been sending them to build the railroad for you."

"We aim to clean the Territories' reputation and develop better practices for a penal colony. It will take time. However, we already have the contract with Mr. Green, and he hasn't done anything warranting a break of that."

"Of course, I understand."

Of course, he doesn't want to admit failure or problems. I wouldn't. I just had to plant the seed, and now I have.

"Tell me, Miss Revere, where were you born?" Millard asks. "It's not here. Your education and diction are too fine."

"I was born in east Saint Laura County, and my mother was from Jezebel. We came here when I was fifteen."

"Ah." Millard nods, and I think he sounds a little kinder. Oh, you fool, I know your kind. "I thought I detected something familiar behind your Rim accent. Saint Laura is lovely. My wife also spent some formative years there."

"Oh, maybe we've met."

"It's a large county, and you're a little young for that." Millard's smile falls into condescension again. He's spent too many years with political men and students licking up his opinions to get ahead or pass exams, and a lifetime of being assured his name makes him special. A name is only as good as what you do with it. Where and what you come into this world as shouldn't matter as much as people want to believe. It's who you become with your actions that counts.

"Well, gentlemen..." I spread my hands on the table and rise. "If you should ever reconsider who you've bought protection from, you can find us through our associate, Raleigh, the best arms dealer in Lideon."

"And if you need something he doesn't have." Leagan drops her name card into Kane's drink with a smirk. "There you go."

He rises with us. "I'll show them out."

My last parting glance goes to the gray and silent Dr. DuPonte. The man unsettles me, sinister as a preacher. I'm undecided on his purpose here, but I doubt it's just for the scenery or the scavenger lizards, like delightful Jonathaniel.

"So will I." Jonathaniel stands in a rush, latching onto my elbow as I leave the dining room. "*Sol*, Tesla Revere. Please give Adelaide my kindest regards, and I'm glad she made it home safely."

I glance back toward the dining room door, and Millard is watching us. Alkaline. "*Sol*, Jonathaniel Swann. We enjoy you very much. Look us up sometime." I offer him my scarred cheek to kiss. "Until we meet again."

"Nothing could be more excellent. You are all delightful."

"I'd like to see some of the weapons you've made," Kane says to Leagan. "Adelaide told me you designed her crossgun."

"And made it."

"I'd be interested in something like that."

"That was just for her. But I have many things."

"I'm sure I can find something I like." Kane holds the front door for me. The wind boils across the new rug, the howl of it human enough to lift hair. "My father hasn't seen what's out there."

"No?" My gambler's eye looks him over, and I see fear. What he wears over it is courage. "Neither have I."

"Adelaide, Navy, and Vesta have. That counts for something. But I don't think any of us have witnessed the true descent of the West Rim."

"Give it to me straight rails then. What's really happening out west, Von Kane?"

He hesitates. "Have a good night."

So close. *Krossus.*

"We'll all just have to be surprised then, won't we?" My wink finds him like a promise. Breakable. "We'll see you on the West Rim."

When Navy's ready to show them all what she's made.

ADELAIDE SITS AT THE WRITING DESK IN OUR ROOMS NEXT DOOR, THE SCRAPE OF pencil transforming blank paper into information.

"Did you have time to miss us?" I ask.

"I cried."

"I stole you this." Leagan brings her a hand pie wrapped in one of Jessa's handmade napkins.

"What secrets of rich men do you have to tell us?" I brace hands on the back of her chair and the desk. She's drawn the rock arches west of Descendants, the place where the wind turns to screams and the ghosts spill from shadows. "Don't build suspense right now, I can't take it."

"It's true." She lays down her pencil to look at me. "The *Exodus Ironclad* is coming. The Von Kanes did order it."

"Fool's fucking gold... Too bad it's going to be late."

FIFTY-NINE
ADELAIDE

I MET RALEIGH WHEN I WAS TWELVE. WE WERE MAKING THE ROCK PASS INTO the South Rim. The Coffin Slots, deep crevices and trees that slashed shadows for miles. I sat spotter in the fire seat while Grandma engineered, scouting the track for debris too thick for our clearing wedge. We were getting close to Windust, enough to see homesteads breaking up the wild brush. I noticed the outline of men and rope stretched across the track while we were still far enough away to pull a full stop.

The two men had the red-haired boy's arms tied to a pine tree on either side of the track so the next train to come by would rip him apart. His bare toes gripped at the rail, fighting to keep balance. As we came closer, the Stranger picked out why. He had only one foot.

"What is this?" Grandma called, rifle in hand but pointed calmly at the ground. I held my pistol with a little more focus.

"This little shit stain owes us money."

Raleigh grinned past his bloody chin. "That's why you should always check the salesman's guarantee. Especially if we don't make one."

"Can it, boy." The knee found him in the crotch and his body tried to curl, but the ropes stopped him, slicing into his thin wrists.

"You have a ghost following you," the bigger man said, nodding to me. "You always let your property carry a weapon? What makes you sure that fox won't turn on you?"

"Is there a reason two full-grown men are out here beating a child, blocking the track, and insulting my granddaughter?" Grandma said. "You're making fools of yourselves and making me late for my delivery."

"Apologies, ma'am." He tipped his embroidered hat. "Feel free to pass right through and on your merry way. He won't put up any fight, and the Rim won't miss him when he's gone. It shouldn't be too hard to pick his leftover bits off the front of your engine neither."

"I've never run over a child, and I don't plan on starting today. I still have a conscience. Though I could get over the both of you."

"With all respect, lady, I'm not a child," Raleigh said. "Been supporting myself since I was eight Seasons, yes ma'am."

The Stranger picked over Raleigh like a new room. He was bone skinny. Most children of the Rim are. All arms and legs, wide eyes the sharp blue of alkaline Ven crystal. He half-smiled at me past his dripping nose and the red humiliation of getting kicked in the balls. I didn't smile back, but he didn't seem to mind.

I wanted to know why he had only one leg. Lots of people are missing body parts, but they were usually older than me. If he was, it was only by a Season or two.

"I think you should leave," Grandma said. Her rifle nudged upward.

The Stranger saw her move, adjusted my grip. I decided which one of them I'd shoot first. The one who called me ghost. The Stranger confirmed it was a good choice.

"Well, then maybe you'd like to settle this little snake's debt with us. Call it your good deed for the day. Providence Almighty likes that, don't He?"

"Or maybe you'd like to keep him," the other said. "Seeing as how you've already got one stray animal in your service. He's missing a few toes, but you won't even notice that."

"You didn't cut his leg off, did you?"

"No boy. He came limping up the street that way, a little one-legged cart animal. We'll sell him to you with a limb discount, how's that?"

"Keep talking," Grandma said. "My conscience is wearing away."

Up at the engine, Aunt Tess yanked on the whistle. Her patience was wearing away.

"Fifty gold. He's yours."

"That sounds fair." And Grandma shot him.

The other staggered back, hand snatching at his holstered pistol. "What the fuck? You said yes!"

Grandma pointed her rifle up under his chin. "I said it sounded fair. But how does twenty-five sound to you?"

"Fine. That sounds just fine. Alkaline, ma'am." His throat knot scraped at the skin as he swallowed, trying to lean away. "Let me be out of your way."

"Stranger, will you pay the man?"

I took the money from Grandma's belt, held it out like I intended to pass it to him, then flicked it into the dust away from us.

"If anyone asks what happened to your friend," Grandma said, "tell them he tried to swindle the Reveres. You recognized a fair price, and we were a pleasure to do business with."

"As you say." He snatched up the money quickly, backing away to the horses tethered near the rocks.

"Go. Go now."

The Stranger watched to be sure he really rode away and wasn't just pretending to.

Grandma shrugged her rifle strap overhead and cut the first of the two ropes straining Raleigh's arm out of its socket. "Where are your parents?"

"Dead and who knows." Raleigh had no trouble balancing on his single leg. I wanted to see how he was going to walk. Hop?

"That is unfortunate." Grandma sighed. "So are mine."

"That's just the way these things go." He stuck out his dusty hand, awfully cheerful for someone who'd skipped death like breakfast. Men usually cried or begged when they thought they were going to die. People are all the same. "Name's Raleigh, at your service. I do have to warn you, though, for twenty-five gold I probably won't work very hard. Maybe for fifty I would have."

Grandma laughed. "At least you're honest."

"I try to be." He rubbed at the blood trying to leak over his upper lip, then offered the opposite, clean palm to me. "Your name is Stranger? I do like that. But strangers are just friends you haven't met yet, so let's shake hands and be acquainted."

"Well, Raleigh, I'd like to help get you somewhere safer before I release you from my service," Grandma said. "Where would that be?"

He gave her the no-bullshit grin I came to appreciate, then respect, then care about. The brother we didn't have. "Ma'am, this is the Rim. Safe is for fools. If it's all the same to you, I'd like to ride along with your people and pay off the twenty-five gold."

"That's not necessary."

"I'm good for it, you'll see. You need something sold, I'll sell it. You need a message delivered, it's no trouble. Those pickers took my ware cart, but I can borrow a new one."

"I'm not asking you to repay anything. It's only twenty-five gold, but if it means that much to you, I won't say no immediately. Although you do have a point. This is the Rim, so I have to ask why?"

"Without my cart, I've got nowhere better to be. I like interesting people, and you seem interesting."

SIXTY
TESLA

We won't hear the *Exodus Ironclad* coming. We'll only feel it. The rail tunnels through miles of rock arches, ancient throats that wind moans through like a thousand broken lovers.

I turn to the cold side of my bedroll, but there isn't one with Travis next to me.

"What's wrong?" He doesn't move, trained not to startle prey and sleep still thick on his tongue.

"Nothing." I pet his beard. "I just need to stretch my legs for a while."

Our camp haunts the ridge above one of the tighter arches, where patches of ghostflower feed on cactus roots and reflect moonlight. Down the other side of the bank, Montoya sits in a bright band of silver. His shirt splays open, blood running black down his chest from a series of cuts twisted up like a knot over his heart. Other, older scars cover the rest of his torso. This isn't the first time.

Poor bastard. I knew he wasn't quite right in the head, but I didn't think it was this bad.

He squeezes the wound, forcing it to bleed harder before scraping out another layer of skin.

"How old are your daughters?" My voice carries downwind. I have the high ground and a safe distance, and I intend to keep it while there's a knife in his hand.

He yanks the flaccid half of his shirt up. "You can't hear anyone approaching with this ambient noise."

"That's the idea."

"My daughters are of a similar age to your nieces, I believe." The sting of clear pine lodges up in my head as he pours it across his blade, flicking the droplets to the brush. From the kit next to him he lifts an already prepared poultice and pins it to his wound. "Please go."

"Since we're about to risk our asses alongside yours, I think it's fair of me to ask. What the fuck are you doing?" Also, do I need to put you out of your misery now instead of waiting for Adelaide to do it later?

"This was a parting gift from my brothers and sisters of poison. A new tattoo to replace the one they took back off me."

"You didn't like it?"

"The ink was made with things from the Garden. Vile things I must cut out of my body before they have their way."

"Fucking Jezebel." And he calls these people *family*. "So, they did kill you after all. And they gave you the pleasure of looking forward to it."

"Die slow, die trying."

I suppose, if that's all you can do. Maybe this will save me from any guilt that might try to grab me later on. "How long do you have?"

"That depends."

"Well, I hope they lied to you."

"They didn't." He lowers his head to me. It's not the first time he's seen this punishment given out then. Maybe he even partook in the justice of poison on another. "If you don't mind, I need to be alone."

"As long as the blood loss isn't going to make you forget your part of the plan."

"I have Adelaide's drawing of the *Exodus Ironclad* here, as well as here." Paper crackles as he pats the discarded jacket behind him and then his temple. "As long as your man Raleigh told the truth."

"Raleigh would never lie about good ammunition." I pause on a heel. "Don't worry, I won't tell anyone about your nighttime activities here."

"I appreciate that."

"We will have to make a short stop to drop the extra weight off before Hannah."

"As you said." His mouth twitches. "As long as no more of your friends show up with new distractions. I'll have to start asking if you're stalling."

"If I wanted out of our deal, I'd take the easy way and wait for your tattoo to do you in for me."

He almost laughs, the way a coyote scoffs to intimidate another scavenger.

"I said we keep our word to our partners, remember?" I say. "It's as good as a contract from your Poisonneur's Order, and I won't poison you at the end of it..." I soften myself. "Don't worry, you'll get to see your family soon."

He nods, already facing the other way.

I didn't see her on the way down, but I do going back up the hill. Adelaide, perched on the rock shelf. From this angle, you could almost mistake her hair for more ghostflower.

"I should have known," I say.

"You should have."

Day warmth still seeps from the rock, scrapes crossing her knuckles from the work we did today.

"I assume you saw enough of that."

She nods.

Even fools know weaknesses are valuable secrets. Now we have to be extra careful because Montoya will be after one of ours to balance out his. And dying men have more to be afraid of, not less as you might think.

Her scowl is canyon deep, part of her. "We shouldn't have made this deal with him."

"Is that what the Stranger says?"

"Leagan says. I don't like it either."

"Then let's prove everyone wrong."

"Her dreams don't have any purpose if you don't listen to them."

"Has anyone ever told you you're alarmingly astute?"

"You have."

"You can kill him whenever the Stranger says the time is right. Once we have the *Exodus*."

That's fair, isn't it?

SIXTY-ONE
ADELAIDE

THE STRANGER FELT THE HUM COME THROUGH THE ROCK TWO HOURS AGO.

Now it's the thunder of a growing storm, the ink flag of an engine run on black gold rising skyward. We cast eight shadows away from the track. Two of them belong to me.

In the slipping light, I bring my binoculars to the engine riding under it. The black nose of the debris wedge surges through a gap in the Rim's red crust, angle sharper than the sun as it drops away.

"There she is." Aunt Tess inhales deeply. "Fool's fucking gold, look at her…"

The train weaves through the valley arches like a widower snake. There's no observation deck like on the *Absolution*. All car crossings are enclosed, either in iron plating or woven bars, rows of holes just large enough to poke a rifle barrel through. Solid, death.

Twenty-five cars.

Storm shutters cover the engine's windows. Their spotter doesn't need to see much. The *Emerald Constellation*'s wedge severed a spine, they could clear a rockslide with this nose plow.

Aunt Tess clicks the stop on her watch. "Shit, she's fast."

"Forty-two?" I say.

"Fifty-five. And that's against the grade, with all that weight."

This is the future Kane and Jonathaniel are so excited for.

"How big is it?" Navy asks.

"Big," Leagan says.

"Well, how big? Describe it to me."

"Longer than any machine you've ever seen," Raleigh says. "When you first see the front, you can't see the end. It will take a long time to stop that thing."

"There's no stopping that thing." Aunt Tess chuckles and keeps at it.

Engineering regulations advise a top speed of twenty-five after dark, but most engineers treat them as suggestions anyway. This is a thing created to break whatever it hits.

I shake off a scorpion trying to creep across the toe of my boot. "Two fuel cars, right behind each engine." Where they should be. "And it looks like they have a backup boiler behind it." The oddly small stack looks out of balance behind the other two. "I see the water reserve tank."

"A nice waste of weight to them right about now," Raleigh says. "It's far too late to turn and run."

"The *Exodus* doesn't need to turn," Navy says.

"Figure of speech. There will likely be five standing guns shooting at us from either side, manual crank with portholes." Raleigh points where he wants my gaze to follow. "That's the one you and Montoya need to watch out for on top. The Exodus Reaper. It's steam-fed and capable of rotating the barrel a full three-sixty radius."

"There's no shield on it though," Leagan says. "That must be where they send the guy they don't like."

At the end rides the reverse engine, its own water and fuel cars attached. Even if the lead engineer and crew are killed, the fallback can still run. But even with all this, they're still as vulnerable as we were. They're still bound to the rails.

"Here it comes…" Aunt Tess shakes her head. "Oh, this is a wretched thing to do to this machine."

The spur of track we chopped the ties out from under will bow under their weight, hopefully jamming several of the wheels but not knocking them off-rail. Any reliable engineer would slow down.

"Are they slowing down too soon?" Manic taints Leagan's voice, and Aunt Tess slaps at her.

"You shut your filthy mouth, ma'am. Don't hex this. Go get into your raptor nest."

The brakes shriek suddenly behind the pop of metal. I feel the jolt in my stomach as if I'm there.

"*Krossus*," Aunt Tess whispers.

Their speed drops. Rapidly.

They stay intact.

Leagan, Aunt Tess and Raleigh spend a minute exchanging a little dance of relief and Aunt Tess plants a quick kiss on Travis. He doesn't return the gesture.

"I never thought I'd like anything better than the *Absolution*, but yes, this will be a suitable replacement." She checks her watch against mine and then Montoya's, then nods. "Forty-five minutes, we'll see you at the top."

THE CANYON GHOSTS CLOSE IN AT NIGHT. IT'S THEIR MOANS YOU HEAR BY THE arches. They leap out of the shadows to eat you when you're busy looking at the moons.

That's what we tell the east bloods.

I crouch against the shadow side of the rock arch like a patch of ghostflower. Canyons and rocky spires look on without mercy. There are no friends here, only strangers, only enemies.

My breath moves through my full-seal respirator like the presence of the Stranger. Everything in my left eye stained white-blue by the glare of a solar quartz lens. The right, plain glass.

Montoya nods to me. Ready when I am. But I listen to the Stranger, counting the fine grain of metal seams as they creak under the arch.

Water car. Now.

From the shadows I step onto the smooth, beetle shell of the *Exodus*. The leather masking the soles of my boots is too squishy, but it gives my weight no voice. I fold back down into a crouch, feel everything, hand on my pistol. It's been a full Season since I rode the *Absolution*, but my body remembers the sway of wheels, how to balance against the wind when everything around you is moving.

Montoya is an eclipse that creeps toward the rear engine.

You could shove him off now.

Would it kill him though? The *Exodus* isn't moving so fast anymore. It might only make him mad.

The flicker of rock passing between me and the moon slashes my vision. But it's doing the same to everyone inside.

Twenty-five.

Metal meets my fingers like cold oil. The Exodus Reaper, the revolving ten-barrel cluster the size of my legs together, straddling a hatch into the car below.

I pull two tubes of Navy's sick smoke from my bandoleer, lay them on the hatch to fall inside and shatter when the gunman drops the lid.

Twenty-seven.

A ladder wraps the curve of the water reservoir, ground flashing silver and black under the iron grate catwalk.

Sandstone scrapes by as I descend, close enough to feel the day heat still pulsing off its face, sucking my hair into the wind.

The Stranger pours off my shoulders, her attention wrapped around the spigot tapping the shadow side of the water tank. I grab hold of the release wheel. It gives.

Water spits a dark line across pale rock. Two turns and it sprays straight, sharp enough to send dirt and stone flying back at me.

Move, the Stranger says. *Now.*

Sixteen.

I place my back to the wall outside the boiler car and draw my crossgun. Ahead, a deep *V* of starred sky marks the gap in the plateau where everyone else waits. If the *Exodus* crew doesn't fall for this, the rest of our plan won't work.

The vibration of the door being unbolted from the inside passes through my spine. The man who steps out doesn't look this way, doesn't feel my presence only feet away, tucking a cigarette into his lip. I catch the door with my toe before the weight pulls it shut, let him take three steps. Then my bolt goes through his neck.

Two.

The door latches behind me with teeth.

Quiet air feels too soft after the wind peeling at my face. The boiler dials glow, heat like day hugging the air. No lamps.

The next car is walled in with fuel boxes, the cubbies layered inside vertically. Crystals are supposed to be wrapped or stored individually to keep them from sparking together. Like we thought, the *Exodus Ironclad* carries enough fuel to complete their delivery without stopping.

Leather seats creak to the rhythm of the wheels. I bar the door from the engine side. They should have.

One crewman snores, face to the wall of the lower bunk. I point my barrel at his head and pull the smaller glass vial from my bandoleer.

The engineer works the lever for the rear mirrors, angling it side to side for views outside the shutter slats. "We're still losing water."

"Could it be a dial failure?"

It's not.

"We'll know when he gets back. That loose track smelled like a picker trap."

A tin voice comes through the speaking tube, mounted between the engineer and fire seats. "We're under attack."

I pull the trigger on the man asleep in his bunk and in the same breath throw Navy's concoction at the ghost quartz green of the engine dials. The two liquids, once separated by wax, fuse in a vein of smoke, comes to life.

"Fuck!" The spotter leaps from the fire seat only to pitch forward, his insides on the way up as the fog grows around my respirator.

"Can't—they're already inside!" the voice in the tube shouts over coughs that distort him.

"That's impossible—" The bolt goes through the back of the engineer's head, splintering the window.

Five.

"Guns up!" the spotter manages to yell before I turn my crossgun on him.

I can hear Aunt Tess now, complaining about how dirty I got the engine. I'll tell her she can use the other one, but there's no guarantee Montoya is cleaner than I am.

The Stranger rolls through the smoke loose in the car, the control wheels and levers, a throb to match my steps. There are more switches than the *Absolution* had, fewer buttons than on Jonathaniel's train.

The outline of the last arch is visible ahead. We have to start slowing before then.

Two valves are open. I close them. Above the speaking tube is a glass-capped dial. *Auxiliary Engine Stop Request.* A bell inside the panel pings when I turn it.

Montoya's Cairosh accent fills up the speaking tube. "The rear engine is ours."

Ours.

Not his.

"Close all the valves."

The *Exodus*'s residual motion begins to settle.

From the ceiling, I pull the brake lever.

SIXTY-TWO
TESLA

SEARCH LAMPS IGNITE ON THE *EXODUS*'S GUN CARS, EYES TO SWEEP THE DESERT for our evil. But the engine drags to a final stop and strands them. Adelaide, she never lets us down.

Blood-crimson bands of aura light unbraid and flex, the storm I prayed for drawing a starless line over the western horizon.

I barely notice the rocks poking into my stomach anymore, Leagan and I sprawled out on our stomachs with our rifles ready. From the dark throats of the gunports, the disembodied clack of the standing gun barrels winds up. Damn, it is a rather frightening sound, but they don't show a face or waste a bullet. Well, neither will I.

Out among the far rocks, Travis lets out the mournful whistle scream of a ghost cat. From this side of the pass, Raleigh and Navy return the cry like an echo. Caught between them, the night feels endless, the air so stiff I could bite it.

Toxic smoke turns to ghosts in the air, silently rising out of gaps in the gun crew car. It seeps from the reverse engine as well, where Montoya did his job.

"You owe me a drink," I say.

"You...shut your filthy mouth," Leagan hisses back. "The night's not over."

A tongue of red lightning forks out west. I click the stop on my pocket watch and observe the needle float across it as I wait for the thunder to roll over us.

"Ten seconds."

"Got it," Leagan says.

"Vent!" A door bursts open on the yell.

"Get back inside," they scream at him. "Johnson!"

"I need air!"

The poor bastard stumbles out, clapping his knees as his stomach empties over his gray jumpsuit and steel-toed boots. The silence inside betrays that they all expected to be shot down instantly, even him.

What are you waiting for? Their fear clots the air when we don't. Unpredictability is far more deadly than over-muscled firepower, my friends.

The next stab of lightning paints the west sky bloody.

"Blessed are those who pass through the fire, Johnson." Death is part of life, and I take aim and count to ten.

My shot punctures the jar of solar quartz set on the opposite slope. False gunshots of white light scatter like fallen stars, flinging shadows up the wrong slope. Meanwhile, Leagan's true shot gets rolled over and lost within the thunder. Johnson's body collapses outside the *Exodus*, without witness.

"North side, fire!"

All at once, the barrels spin to full speed. Pale orange light explodes into the night, jagged new shadows tearing up the wrong slope, just like I wanted. Ha ha.

Leagan fires and racks again before I even see another man outside the car.

There's so much hemorrhaging of light, and now it's hard to know what to focus on. I remind myself to take a breath.

Leagan's mouth moves, but whatever it is, I can't hear her. I can't hear if the barrels wind down again. I can't hear anything but the gunpowder and lead shattering everything in its path. But it's very obvious when the sky and rocks stop quaking with man-made light.

Fucking Jezebel, am I deaf?

Smoke drips from the bottom corners of the door Johnson left open, a leg wrapped in a knee-high boot dangling from the dark interior.

Downgrade, steel rail and splinted ties rupture skyward as Raleigh detonates the bundle of demo sticks we laid below the last rock arch the *Exodus* passed through. Dust air hits me like a brick wall and keeps going, on course to collide with the storm.

Now there's nowhere for the *Exodus* to run but deeper west, even if Montoya tries to snake her out from under us. Adelaide sits at the lead engine. I took no chances here.

While all eyes are on the dust caving from the sky, Travis rounds the nose of the engine, crouched below the gunports, well below their line of sight at such close range. He lets out an animal howl before he springs into the open gun car, hatchets drawn.

SIXTY-THREE
ADELAIDE

THE *EXODUS* VIBRATES AS THE INTERIOR STANDING GUNS SPIT FRESH FIRE, BUT they can't undo what Raleigh just did to the track. The Stranger rubs over every cornered shadow, even though I've double-checked that the engine, boiler, and fuel car doors are all bolted from the inside, gone through the pockets of the dead engineers. The tang of gunpowder and now iron from the door bars taint my hands.

I'm the safest of us all right now, sealed in here. But that's what she doesn't like.

Travis screeches like a deep west bone picker somewhere down the line, and the rapid fire of modern guns cuts out, a severed thread.

It's so quiet.

"Greetings." Montoya's voice makes me flinch. "Honorable crew of the *Exodus Ironclad*. While I'm certain you will still try, you have already lost your fight here. You will not be outgunned, but you have been infiltrated, and both your engines now belong to us. Stand down your weapons and have your commander step outside. The Widow will negotiate your peaceful surrender."

"Who is this?" This voice comes from a car closer to me, clearer in the speaking tube than Montoya's.

"I've worn different names, as I've worn different clothes. Discarded and picked new ones that fit better, as do we all."

The knock blooms across the back boiler door. Two fast, three slow.

I stop, hand on the bolt draw. "Who am I?"

"A Stranger," Navy says, voice turned to a vibration in metal.

She and Raleigh bring dust with them as they step inside, follow me up to the engine.

"This is cozy," he says. "Travis is on the Reaper. It's safe at this end for now."

"You sound jealous," Navy says.

"I'll make sure I get my turn, don't you worry." Raleigh's boot skids in the blood smeared on the floor. "Shit, I should've known. Be careful, Rook."

"This will not be a surrender, bone picker," the *Exodus* crewman says. "And we do not negotiate."

"And you are not the commander," Montoya says. "We speak to no one but him."

"Fucker, you have no idea who I am."

"No one but him."

Raleigh glances at me. "Sell the lie? Like Moira used to."

Be what they fear.

"Yes."

He sits in the swing chair that faces the speaking tube. I feel his pause gather. It settles over all of us, a storm shadow. "You are not alone onboard this train. There's a ghost among you."

The smile begins in his blue eyes and expands under his respirator.

"You really should have read up on the dangers of where you'd be traveling. You heard them wailing on the wind, didn't you? Wayward spirits."

"Is this a joke?" a man says.

"You're not scaring them," Navy says. "They know you're lying."

"Ghosts can't cross moonlight, but shadows make a bridge for them, and that's when they attach themselves to you." Raleigh looks to me again, the grin in his eyes brighter. "Maybe you felt her touch, and that's what made you sick just a little while ago? Maybe you've even heard her name. She's known on the Rim, whose face you'll only see before you die. They call her the Stranger. This ghost answers to no one but my partners, a mistress of clever blood, a lady of chemicals, and a reaper of futures. But..." His tone shifts abruptly from one of a ghost story to fact. "If it is your dream to die in this metal tortoiseshell, for a company that does not even know your names, don't let me dare stand in your way."

The empty scream of Travis's mountain-cat whistle ricochets off the top of the train. Muted male voices rattle against each other like a pump running out of water.

"This is Marshal Donnerick Edwards of the Exodus Arms Company. *I* am the commander." With boom of authority to back him up. "Who am I speaking to?"

I nod.

Navy leans in to reach the tube. "Our name is Revere... If your men cease fire you can step outside with your hands up and walk toward the front engine. The Widow will meet you there."

"It is not my personal position to negotiate with outlaws and other degenerates. The Exodus Company does not either, I assure you. I'm certain I can wager what you came for, but you're going to be disappointed."

"We just want the guns," Navy says. "Not your lives."

"I believe you, Marshal Edwards," Raleigh says. "You can trust in the word of the Rook too. She always tells the truth." He stands, prepares to close up the speaking tube. "But we will take both if that's required."

"I know where he is." I start toward the door at the back of the boiler car. Edwards's voice was also clearer than Montoya's. He's on this side of the freight cars.

Thirty-seven.

The other gas sticks we planted on the rails bleed new smoke, but the storm has shifted, wind ripping away pieces of the lifeless fog. Bodies tangle the floor of the crew cars, the leather tied over my boots slipping in blood too dark to be seen.

The Stranger marks out the seventh car, windows blinded by pinhole storm shutters. The one with the Exodus Arms logo branded in the steel outside. Immediately behind it are the freight cars. The boss would be near his goods.

The crossing is encased in steel, but the interior door is wood. It shatters under the spray of my crossgun enough for me to dislodge the knob with a kick.

New glass, not reformed, bends colors like pearls from the lamps.

Wood panels seamless as satin, a desk full of drawers, the comforts of a company boss.

Marshal Edwards crouches in the next crossing, a scarf tied over his nose and mouth to keep out Navy's smoke. Metal scrapes as he uncouples the joint to the freight car. Sneaky bastard.

But not enough.

The wool rug eats the weight of my footsteps.

Twenty.

I touch my crossgun to the base of his hairline. The reflex to freeze with air still in your lungs at the cold brush of a muzzle is one of the few things you can count on in this world.

"Hold your fire." His voice sounds calm, but the Stranger finds the flutter in his neck, beat faster, proving that he's scared of death like everyone is. "Let's settle this like men, not bone pickers."

We'll settle this how we do things on the Rim.

In blood.

"Hands up."

My female voice startles him at first, then changes odds in his mind for what he'd decided to do about me. He rises slowly, only one hand showing.

I step back.

Shoot.

He rounds, arm up to knock my barrel away, left hand around a pistol.

His white shirt floods red beneath his brushed wool vest, shot scattering its silver buttons and sparking off steel behind him. He stumbles into the plate wall, knocking the strength out of his legs himself. Not dead, but he will be.

I kick the pistol out of his hand, unholster his second, the push knife from his ankle sheath before I reload myself new shells.

"What is wrong with you people out here?" Blood flecks his lips as he coughs. "The Rim rots your brain, doesn't it?"

He doesn't waste breath trying to bargain with me as I peel off his belt and figure-eight it through his wrists, cinching them to his neck. He knows he's going to die, and I'll take what I want anyway.

The iron pins that lock the coupling joints are very similar to the ones on the *Absolution*. Some things designed to accommodate the stupidest among us make taking things simple for the intelligent.

Like him. He thought I was an easy target because I'm not a man. They always do. They're always wrong. At this point I don't have high expectations that they'll ever see us any different. It doesn't matter. I'll keep doing what's best for me and us.

I grab the front of Edwards's vest.

One of the crossing's armor plates has hinges, a seam only visible from this side. Bolts retract as I twist the locking wheel and the section peels open, moonlight blinding to my solar quartz eye.

He balks. "I hope this is worth it."

Yes. I put my foot into his backside.

He hits without hands to break his fall, rolls from his stomach to his side with a groan. The secondary gun car on the other side of the freight section is dead silent. It's possible they're all unconscious, but the Stranger doesn't assume that without proof and neither will I.

"Don't touch me. I'll go where you want."

I point forward, the lead engine. Edwards turns mechanically, head pulled up even though his breaths become more pronounced as the grade sharpens. The belt chokes him otherwise. He barely looks anywhere but forward. I trail him until the ground breaks beyond the channel of rock we trapped them in.

Aunt Tess steps through a gap in the rocks, revolver in each hand, the smirk of triumph behind her mask a pink glow the Stanger sees. "Hello there. Let's talk about how we all get out of here alive, shall we?"

SIXTY-FOUR
TESLA

THE MAN ADELAIDE BRINGS TO ME BLEEDS FROM SO MANY FRAYED HOLES IN HIS chest. His hair is half gray but was once all black, eyes the kind of brown you don't mind trusting, lashes so thick it's a pity they're wasted on a man.

"Marshal Edwards," Adelaide says.

"You are undeniably alkaline at what you do, my dear."

"I know."

With our backs to the moan of the arches, even I start to hear voices in the wind if I put my attention to it for too long, the hair on my neck tingling.

Edwards winces as Adelaide tugs the scarf off her head. The shaft of moonlight falling through rock turns her to silver as she takes her place at my side.

"This is the ghost?"

"She repels them." I take a step closer, one revolver leveled at Edwards, and he responds by stepping back. "Get your folklore right."

"And what kind of devil are you, commanding one?"

"There are many devils that prowl the Rim, Marshal Edwards. We're the least of your concerns." I hope he hears the smile behind the shell of my mask. "My name is the Widow. If you haven't heard of us, we are the Reveres, and the *Exodus Ironclad* belongs to us now."

"The *Exodus* and its contents are the property of the Exodus Arms Company. Its loss would be—"

"Substantial."

"I was going to say retaliated."

"Against you." I close more distance between him and the cliff, Adelaide keeping pace with me. "You appear to be bleeding out, sir."

"There's nothing for me in this if I'm dead."

"True. I acknowledge your difficult position, Edwards. You're dying, but if I offered to let you and your men walk away if you surrender to us, would that make your choice a little easier? At least die a free man."

Edwards glances behind him at the approaching nothing. "It's not that simple."

"It's not? The Rim is the edge of the map," I say. "All of you can easily vanish into the wind, operate an alkaline quartz mine, work on the new railroad, sit in the sun all day eating prickly pears if that's what you like. The Exodus Company will never be able to divine your fate and pursue you."

"My men have families. I have a child."

"Don't we all? Tell the rest of your men to surrender, and I'll have my Menace try to save you. He's from Cairo, he might have some Poisonneur's witchcraft up his overskirt."

We have him backed to the round edge of the rock. Wind ripples in the folds of his pants and sleeves, moonlight reflecting off blood.

"I'm not the fool you think I am." His chest rings with the same emptiness Mother's did as she died. "I know I won't survive the night. Not even the God of Mercy or the devil's black magic could fix this." He looks past me to the train that was once his, and I know all of his bitterness. Of ends, of loss, your future slipping away and you being powerless to stop it.

"All things end," I say.

"Go back to the engine and ask for Shaw. He's the first gun in the auxiliary crew. Tell him I asked you to have mercy on my men, but I won't have anyone saying to my son I died a coward. You kill me now, or so help me God of Mercy."

"Done."

His gaze fixes on Adelaide. "I want the fox to do it."

"That's up to her. Stranger?"

She flicks the trigger switch on her crossgun and places the stock to her shoulder.

"Dust to dust, ash to ash." I cross myself.

"I know where I'm going." He nods and shuts his eyes. "You will reap what you deserve someday too."

"Blessed are those who pass through the fire, Marshal Edwards, for they shall be refined."

Fool's fucking gold, he was a brave soul.

SIXTY-FIVE
ADELAIDE

Idle steam lists from the *Exodus*'s front boiler stack, the reverse engine still at running warmth, even though the soft hiss makes it sound asleep.

"Find one more of them to shoot in here, Stranger," Aunt Tess says through the speaking tube, up at the front. "You missed a little bit of the ceiling."

"I knew you were going to say something about that."

"If you knew, why weren't you more careful?"

I step over a long red streak on the floorboards of the rear engine. "It's not who I am as a person."

"This is why we can't have nice things."

"Just wait until you see how Montoya fucked it up back here," Leagan says.

His eyes narrow, a smirk or a sneer behind his respirator. "Just doing as I was told."

"Really, dear, I expect this from the Stranger, but I thought a Poisonneur would be more delicate," Aunt Tess says.

"Dying men bleed and piss themselves. I'm an assassin, not a magician."

"Well, let's never confuse those two things."

The Stranger doesn't settle once I've looked at everything on this end.

She focuses on Montoya. My nose likes his orange oil cigarette less than I like him. He watches Leagan and I with the same sharp scrutiny as Horne used to, never puts his back to me. Waiting, like I'm waiting. For the right time. At least I have Leagan to help watch him.

"How does the little sister engine look?" Aunt Tess asks.

"She's ready when you are." I assume as long as I don't pull my brake lever or engage my end's driving rods, engineering a double engine is close enough to a single one.

"Alkaline." Aunt Tess clears her throat. "Hello, remaining crew of the *Exodus*. I assume you heard all of that, but let me introduce the family. My name is the Widow, and we are the Reveres. I'm looking for Shaw, the first gun. If you're still among the living, I'm told you are now the highest-ranking man onboard—congratulations. Would you be interested in a deal?"

We wait.

The voice is rough, someone who smokes often and survived an event like this before. "The marshal's dead then?"

"He died with too much honor to take our offer, but he told me you might."

"Yes." No pause. "What are you offering?"

"Leave all your weapons on the floor and come out of that car. We'll let you walk away as long as you go right now and behave."

"That's it? You'll let us walk. No tricks."

"No tricks. We like to leave some alive to tell the tale."

"That's easy to say. You could lie, or let the desert kill us for you."

"Yes, you take a chance either way. I leave it up to you to weigh those odds. You sound like a resourceful man, I'm sure you can figure something out."

"On the other side of the moon diviner, we could wait each other out."

"We could...but I wonder which of us will run out of water first? Or I'll just have the Menace poison you before the sun came up, if the Stranger doesn't kill you first."

He covers the speaking tube. Voices move in the space of that car, but they're all jumbled up by it.

"Good idea," Aunt Tess says. "Take a vote, gentlemen."

Their search lamp cuts out.

"We have a deal," Shaw says.

The slide door sends a vibration across the *Exodus*. One man walks into the blackness filling the pass like dust. Then more. Their shapes disturb the ink, dashing toward the rock cover.

The Stranger counts heads.

I think they know Marshal Edwards tried to uncouple the train in the middle. They believe they'll still have this engine once we try to pull away. It's the only way I'd surrender a fortified position under circumstances like this.

Seven.

"I can't believe that worked," Leagan says. "Dum-dums."

"Let them go," Montoya says, eyes warning. "You made them a deal."

"I never said anything to them." I know exactly what else she's thinking by the look she gives me.

"We thank you for your cooperation," Aunt Tess says, even though the *Exodus* men can't hear her anymore. "*Sol* gentlemen, and if anyone should mention the name Revere, tell them they'd better remember it."

SIXTY-SIX
TESLA

I RUN MY HAND ALONG THE *EXODUS*'S HARDENED RIBS AS I WALK THROUGH THE Boneyard, white and blue sparks snapping below stacks of metal scrap high as hills. The wall around the yard is almost as tall, welded from every type of metal the Boneyard pickers were able to get their hands on. Some of it is twisted from wrecks, some sections corrugated, wheels still attached to undercarriage slabs, but all of it is topped with five-foot spikes. Here, behind it, the *Exodus* is safe as anyone can pay to be on the Rim.

She is so beautiful. Not fine velvet and crystal touches, or even the worn charm of the *Absolution*, she is ruthless and devastating, and she's ours. We can give her the human comforts, after all. That's the easy part. I haven't stopped smiling since I touched her engine step last night.

"Do you know why they call it the *Exodus Ironclad*?" I ask.

"Because it's covered in metal?" Navy uses her walking stick to guide her steps, the dirt knotted up with nuts, bolts, shards, and springs.

"Because people get out of the way when they see her coming."

The Boneyard boss is a man known only as Lumpy Jord. Jord, short for Jordannias. Is that the name his mother gave him? Possibly. I've never asked because that would be rude. But he is a lumpy man covered in grease that is covered in dirt, and missing the front half of his nose. I think he looks like a potato and he'd be governor of the bone pickers if they had any desire to listen to one.

He gives me the engineer's salute, then one for Navy with fingers absolutely grease-black. "You don't disappoint, Widow."

"I wouldn't dare."

I don't ask him if there are any pieces of the *Absolution* lying dead here. It will only make me depressed. I wish I'd had the chance to stash her here for safekeeping like Mother and I discussed before the derailment. Which is why I'm doing so now with the *Exodus*, but I hope her sacrifice gave new life to some other machine.

"What would you like me to do to her?"

I pass Leagan's design for retrofitting one of the freight cars into her workspace, another for Navy's lab. I'm taking Marshal Edwards's, and Adelaide will have the rear living car. "Are you excited to pull her apart?"

He rubs his big, greasy palms together, half his smile made of steel. "There's nothing on the Rim I'd rather put hands on."

"Will two hundred crates of ammunition and five freight cars of sacrificial metal buy your silence and cover the modifications?" It will make the *Exodus* significantly lighter.

"Do you like getting fucked or do you always start your bargains that high?"

"I don't like to insult my friends. Your services are worth the price." A high bribe ensures he won't rip the *Exodus* out from under me in search of a better offer. I think that would kill me.

"You're trying to make me blush." He strokes the goiter bulging from his neck like a swallowed fist, an ink grin tattooed onto it. "The god of scraps and rust accepts your sacrifice. I'll get my men and a winch and make sure their mouths are welded shut myself."

I kiss his creviced cheek. "I've always liked you, Lumpy Jord."

"I've never liked you more than I do now."

"That's what a lady wants to hear."

Leagan and Raleigh sit on the top layer of crates, several guns disemboweled from their cotton packing.

I hike my skirt to make the necessary step and then pull Navy up. "How's our cargo?"

Raleigh disassembles a barrel from the firing chamber, examining the inner scoring and maker's mark. "They're authentic. A testament to the greatest heist the Rim hasn't even seen yet." He tucks the yawn behind his sleeve. "Excuse me. Now I'm looking forward to a nap. It's been a long time since I was awake all night."

"Yes, we've earned a good sleep. But first I'd like you all to appreciate for a moment that from now on, the legend won't be no one takes the *Exodus Ironclad*, it'll be when the Reveres took the *Exodus Ironclad*." I dare the Rim and these east bloods to deny our presence now.

Leagan claps against the side of the crate.

"And now you honor our part of the deal."

I didn't feel Montoya in the shadows.

I hold onto his gaze once I find it, the change in light from outside to inside sharp. He won't see any traces of a lie in me. "Of course. With this train, we will smoke Rafe from Hannah and you'll get to see your family again."

"It smells like your kind of place in here, Raptor." Navy says. "But not as good as science."

Leagan lowers the rifle she was sniffing. "Good?" She hops off the stack. "Feel this. It's a virgin, and it's prettier than me."

"That's not true."

"Yes, it is. Look harder."

Adelaide returns from the neighboring car, manifest in hand.

"Give me the good news. How much ammo did we get?"

"Seven thousand crates." Her satchel bulges with things that once belonged to Exodus men. "Two hundred fireboxes to a crate."

"Exodus packs five hundred rounds to a firebox..." Raleigh's grin dies off as he tries to calculate that math. "Fuck..."

I don't even try. I don't have to know it's more lead than we've ever seen. Collectively, ever.

Adelaide passes me the manifest. She's done the math.

"*Farce.*" I can swear in five different languages, but right now that doesn't seem like enough. Seven hundred *million* rounds. "I may need to sit down, God of Mercy."

A tremble infiltrates Raleigh's laugh. "What are they fighting out there?"

"Monsters," Leagan says.

Navy's hand pauses against another crate. "Starting another war."

"The last war probably didn't have this much ammunition."

"Lumpy Jord is on his way to collect what we owe him," I say. "Would you keep an eye on that, Stranger and-or Raptor? Then go get yourself some sleep."

There's something else I have to do first.

TRAVIS IS WHERE I EXPECTED HIM TO BE, EATING MEAT OFF BONES IN THE SHADE of his tent while his firepit smokes.

"It must be nice to have all your work done," I say.

"Don't pretend your ass is sore because you have more to do. You can't sit still for more than a day."

I sink next to him, my skirt a blue *Sol* flooding the grass behind me. "I wouldn't be the person you loved any other way."

He kisses slowly. Rabbit grease coats his lips, the odor of skunk rising out of his clothes, but I've always overlooked that because being in his arms feels so right. *I* know he still loves me, and I love him. He always will, and so will I. It's not such an easy snare to escape. I did hope he'd be able to say it back, but I won't waste any more tears if he won't be honest with me and himself. It's Moon Season, and water is about to become too scarce.

"Are you leaving tonight?" I ask.

"It's going to be a long road south."

"You were very good on the heist last night. We'll make an outlaw out of you yet."

He snorts.

"You can't fool me, you enjoyed it a little." I run my fingers through his dark beard. "Would you consider riding with me a little longer?"

"Going north, as in Hannah?"

"Yes. We could use the extra gun."

"I thought you all sold the protection around here."

"Oh, we still do, but I believe in having friends to go with family." The sky is faultless blue, golden poppies nodding to the wind between the grass stalks. I miss her. "Do you remember when I told you how my mother saw the future in her dreams. It turns out she wasn't alone with her gift."

"You?"

"Not me." As long as I know where I'm pointed, I've always been able to create the steps necessary to get there, it doesn't bother me having my mother or Leagan as the compass. Seeing the outcome myself would feel like cheating, and not the fun kind. Getting a little hint now and then is different—it still requires cleverness.

"I need you to come with us." I lace my fingers through his, the calluses on his palms so thick, it would take a very sharp knife to cut through them. "Our survival depends on it."

"Your mother was never wrong before?"

"Never." I still wonder what she saw the night she died. Fearful is not a word I'd use to describe her, but whatever she saw ahead of us frightened her. It frightens me, a hole that's cold and gut deep as the one Leagan described.

"What does your new diviner see?"

"She dreams of bones, deep caverns. And of getting her hands cut off."

His sigh reverberates through his chest into mine. "You believe this is true. Can you be more specific."

"Sorry, it doesn't work like that."

"Maybe she should stay home."

"We don't have a home. These men took it. Would you let your family go without you?"

"I'd keep my family where they were safe."

Even if he can't tell me he loves me, the truth is in his eyes. Still, this is the rail he'd rather lose me to than follow me down.

"You know how I feel about what it is you do," he says. "I know you feel there's no other way…"

"Please."

"Let me finish. I told you I'd be here if you needed me. I meant it."

I let my head rest on his shoulder. "Thank you." The weight of my body suddenly feels like too much to move, and the ferocious stink of animal and man sweat has its sweet moments. "I'll just stay here a little bit longer. I'm getting old. I used to do better with less sleep."

"Just this once, Tess. Don't come to me with these fortune teller stories just to get your way."

"I won't."

"Look at me and say it."

"I don't lie to you." I never have.

Leagan's dream doesn't mean we fail, it just means we have to be smart. We have to be calculating. We have to be ready.

And we will.

Green and Millard Von Kane expect guns for sale onboard the *Exodus Ironclad*. We will deliver guns and the *Exodus Ironclad*.

CHAPTER
SIXTY-SEVEN

Greetings, distinguished friends and businessmen of the Rim:

Mr. G. Rafael of Hannah Mining Co., Hannah;
Mr. C. Green of Green Contract Co., Vantage / Descendants;
Mr. Raleigh, special arms dealer, Lideon;
Millard Von Kane, Von Kane Industries, Oath / Jezebel.

Announcing the back-market sale of the Exodus Ironclad's *cargo manifest, unauthorized by Company and EASTERN TAX FREE:*

- *750 virgin Exodus Reliable Revolvers*
- *500 virgin Exodus Repeater Rifles*
- *2 Exodus Standing Guns*
- *1 Cannon*
- *3,000 cases of fresh Exodus ammunition (standard caliber)*
- *1,000 cases of Exodus Standing Gun ammunition*
- *5 cases of 10-pound cannon shot (6 each)*

Only the above parties are being considered. Don't let this steal fall into your competition's hands.

This sale will be made and bound by all our combined honor to the highest bidder.

Send your offers to the Express Office in Descendants, and soon.
Best of luck!

Sol,
Marshal Edwards and the crew of the Exodus Ironclad

SIXTY-EIGHT
ADELAIDE

I ENTERED HANNAH ON A TRAIN. THE NORTH RIM, GRASSLANDS TRAPPED under the blood sun.

I left Hannah on a train.

Now I'm back with another one, and this will be the last time.

We go in dark. No front lamps, no interior lanterns.

Raleigh helps me drop the ramp onto the berm outside.

Aunt Tess steps into the saddle of a dusk-gray horse. A white star blazes across her forehead, muscles packed on her shoulders. Her dark brown sister bumps my arm, wanting more of the carrots I brought them earlier. Sorry, they're gone.

I let go of her bridle as Travis approaches. His smell is thicker than the river air in Lideon.

The Stranger doesn't see the danger in him I find in most men without trying, but that doesn't stop me from looking. He broke Aunt Tess's heart.

She reaches down, hand to my shoulder. "Whatever happens to me, don't let anyone take this engine from you."

"*Sol sana.*" I nod. "They won't."

Aunt Tess salutes back. "See you soon."

SIXTY-NINE
TESLA

THE WALL AROUND HANNAH APPEARS LIKE NOTHING BUT A DARKER BREAK IN the moonless prairie until we're quite close. It's not unlike the one around the Boneyard. The route becomes less jarring as I make my horse drop the hard canter for a walk. Something she's displeased with if the snort is any indication.

"Now you'll get to see how good I really am, sir." I lift the bugle and blow two sharp notes, the white and black flag of the Express Riders streaming from my other hand.

Travis scowls at the guard towers rising above the sharp wall. "If we see them, they've already seen us."

"Just trust me."

There's the thrum in the air Adelaide described. It vibrates like the roll of wheels on steel, yet wider somehow, everywhere. It feels man-made, mechanical, and it doesn't just fill my ears—it pushes back like storm pressure, present in a physical way.

A lower section of the gate cracks, storm dust crumbling off its edges. The break in the wall appears gradually. Light as red as roses flourishes on the other side, each lantern a beating heart.

"Look at little Hannah." It makes me draw back the breath I just let go. Nothing looks familiar, and all of it has expanded. The double refinery stacks rise like cigarettes to kiss the black cloud they exhale. Astride the hill of mine waste, rows of dwellings crowd together, patched with various types of material. "All grown up."

Montoya strides from the gate tower a few paces behind us, overskirt snapping to the tune of his legs.

There's something else in the air that Adelaide didn't mention. It bleeds through my half-respirator and the scarf hiding it.

"Do you smell that?" I whisper.

Sweet tar. That's fresh black taffy pitch, an impressive scent you'll recognize anywhere if you've smelled it just once, and Hannah reeks like the warehouses in Descendants.

Rafe knows we're coming.

Travis brings his mask down to sniff deep, the hair on his lip trembling. "There's a lot of crystal moving here. They should be prepared for fires."

"This is new." Black taffy is too thick to burn and therefore takes several Seasons to dry out. "If it was this thick before, Adelaide would have told us."

"We all miss things."

"There's no way she missed this." Not her.

I had my suspicions, Leagan and Adelaide theirs. It appears that we're right.

The flutter of anticipation hits in my bones. I feel exposed stepping out of my saddle, vulnerable with my two feet on the ground. Hannah is bigger than any settlement on the Rim, broader than the town I grew up in back east. Here we are all small, dust under a rug of cooking oil, shit, perfume, and the refinery ash.

Despite the many lanterns clinging to posts and doorframes, the darkness feels very close to us, the night so much deeper without the moon or stars.

Travis puts his back between me and Montoya on the way up the hill. The black taffy pitch is ripe here too, but as with Green's warehouse in Descendants, it only protects you if the fire starts outside.

"What's that smell?" I look back at Montoya just to see his reaction. "Do you smell it?"

He pulls down his scarf to sample the air, a daintier taste than Travis took. If his Poisonneur's senses are actually acute enough to catch poison dried on porcelain like he's always bragging about while sniffing his teacup, a pall this thick should be obvious. "Something sweet?"

"Maybe it's bread… Um, one note, would Commander Edwards carry a Cairosh sword?"

"He does now."

The hours I spent memorizing Adelaide's maps showed Rafe's bedroom connected to his office in the southwest side of the main Company building, accessible by a private staircase off the first landing. That dark red line of windows looking down on us are his.

Two men stand guard behind the compound's iron gate. The one to spot us puts out a hand. "What do you want?"

Travis and I step aside and allow Montoya to pass through first.

"I'm Commander Edwards of the *Exodus Ironclad*," he says without his Cairosh accent. It doesn't suit him. His voice sounds naked without it. "Gerard Rafael is expecting us."

"Right." The man moves his hand off his pistol. "You picked an unusual time to come."

"A back-market sale would be unseemly during the day."

The guards toss a glance between them like a piece of hot fire quartz. "You want to wake up the boss?"

"Not if you won't."

"He'll be angrier at you for not waking him if don't wait and I sell to someone else." Montoya offers his hand for the bag I carry with the disassembled Exodus rifle inside. "A sample of our wares."

Rafe's man doesn't notice. He's distracted by the weight of the bag, but I catch Montoya flip the point of a knife around so it scrapes the man's knuckles during the exchange.

"*Sol.*" The other guard chuckles as his partner has to take lead from us now that he's saddled with the bag. "Maybe Boss won't kill you in front of company."

The private staircase isn't buried as deep in the compound as I was envisioning. It's right next to the kitchen and ends in a windowless parlor glistening with black wood.

"You can wait here," the Company man says.

The emerald velvet covering the couch is one of the softest things I've ever felt. Sure of itself with springs that rebound, not cotton scrap stuffing like most of the furniture around here. "Oooh, I want this. We'll be needing some furniture for our new home."

"It's too fancy," Travis says.

He wouldn't say that if I promised to let him fuck me on it.

"One of us should remain here," Montoya says. "To guard our exit."

"That sounds logical."

"You and I will go in, as that is what we planned." Montoya's gaze brushes against Travis. "You will stay."

Sounds logical, and is from the point of view of a person outnumbered and up to no good. "That's why I brought him."

Travis doesn't give up his glare as I pat his chest, but he generally looks a little grouchy because his eyebrows are somewhat overgrown. He seats himself in the only wooden chair, put away in the corner because anyone else would rather sit on a cushion. The blade of his hatchet rings as he sets it across his knee and picks at it with callus-armored fingers. "I'll be here, guarding the way out if you need me."

The words sail past Montoya to find his only intended target: me.

I unfurl my legs as the office door opens.

The man rubs his hand as he allows us inside, the cut draped across his knuckles like a red thread.

He sits behind his desk, a silk smoking robe over a white shirt, wire spectacles, and the flecked hair of an aging man.

Well, well, Gerard Rafael, the grand boss of Hannah himself. That's what I would say but don't, because he'd know me for sure by my dead-shot mouth.

The scar that jumps my eye and continues its gray line beneath my scarf works in my favor today. Even though it's been close to nineteen Seasons since we were last together, he'd recognize my face naked and in the sunlight. Wearing loose men's clothes in thin quartz light, scarred and silent as a rabbit, he'll need luck.

Note, I've aged better.

"Commander Edwards." Montoya removes his hat with a checked bow. For one syllable, his accent slips. "And my spotter, Miss Thorn."

"A woman. That is forward of the Exodus Company," Rafe says.

"I have found the presence of a woman to be good for luck and diplomatic relations."

"Well, I'm pleased to see you accepted my bid, and I welcome you to Hannah."

I curtsey, the lady my mother once intended me to be.

Rafe weighs me with a longer stare than the one he gave Montoya. "I don't mean to slight your character, but I was betrayed recently by some women I used to know. It leaves me less than trusting of the others. Would you mind removing your scarf and showing your whole face, Miss Thorn?"

"Miss Thorn unfortunately had a run in with some pickers years back who removed her tongue and scarred her deeply, as you see here." Montoya gestures to the upper half of my face. "The worst she keeps covered for decency's sake, but I like her for her...unique debility. It hurts my ears to hear women chatter."

I release a very unfortunate hiss from the back of my throat and almost make myself laugh.

"Ah. That is a shame indeed. The Rim is a savage place."

It takes me a moment to place the subtle click that happens whenever Rafe talks. Then I remember, his jaw is copper now.

A bell in the wall dings, and as it does the scent of coffee drifts up the dumbwaiter.

"This is the product?" Rafe opens our bag on the desk. "Tell me about them."

"This is the Exodus Repeater. Standard caliber." The information doesn't roll off Montoya's tongue with the knowledge of Leagan or Raleigh. Not as smooth with guns, are you Poisonneur? Shame, shame.

"I see." Rafe pulls the rifle's last disassembled part from the satchel and begins fitting them together. "Magazine capacity thirteen?"

"Thirteen," Montoya says. "Lucky."

"Would it be possible to view the rest of the stock before exchanging payment?"

"If you wish."

"I do."

It's not so easy to see a clear picture of Hannah outside the wide bank of windows, the reformed glass bubbled with air pockets that fill with orange and red light.

Rafe's man puts out his arm to stop me from wandering further around the office. Itch lines stain the back of his cut hand red.

Rafe runs his palm down the rifle one more time and then lifts his eyes to me. "Do you think I'm a fool?"

"I know you're not."

My feet catch on the rug as Rafe shoves me at one of the leather armchairs. His arms plant on either side of me, sour breath flooding my nose. His fingers catch on the respirator as he rips down my scarf but I don't fuck around. I sink my pistol into the hollow under his chin.

For a moment, pent-up steam blinds me. "It's about time, you piece of shit."

"So this is how it ends, Tesla Revere."

"I have the gun in my hand right now."

Rafe wraps his hand around my wrist. "This is my house, and you can rest assured I keep traps for snakes like you."

"I wonder which is faster? I bet it's my finger blowing your brain out." Fuck, I didn't expect my stomach to burn me when I looked at him. "You forgot I made all this possible for you, didn't you? My mother always said leaving you in charge here was a mistake."

"Now we get to the bottom of things. You still want praise and validation for something you did years ago, but without me your information was worthless anyway. You were just along for the ride to get your mother and sister back. I did *you* the favor, you conceited bitch."

I laugh in his face.

For all the nights I cried myself to sleep, the mornings I woke up with sun on my face but worried my smile might never be real again.

You killed two people I loved more than the world because someone lied to you.

Rafe shakes his head at me. "Don't you come here and judge me for doing exactly what you've done for years. There's blood on your hands too."

"The only blood I care about is on yours."

"I offer no apology for the events of the past. We all knew there'd be consequences for our actions."

"I never got to say goodbye to my daughter. Your men gunned her down in the street, and her sisters watched her die." My voice catches on feral memory. "Meanwhile, I got to watch my mother bleed to death, then leave her body behind to be sold for blood money." It all comes down on me and I choke, tears burning from my eyes like morning salt, each breath hard and hot as heartbreak. Don't mistake this for weakness. This is rage.

"Hannah is your child. Now you get to watch her burn."

"No." He breaths damp heat out on me. "You want me to beg."

Montoya stands by, a pillar of salt and flesh, emotionless as stone. Go on, you bastard. This is your move, watching? Make it a better one. There's nothing more disrespectful than a weak betrayal.

Rafe slaps my gun away, the impact enough to tighten my finger on the trigger, ghost pain firing through my weak wrist. The shot nicks his ear but gets lost in the ceiling.

He turns back to me, malice like the slow drip of blood from his earlobe filling his snarl. "You're as predictable as the fury of Moon Season. I know you buried explosives. I know where."

"You think you know." I can't help myself.

His gazes up and out across the windows. "She's lurking out there somewhere, isn't she? Your niece, the fox. Well, I'm ready to take my chances that my men find her before she does whatever it is you have for her."

"You have no idea what's coming."

"I know enough."

The glass filling the cabinets rattles as something impacts on the other side of the wall. It felt like a body—hopefully not Travis.

"You came in on a very distinct train," Rafe says. "And when your girls show their faces, my men have their orders. No prisoners. No deals this time."

"My mother and I taught them well. We're survivors, and we will never stop."

"They're already dead."

"Like hell they are."

Rafe turns. Yes, it is to look at Montoya. "Make sure that other bastard she brought with her doesn't cause any trouble."

SEVENTY
ADELAIDE

WE MOVE WITH THE DARK, THE NIGHT OUTSIDE THE *EXODUS*'S SHUTTERED windows unbroken. Black like my sight edges when the Stranger is angry. Moonlight can't puncture it. Only us and pale green pressure dials, only the faint red haze of Hannah creeping above the wall.

Leagan holds out her hand in the fire seat, twisting it against the ghost quartz glow each time she exhales smoke from her pipe. She smells like memories. She smells like today. Rose and burnt pages, Grandma and gunpowder.

"Is Navy asleep?" Raleigh squints at her in the backup engineer's seat. Her forehead's propped against the wall, but she's still upright.

"Probably," I say.

"Let's find out." Leagan collects a handful of date pits from her cup and places one on Navy's shoulder.

"I didn't mean to wake her up," Raleigh whispers. "Leave her alone."

"She won't wake up." Leagan balances another pit on the back of Navy's hand. "Watch this."

Lead rings against the *Exodus*'s armored body. Out of tune, a bell that has cracks. My heart punches up into my throat just so it can fall back down as I grab the solar quartz scope pushed up on my head.

Raleigh lurches to his feet and shakes Navy, the date pits tumbling across the floor.

"What do you see?" Leagan whispers.

"We're still too far out for it to be someone on the watchtower. They must have a scout in the grass somewhere. What do you see?"

They know we're coming.

Leagan adjusts the focus dials of her sniper lens. "Nobody."

Raleigh turns. "I'll get on the standing gun."

"Hey, you just want an excuse to shoot it first!" Leagan chases after him.

"Don't we all? Don't trip me, there's one for each of us."

"What did you do to me?" Navy asks. "My hands are all sticky."

"Nothing…" Leagan yells back.

"I know it was you. Stop fooling around, this is serious."

Rafe told me he set a trap for us, and even though our plans have changed, I know he hasn't let his guard down. This isn't over. His words.

Navy leans forward like I do, her breaths butting up against the dark air. You don't really disappear in darkness. But darkness that comes from sky being covered like this, like storms and the ground swallowing you whole, makes you feel like you might.

The Stranger reaches into the night. It's as thick as her, and her pulse goes through me like a dropped stone hitting water.

Someone's coming.

I grab the solar quartz scope again.

A string of freight cars rides the opposing track toward us. Four of them, towed by a boiler-fed handcar.

If I was doing this, the side-rake would be a distraction while someone climbed onboard from the other one or behind.

"I have to go."

"They're coming after us?" Navy says.

We're only nine miles out. If I speed up to outrun them, we'll hit Hannah too fast. This is a war machine, not the *Absolution*. Let them shoot us. There's less glass to worry about.

"They don't know what we're driving," I say.

"I wish I could help you."

"You can." I twist the pin on the side of the engineer's stop clock. Hannah's light is red. I'm not sure she'll be able to see it, but she can hear just fine. Twenty minutes. "If I'm not back when this rings, close the valves and pull the brake." I guide her hand to the pressure control panel, then the main brake lever protruding from the floor.

"If you're not back..."

The fear that flickers through her voice reflects in my stomach. I shouldn't have said that. "It'll be because I like the standing gun too much."

Before I go, I open the cap on the speaking tube so she can talk to us.

Forty-nine.

When we unhooked the freight cars of ammunition in the Boneyard, we also switched the gun car with the water reservoir so we wouldn't have to cross the exposed catwalk to reach the standing guns. No one can do the same thing to us that we did to the *Exodus* crew.

"Wait." Raleigh pries off one of his cotton ear-mufflers. "If you're here, please don't tell me no one's engineering this thing."

"Navy knows what to do. As long as they don't blow us off the rails, we'll be fine."

"Why would you even suggest such a thing?"

Leagan bounces on the front half of her feet, ear-mufflers sloshing around her neck. "And even if we run into something, the *Exodus* can cut it in half."

"While I enjoy your confidence, I don't know if I share it."

I point ahead, northwest, and grab another set of gunner's ear-mufflers. From this angle we can't see them yet, but they're going to pass us soon.

The gun port on Raleigh's side faces out across the plains. Shadows and grass stand flat on top of each other.

Raleigh holds out his fist. "I'll play you for the better side."

"No. That first shot came from your side."

"Don't spoil my fun."

"I don't like games."

Raleigh taps his closed fist. "Three, two, one, shoot."

There are three options in this game.

Raleigh points with two fingers. Gun. I hold out my flat palm. Drought.

"Drought beats the hand that holds the gun." I pull the safety pin from the barrel crank.

"Rub it in."

I wipe my palms dry and plant my feet. The barrel crank ticks. First like a nail on a window, then a hive of stone beetles chattering. The trigger snaps forward once it's picked up enough speed.

A deeper shadow crosses my gunport. We slip alongside each other, daring the other to strike first. I wait for the Stranger. Breathe.

Three...four...fire.

The sash of bullets attached to the chamber ripples. Fire spits horizontal from the barrel, drawing ammunition in like ribbon as the gun inhales them. Vibrations punch through the grips, my arms already numb. If thunder could be held, this is what it would feel like.

We pass each other in flashes. Glimpses. Steel rivets, open slide doors, limbs ducking for cover, poorly retained memories illuminated by gunpowder.

Their boiler ruptures. Steam hot as noon burns the backs of my hands, floods my lungs. The taste of shredded metal overpowers the gun smoke in the air, dead on the track.

We clear what's left of them, and no one else shoots back.

My barrel and Leagan's barrel stop firing almost simultaneously. Smoke drifts from spent shells around our feet. Raleigh's too.

"They came from that side too, didn't they?"

"Three or four of them," he says. "On horses. They never got close enough to jump on."

It's what I would have done.

"So, what do we do now?" Leagan asks.

I close my gunport, face the speaking tube. "I'm going back to the engine. You can stay here if you want."

If Rafe has anything worse up there, I better see it coming.

SEVENTY-ONE
TESLA

I SHOVE MYSELF FREE OF THE CHAIR WHILE RAFE PLANTS A HAND ON MY shoulder to shove me back into it.

"I hope you didn't bring anyone else you care for around here," he says. "You should know better by now. I'd hate to kill every last person you know."

"I don't suspect you've ever loved anyone other than yourself," I say. "With the exception of your mother—"

He grabs my jaw, a knuckle popping as he squeezes. "Don't. If you say her name, you unrighteous whore—"

"Willa." I thrust my knee up into his groin, ripping the revolver from the holster under his robe as he staggers off.

"Bitch."

"Took you long enough to recognize me."

"I've always known exactly what you are. I paid you respect you didn't deserve by not saying it until now."

I give his revolver chamber a flick with my thumb to hear it whiz. "Ah, a ten-shot. A sure sign of overcompensation in my experience. You first." I level out my aim and find Montoya, still a stone. "Then you."

The bang comes from across the room. Sharp enough to rattle the cupboards. The man Montoya slipped the cut on earlier is on the floor. His arms flail like two eels, his back an arch as his heels dig for purchase on the wool rug without luck.

"*Vacca voya…*" Cold bumps cover my skin.

White foam bubbles from his mouth, his spine curling to almost a full circle as the rest of him thrashes to break free. The snap is audible, violent. You don't forget the sound bone makes when it breaks. And I haven't.

"Fucking Jezebel." And all the others I know. I only expected him to drop dead once the poison took hold, not snap from the inside out.

"What did you do?" Rafe says to me.

For once in my life, I can't think of any words.

Montoya rounds suddenly, bringing his red steel blade to Rafe's neck for a kiss. "Have a seat in any chair, then don't move again."

"Ah." Some of the shock tremor drains from Rafe's voice. "Now I see clearer. You did the deed that has been done."

"You built up the suspense long enough," I say. "How long have you been straddling both sides of the rail?"

"It's called working from inside the garden," Montoya says. "I thought you'd notice I didn't respond when he called on me to turn on you."

"I did notice. I assumed you would get around to it and were just too proud to be told when."

"How little faith in people you really have for someone who preaches so loudly about family and trust."

"I have the same amount of faith in people as everyone who's lived on the Rim as long as I have." That would be next to none. That's why family is so important, and one like mine so rare.

The Wells were a family too, remember. Amnesty Wells created the pestilence to kill them and the rest of Eden after being hurt and abused by people that should have cared for each other for too long.

"I needed my own insurance this could still be done with or without you. In case anybody died during this outing or the *Exodus* heist."

I didn't ask, yet he explains.

Travis doesn't come blasting in, even though he had to have heard my gun go off. Assuming he's still alive. I won't consider that now. He respects my independence and capabilities, and that's where I'll leave the matter. Rafe is a shifty bastard. If I give him one blink that looks like hesitation, he'll take it.

I flip open the satchel that contained the rifle while doing my best to keep an eye on both of these snakes. When we claim land against the Von Kanes on the West Rim, I want every advantage I can get my hands on. Contacts will make us strong, not necessarily the black gold alone.

"Get up. Put this Season's Company books and letters into that bag."

Barely halfway through the task, Rafe swings around, the satchel colliding with me, but not before my bullet punches a hole in his shoulder. Tumblers and a whisky decanter scatter and fracture as I break my fall on the shelf.

Montoya's sword slashes through the tendons in the back of Rafe's calf, dropping the leg out from under him.

Rafe catches one elbow on the desk. "Fucking foreigner."

"There are no foreigners here, no friends. Only the dead, and those who aren't quite there yet." Montoya's sword shivers metallic as he returns it to its scabbard. "Are you hurt?" He grabs my wrist and pulls me up.

I see too late.

It's a curved and elegant raptor talon. A knife so sharp I don't feel the sting of the cut until I see the line on my forearm, the same red steel as the sword on his back and the blood it draws. We are fragile, but this can't be happening to me. Not now. I have more time. I did not come this far to fail.

Without my consent my eyes turn to Rafe's man, dead on the floor, bones snapped inside his intact body, bile turning to crust over his lips.

"Fuck you." Nausea swells up my throat. The urge to run hammers against my chest, but toward what?

My skin is slick and my fingers slip as I spread the wound. Maybe I can siphon the poison back out if I bleed enough. It's possible.

"I'm sorry." Montoya flees to the other door. There must be another way out of this shithole, and he knows where it is. I have to let him go.

"Oh fuck." I breathe deep to give myself the courage to dig my knife into my arm.

The first shots didn't bring Travis to the door, but my scream does. Wood splinters off the bite of his hatchet.

Rafe spits laughter past his false teeth, gripping the desk to help him stand. "Justice is swift."

I let the knife go to point both guns at him. If I die, then that's what Providence meant to be, but this is not getting taken from me. "Blessed are those who pass through the fire, Gerard Rafael. For they shall be refined, except for a piece of shit like you."

I thought I might cry once it was done. But I don't shed one drop, gunshot still cold ringing in my ears. I don't feel relief, either, Travis's hand as immaterial a memory as he grasps my arm. How anticlimactic. I've waited to kill this man for a whole Season and it's not enough. If anything, I'm emptier than I was before, and now I'm going to die an absolutely wretched way. There are so many things I still need to do, and that loss feels so much more real than anything else at the moment.

Damnation, Evangeline. Why are you always right about the shittiest things? Let me be bad for the right reasons for once and get away with it.

"Where is he?" Travis starts to look for Montoya but at least I have the sense to grab his arm. It slips away because it's too thick and my hand too bloody.

"Don't get too close to him. His knife is poisoned."

I could shoot myself before it happens, but that would be doing Montoya's dirty work for him. He couldn't even bother to stay and watch me convulse myself to death.

Not if I have anything to say about it. And I always do.

My hands shake as I pass through the bathroom plated in copper to the balcony beyond Rafe's bedroom. How the hell do I know if that's the poison working in me or my reignited rage? I don't, and I hate it.

The blood dripping off my left arm leaves a trail on the carpet like the empty fortunes Mother used to cast with her moon diviner.

"Hey." I take shots at Montoya's back from across the bed and miss. "Get back here and finish me like you would a man, you coward."

He melts like a specter somewhere near the wall. I shoot at that too. I shoot into the darkness so exquisite the flash of my muzzle barely touches it, but he won't fucking die.

"This is what you do," he calls. "Sell helpless *imbecilios* protection before you murder them. You knew this was coming."

Travis creeps that way. I shake my head. Knives are too fast for hatchets or trappers, this knife was too sneaky for me.

"You bet your last fucking breath I did." I'm willing to bet the truth is rather obvious, like he's turned out to be. "You told Rafe where the Stranger was hiding the explosives to make him trust you, am I right?"

His breath shudders, wet though the nostrils.

"Oh, don't cry, you pathetic baby."

"This is not personal. I love my family. This is the only way I'll see them again."

I laugh, the only thing keeping me from screaming, so painfully aware how I'm going to die thanks to him. "Well, you enjoy the memory of that family, because the Stranger buried more. You're never going to see them again. And I hope that haunts you 'til the second you die."

Because nothing he believed was ever the plan to begin with. It was never his plan. It was ours.

The silence rings hollow and wrapped around my throat at the same time.

Fire pricks at the fingernails of my cut arm.

"Oh Providence, no."

I want to see my family again too. I'll claw off any face that stands between us if that's what it takes, so watch me. I press my knife into the open wound and force it to bleed. For everything I wanted to accomplish and the space in this world I have the right to claim.

The knife slips, flaying my forearm wide open and biting into bone. My scream is too late to save me, my whole arm livid red and pumping fire.

"What are you doing?" Travis rips my knife away. "Are you insane now?"

"You don't understand!"

"Don't worry," Montoya says from where I thought he'd left. "I won't make the girls suffer. I'll kill them with dignity, and do it quick."

SEVENTY-TWO
ADELAIDE

WE RIDE THE *EXODUS* DOWN THE YAWNING THROAT OF THE TUNNEL. THE PLOW shears through the metal gate, dropped across the track like a sharp knife through paper.

Shocks of white light change the shapes of the rail yard, Leagan and Raleigh on the standing guns. Bullets skip off the angled storm shutters as I bring us to a stop at the track switch. Left goes to the crystal-loading yard, right to the station for its barons. I choose neither.

If Aunt Tess was able to reach Rafe, she was supposed to set the Company compound on fire on their way out. Hannah smolders. It always does, an ash blanket hung over the refinery hum. But it's not burning.

I close the final valve and drag down the long gear reverse lever that turns the work over to the back engine.

The Stranger counts the bodies lying face down in the black dust, what's left of their standing guns' barrels smoking, but no one to turn them.

Twelve.

This is a trap. Rafe told me so, but I still can't see teeth sharp enough to pierce an *Ironclad* shell.

Was he lying?

No.

Navy eases her fingers from her ears as the hammering metal on metal slows. Stops. She leans forward along with me, even though I don't know how much she can actually see.

"It's so dark," she whispers. "It stinks like smoke."

"It always smells like that." But it didn't always smell like black taffy pitch. Now it does.

"We're not early," Raleigh says.

"No, they're late," Navy says.

Black flakes drift, collect like dust on trim, brush glass like moths.

Leagan sits on the other half of the engineer's seat with me, breathing close. "Do you think this is what snow is like?"

"Maybe."

"I've read it makes everything so still and quiet, like being caught inside glass."

That's not what Hannah is like, but right now all I feel and hear is the tick of the Stranger spreading out against the walls.

Something is wrong.

"Where is she?" Navy asks.

"Montoya got them both," Leagan sighs. "We knew he was going to do something shifty. Aunt Tess didn't want to listen to me. He read *Rook and Ladder*, remember?"

"So have you."

"That's right. That's how I know."

We can still light the explosives.

"Come with me," I tell Leagan. "Rook, you go to the reverse engine and get ready. Raleigh will keep shooting until we make it out. Then get outside the wall."

"We're not leaving you here."

"No. You're not leaving us." I just want anyone watching to think we are.

Navy puts her arms around me and Leagan at the same time. "I love you, and I love you."

"Love you too." I break away because I have to.

"Be careful." Navy offers us each a tube of tear vapor from her bandoleer. "Be prepared. Don't light yourselves on fire."

"Don't tell me how to die," Leagan says.

"That better be a joke, and if it is, it's not funny."

A smuggler's drop cache lies in the floor of the boiler car. I found it when we brought the *Exodus* to the Boneyard.

I slip through the bottom hatch first, onto the track below the *Exodus*'s steel belly plates, crawl until there's room for Leagan to follow. Ash rises up my nose, rock catching on my pants. The deep churn of the refinery fills the back of my head like an ache. I was here long enough I stopped noticing it so violently. Now I do again.

The crack splits me as Raleigh cranks up the standing gun, even though I knew he was going to fire it.

The Stranger sets her sight on the baron station platform, her shadow ahead of me, not behind. Leagan fills that place.

Ninety-one.

Any men Rafe had guarding the station door either decided he wasn't worth dying for or are already bleeding by the *Exodus.*

I shoot a hole in the seam of the double doors while Leagan aims at the overhead and twin lamps in motion. The end of her barrel belches a bright star of orange flame, the sharp explosion of the gunshot dying against the roar of the standing gun. Hot crystal collapses on the wood of the station lobby.

Hannah opens up past the severed doors, a mess scrawling out in three directions. I don't have to work to avoid the red spill of the lanterns. The Stranger learned how to evade them cycles ago.

I have Grandma's voice in my head. She says I shouldn't try to avenge her, that Rafe isn't worth the effort. Or my life. But even she didn't know everything.

Walking here with Leagan feels bad in a different way than being alone. I'm afraid for her.

When we get close enough, the air turns thick. "This is the soup camp."

"Tasty."

She holds back the lid of the bone well with both hands so she can lean inside, see the bones with no end while I draw the bag. Gunpowder, a disassembled rifle, flash fire, and demo sticks. They're still here.

Eight ninety-nine.

The black dust of Hannah hides the lines we draw with powder.

The waste hill still has the press of a shadow, even in the dark. The mine yard, the shaft elevator, both are secure inside their fence. Their only weakness is that something higher up looks down into them.

My fingers sink into dirt. Thick, sticky.

The slope comes loose without much pressure. Real dirt, red and brown from inside the earth that sheds its ash coating to our touch. Chunks of mine slag are the only solid thing to grab onto, everything else sinks. For every three feet gained, Leagan or I slide back one.

My legs burn as I drag myself over the top, boots filled with dirt. I let myself sit.

"I'm sweating." Leagan takes a sniff of herself.

"How is it?"

"I smell like that soup."

Boots emptied, eyes forward. The mine's steam-fed waste ladder. Trough-sized buckets rise on a massive chain to feed the hill. One every fifteen minutes.

"I wish we could ride that," Leagan says. "It looks fun."

I take the two demo sticks, remove the brass tube around the flash fire, a rock heavy enough to shatter the glass vial. Leagan binds them together with string.

Life is a slow death.

I stretch my arm out over the shaft. "Run."

And I let go.

The bundle drops into the black. Down, deep. How far? I don't know, but it's falling and I run.

A deep-throated crumbling rolls across the ground. The beat of the Stranger tightens. The waste hill shifts, parts. I fall headfirst down the backside while the other half floods over the mine, its yard, sliding faster than dirt should be able to move. It touches the wall of the refinery. Stops.

The mine lies buried, a grave of its own bones. I hope it's forever.

Turn around. The Stranger's whisper nudges me a second before Leagan does.

She points through a gap between rooftops, the plume of dust a slightly different shade than the smoke sky. "What is that?"

Over the rail yard, too late to stop even if we run back now.

"Let's find something to climb," she says.

Aunt Tess wanted Rafe to see Hannah burn from outside, but I'm not giving this situation the chance to turn on us. I place the final tube of flash fire into a red lantern, set it on the tracks of gunpowder we laid to connect to the explosives I buried without Montoya's knowledge. Before it boils, the glass vial will break.

Sixty-one.

I shake the railing before I put weight on it, cross a slanted plank to reach the adjacent roof, Leagan after me like a cat.

Dust still drifts across the rail yard, no wind strong enough to clear it. I pin the solar quartz lens to the end of my scope. It amplifies even Hannah's feeble light, shadows harder black and illumination hard white-blue that hurts my eye after so much darkness.

The *Exodus* is gone.

Not *gone*, we don't know that yet.

I start at the watchtower for orientation, sweep my scope down the wall to the mouth of the tunnel. But it's not where it was either. A slope of dirt and collapsed beams fills the once-hole.

"*Farce.*" My limbs start to tighten, but I turn my scope farther south.

The *Exodus Ironclad* breaks the flat landscape of Hannah's everlasting night. A lampless shadow beast aligned with the southwest wall, out of reach of the Slash gate guns. Debris clings to the roofs of the back cars but Navy and Raleigh are out.

"Now we're locked in," Leagan says.

"Not for long. I know where they keep the horses. Let's get them now."

The flash fire in the lantern reaches its boiling point, ruptures. A spark that looks like daylight ignites, throws long shadows up walls and the stab of burnt-orange oil through the air like a punch.

The trail of lit gunpowder hisses along the street, a snake made of sunlight.

I draw my pistol. "Let's find Aunt Tess."

SEVENTY-THREE
ADELAIDE

PEOPLE SCREAMED WHILE RAFE AND AUNT TESS TOOK HANNAH WHEN I WAS young. I didn't like that. They scream now. I'd plug my ears, but I need my hands to climb, hold my gun. So I let the pulse of the Stranger throbbing black at the edges of my eyes fill up my head until it's not so loud and she's the only thing I hear.

One hundred and seventy-nine.

The fresh blast staggers me, stuns glass. The bunkhouse walls, roofs, and anyone inside it rip apart. Shards of debris come down hard the way *Solace* rain does, falling framework knocking the next piece of the row off its foundation. Seething drops of light fall, the flash fire that instantly scattered, boiling into whatever they touch. The warm satisfaction of the Stranger spreads through my chest. All my cycles of dirty work.

Horses.

A second demo stick explosion breaks the air. Wood split open, raw white flesh inside the black taffy crust of the outer wall. Always have a second way out, Grandma said.

I touch Leagan's arm, stop her before she steps onto the Slash. There.

A man walks the perimeter of the Express Rider stable, another the bunkhouse, shotguns in hand. The Stranger latches on as they move, picks apart the pattern, thread detaching from fabric.

The far one circles out of sight again, another round beyond the bunkhouse.

Now.

I slip behind the other, my knife through his neck, one breath.

Leagan grabs his other foot, and we drag him into the barn while he finishes bleeding out.

The warm musk of grain and horses softens the air, my feet sinking in the loose hay.

Thirteen.

This isn't the time, but the Stranger's instinct doesn't let me go. I pick through his pockets as Leagan draws open the stall doors, leaves them that way for the horses we don't need to escape at their leisure.

Express Riders always keep at least two horses saddled and ready at all times. I can't tell what exact color he is without light. Dark.

"That's definitely blood. Did you see anything?"

I go still, my hand around the bridle.

"No. Did you?" Their hushed voices carry despite Hannah's throb. "It was her. The row ghost."

Fire quartz sweeps bars of light across the dark that tries to hold onto itself. I put my eye to the seam of the barn door and wall, but can't see them.

"Who?"

"An evil Tov spirit. She kills men when the moon cycle changes. She *only* kills men, check yourself for bite marks."

"Don't waste my time with a wives' tale you picked up at the soup camp. Just find him, fool."

"I'm warning you. Be aware."

"I'm warning you, don't talk to me about this shit again."

Four—

The gunpowder flash of Leagan's pistol illuminates the rafters. The rider she just shot barely a step past the back entrance of the barn.

"Still the fastest gun on the Rim, fool."

The whistle used by Express Riders to call their mounts is a low, wooden chirp. Something high-pitched would annoy them. Leagan's horse wheels around to obey it, thick shoulder connecting with her body.

"Shady horse thieves."

Even from the ground Leagan's gun hand is faster than mine. The second rider falls, horse dancing four feet sideways to avoid stepping all over him.

"What did I just say?" Leagan shares a look with her revolver. "They never listen to me."

The horse doesn't run like another animal would when I approach him again, ears pricked forward. He comes to my open hand, soft feet, hair tickling my palm. I nod to Leagan, one foot in the stirrup. Go.

We clear the barn overhang. At the gatepost both horses lunge for the open Slash, a route they've run a thousand other times, dent worn into the ground to prove it.

Up the hill, the undulating light of flames at work ripple against the windows of Rafe's office at the top of the Company compound. Gunfire sparks in the yard below it.

Leagan touches her left shoulder.

The scar rips open all over again. The rest of my body falls away like shed skin, but my arms and legs feel like they're dragging me off the horse, a pulse in them that's pressurized and acidic. Vesta's hands pull at me, the wet rattle of her lungs forcing bubbles through the blood where her nose should be. Gunpowder, rotting flesh, blood and juniper.

Don't stop.

"Are you okay?"

"Yeah."

I see blood. Panic ruptures like ink through the center of my vision.

The horse's hooves slide and trail dust as I drag his head back.

The Stranger says something, distant lightning without thunder. I can't go through this again. If I lose another sister...the holes will be too big and what's left of me too brittle.

"Why are we stopping?" Leagan asks.

Ash, saddle leather, horse, and lye. Smells can't lie. I use them to root me here, repel the ghosts that haunt me. Soap residue clings the lower wall of the bathhouse like congealed fat where they empty used water through a gap in the floor.

I touch my arm, same place she did. "Show me."

"I fell on something in the barn when the horse knocked me over. A nail or something. It's not that bad."

It's not safe here.

I feel it too. Eyes, watching.

The last time, in Winchester, we tried to run. It didn't work.

We need to get somewhere safe. I need to think.

A group of men run at us, the bodies they leave like bare branches rising out of the street ahead. "Hey, give us those horses!"

"No!" Leagan yells back, kicks off.

As my horse follows hers, I pitch Navy's vial of tear vapor back at them, round the corner before it spreads.

Three fifty.

On the other side of the crossroads, I ride toward the wide screen porch and blunt corners of the tea house's single story. The only tree for miles clings to life, even though Joelle, the one who cared about it, is dead. Together they block most of the rear garden area from view both ways.

"What is this place?" Leagan asks.

"The Pinings. The tea house."

"Where your friends are, the chemical dealers."

They always left a lamp burning all hours. Now the windows are flat behind storm shutters. "No one will see the horses back here."

I tie the reins to one of the tree's hooked roots, an arched spine protruding from the dirt.

The back door drifts at the hand of the wind.

I'm glad no one is here. I didn't plan to come back, face Thadie or Saraline and Solstice again. It's better to fade. I'll remember them as help who made this place somewhat bearable.

Nineteen.

Dried herbs coat the air from my first step inside, not ash. Laundry dangles like skin, jars still missing from the shelves after the ransacking. My presence spreads up the length of the floorboard.

Blood. It hits the back point of my throat, rust.

She lies face down by the iron stove. A pool of gold hair, a mirror of black reflections. Constellations and poppies and lace in black ink ride her skin, making it more hers than it already was.

Saraline's ghost is a weight that sinks. The kind that says goodbye and fades.

But Solstice isn't here. Thadie isn't.

Leagan sets her cheek to rest on my shoulder, arm around my waist. "You still have me."

I'll always rather have her. "These things happen."

"We should probably look for Aunt Tess."

Yes, but first—

Wait. The Stranger's voice stings.

"What is it?" Leagan whispers.

There are many silhouettes running out of Hannah's seams. Some escaping from the fires, some going toward them. Not as many guns. The Stranger lifts to the touch of eyes on my back. She knows these ones now that we've felt them enough. *Here, Winchester.*

It's time.

I turn my head away, to Leagan. "Montoya's out there. Let's kill him."

She blinks slow like I did. "Fuck yeah."

I creep to the edge of the room. The gaze doesn't move. One of these glass-flat windows or shadow-cast alleyways, watching.

The bead curtain covering the inner doorframe ticks. Once. Twice. Nothing. Leagan steps toward it, pistol up.

Don't go in there.

I grab her. "Don't."

The Stranger would usually tell me to look in every room. I trust her. Back away.

Boards moan. I whirl around, aim at the silhouette brushing shadows. Just loose flyscreen, torn from the frame.

"Is he back there?" Leagan's whisper barely moves the night.

I nod.

Leagan picks up a stray honey bowl, throws it out the open door. "He's not dumb enough to go after anything but a person. That was fun though."

"I'll go first, and hopefully he'll follow me. Then you can shoot him."

Seventeen.

I make it to the horses before the Stranger snaps around me. Glass to my lungs, sudden as falling. *Leave. Now.*

Leagan feels me tighten in, runs her last few steps. "What?"

I untie both sets of reins. "I think we should both go."

"I'll get him if he shows."

"Head back the way we came in." I want her in front so I can watch her back.

Two sharp blasts and one long pierce my head. The Express horse whistle. It comes from somewhere above. Somewhere close. The horse whips around, all muscle and hooves. Leagan manages to hang onto her saddle, but the horses bolt east. Back the way we came.

I see him as my horse tramples lemongrass to get around raised garden beds to the road. A curve of iron that blocks out orange sky. The backward spinning kick lands, and his arm tangles mine. Pulls.

SEVENTY-FOUR
TESLA

THEY DROPPED THE BEAMS THEIR OWN RAIL TUNNEL. DIRT AND DEAD MEN LAY all over the yard, anointed in spent Exodus ammunition shells. I pray my *Exodus* is on the other side of the wall, not under it.

"You're fucking with me from beyond death, Rafe." I turn away from the station's iron fence.

"You're bleeding out." Travis stretches my skin in a downward pattern and twists the snakebite tourniquet that he apparently didn't make tight enough upstairs. I barely feel the scrape of his rough hands. The blood rolling down the back of my hand quietly splashes across the ground to dissipate, mixed with another, milky fluid.

"Good." The flap of hanging skin is a burden on itself, fresh pain to remind me the wound hasn't gotten any better in the last few minutes. That sensation quickly goes away under the pressure of the tourniquet threatening to pinch my arm off. "There's poison inside me. Let it bleed."

"No." Travis catches my other elbow, but it's my own sob that catches me off-guard.

"I'm going to die."

"You're not." His thumb put pressure dents in my cheek. "You're not going to die. You planned for this. The girls made us another way out."

"I didn't plan for this." I hold my bloodied arm close. It catches light from the signal fire I made of Rafe's office, but it's not the only fire throwing smoke into the already thick sky. "We're already late and Adelaide went ahead with the demo sticks. Montoya will see this too. I feel sick. Let's find that bastard. He can't have gotten far."

"There she is. That's the Tesla Revere I know."

"If I start convulsing, you better fucking kill me."

He hesitates.

"Please. Don't let me suffer. Then promise you'll kill that son of a picker for me."

"I will."

"And make his death slow." I give my horse a quick bump to the ribs, and she takes off, the road sweeping down the last bit of hill like a dried-up *Sol*.

Where would Adelaide go that Montoya is confident enough to catch her?

I swing right, aiming for the lowest smoke above Hannah, away from the other fires staining the black sky orange, Travis only a beat behind me.

The throb of my arm swells with every bump in the road, the wound I gave myself burning like I dipped it in boiler steam. I just hope I hold it together long enough to get back to the *Exodus*, even if it's just to see the girls one last time.

"I have one idea—" Travis calls, but I stop listening as the flash of white hair grabs me.

"Oh, *farce*." My horse grunts, tearing up the dirt and gnashing at her bit as I stop her too hard.

Montoya drags Adelaide's head back, exposing her throat to open it. My feet hit the ground, and she rams her elbow back, like the blur of a predator striking, ferocious and repeating. But I've seen knife fights end faster than gun duels, and that blade is poisonous.

Her other arm rises up, clearing his knife hand and allowing her to slip out from under him. Montoya sweeps his leg out, clipping hers, and she falls.

"Motherfucker!" My scream tastes like stomach bile. It burns like it too.

Adelaide rolls aside and up, anger coiled around her, so potent I could grab onto it. He doesn't give her the chance to recover or draw her gun. Already on top, he swings across to gut her.

She lets herself fall back, narrowly avoiding the red hook. I want to believe in her, but she can't win, not against someone like him in a fight like this.

Travis and I both try to take aim, but mine is all over Adelaide too, my solo hand shaking too much to be trusted. Garden beds of twisted herbs and corner of the building they belong to block my view every other time they move. The best Travis can do is fire a few warning shots at the dust and the tree behind them. Montoya doesn't even flinch.

Somehow Adelaide manages to keep out of Montoya's way. Or somehow he's managing to miss her when he swings.

Leagan comes riding up the opposite street, shrieking. I race to stop her from getting too close. My legs give out. "Raptor, shoot him!"

Adelaide drops below Montoya's arm to her knee and onto her back, her foot driving up to stop him from falling on her. For a beat, my heart stops. There's something darker than black wrapped around her, like a shadow's shadow. The taste of it is dry and singed, like the charge in the air before a storm rips through you. I've brushed up against it before, but was never quite sure whether it was real wind or one of those things that happen without a solid explanation, like Mother's dreams, like churches. Something only given power because you believe in it.

The Stranger.

SEVENTY-FIVE
ADELAIDE

On my back the sky is blood. The Stranger wraps me, burning curls of paper as Montoya steps on my arm, presses me into the wall.

My fingers scratch against the tea house underboards while the others fill with dirt. I left that last vial of flash fire under here because I wasn't cold enough to set a fuse. Maybe the Stranger knew. If I can reach it—

His knife is red.

Spider webs.

Glass.

In the still of the black, I kick, direct away Montoya's knife arm. He spins, and I come up. Dirt in one fist, vial in the other, thirteen drops of flash fire.

One.

He flinches inward as the dirt hits his eyes and my other arm swings around. His body has to...

Turn away.

The glass shatters against him. The head of the fireball shoots up, but the tail comes slashing back at me. Oranges, bitter. A shriek like shaved metal.

I peel out of my jacket and glove as they ignite, roll, hit the tea house wall again.

Right behind me, a gun goes off. Montoya staggers to his knees, bleeding fire, not screaming anymore.

I rip off my single solar quartz goggle, white pyre still stabbing a hole in my eye. Leagan rushes in, drags me clear, all pistol smoke. The Stranger recedes to her usual space in my head as we stagger away. She latches onto Aunt Tess's left arm, saturated in blood.

Twelve.

It always feels like I've been gone a long time when I come up from the black. But I know I was here the whole time.

"He cut her," I hear myself say, picking the glass shards embedded in my palm so I can help.

"His knife was poisoned." Leagan moves with me, terror bright as day in her hazel eyes.

Shock rides my arm as Travis grabs it from the side, the Stranger still livid and raw. "Find crystal. Any but Ven."

DON'T touch me.

He's trying to help.

"Wait." Aunt Tess's hands slip off my face as she tries to grasp it, tears pouring down hers. Below the snakebite tourniquet, her skin is purple. "If I start seizing, I want you to shoot me. Stranger, are you fucking listening to me?"

"I'm listening."

But I feel Vesta. Dead in my arms again. The day before that in Dr. Pike's office, realizing I might have to mercy kill her myself and knowing I could never do it. I see her ghost in Aunt Tess, only this time she's begging me to kill her before something worse does, not denying it's happening like Vesta did.

And I love her too. Not like a sister, but like someone who has always looked out for me.

"I saw how it happens… I don't want to die." She gulps air. "I'm not ready."

"I said get crystal." Travis, deep like an animal. "We need to cauterize this."

The Stranger lashes out with my glare. You don't love her, we do. And I won't leave her. I point to the tea house. "Find it yourself."

"I'll get it." Leagan darts away, her boots colliding with the porch.

"I know one way." Travis pushes Aunt Tess's black hair off her face, trying to hold her other hand as she holds me. "It's not a sure thing, but I've seen it work in the past. If I cut your arm off and we got the bite kit on in time, the poison comes out."

"Take it," she says.

"Do you understand me? You understand what this means? You won't have your hand—"

"I said do it."

He picks her up from the legs. "Over here. I'll need your help, Stranger."

Nine.

The tea house porch. Wide and flat.

"Hurry up in there, red," he hollers at Leagan.

"Mind your own business and fuck yourself," she calls back.

Travis unhooks his hatchet and slips his belt up past Aunt Tess's elbow, giving her the tail. "Bite this."

I'm glad it's him, not me.

He kisses her as she turns her face away, flattening out on her back. "You should swear in every language you know. And maybe some that you don't."

"Just do it!"

Leagan kicks the loose door out of her way, arms full of a firebox, iron pan, and clump of towels. "What are you doing?" She drops it all in my lap as Travis draws the hatchet off his belt, puts it to his sharpening stone.

Milk green, ghost quartz. Ends wrapped in cloth, I slide the two biggest crystals together.

Travis puts his knee to her shoulder and pins her arm down. "Hold her other side. Deep breath." He tests his swing, blade out. "Don't move."

"Holy shit." Leagan watches too.

Aunt Tess's back arches. She must scream, but what I hear is the dull thud of the ax breaking through her bone just below the elbow into the wood floor below. I swallow the sour lurch of my stomach, but it was close enough to taste my last meal.

Sparks shed off the ghost quartz into the iron pan, some melting on wood. The crystal glows clear green, becomes white, heat seeping through the cloth as sweat picks my neck.

Travis lets her bleed a second, then cinches the leather tourniquet so tight she writhes again. "Stay with me, Tess."

I can't hold onto the incensed crystals anymore, hot to the brink of combustion. "Move."

Her gasps become a shriek as the quartz melts flesh and boils the blood seeping free. I want to stop, but I can't. Won't.

"That's enough." Travis rips off one of his sleeves, wraps her bloody limb. "Tess."

"That's sanitary," Leagan feels out her pulse.

Farce, I've never seen someone who wasn't dead this shade of gray. After all this, she can't die, but that's not true. Vesta did. Grandma did. The Rim breaks anyone it wants. Merciless.

Pain like needles begin to break through my skin. My hands from the crystal, my arm the flash fire, sweat all over my body. I should stay to watch, just in case, but suddenly I can't.

Ten.

The pump handle feels sharp to the touch as I work it, even though the metal is smooth. Relief lasts only as long as the water does. Blisters are already rising, somehow whiter than my natural skin tone.

Leagan comes to me, whatever her face says hidden by her mask. "Oh, your poor hands." She wets one of the towels, wraps my arm in it. "You deserve a cookie when we get back to the train."

"How is she?"

"Weak, but her pulse is steady..." The bright spark of fear in her eyes doesn't go out. "I think she's going to be okay... this is what I saw."

My breath still won't move farther down than my middle ribs. Leagan pats my shoulder. We don't say it.

Glass ruptures down the row behind us, more frantic yells. We can't stay here.

Eight.

Travis holds Aunt Tess, her eyes shut. I've never seen her this vulnerable.

I let my firelight shadow and the Stranger's loom over him. "Get the horses."

OUTSIDE THE WALL, WE WATCH AS HANNAH BURNS.

Aunt Tess rests against Travis's back, eyelids heavy but open. Strips of cotton cap her severed arm, cradled in the front of her shirt. She reaches for me. "Rafe is dead."

"I assumed."

Her fingers tighten around my forearm. "Do you feel relieved?"

I don't know. I feel more relieved Montoya is gone. The Stranger never stops reaching.

"Evangeline said I wouldn't." The smile is in the corner of her mouth, not with her teeth, takes a moment to reach her eyes. "I get to tell her she was wrong."

The dappled gray horse digs at the ground impatiently. Her ears turn away as I handle the reins, displeased by the bright light in the sky that's not the sun.

"I know, I'm sorry." I steady her nose with my hand so Leagan can mount. "We're going now."

She sniffs me, snorts.

"Rude," Leagan says.

I look one more time, not at the smoke or the ash, but at the fire.

The crystal-hungry east bloods will never let go of this place, but you'll stay proud of me, Grandma. I'll do my best to never let you down.

The Stranger wants what she's always wanted.

Out there. Out west.

SEVENTY-SIX
TESLA

THE ACTUAL SALE OF THE WEAPONS WILL TAKE PLACE IN JUNCTION.

My mind still hasn't fully grasped the consequences of losing a limb, but I'm not a crispy body in Hannah, so I win, Montoya.

Junction's underground hotel is a coil of buried train cars, protected from the heat of the sun and raging storm debris. In place of windows and sunlight, lanterns of reformed glass in every color hang from the blank spaces.

Kane closes his book to rise as we enter the rug-cloaked room. What a fine gentleman he makes. "Tesla, Adelaide, Navy, come in, how are you?"

"Von Kane, the younger." My sling disguises the fact that half my left arm is missing. No need to draw attention to myself that way.

I place Navy's hand on the chair's velvet blue armrest so she can find her way to the seat, then help myself to its mismatched orange cousin.

Adelaide stalks around the wheel and pipes now living their second lives as a tea table, lifting the lids on the honey and fresh mint bowls.

"Help yourself." Kane pulls out the remaining engineer's chair turned parlor furniture. "This is for you."

She takes up a defiant stance behind Navy's chair.

Some response rolls around behind Kane's eyes, but her silence seems to frighten him from letting it out.

Oh, I could watch them hate to want each other all day. Sadly, we don't have the time. "I don't think that chair is haunted, Stranger."

"That shouldn't be a problem for her, right?" Kane tries to smile at her but remains on his feet as well. "I admit I was surprised to hear from you."

"Well, you shouldn't be," I say. "We're friends now. Friends check up on each other. Where's your father?"

"Back at home, he had meetings, and my mother missed him. I'm responsible for the surveyors and foremen."

"Well, he clearly believes in you."

"I must have done something right." His gaze turns from my bandage to the one protruding from the sleeve of Adelaide's yellow cardigan, wrapping her flash fire injuries. "What happened to you two?"

I tilt Adelaide a smile of unrepentant wickedness. "You first."

She scowls, looking to the wall. And that is why I do it. Ha ha.

I turn back to Kane. "To be honest, I'm glad to see you alone."

"So am I." He clears his throat, closing his hands around the back of the questionable gray chair he and Adelaide are both too scared to sit in. "I heard a rumor when we got back to Vantage. After the expedition…"

"Oh, did you now?"

"Your train was derailed."

The *Absolution* was mine more than anyone else's, and I will always think of her fondly, but I won't have customers pity us. "A rumor that's unfortunately true, but we fixed that, didn't we, girls?"

"Yes, we did," Navy says. "You'll be very impressed when you see the upgrade."

"I also saw the bounty. It was…substantial."

Adelaide's sidelong gaze slips across mine.

We *could* tell him Green put the target on us right now. Appalled, he'll tell his father that Green tried to clear the rails by killing women, a rare enough commodity, and our dear Mr. Green will lose his powerful allies to us in one shot. But I have a stronger feeling this conversation is only surface deep, a skin so he can continue believing he's a good man with righteous morals.

This pause grows up to be awkward silence.

"The Rim is a dangerous place," I finally say. "But I don't have to tell you that this time, do I?"

Kane doesn't flinch. "No, ma'am."

"I'm lucky to have survived this long." I trail my widow finger down my cheek scar just to feel it tingle. "If I live much longer, I'll be considered old, isn't that frightful? Those bounty hunters will have to do better if they want us."

"I don't know if I'd be so casual about that."

"I'm not saying we didn't deserve it. I'm not saying we did either."

We didn't.

"I wasn't asking. It doesn't matter to me what you did to someone else, as long as you respect me and aren't here to cause trouble. I don't like that someone was trying to have you killed. That seems…excessive."

"Because we're women?" I turn my smile to level him. Have some respect now, Kane. You were just a starry-eyed fool wishing on moons you didn't know when you came here. We taught you the ways of the Rim, and that's treachery. Adelaide was only kind enough to not kill you at my suggestion.

"Yes." Kane's tongue staggers over itself. "I suppose that's part of it. You…I just don't agree that you're wholly bad people with no redeeming qualities. Death is…final."

"There are no gods to men here, only death. And women are killed every day with no mercy." I tug apart the strings securing the leather folder in my lap. "Some people kill for free. The smart ones, however, kill for money. They don't care who it is, as long as they get paid."

"That doesn't make it respectable."

"Just business."

The crusty hinges make their own appearance as the door opens.

"Sincerest apologies that I'm late. I hope that I haven't—by all my lucky moons!"

Navy jolts as Jonathaniel claps our backs. I saw it coming, she didn't.

"I thought we were to meet that mutinous rapscallion Edwards, but this is a far better turn of events. I told you we'd meet again. Let us hope this is the last time you doubt me, Adelaide Revere."

"I didn't realize you knew each other," Kane says.

The gray of Adelaide's eyes is colder than they were looking at Kane, the tight line of her jaw deeper. I'm sorry, I did not realize he'd be here. I hope she sees that in gaze.

"I thought you'd be headed back east by now, Jonathaniel," I say. "I heard the *Emerald Constellation* left six days ago."

"Well, then you, madam, thought wrong. I came to my senses and realized it would be a sin to waste this black gold opportunity. Fortune clearly wanted to stop my leaving and sent those bone pickers to block the rails. Once the track was finally cleared, I shipped that old fool Montgomery back east with my train. Not an hour too soon. Providence knows I could not tolerate another minute of his whining. And I have been enjoying myself handsomely ever since."

Kane pockets his grin behind a balled fist and a fake cough, but it's not so easy to slide a tell like that past a card-counter, dear.

"I sense an egregious amount of tension in this room. Dare I even ask?" Jonathaniel swaps looks between us. "Have I interrupted something I shouldn't have?"

"Not at all." I draw the modified *Exodus* cargo manifest from my folder and place it in front of Kane. "For you, sir."

He reads like a good businessman does, then his eyes lift. "You…"

Now Adelaide smiles at him, but it's not friendly.

"You didn't."

"Oh, yes." I smirk. And after all the trouble and shit we've had to dig our way out of, this moment feels particularly good. "Surprise."

"If you don't mind, my good man." Jonathaniel clicks his fingers for the manifest. "Thank you."

"What happened to Edwards?" Kane asks.

"Oh, he's dead."

"I was afraid of that."

"Well, well, you lady devils." Jonathaniel flings the manifest at the table. "I am thoroughly shocked…no, dare I say impressed. Damnation."

"There was no mutiny against the Exodus Company, was there?" Kane says. "You sent the shadow sale letter."

"You catch up fast, Kane."

"This is also significantly less ammunition than we ordered."

"A smuggler's tax, my dear. And we're keeping the standing guns." Naturally. Leagan would have a fit if we didn't.

"You do realize how much money this cost the endeavor. My father went back east to tell the investors."

"Yes, but we're willing to make a deal. Would you like to see the guns?"

Kane stands, reaching for his hat. "I would, actually."

"Goody. Follow me."

SEVENTY-SEVEN
ADELAIDE

We lead them to the Boneyard.

The wind rides hard across the valley, moans in the rock arches that lie between here and Descendants. They say those ghost shrieks will drive you mad, and that's why people become so depraved after spending too long here. But Descendants just uses that as an excuse to be wretched. The Stranger recognizes the difference between what's real and what isn't. In my experience, people are still more uncomfortable with silence than even disembodied voices.

Kane walks too close to me. I feel the rise off every breath he takes. "I can't believe you did this."

"Did it, or got away with it?" There's a difference.

"You could have been killed."

I could have been killed many ways by now. The scars from Hannah, the flash fire burns, the way I came into this family, all intimate reminders of how close death and I have been. We breathed on each other.

"Believe it, my friend." Aunt Tess clears the field of scrap metal hiding the *Exodus Ironclad* and spreads her good arm. "Behold."

Nine seventy-nine.

"Fool's gold..." Kane's steps falter.

Fool's gold, not sweet Jezebel. He's becoming one of us.

Aunt Tess won't stop smiling. "You've never seen an *Ironclad*, have you, Kane?"

"She cuts quite the intimidating figure, I dare say." Jonathaniel breathes out a chuckle. "May I touch her?"

"You may, but I can't promise she won't bite back."

I get ahead of them, away from them, enter the car and find a wall to lean against. Fuse with the shadows.

Nineteen.

Raleigh waits at the ramp, Leagan straddling one of the open crates. "Afternoon, Mr. Von Kane. And Mr...."

"Swann."

"Please, feel free to just call me Kane."

"I'll be sure to do that. My name is Raleigh, munitions and pearls are my main vices. All of these are certified Exodus-manufactured, alkaline and ready for use. The Raptor and I checked each weapon individually and can confirm none of the parts were substituted with bastard Eos pieces."

Leagan nods with him. "Or that sludge the Smythe and Matthan-Atlas Company tries to say is weaponry." She passes a rifle to Kane, Raleigh one to Jonathaniel. "All their men still carry Exodus."

The Stranger can't decide which of them she dislikes more, different reasons. Honestly, I prefer Kane. Jonathaniel talks too much.

They're both fools. They're both dead.

Probably.

"If you're not satisfied with the quality, I don't deserve to call myself a purveyor of fine arms," Raleigh says. "Feel free to inspect them at your leisure."

"I'll take your word for it." Jonathaniel lays the repeater back on the crate with barely a fingerprint. "Shooting hurts my ears, although the scent is quite nice. Perfume of the modern age."

"Isn't it?" Leagan puts her nose to a removed barrel. Black lipstick in case Jonathaniel misreads her smile. "Did you know, holding weapons makes you more attractive?"

"I would have to agree with you there," Raleigh says. "Oiled and pure, no bastard alloys."

"Where's the ammunition?" Kane asks.

"Would you like to see it?" Aunt Tess says.

"It's still wax-sealed," Leagan adds.

"In a minute." Kane slides the bolt action with a tilted ear, checks that it's empty, and tests how the trigger feels. He sights down the barrel before picking another to repeat the process. "What's your plan here?"

"Oh, we were always going to sell them to you."

"Minus your cut."

She flicks him the engineer's salute. "The railroad expansion is good for our business too."

"The back-market auction announcement was just a ploy to drive up the price."

"Not exactly." She rolls the truth across her teeth with the smirk that makes me ache for Vesta. "We needed that cover for a different reason. We're not your enemies, Kane."

"I don't know if I can believe that."

"You've grown up, sweet adventurer."

"You all had nothing to do with that." He looks at me.

Never say sorry.

I wasn't going to.

"Fair point, I amend that statement. We're not your enemies anymore," Aunt Tess says. "Some lessons need to be learned the hard way. Now you're wiser for it, and so are we. You're welcome."

Kane drifts deeper, a hand put to each crate as he counts them. He's been counting our faces too. It won't take him much longer. He's smart. It's only a matter of time before he figures out that he wasn't the only one who lost people. But we don't owe him that information. Horne and Randy were just his hired guns. Maybe his friends at best. Grandma and Vesta were family.

I know what he's going to say. *I understand.* And I dread the day his pity comes.

He rubs the maker's mark of the Exodus Company, etched into each rifle butt. "What's your price?"

"That's something I have to negotiate with your father," Aunt Tess says. "But you can tell him what you've seen here, and that we're willing to deal in things other than money."

"He's harder to impress...I would know."

"Don't depreciate yourself now."

"You've just embarrassed him and everyone else between here and the Exodus factory, and he's old-fashioned."

"He obviously trusts you—he put you in charge here. I think he'd listen to you if you persuade him to hear me."

They need these guns. I spent enough time with him. Whatever's going on out there, it's making him nervous, and his father isn't listening to him.

"I'll make him aware of the situation," Kane says.

"That's all I can ask. About Green…"

"Green had the contract first. I'll give you this piece of advice. My father doesn't like to be pushed or made to look like a fool. And you've already done that."

"Oops."

"Make your deal for the guns, don't try anything else. It won't work, you'll just ruin any chance of him ever respecting you."

"Doesn't he want people who get results?" She sweeps her hand across the haul. Inside the sling, her other arm twitches. "Clearly, we can."

"It doesn't work like that." Kane's shoulders barely move as he breathes, rigid inside his shirt. "You'll hear from us about the weapon deal soon."

"So he says." Jonathaniel tips his hat to us. "*We* will be in touch, Ladies Revere."

"That sounds promising." Aunt Tess touches him on the arm as she escorts Kane down the ramp.

"A wise woman once told me I was foolish for traveling without bodyguards," Jonathaniel continues.

Aunt Tess turns a wink at me. "One I know?"

"I believe you do."

Kane turns. "I can't hire you for the Company…however, I can't stop you from being where we are."

Aunt Tess just won her game.

"I'll take your advice." She lifts her two fingers. "*Sol*, Timothy Von Kane. It will be a pleasure to see you again, as usual."

SEVENTY-EIGHT
ADELAIDE

NAVY KEEPS A HAND ON THE OUTSIDE EDGE OF HER WORKTABLE WHENEVER SHE moves in her Damascus lab. She doesn't look at faces when she talks to people anymore.

The sharp smells bring me back to the *Absolution*. Pure alcohol and smoldering herbs, paper and book glue. Glass tubes grow morning salt crystals. A scale and silver tongs, cold to touch, surgeons' glass with a complete set of amplifying lenses.

"This is better than what you had before," I say.

"I ordered some books from the University, and I've been studying the notes in Amnesty Wells's journal. It's not in very good shape, so we copied it. And Leagan's a very good assistant."

She stops playing with a set of glass sticks and droppers. "I know how to follow directions, and I promised not to drink anything."

"No," Navy says fast. "Please don't."

"Only if it smells salty."

"No."

"Only for science."

"No, don't ever." Navy presses her hands into her lab apron's deep pockets. "I thought I should warn you, I sent a letter to Dr. Pike."

I control my first instinct, the Stranger's flare of anger. This is Navy. "He wrote back?"

"It took so long I didn't think he was going to respond… I know you're not happy about this. You don't have to be."

"I didn't say anything." This isn't about me. She was brave enough to collect the skin, hair, and blood samples from Vesta. I couldn't even look at her once she was gone. "This is your project."

"I thought you'd be mad."

"I trust you." It's Pike I don't trust. This will be my chance to find out which of us is right. I took Montoya. I can hold my own against a doctor.

"I'm just letting you know because I know you don't like surprises," Navy says. "You did try to kill him."

"We've killed a lot of people," Leagan says. "It's not exactly a new thing for us."

"That's true…but we didn't find Dr. Pike on accident. Or that Grandma told his fortune years ago, or that he trained in the Yellow City. It all means something. He operated on Vesta. I wanted to know if he noticed anything unusual."

I can read her tone. "He did."

"Yes. The pestilence does show internal signs before it…does those other things. He said the count of…something I can't remember the name for, in Vesta's blood was off."

"How much did you tell him?"

"He knows we went on a survey to the West Rim, but I didn't tell him where specifically."

He seemed smart enough to guess.

"Did you tell him about the journals?"

"No, and don't worry, I won't," Navy says. "I can keep secrets too. Now, would you like to see what we made?"

"It was evil of you to make me wait this long."

"See, I can be evil too. Sometimes. For science."

"For science!" Leagan pulls up the bottom shelf of the bookcase and sticks her arm into the gap under it. A moon diviner's case.

Navy uncovers the dish from the cold storage box.

Blood.

A milky liquid rolls against the sides of the diviner's center globe. Thicker than water, but it moves with more ease than honey.

Leagan holds onto the pins, keeps the diviner globe from turning inside its ring axis, extends it at arm's length. Pricks of glow come to life in the milky center, like bastard ghost quart. So do silver-green flecks in the blood.

Fool's gold.

"You like it?" Navy asks.

The longer the diviner and blood hover near each other, the harder the light gets.

Leagan smiles. "She likes it."

"She's speechless." Aunt Tess shuts the door behind her. "Shocking."

"Not for her," Navy says.

"Yes, darling. I'm just teasing her."

"Who needs the University now?" I say.

Navy covers the red rush in her cheeks. "Our next project is making these in a smaller scale, so we can all wear one when we go back out there."

"I was designing an arm compass," Leagan says.

"Or a pocket watch," I say. "That would be more secretive."

"But this one is fun to play with."

"Just don't break it," Navy says. "We can use this to test the water and the areas where we camp. If it works the way I want, it will glow in proportion to how contaminated a source is...I'd ask you not to go at all... but I know you."

"You do." Despite what we've been through, and whatever else is waiting out there, there's nothing that will allow me to turn back. This is a fate I can't escape.

Leagan brings the diviner to me. "Now hold out your arm."

The concoction inside stays neutral.

"Nothing," I say, for Navy's benefit.

"Oh, good."

"But we were all exposed to it."

"Yes, and you had your mask off for the longest period of time," Navy says. "This is the question I've been trying to answer. We know it was in the water because of the journals, but Lake Amnesty was all dried up. I've been over and over what happened, so many times. What Vesta did that you and I didn't."

I know exactly what she did that was different without saying. The memories resurface for me anyway.

"There was only one time we were separated from her," Navy says. "You remember."

"Yes." Other than the night I spent trapped in the mine with Kane.

"But we were the ones who dug up the Wells's graves," Navy says. "If I was a gambling woman, I would have said they would be more contaminated than the air or the ground, and maybe they are."

"As an actual betting woman, I agree with those odds," Aunt Tess says.

"Isobel Carlisle and Amnesty designed the toxin based off the assumption that the Tov were cannibals. It seems logical that the pestilence spreads better if it's ingested. We didn't eat the Wells's bodies."

"No, we definitely didn't. But Vesta didn't eat anyone either."

She fucked Randy.

Aunt Tess braces her one good arm on the worktable. "She found one of Kane's boys she liked, didn't she?"

"Randy," Navy says, reluctantly.

"Do I know my daughter or what?"

"*Him*?" Leagan cringes. "The short one? With the neck beard? Oh, gross. She could do so much better than that."

She would have said it to Vesta's face too. It wouldn't have helped.

"All we know for sure is that she went somewhere we didn't," Navy says.

I fold my arms. It holds back everything unpleasant inside me. "Randy was infected too. Kane told me."

"That's what I keep coming back to. It's the only theory that explains most of the happenings. There are hotspots."

A chill passes through my body. Even the Stranger goes still.

"All that water in Lake Amnesty went somewhere. Logically, into the ground."

I see Eden, the dry lake bed, cracked like sunburned lips.

"If I'm right, and I really think I am, some parts of the West Rim are more poisonous than others. And maybe some aren't poisonous at all. The pestilence contamination is congealed in whatever environment attracts or feeds it. I haven't figured that part out yet. But I have theories about it too."

"*Farce*." No one but my sister stopped to consider this until now. She's right, it's only logical.

Aunt Tess smiles on her. "A bright mind solves problems."

"Thank you. Now I just have to prove it."

"With Leagan's help," she says.

"With Leagan's help, of course."

"But?" I ask.

"The notes are incomplete," Navy says. "Amnesty was a cultist, her science isn't reliable. Isobel, aka Benjamin Carlisle, was the chemist. She did the real science. Her journal is the one I need."

It wasn't in the lab where I found Amnesty's.

You didn't finish searching it, the Stranger reminds me.

"You're certain these notes exist?" Aunt Tess says.

"They were working on a project that literally changed the outcome of the war," Navy says. "Even foolish scientists take notes."

She's right. This story has three parts. We have Zachariah's, we have Amnesty's. Now we need the final piece. Isobel.

"You hope that Isobel's notes tell exactly how the pestilence was created," Aunt Tess says.

"Exactly. Then I'll make an antidote."

"Well, we already know they had one that didn't work," Leagan says. "The opposite of that, actually."

"Then I'll know what not to do."

The Stranger and I don't believe in many people. I don't believe in Pike or Isobel Carlisle. But I believe in Navy. This time will be different.

She touches the chair to find the desk against the stone wall. Drifts her hand along the shelf until she contacts what she's after.

My journal, Kane's journal.

"I thought you might want these."

Seven.

The weight of leather and paper feels good in my hands. I can tell which pages have been out in the sun longer. They're yellowed slightly, crinkled. Dust between them.

I fold them against my chest. "Grandma told Pike's fortune when he came to the Rim. She told him he would do good things here. She knew."

Navy nods, tears up in her throat. "She's still taking care of us."

Leagan touches Grandma's pipe through her pocket. Me, the black pearl ring on my first finger.

"We are the daughters of a great woman," Aunt Tess says. "She made us strong and unapologetic for it. Let's make her proud."

Take everything we can.

SEVENTY-NINE
TESLA

THE *EXODUS IRONCLAD* SITS ASTRIDE THE TRACK, THE WORK OF THE BONEYARD welders' steel sorcery. She's fitted to be our home now, a beautiful beast of fortune, ready to leave Covenant when I say so.

"I told you I'd get another train." I link my good arm through Evangeline's. "Thank you for watching our things while we were gone."

"Of course, my friend." She smooths a hand across the shoulder supporting my sling. "It's just a blessed relief to see you alive."

"The cost of vengeance, like you said."

"I didn't wish this upon you."

"I know. It was worth it."

"I'm glad for you."

Navy sits on the platform's block steps while Leagan wades back through the silvery grass and tombstones out past the track. She disappears briefly, coming up again with something cupped in her hands.

"You've made the start of a nice life here," Evangeline says.

"Don't start that with me." It's been hard enough after...what happened with Travis. I have to fight off the tears that build up even thinking about... that bastard. But I can't let go of him. I'm afraid I never will.

"I know." She smiles and her stare moves deeper into me where he lingers behind my everyday thoughts. "You have to do this, but you can always change your mind. And you can always come back."

"There's nothing left for me here. Except you, of course."

"Look what I found." Leagan takes Navy's hand.

"What was that?" Navy yanks back, the lizard taking its opportunity to escape. "You are rude!"

Leagan just laughs.

"Don't ever hand me something alive. Or dead."

Adelaide pushes out the hatch between living car couplings, wedging herself so the lid forms a shield. She has her crossgun in her hands. "Someone's coming."

A four-horse stagecoach angles through a previous trail torn in the grass. Two men ride the top seats, another clinging to the back hitch rack and getting bounced around more than his companions.

"Cover me." Grass stalks snap as I hike to stand at least a little higher on the platform, my skirt snaring bugs and seeds.

They're unremarkable, common lumps of flesh until they stop just within speaking range, and their sage railroad bully uniforms and rifles make me pause. One aims at Adelaide from his seat while the other two lift rifles to Evangeline, Leagan, and I.

"Don't." Raleigh's face appears within the shade of the coach behind the iron bar windows. Generally, they keep pickers and roadmen out, but occasionally will hold prisoners in. Like right now.

Lurking behind him like foul breath is the next man I plan to murder now that Rafe is dead. The glint of a revolver barrel caresses Raleigh's lower skull, a steely crescent moon peeking between his red curls.

"Carrson fucking Green." Each one of those syllables leaves my mouth tasting of dirt. "Hello, you greasy piece of snake shit."

Green slides his arm around Raleigh's waist, keeping his body close to protect him from Leagan's deadly aim.

"Well, doesn't this feel familiar?" I say. "Just like the last time we spoke, still a coward, hiding behind everyone else."

"Don't keep me in suspense like this." Raleigh lifts his chin as Green's breath moves the hair by his ear. "Blow my head off. I'll hang around long enough to watch them turn you into a cheese grater."

Green doesn't bother looking directly at us. His gaze points off at the white line of the Salt Waste.

"Do you want to know why I'm the best gun on the Rim?" Leagan says to the pistol in her hand.

"Don't," I warn her. She may be the best gun on the Rim, she can make two shots for every one made by anyone else, but there are three rifles aimed at us at the moment.

"Put that iron away or I'll remove this boy's head," Green says.

"Steady now, my friends." Evangeline puts a lone hand out, wide and strong as any man's. "You're standing with believers in the God of Mercy. Let's all practice some, shall we?"

"Providence left the Rim to its own devices a long time ago," Green says.

"I was just itching." Leagan rubs one finger up her chin. Her middle finger.

"As much as it would relieve my burdens," Green says "if I intended to kill you, I would've had you shot immediately and from a distance so I wouldn't have to listen to you whine."

"Then what do you want?" I ask. "Or did you just come here to waste my time?"

"My own, but it's time we had a conversation. You and I, like civilized people with a begrudging mutual respect for each other. This hostage situation is just to ensure my own protection."

"Oh, I thought we had something special," Raleigh says. "Have I mentioned you smell nice? Like Eosin cedar."

"Well, we're all here." I offer him a look at my teeth, nothing but disgust in me. "What did you want to say?"

"I've had enough of you and your vengeful bullshit."

"Oh, didn't you like the gift I left for you?"

"That—" Green steadies his grip on his tongue. "—is what I'm talking about."

"Fool's gold, I do believe he's terrified," I say to Leagan.

"Pissing himself through his clothes."

"It's probably getting on Raleigh."

"Ha, good."

"Somehow you've managed to survive another Season," Green says. "I'd count myself lucky and walk away with my life. Know when you're beat, Widow. Your fortune can't last forever."

"You go right ahead and do that." If he thought he could beat us, he wouldn't be here trying to convince me to run. We made that mistake last time. "I have to say, it wasn't a bad plan, getting Hannah to pick us off for you. Just not good enough."

"Yes…" Green gazes across the thin strip of field to Adelaide through lidded eyes. "My company has been investigating the question of the arson that destroyed Winchester. They say it was a ghost."

"If you want to make an accusation, then do it." This isn't Vantage, and we're not the Meades, disposed of with lies, a rope, and the justice of an ignorant crowd.

Green's lips pucker like a worm under his moustache. "I had my suspicions something else had gone east when no trace of the *Exodus Ironclad* was found, except a rumor echoing from the North Rim. There's scorched earth in Hannah."

"That I'll gladly take credit for."

"I wonder if you don't underestimate the flood reach of what you've done. Black gold prices are already surging back east, investment values falling. You're driving them west, and I understand you're now leveraging the Exodus weapons in order to market your protection services to the Von Kanes."

"That's right."

"Then allow me to give you some advice. If you intend to join the ranks of east blood business, then you are also done acting like common bone pickers. Done destroying my facilities in Descendants and killing my men for doing their jobs, breaking into my home, and leaving snakes on my desk. I would buy you off if I thought that would be effective, but I know you better than that."

"I don't know. Pay the right price, and we offer protection from anything and anyone who might cross you." I look to Adelaide with a leading smirk. "Even ghosts. Winchester forgot to pay."

"You're no fool, Tesla. You don't really believe you can shake me down like a common prospector, and this intimidation ploy isn't going to work either. It's not a good look for you."

"Oh, do you think that matters to me? You're mistaken, darling."

"Step on me one more time and I'll tell Von Kane and the rest of them exactly what you are," he says. "Thieves. Frauds."

"Millard Von Kane seemed to like me. His son definitely does."

"Only because they don't know you like I do. You're the kind of sludge they hired me to chisel off the rails."

"What exactly are you going to tell them? Let's think about that, shall we? In order to clean up the rails, you had six women hunted by rapists and killers across the Rim. You had my mother, a grandmother, shot to death when she was injured so bad she could barely walk. My daughter framed for theft and murdered, all so you could secure a position with the railroad expansion. I'd check your logic, Green, dear. The Von Kanes are old-fashioned chivalry."

"You're hardly defenseless."

"That doesn't matter." Kane said it himself.

"You think your lives matter to any investor back east?"

"No. We're dust to them. But our lives matter to me. And I will make it so."

Green pauses, oily mustache pinching as he rolls his wormy lip again. "There is one thing I do regret. I was not happy when I heard what happened to Vesta...it is a shame."

My breath trembles as I force it through my nose. You think you're safe with your disgusting little snake thoughts so well hidden by this salesman mask, but like any good mother or sister or intelligent woman, I see them. Adelaide's glare prickles on the back of my scalp, hate that burns so deep you shiver.

You've only fooled yourself, Carrson Green, and by the North, South, and West Rims, we will fucking end you.

"What did you think was going to happen?" Only rhetoric. I don't want to hear his justification. I could let myself imagine, but I won't.

"The Stranger and I were with Vesta when she died," Navy says.

I didn't realize she was standing behind us, her voice surprisingly strong despite the pain that marks her face below the goggles.

"We held her hands. It's something I'll never forget."

Green clears his throat, shifting the arm in his pearl button sleeve. What can he say to that?

"As much as I hate this admission, you are good at what you do here." He pauses over words that sicken him, like me. "You were powerful. Cunning and dangerous in an uncivilized place. Bastards like you do not allow the Rim to move forward. I'm not sorry for what I did to you."

"You're sorry it failed."

"Yes."

"Well…" My fingers rise and fall against my hip.

If there are times to lie, and I do believe there are, then there must also be a time for honesty, and something to be gained from it.

"My mother always said don't be sorry, it's not usually worth the effort." I think she meant that we have to learn from our choices, good or bad, because life has very few takebacks. But I think she missed another important truth in the heart of her favorite response. Never apologize for being as ruthless as your enemies. My gaze lifts again. "But I am not my mother."

The words sting my tongue, they bruise my heart. They taste like betrayal, but they are the truth. At her core, my mother remained merciful, like the dawn. A light shining through every kill, every theft, holding out for a day when we wouldn't have to. I want those things too, but the way we're willing to get them is where Mother and I diverge and Adelaide and I collide.

I am the night. Dark and lovely but full of teeth, and the Stranger capable of things I don't think Mother wanted to imagine.

"I'm not sorry either."

If there are times to be burned by trust, then there must also be times that betrayals protect. Respect is not a birthright. You have to earn it, and if that fails, take it with force.

"Then we agree," Green says. "The time has come for this aggravation of each other to be done."

"Am I having a fit or are you suggesting a truce?"

"Yes." Green transfers the gun from Raleigh's neck to his kidney. "Like it not, we all work for the Von Kanes and their east blood friends now. It's in all our best interests if we find a way to coexist in this new world we're building without further antagonizing each other to ruin."

"I think…" And I judge every breath that comes off his lips to ruffle Raleigh's hair so carefully. "That we want what you want. To keep what we built here because we were here first, brave enough to face the Rim while it's still wild. Travelers with nothing. The Von Kanes of the world will never understand what that takes."

"No," Green says, and I sense the same untamed pride in him that's swollen in me. "They will not. Do I have your smuggler's promise?"

"I swear on the *Absolution*'s rusting shell." My smile is prickly, sour as pear jam as I give him the engineer's salute. "Now let our sweet Raleigh go."

Green taps the roof of his coach, drawing Raleigh back into the caress of shadows with him. "I know how loosely you treat your promises when it serves you. Raleigh will travel with me, and we will be accompanying you onboard the *Exodus Ironclad* to the West Rim railroad camp."

"The fuck you will."

From the depths of the coach, Green's iron gaze bores into mine. "An insurance policy, guaranteeing we all make good on our word. Can you argue with that, *Widow*?"

I'd like to. But I'm smarter than that.

"Well, you're in luck, we just got our guest car upgraded. You'll have your own toilet."

"He will be treated respectfully, the guest of a gentleman."

"Gentleman?" Leagan scoffs. "Liar, liar, long johns on fire."

"It's okay," Raleigh says. "I'll go peacefully. Nobody do anything you won't live to regret."

"Hey," Leagan says. "Don't we get one of your guys?"

"We don't want them," Navy says.

"But that's how this is supposed to work. This isn't fair."

"I hope there's peach jam," Raleigh says. "I do love some quality preserves."

"This isn't a hotel." She shows him her middle finger with the purest Leagan affection.

A quiet tear slips from under Navy's goggles, down her rosy cheek.

Of course, I care for Raleigh, but this situation would be worse if it was one of the girls Green had. I do know how to quit while I'm ahead.

"We'll go make sure your beds are made. We leave in thirty minutes. If you're late, I leave without you." I back off, first wiping Navy's face and inserting her hand into Evangeline's, so I can make sure Leagan comes with me. Having one less hand causes trouble in unexpected places. "You enjoy him, Green. He likes a bedtime song."

"It's true, I can't sleep without it." Raleigh leans out to smile at us one last time. A brave, loyal soul.

"Come along, little darling." Evangeline puts her other arm around Leagan to help me guide her away. "Worry about it elsewhere."

"What a swindle," she scoffs.

I can promise you one thing, Green. Everywhere you go, we will be there. Everything you try to build, we'll be waiting. You will be haunted by our ghost. And one day, a woman will come for you. She may be a Widow, or a Stranger, a Raptor, or possibly a Rook, but her name will be Revere.

I swear on the *Absolution*'s rusting shell, and my eternal soul, you motherfucker.

"*Sol*, you slippery bastard. We'll see you on the West Rim."

EXIT

I sit on the roof of the *Exodus*.

Red stone, cliffs and mountains, fading to gold, fading to blue, fading away.

A hidden empire. A Shadow Nation. The queens of the desert. Lost.

All that space knows my name. I don't know what it wants, but I'm going to find out.

Welcome to the end of the map, Stranger.

Thank you for reading! Did you enjoy? Please add your review because nothing helps an author more and encourages readers to take a chance on a book than a review.

And don't the last chapter of *The Revere Trilogy* from J. L. Delavega with SOLACE BY FIRE. Turn the page for a sneak peek!

You can also sign up for the City Owl Press newsletter to receive notice of all book releases!

SNEAK PEEK OF SOLACE BY FIRE

I once told you, I have two shadows. One of them is from sun. The other is there even in the dark.

Leagan wears a leather welding harness to hang off the ribs of the *Exodus Ironclad*. Our train. A jar of white paint is holstered on her hip, splatters of it on her face, hands.

I hold the tension line so she doesn't fall into the wind. Air floods the pages of her books and weapon designs as a cascade of steam rolls past the open slide door.

"There." Leagan wraps her leg around the doorframe for leverage, and I walk the tension line in. "Do you like it?"

I check for rocks, then lean out to see her finished work.

The lady has a skeleton face, curly hair piled over it from lines of welded metal. Now she glows, moonlight white on black.

The weight of the wind pushes against the air in my lungs. Sun cracks across the red surface of the Rim, rock shadows and canyons a web of dark scars. They all point one way.

The striated cliffs that were faint shadows yesterday are blue and orange and not so far away now.

The West Rim.

The Stranger beats in my throat, my stomach empty and longing. Reaching.

"You're right." I pull myself back inside and bolt the armor-plated slide door. "You can see it better painted white."

"And now she looks kind of like you," Leagan says. "If Aunt Tess gets mad, I don't care. Thanks for helping me. You can go give Raleigh his breakfast now, before he complains that he's starving to death."

It's time to make sure Raleigh is still alive.

Three hundred.

The roll of the *Exodus Ironclad*'s wheels is louder within the metal plates enclosing the car crossings than in the open wind. I raise my fist to the iron-banded door of the spare car. Two knocks.

"Who is it?" Green asks somewhere behind the peekhole.

He knows.

"Let her in."

Seven.

The car stinks like men.

"Pleasant morning, Stranger." Green's dead man's gaze trails me from the bunk he sits hunched on, nothing pleasant about it.

This living space was good enough for the Exodus Company men who left their blood to haunt the floor. It's good enough for him and his hired guns.

"Your visitor's here," the one posted by the open bathroom says. "Hurry up, you've got no one to impress here."

Raleigh steps out, dabbing flecks of shave cream off his chin. "Just because I'm a hostage doesn't mean I have to look like one. Greetings, Adelaide."

I move closer and Green watches.

Seven —

He shifts his stony shoulders, so do the guns staggered around the car. They all face me.

"Three feet away, same as yesterday," Green says.

Like you said yesterday, the Stranger says, her voice a dark echo, a shade of my own.

I stop, face Raleigh, then circle him. Slow.

"I'm all right," he says.

I'll make up my own mind. The Stranger picks apart his collar, open from shaving. Rolled white sleeves and satin suspenders, pink like crushed rose petals. No blood. No bruises. Visible ones, at least.

"You know in any other circumstances this would be considered creepy." His smile feels real. "What did you bring me today?"

I hold out the tray. Eggs and a biscuit. Pear jam. Coffee.

"Did you make these, or did Tess?"

"I did."

"Alkaline, I can tell. They're fluffy."

I stand where I am while he eats it. I look at Green. He looks back, and every time he breathes, the muscles stringing his neck to his shoulders pull tighter.

"Don't you have somewhere more important to be?" he asks. "You won't intimidate me this way. I'm not afraid of you. Any of you. You least of all."

If that were true you wouldn't have to say it.

"The Raven used you as her shadow puppet and that spook tactic worked on fools from back east, but you're only a sad façade that no one else will ever want around."

"Well that's rude and uncalled for," Raleigh says. "You ask if she has somewhere more important to be, but if that's true, you should actually be honored she's chosen to be here with you right now. Think about it."

A scoff peaks in Green's throat, cools quick. "It's safe to say none of us are comfortable with this situation, but that's a luxury for another day. If we all do our jobs for the Von Kane Company, we protect our futures. You're all smart enough to see that. Remember why we're here."

The Stanger taints the car in all shades of black, seeping into nostrils, smoke none of them can see.

Maybe you don't always remember, but I haven't forgotten anything.

I remember little pins of sweat along your nose, breath too shallow, eyes too black when you would look at Vesta.

I remember how loyal Grandma was to you, delivering you favors even when we didn't need your work anymore. She took that reservation you framed us with because she believed in honor. She died for it.

Aunt Tess and I don't.

Maybe I'll die for the opposite of it.

Raleigh's eaten two thirds of his breakfast. Even if one of Green's bone pickers steal the plate from him now, he won't be hungry. He just won't get to finish his coffee.

I smile at him before I go. Only him.

Three.

My passing stare chips off Green like a rock. "The Widow says we're stopping in Junction."

If you get out, she'll leave you.

Don't stop now. Keep reading with your copy of SOLACE BY FIRE available now.

Don't miss the last chapter of *The Revere Trilogy* series with SOLACE BY FIRE available now and find more from J.L. Delavega at www.jldelavega.com

All things come to an end.

Adelaide has always dreamed of one thing: freedom. Now, deeper in the West Rim than ever before, her second shadow—the mysterious Stranger—grows more restless, bloodthirsty, and dangerously real.

Tesla's fight to carve a future for herself and other women like her reaches a turning point. Will her vision of a new world for women succeed, or will it crumble beneath the weight of ruthless progress, just like the Tov Shadow Nation before them?

But the dangers don't stop there. An evil hunger haunts the storm-ravaged canyons of the West Rim, and the man who almost destroyed them two Seasons ago is still a looming threat. Alongside the deadly pestilence, the Revere women must rely on one another if they want to survive.

ACKNOWLEDGMENTS

My family: Kirsten, Olive, Hollie, Jess, James, and Dustin, you give me love, food, and couches to sleep on. The Reveres decided to bring some men onto their crew, and look, we did too.

My Grandma, whose wisdom and humor made Moira so damn close to my heart. She even got her neighbors back east to read my book. May we all have someone who never lets us feel wrong for being exactly who we are.

And to the best of the rest: Mom, aunts, cousins, friends of old and the fresh who have always been unflinchingly supportive of my creative endeavors. Thanks for never telling me to my face I was weird. It's okay if you think it.

My editor, Tee, who as usual forces me to do better, as well as the rest of my accomplices at City Owl: Tina, Heather, copy editor, and the many authors I've had the pleasure of getting to know.

Beta readers, Dino Derek and Olive, I hope you know how much I appreciate your time and undying enthusiasm for this series.

My ARC Crew: you guys are all amazing! The effort you put into championing someone else's work gives me hope. Maybe we'll get to meet in the real world someday.

Thank you, Matt, for being the first eyes besides mine to read this even though you were on the brink of agenting retirement. I'll miss your insight. You'll always be my first agent, who understood Adelaide best besides me, and the one who sold this series.

But to Sarah, my new agent, I'm so pleased to now have access to your insight. I hope there are many books in our future.

And especially, thank you everyone who read Smoke and Other Storms and loved the Reveres enough to keep riding with them. You are all alkaline. Moira is proud of each of you for exactly who you are.

See you on the West Rim.

ABOUT THE AUTHOR

J.L. DELAVEGA is the award-winning author of feminist bloodbath THE REVERE TRILOGY.

Her work has been recognized for its unique blend of western gothic meets dark fantasy and horror. *Smoke and Other Storms* has been nominated for numerous awards and won the Reader's Favorite silver medal for western fiction (2024).

She lives in the Las Vegas desert and could say she makes all her own clothes but that would be a lie.

www.jldelavega.com

facebook.com/Ninjenaiyauthor

instagram.com/ninjenaiyauthor

threads.net/@ninjenaiyauthor

ABOUT THE PUBLISHER

City Owl Press is a cutting edge indie publishing company, bringing the world of romance and speculative fiction to discerning readers.

Escape Your World. Get Lost in Ours!

www.cityowlpress.com

facebook.com/CityOwlPress

x.com/cityowlpress

instagram.com/cityowlbooks

pinterest.com/cityowlpress

tiktok.com/@cityowlpress

www.ingramcontent.com/pod-product-compliance
Lightning Source LLC
Chambersburg PA
CBHW022347020726
47500CB00002B/166